Frank Coates was born in Melbourne and, after graduating as a professional engineer, worked for many years as a telecommunications specialist in Australia and overseas. As a UN technical specialist in Nairobi, Kenya, he travelled extensively throughout the eastern and southern parts of Africa. During his time there Frank developed a passion for the history and culture of East Africa, which inspired his first novel, *Tears of the Maasai*, published in 2004, after which he became a full-time writer. *Whisper at Dawn* is his eighth novel.

www.footloose.com.au

Also by Frank Coates

Tears of the Maasai

Beyond Mombasa

In Search of Africa

Roar of the Lion

The Last Maasai Warrior

Softly Calls the Serengeti

Echoes from a Distant Land

Whisper
at Dawn
Frank
Coates

HarperCollins*Publishers*

HarperCollins*Publishers*

First published in Australia in 2014
by HarperCollins*Publishers* Australia Pty Limited
ABN 36 009 913 517
harpercollins.com.au

HarperCollins*Publishers*
Level 13, 201 Elizabeth Street, Sydney NSW 2000, Australia
Unit D1, 63 Apollo Drive, Rosedale, Auckland 0632, New Zealand
A 53, Sector 57, Noida, UP, India
77–85 Fulham Palace Road, London W6 8JB, United Kingdom
2 Bloor Street East, 20th floor, Toronto, Ontario M4W 1A8, Canada
10 East 53rd Street, New York NY 10022, USA

National Library of Australia Cataloguing-in-Publication entry:

Coates, Frank, author.
  Whisper at dawn / Frank Coates.
  ISBN: 978 0 7322 9232 4 (paperback)
  ISBN: 978 1 4607 0179 9 (ebook)
A823.4

Cover design by HarperCollins Design Studio
Cover images: Landscape © Roy Toft/National Geographic Society/Corbis; Elephant by
shutterstock.com
Map by Laurie Whiddon, Map Illustrations
Author photograph by Belinda Mason
Typeset in Sabon 10.5/14.5pt by Kirby Jones
Printed and bound in Australia by Griffin Press
The papers used by HarperCollins in the manufacture of this book are a natural, recyclable
product made from wood grown in sustainable plantation forests. The fibre source and
manufacturing processes meet recognised international environmental standards, and carry
certification.

5 4 3 2 1   14 15 16 17

To Wendy ...
Ever mine

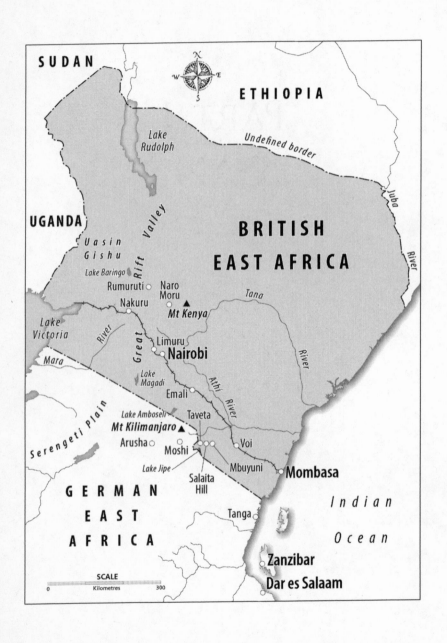

PART 1
DAN

CHAPTER 1

1902

It might not have been the biggest bull he'd seen since arriving in Africa nearly a year ago, but this was the first Dan Sullivan had met while on foot. The buffalo lowered his head and glared at the intruder from under the heavy boss that sat between his horns like a cast-iron rampart, and the herd, fifty or more strong, were assembled in support columns, watching as the bull stood his ground. From his jackaroo days, Dan knew the beasts wouldn't move until their leader did.

The animal gave a belligerent snort, raising a puff of dust from the track. Dan raised his rifle to his chest. He didn't want to shoot. The bugger looked like it would tip the scales at three-quarters of a ton and, although the 303 might stop him, the shot would alert every Boer commando unit within miles. He could only wait until the buffalo decided the next move. It was a hell of a choice, but Dan had been in hell since leaving the company a month ago, after watching Meg die.

Recruits are required to be good shots, good riders and practical bushmen of experience, the poster had said. *And to have good eyesight and hearing, and otherwise to be of good physical condition.* Dan was that, and was also between five foot ten and six foot, as required. Unfortunately, he wasn't of age. Not even close. But at sixteen he'd been big enough to pull down a year-old heifer.

'You don't look twenty-one,' the recruitment officer, a red-faced man with a lantern jaw had said, eyeing him reproachfully.

'I have my own horse,' Dan replied.

The recruitment officer stamped his application, and three days later, Dan was in the mounted infantry training camp just outside Brisbane. That had been the best of it. The mateship; the thrill of a long sea voyage — his first; seeing new places; and the excitement of meeting the Boer in battle.

It all began to pale, though, early in 1901. The British and the troops from her colonies had by then captured all the major towns. Talk among the Queensland Imperial Bushmen contingents was that many of them would not see a twelve-month of duty ... but the Boer wouldn't stand and fight. He would engage in a furious skirmish, then mount his pony — a puny animal that could go for days on the smell of a chaff-bag — and disappear before the guns could be brought to bear. It was like fighting a will-o'-the-wisp.

The military hierarchy changed tack. More than once Dan's company came in contact with long lines of Boer civilians — mostly women and children — trudging to makeshift camps the British had set up for them. Whole areas were swept clean of farming communities, concentrating them into large camps — *concentration camps* they were called — to stop them provisioning their troops. Rumours spread that many thousands were dying in these camps. It didn't seem right to Dan. He didn't want the farmers to pay for the actions of their Boer leaders. Now that he thought about it, he didn't even fully understand why they were fighting the Boers at all. Back on the Darling Downs it had seemed a bit of a lark: a break from the stultifying monotony of droving cattle.

The British colonels and generals had started to make mistakes, or at least that's what it felt like to Dan and his mates. In an attempt to catch the elusive Boer commandos, flying squadrons like the Queensland Imperial Bushmen were sent to cut them off, but in so doing became themselves cut off from the main force. Thus the stupidity of the officers went from being a topic of sarcastic infantry humour to costing lives, as the Boers cut the isolated contingents to pieces with ruthless precision.

Through all those days in hell, Dan never once thought about leaving.

The bull's nostrils flared, and his drool fell in slobbery tendrils. He was sniffing the air for a taste of fear. Dan knew he'd find a touch of it on him. It was hard not to be scared facing naked aggression from such a large animal. It was different from engaging an armed man in hand-to-hand combat, where you could see the very same fear in his eyes that you couldn't keep from your own. This beast was angry; it could not afford to be afraid: it must fight or die.

Disaster had followed disaster on the military campaign. During a period of rest in the captured town of Bloemfontein, a thousand men died of typhoid fever — their water supply had been contaminated by corpses and human waste.

In the empire's haste to pursue and engage the mobile Boer forces, British supply lines were stretched beyond capacity. The men were often hungry and began looting food from civilian towns, and seizing whole herds of cattle. Their mounts, driven beyond fatigue and unable to recover on the poor native grasses, fared very badly.

A distressed horse seems to know its time and no amount of coddling can save it. When his mare, Meg, who had been his workmate and sometimes only companion on long hard drives on the Darling Downs, dropped her pretty head, Dan began to fret. He cut bundles of sedges in a desperate attempt to find something the horse could eat and tolerate. But she faded and weakened. He watched, could only watch, helpless as a parent watching an only child submit to the inevitable, until dear Meg fell. It was at that point that Dan decided to leave.

The buffalo emitted a low grumble and Dan's attention returned immediately to the present. It was no time for reveries. The bull snorted and scuffed the ground with his hoof, sending a dust cloud dancing away on the breeze.

Dan raised the rifle again, taking aim between the buffalo's eyes. He wondered if the 303 could even penetrate such a thick mass of bone and horn. Sweat ran down his forehead. He lifted his index finger from the trigger guard to wipe it away, and as he refocussed his aim, the bull was coming at him with startling agility and speed.

Dan pulled the trigger.

The crack of the rifle shattered the silence of the surrounding hills like a silver platter dropped in church.

The buffalo's charge ended as abruptly as it had begun. The enormous head and horns crashed to the dirt and the beast lay motionless where it landed.

Dan let his breath escape in a rush.

The echo of the shot bounced around the encompassing hills. Dan ran his eye along the hazy demarcation between the veld and the sky, half expecting to see an immediate cloud of dust arise as a Boer column charged down upon him. He could find nothing, but it would not be prudent to stay. He was in danger from his own troops as well. It would be capture and imprisonment on the one hand, or a court martial and British firing squad on the other.

Deserter wasn't a term Dan would choose to describe himself, and more than once he'd regretted his impulsive decision to leave. He'd made a commitment to the army. They had an understanding. Dan would place his life on the line. He would stand with his mates and fight the Boers for king and country. But he'd not agreed to watch his horse die of starvation — a sad and ignominious death — on the South African veld. He would have liked to explain to the hierarchy that he was just sick and tired of the war, and disgusted by the looting, and that his horse dying was just the last unbearable straw, but he imagined it would now be impossible to escape the consequences. He knew enough military law to know that the British authorities would be pedantic about such things. They could not make exceptions.

So he didn't retrace his steps to the Cape: too obvious an escape route. Nor did he head for the port of Durban to make his way back home. There would be officials there demanding to know who he was, where he was going, and why he was leaving. He decided instead to head east to Lourenço Marques, where he hoped the Portuguese would be less pernickety.

Dan had thrown his street clothes into his pack and walked into the bush. He had a rough map, a knife, his 303, a box of matches, a few days' rations, and a little more than thirty bob in his pocket.

The herd was thundering off. He took one last look at the buffalo corpse. He couldn't initially see the entry point of his bullet, but on closer inspection he found it. He'd aimed at the centre of the buffalo's forehead but had hit him in the eye.

Dan shrugged. It might not have been his best shot, but it had been effective.

He reloaded his rifle, and resumed his march.

* * *

Within half an hour, he was in more trouble. It hadn't been there even a moment earlier when he checked the skyline but on the hills to the west there was now a plume of dust. He watched it grow and waver in the wind. He couldn't see what it was, but it was clearly coming his way.

He scanned the surrounding savannah. He couldn't outrun a mounted column so he searched for somewhere to hide. The only feature that broke the monotony of scrub was a dry creek bed; he headed towards it in a low crouch.

He slid down the bank and hastened along the watercourse, still searching for a place to hide. A thick clump of bush. Even a tall stand of reeds. Just as he heard the sound of approaching hooves, he found a large hole in the bank, partly concealed under a log. He peered inside before backing into it as far as he could go before the burrow's width restricted him. His head was only a foot from the opening, but by drawing back into the shadow he thought it might do.

The horses gathered in the creek bed before him. The guttural Afrikaans voices confirmed it was a platoon of Boers on a reconnaissance mission. They'd undoubtedly heard the rifle shot, probably recognised it as a Lee-Enfield, and ridden out to investigate. They milled about, discussing their next tactics.

Dan held his position, barely daring to breathe.

A low growl came faintly to his ears.

For a moment he tried to convince himself that the sound had come from outside the hole. He dared to peep out. By their behaviour, it appeared the Boer soldiers had heard and seen nothing.

The growl came again, and this time Dan was certain it had emanated from behind him, deep in the burrow.

The Boers hadn't dismounted and Dan prayed they wouldn't. If whatever was behind him attacked, he would have to bolt or be torn to shreds.

Although he was sure the creature that had made such a blood-curdling growl was in the burrow with him, part of his reasoning rejected it as simply too preposterous; nobody could be so unlucky. But as if to immediately allay any such hope, the growl returned, more insistent.

Dan felt a solid tug on his right boot. He almost shrieked in fright. Then the something behind him shook his foot and snarled. He could feel teeth compress the leather of his tough army boot. The tip of an incisor pierced the upper just above the sole and he gasped as it pressed into the lines of fine bones, puncturing his skin and sending waves of excruciating pain up his leg.

There was a moment's respite, during which Dan dared hope that the creature had given up, but it grabbed his boot again and gave a tremendous tug, pulling Dan further into the hole, and threatening to wedge him there. It was now quite possible that neither of them would escape the burrow.

The Boer contingent were talking, and making moves that perhaps indicated they were about to leave.

Behind him, the beast's snarl gave vent to its rising anger.

The Boers reformed their line and galloped off.

Dan waited as long as he dared, then dragged himself free of the constriction. He scrambled out of the burrow and, with no alternative refuge in the creek bed, he swung his body up onto the fallen log.

He expected a lion, a hyena, or at least a leopard to charge out after him, but it was none of these. In fact, it was no animal he'd ever seen before. It was less than a yard long nose to tail, with short legs, a black body and white back. It was still growling as it came out of the hole, but now ignored Dan as it scuttled away, snuffling the sand of the riverbed in search of more amenable prey.

* * *

The experience with the buffalo and the platoon of Boer commandos convinced Dan he couldn't use his rifle again. If he could, he might have bagged a feast of game meat. There were herds of antelope of various types and they allowed him to approach quite close before throwing their heads back and galloping away. Several times he raised his 303 before his caution overcame his gnawing hunger.

He passed near several towns and villages, but daren't trust the reception he might receive from the inhabitants. He could replenish his water bottle at any one of the many streams and rivers he crossed, but, although he rationed himself, after the fourth day his tinned supplies were finished.

Occasionally he would come upon a large warren of small furry animals, much like mongooses, but able to stand on their hind legs; they would watch his progress in a most curious manner. They were skinny, but he couldn't be picky — by the fifth day he was weak with hunger.

In desperation, he tried a number of times to ambush one of the sleek furry creatures, and to chase it down, but without luck. Even without the nagging pain of his injured foot, the creatures were far too agile.

It occurred to him that he might use a trick from his childhood to catch one. In those days he would place a snare — a loop of wire or cord — over the entrance of a rabbit burrow. Then he'd wait for the inhabitant to emerge from its hole before scaring it into hasty retreat. The rabbit would dash to its warren and usually get caught in the trap.

He made a crude snare from his shoelaces, and placed it at the opening of the little creatures' burrows. He then spent a frustrating hour rushing after them like a demented fool to send them scuttling into the snare. They were quite slender creatures, and even when he managed to snag one, it always found a way to slip the noose. Throughout the remainder of the day he worked to refine the setting, and it was almost dusk when he made his last attempt. It was a success. He quickly despatched the animal with his knife, and danced a jig, whooping and leaping and rolling on the ground with his feet kicking the air like a child. Then he laughed at himself for the bizarre image he would present to anyone watching.

As the moon rose, he roasted the scrawny carcass over his campfire. It was meagre fare, tough and stringy, but about the best meal he could remember.

* * *

Dan opened one eye. It was still dark, but the dawn was spreading its colours across the starlit sky. He was on a freight train and its sudden stop had woken him. He remembered hiding among the logs at the Portuguese East Africa border, presuming the train was headed to a sawmill and a port. He'd fallen immediately into an exhausted sleep.

He lifted his head and scanned his surroundings and found he'd guessed correctly. A hundred yards away, beyond a scattering of huts and the small number of ships at the port, the Indian Ocean's opalescent waters ran pink and mauve towards the dawning sun.

He picked up his swag and rifle, swung his legs over the topmost log and lowered himself down to the track. He was captivated by the serenity of the ocean and recalled his first sight of the dawn over the Pacific while chasing brumbies with his dad on Stradbroke Island. Perhaps that was when he first became aware of the enormity of the planet and his inconsequential presence in it. It kindled his desire to explore it — a desire unrequited until he volunteered to serve with the 4th Queensland Imperial Bushmen.

He was lost in thought, wandering idly towards the huts collected around the port, when the piercing call of a bugle brought him back to reality. It was reveille. The shapes silhouetted by the brilliant dawn were not small huts, but tents, and being hoisted on a flagpole not fifty yards away was the Union Jack.

Dan backed away, his heart in his throat, and quickly scanned the camp for the sentries. He could see none, and by pure luck, none had seen him.

Keeping low, he ran back to his hideaway among the logs.

The sun pounded him relentlessly through many long, hot hours. He was soon without water, and the space between the logs became an oven, but each time he peered out he found he was surrounded by men in uniform.

When his thirst pushed him almost to the point of surrendering to the soldiers, thereby trading his life for a ladle full of water, the train jerked into motion.

The forward motion moved the hot air and the staccato clatter of wheel on rail soothed him. He didn't care where the train was headed; it could be no worse than the furnace he was already suffering. He drifted in and out of consciousness, delirious with dehydration.

A strange sound roused him from a fitful sleep. The train had stopped. The air around him was marginally cooler, and the sound, like the distant boom of cannon fire, drew closer. Dan simply wanted to sleep, but the noise persisted. He could feel the train carriage shake as it approached, and another sound joined the first — a metallic clank. The latches securing the heavy thick chains that held the logs together on the flat-top carriage were being undone. In a moment, the roughly stacked logs would tumble from his freight car to the ground, taking him with them and almost certainly crushing him as they did.

Dan scrambled up as the workmen sprung the latches on his carriage. The topmost log, on which he was standing, lurched. Dan was carried with it, and just before it bounced and collided with the others, he leaped clear.

The startled workers saw him climb to his feet and stagger from the timber mill.

Dan stumbled along the only road out of Delagoa Bay until he found a stream about a mile away. He threw himself into the water beside the timber bridge and drank his fill. After bathing and washing his clothes, he lay on the bank to dry. After a time, the sound of voices — English voices, loud and cheery — came from the dirt road. He scuttled into hiding under the bridge, and held his breath as a bullock wagon carrying soldiers rumbled overhead towards the camp.

Dan guessed the men were returning from leave in Lourenço Marques. The town was therefore not the safe haven he'd imagined, but he had no other choice. He dressed himself in civvies and buried his uniform in the sandy riverbank.

* * *

Lourenço Marques was a town like no other Dan had ever seen. The houses were very grand and of a most unusual architecture. He imagined they were typical of buildings in Portugal, but he could only guess. They had arches, columns and edifices of stone, and life-size heroic statues. Many houses had little fences of thin iron railings around upper-floor windows. Everywhere the impression of wealth and style pervaded.

Dan was fascinated by the town, but he kept a wary eye. He didn't want to attract the attention of the military police, who would have an interest in any English-speaking man of his age.

He gorged himself on roasted lobster he bought for a few coins from a hawker on the beach. Perched on the high cliffs above him were the impressive colonial mansions. Facing him was the Indian Ocean where, some five thousand miles beyond the horizon, was Australia. He felt homesick, although he couldn't say why. His mother had died when he was thirteen, and the only family he had was his perpetually absent father, droving somewhere in the outback.

He had to get as far away as possible, as soon as possible, but where? How? To sail on any British or allied ship risked exposure. Even ships carrying a Portuguese flag were now suspect given the presence of the British military camp at Delagoa Bay.

Rocking on its mooring about a hundred yards away was a strange craft. It had a sail furled around its single mast, and a square stern that rose high above the water. It carried no flag. Its lines made a graceful arc forwards from the stern, ending at a bow that nosed upwards, though not as high as aft. Dan wasn't a sailor, but he sensed the ship would have difficulty managing heavy seas.

He spent the remainder of the day watching the craft. Nobody boarded or disembarked until around late afternoon when two men pushed off in a small dinghy and one rowed them towards the beach.

They were Arabs. Dan approached them, and the one who'd sat in the bow of the dinghy acknowledged his greeting.

Language difficulties complicated the discussion, but Dan made it known he wanted passage north. It came down to price. Dan showed the only tradeable goods he had. His rifle had been lost when he hastily abandoned the rail car, but he had his knife and a small amount of cash.

The Arab made a face and shook his head.

Reluctantly, Dan produced the gold watch he'd bought in Cape Town. It was a going-home gift to himself, and he'd not yet worn it.

The Arab smiled.

CHAPTER 2

Bill Freeman spat in the dust. Without taking his eyes from the elephant, he wiped the back of his hand across his lips. It was the best tusker he'd seen in many a long year. From under his craggy grey eyebrows he squinted into the sky. He had an hour before the equatorial sun plunged into Lake Rudolph like a fireball. Time enough to find the animal's weakness, to stalk him, to outsmart him, and to bag the tusks that the big fellow carried like a pair of ivory scimitars, the tips grazing the dirt. He needed that ivory and this bull could be the difference between a good profit and financial ruin. Again.

The elephant was unaware of his presence. He dipped his trunk into the powder-dry earth, swept it smartly behind an ear the size of a gaff-rigged sail, and doused in dust the parasites that drove him mad with the itch. A golden fog surrounded him as he shook his enormous head, making light of his pair of hundred-pound tusks. Ivory was worth a pound a pound in Nairobi, and a fortune in Calcutta for anyone able to shape it into billiard balls, piano keys or a Chinaman's ornate signature chop.

As the sun sank, the air rising from the baked earth sucked a breeze from the lake. Freeman grunted his satisfaction. It meant he could safely circle behind the bull without his scent alarming the animal.

He turned to his men, signalling the porters to stay and his gun-bearer to follow.

Freeman wasn't a person to blame luck for all his many misadventures, although there were times when he felt he'd been dealt more than his share of ill-fortune. Like the time, as a young man of twenty living with his family in the goldfields of Bendigo, he went secretly one night to test a claim to see if its yield was as good as the American owner said it was. He panned a few buckets and found enough colour in the lamplight to make it appear worthwhile. He'd dug up the cigar tin containing his father's retirement nest egg — after the crash his father swore he'd never again trust the banks — and bought the American's claim. By the time he'd found all the salted dust specks the Yank had scattered throughout his claim, the crook was halfway home to California.

A couple of years later it wasn't bad luck that left him broke, but the rapture of a love affair.

They said there were fortunes to be made in the South African diamond fields, but by the time Bill arrived, Cecil Rhodes and his cronies had grabbed all the best lots and had a stranglehold on the market. But Bill had worked hard in the mines and, when he left, he took a reasonable bankroll to the nearest town to wash away the dust.

He hadn't had a drink in months and the music coming cheerfully from the bar opposite his boarding house drew him in. There was a happy crowd around the piano and Bill felt good as he drank his lager, tapping his feet to the jig. Tomorrow he would board the ship that would take him home with enough money to repay what he owed his father and a little extra to set himself up in Adelaide.

She was a pretty young thing, not a beauty by any means, but he was a young man long removed from female company of any form, so his heart gave a funny jump when she spoke to him. He didn't fully understand it then, but much later recognised that the rapture he felt during sex was similar to that experienced while hunting dangerous game. It started in his groin and spread through his body until his toes tingled and his eyes glistened. It was the reason he was a hunter.

He noticed she was a little too well known to the men in the bar, but this fact was soon forgotten as she ignored all attempts to distract her from her exclusive interest in him, Bill Freeman.

He was flattered and made awkward conversation for a while, discovering that her name was Dulcie and she was a ladies' hairdresser at the Kimberley Salon just a block away.

'Would you care for a drink, Dulcie?' he asked, above the wheezing sounds of a button accordion.

'Oh, I couldn't ever drink beer,' she said, fanning her hand in a futile effort to clear the stifling tobacco-laden air.

'Champagne then?'

'Now you're teasing me,' she chided. 'How would a young fellow like you afford such luxuries?'

'I've done all right,' he said, feigning modesty. 'Well enough to buy a lady a drink on a night such as this.'

She giggled delightfully.

And drink they did. Dulcie became quite animated by the wine and appeared to know all the songs. After they finished the first bottle, Bill bought a second.

He had been a little unsteady on his feet when she said it was time to go, but Bill didn't want the night to end and insisted he walk her home. At her door, a rough wooden thing on the front of a flat-faced guesthouse off the main road, he took her hand and drew her to him. The champagne, or the feeling of her slightly parted lips on his, sent his head into a spin. He stumbled through her door and they were in a room with nothing more than a bed to furnish it. Somehow she'd closed the door and put the light to a lantern with a heavily smoke-stained glass before he had a chance to reclaim her in his embrace. Their shadows danced in the flickering light and the room threatened to twirl him off his feet.

He kissed her and the hot spot in his groin stirred. He ran his hands up from her hips to her breasts and she pressed them there.

While she undid his belt, he attempted to slide her shoulder straps free, but there was a catch somewhere and she escaped his hands for long enough to shrug off her dress, revealing a delightful pink chemise.

Dulcie insisted he remove his boots and trousers, which he attempted to do while performing a one-legged jig before they both tumbled onto the bed laughing.

She was above him, her hands and her mouth everywhere.

Rapture.

He had awoken late the next morning in a bewildered state, *sans* Dulcie. He searched his pockets and was relieved to find he still had the receipt for his passage home, but his wallet and savings, except for a small amount he'd left in a shirt pocket, were gone. His one night of passion had come at a cost, but it didn't daunt him.

Freeman seldom pondered the convoluted path that had led him to his latest adventure — stalking approximately ten ton of elephant in the immense expanses of British East Africa's northern frontier. If he'd been so inclined, he would have realised it wasn't one, but a string of failed ventures.

After returning to Australia from Kimberley, Freeman met Harriet Robinson and later married her in a bluestone church in the hills above Adelaide. Their son, Walter, was born a year later.

Bill worked at a number of jobs over the years, never sticking at any of them for more than a few months. He could always see better opportunities elsewhere. Meanwhile, Harriet had developed a small but modest income, sewing and mending ladies' clothing. She was a resourceful and talented woman: she expanded the business into fashion design and was eventually able to hire a small staff to do the menial tasks.

For several years Harriet's business flourished and kept the family comfortably situated, then due to complications he never fully understood, it failed and she was forced to start all over again. She never quite recovered from the setback and, in Bill's opinion, became an embittered woman. The marriage, which had never been a joyous one, also suffered. Bill felt he was a failure both as a breadwinner and a husband and wondered why they should continue in a loveless marriage once their son, the only reason for keeping the home together, was making his own way in the world.

Meanwhile, news from South Africa again captured Bill's imagination. The roads to the Witwatersrand were paved in gold and Bill followed stories of big strikes in the newspapers, itching to pursue the fortune that had eluded him in Bendigo and on the diamond fields. When he finally found the courage to reveal his ambitions to Harriet, who was consumed by the task of rebuilding her business, she told him to *Just go*.

Gold mining in the Rand was no more profitable than Bendigo and when, in 1899, a year after arriving, the British Empire went to war against the Boer, the game was up. At fifty-four he was too old to enlist and too broke to return home yet again with his tail between his legs.

An advertisement calling for managers on the construction of the Uganda Railway caught his eye. He was offered a contract, and the day before he boarded a ship to East Africa he sent a letter to Harriet informing her he'd taken up a two-year contract as a hunter.

His job was to supply the railhead coolies with fresh meat. He enjoyed the life, and learned a lot about the country. Under the expert tutorage of Robert Turk, he also learned all there was to know about wild animals and how to hunt them.

Ivory was in great demand and Bill heard from men he'd met on the hunt that a few big tuskers could earn a man a fortune. He decided to try his hand and declined to renew his contract.

His problem was that a safari to the best hunting sites required money for porters and supplies, and he had insufficient for more than one hunting expedition. It meant that the Lake Rudolph area, with its large tuskers and savage Turkana tribesmen, was the best of his limited choices.

The Turkana were true desert dwellers. Tall, proud and fierce, their ribs shone in the northern district's unremitting sun like rods of polished ebony. They wore their plaited hair long, adding tufts from their ancestors' braids, using dung and the fat from their sheep's tails to form a wide, flat, oval plate. These elaborate hairpieces were fixtures for life and the warriors were obliged to carry a small headrest, something like a tiny stool, to enable them to put their head down at night to sleep.

When Freeman met a group of Turkana to parley, he saw the warriors were wearing innocuous-looking wrist ornaments that, upon closer inspection, were far more treacherous. They were discs of iron, clasped in the palm of the hand, from which curled a sharpened blade encircling the wrist. He had met the Turkana to offer *honcho* for safe passage through their territory, and hoped his offering wasn't considered too miserly, otherwise the wrist knives could slash him to ribbons in a thrice. They also had metal spikes on their rings. He wondered if these were used when discussions proved unsatisfactory, but not so badly as to warrant the wrist knives.

He'd already been on safari for six weeks with little to show for it. His provisions were low and his money almost exhausted. This one bull elephant and his ability to bring him down would determine his future.

He was on the landward side of the elephant, feeling the brush of the hot breeze in his face as he searched for the cover he needed to approach to a safe killing range. He knew the elephant had not caught wind of him, but was heading towards a gorge thickly covered with scrub. He had only a half-hour of light before his trophy disappeared from sight. Freeman began to sweat.

As he and his gun-bearer approached the gorge, the terrain rose slightly, giving him the chance to edge forwards, using the rocky outcrops as cover. He had to move faster than he wanted and worried about making a sound that would startle the bull into a quick retreat. He silently cursed himself for not having removed his boots.

A boulder up ahead offered his best and perhaps only opportunity to set himself for the shot. He kneeled behind it and took three controlled breaths. He removed his hat and peeped over the rock. The bull was moving along the lake and would momentarily present himself broadside to Freeman's line of fire. He was sixty yards away; a little more than the ideal range, according to Turk, but he had no choice. He carefully raised the rifle to his shoulder and peered down the sights.

The sun was ruthless. A trickle of sweat crept down his forehead and threatened to enter the corner of his eye. He blinked. It burned his eye. He quickly wiped it and reapplied his eye to the sights.

'The brain shot works well on a big tusker,' Robert Turk had told him, 'but be careful … a near-miss might knock him out without finishing him.'

He placed the bead on the line between the elephant's ear and eye.

Again Turk's words were in his mind. 'An elephant's brain is like a football. Not one of those round things, but a real football.' He went on to describe its position as forwards of the ear, just above the musth hole. 'But if you're not directly side-on for the shot, you have to make allowances for the fact that it's a small target inside a big head.'

Freeman forced himself to wait until the bull was squarely side-on. Then he took a deep breath, slowly exhaled, and squeezed off a shot.

The magnificent beast crumpled at the legs and fell to its knees, where it lingered as if in need of a moment's prayer, then slowly toppled to its side, sending an explosion of dust into the languorous hot air.

It was Kimberley town again. Dulcie sat astride him.

His toes tingled and his eyes glistened.

* * *

Bill sat on the dead elephant's leg — the size of a fallen tree trunk — and studied the pad; it was nearly two feet across, meaning the bull had stood about eleven foot high. It seemed implausible that the pad, and its neat toenails, could support the massive bulk — the weight of more than sixty men.

It was not the first dead elephant he'd sized up, but he again marvelled at the enormity of the animal. He felt a strong sense of gratification or even, if he indulged himself for a moment, just a touch of self-importance, knowing he had brought death to such a giant.

A blob of dried mud clung to one enormous ear — the residue of its early-morning bath in the lake. Flies had already begun to gather around the hole in the side of its head, buzzing in dizzy excitement at the feast.

Bill's ears rang long after the explosive sound of his Nitro Express until, slowly, the profound silence returned.

Soon the porters would arrive with their cutting tools to extract the ivory, and they would then start back to Nairobi. Bill was in no hurry. He relished the opportunity to reflect upon a lifetime full of courageous acts taken against the odds, but seldom vindicated by success. At last his luck had changed and he'd scored a unique triumph. Now he could dare to dream.

He was a hunter, and loved it, but he'd been forced to relinquish his ambition to run a safari business because he could see no way of securing the necessary funds. To start operations he would need equipment, wagons, pack and haulage animals and supplies. He would need to be able to make advance payments to maybe a hundred or more porters before taking on his first paying client. It had been beyond his wildest dreams — until now.

There remained a *slight* complication. Prior to coming up with this inspired expedition, he'd abandoned his hope of starting his own hunting business and decided his best option was farming. But even here he was short of the necessary funds. He needed a partner, and he'd written to his son, Walter, offering him a share of the proposed venture. Settlers were starting to arrive in numbers, he'd said, and the best land was being rapidly taken up. The authorities were spruiking the huge possibilities the land offered, and if the farm delivered only half of what was in prospect, they would both become wealthy men. Walter had agreed, and was already en route to British East Africa with his family. It was a complication all right, but Walter was a hard worker and Bill felt confident he could make a go of a farm on his own while his old dad got on with building his dream safari company.

The sound of voices and laughter came faintly to his ears. The men were already anticipating their return to friends and loved ones. They would have money in their pockets and tales to tell their children. Their stories would rob him, the *bwana*, of any significant part in the adventures of the safari; they would remove from him all the bravery and skill that had resulted in a successful hunt and instead install themselves as heroes. One would tell of the deadly green mamba that might have struck his fellow porter had he not been there, brave in the face of deadly danger, to save him. Another might say he saved the whole caravan from violent death in the murky waters of the Ewaso Ng'iro by seeing, with his own keen eyes, the stir of turbulence that revealed not a subtle change in the current of the waters, but the wake of a submerged crocodile.

Freeman didn't care what the porters claimed. He knew he'd shaped success from impending failure by that one magnificent act: the precise placement of his 450 Rigby into the brain of this mighty beast.

The men arrived and set to work; Freeman took his pipe from his pocket as he strolled away. He unrolled a short length of Samuel Gawith's black, and screwed it into the bowl, taking care to tamp it properly because otherwise he'd have the devil of a job to keep it alight. When the evil-smelling wad was smoking vigorously, he turned his attention back to the men. The elephant's 'hand' — the finely tuned appendage at the end of the trunk that was the animal's third eye, nose and dexterous fingers — had been thrown about twenty paces away. While it remained on the trunk the men would not feel safe, for if the elephant wasn't dead, the hand could break a man's neck in an instant.

One man was wielding the tree-felling axe into the face of the elephant, digging for the core of the tusks — there was at least two foot of ivory concealed within the skull. Hunks of glistening white fat, speckled by globs of blood, fell away under the blade.

The work was strenuous and the first man handed the axe to a second, who attacked the deepening hole with gusto. The thick leathery hide fell loose in chunks, teeth shattered and the hidden ivory, pink with blood, slowly became exposed to the baking sun. Having found the root, he applied the blade to it, sending splinters of bone flying in all directions until the massive tusk was freed.

They now needed to turn the elephant onto the other side to gain access to the second tusk. The men used their spears as levers, and, with lengths of rope attached to the elephant's legs and Freeman's added weight, they laboured for half an hour without success.

'It's the legs,' Freeman said, and ordered the men to amputate them. After a further fifteen minutes, during which time two of the legs were hacked from the body, Freeman said to try again. This time they were able to tumble the carcass over, and the men set to work wielding the felling axe again.

Above the sound of the falling axe Freeman heard a clamour of voices. A troop of chattering and cackling natives came scuttling towards them. They were not the tall, aloof Turkana people who had lived on the shores of Lake Rudolph for as long as time could recall; they were stocky, intensely dark people, who were almost completely naked.

Freeman's men took little notice as the newcomers set to work on the torso, hacking and sawing at the tough hide of the elephant's belly with their simple iron implements. In the space of a few furious minutes they had carved a hole into the steaming inner cavity, at which point several of the men threw off the small skirts that shielded their privates, and began to tear at the still-warm inner organs which spilled from the carcass like huge writhing pythons. When the hole had grown deeper and wider, one of the men slid inside the abdominal cavity, from which he thrust out yards of entrails. Eventually three more men joined him and the internal dissection continued apace. They shovelled out lumps of the heart, kidneys and lungs, while the women laughed and made a game of trying to catch the slimy meat before chopping it into manageable sizes.

His porters freed the second tusk shortly after the industrious meat hunters had completed their task and decamped, loaded down with chunks of meat, fat and offal.

As his men headed to Lake Rudolph to bathe in its shallow warm waters, Freeman gazed back at the remains of the elephant, which now lay like the shattered wreck of a once stately galleon.

The bull elephant, which had retained its grandeur even unto death, was now a collection of white ribs, dismembered body parts, steaming offal and sagging, shit-stained skin, indistinguishable from any other pile of rotting carrion.

CHAPTER 3

The sou'easter filled the lateen sail, carrying the dhow past the entrance marker to the old Mombasa harbour on a single, long tack. Dan thought the vessel had looked heavy in the water at Lourenço Marques, but with the trades in her three-pointed sail she seemed to lift her skirts and dance across the Indian Ocean, leaping the blue deep-water rollers and spuming down the leeward flanks in a dash before the wind.

Dan stood at the stern against the rail, his sun-streaked dark hair tossing in the wind, and his eyes narrowed on the old town now coming into view beyond the point. A pile of gleaming white coral-rock buildings lined the waterfront amid palms, coral trees and bougainvillea.

Mombasa already looked typical of the other ports of call on their route from Portuguese East Africa: Lindi, Kilwa, Dar es Salaam, Zanzibar. Only in Zanzibar did Dan find the Union Jack flying from the governor's palace, and only in Zanzibar did he decline the invitation to go ashore.

Here, he had no choice. Captain Abu had only agreed to take him to Mombasa. As far as Dan could understand it, in Mombasa his ship would be joined by a Moslem eminence and his entourage, and it would not do to have an infidel on board.

The captain shouted to his crew from his position at the tiller arm, and they dashed forwards to make the tack. Dan had seen the manoeuvre performed many times during the voyage, but it still intrigued him. The crewmen spilled the wind from the sail, loosely furled it, then pulled the trailing end of the yard in, making it stand almost vertically alongside the mast. They then danced around the mast with the yard, avoiding the rigging, to the leeward side where they lowered it. The sail filled and the vessel's response was immediate. The dhow rose like a waterbird taking flight, lifting its bow to again surge through the waves.

Captain Abu had timed their arrival perfectly. The sun was about to disappear behind the hills rising a few miles inland. He luffed up to the wind and the crew loosened the sheets and secured their mooring.

A lighter boat came alongside and the operator exchanged greetings with the captain.

Dan watched as the pair engaged in animated conversation. They were obviously well acquainted, laughing as the dhow's crew transferred cargo to the lighter. Dan spotted his haversack going over the rail, and the captain waving him to disembark. It was rather abrupt. Dan had expected to spend the night on board, during which time he would have planned his arrival and how to avoid the attention, if any, he'd receive from the government authorities.

Instead, within minutes the lighter man deposited Dan and his modest belongings on the stone dock. In the space of half an hour the afternoon had become evening. A breeze sprang up and sent a cloud of leaves and litter tumbling down the cobblestones.

Dan watched the lighter man's crew unload the vessel for a few moments, uncertain what else to do. At the far end of the dock were darkened storerooms and shopfronts. He was reassured to find there was no sign of the authorities. Maybe they didn't bother with the small Arab trading vessels. The lighter pushed off for another cargo, leaving him alone.

Dan bent to pick up his swag and found a page of newspaper wrapped around his leg. He peeled it off, releasing it back to the wind, but as it drifted away he caught sight of the headline.

He took a couple of swift steps, pinned it under his boot, then picked it up.

The headline almost filled the page: *Boer War Ends*.

* * *

Bill Freeman stood at the counter beside the weighing scales and watched the old Swahili count, for the second time, the pile of notes in front of him.

'Hurry up, will you?' he demanded, sweeping his eyes around the darkening warehouse to the open doorway. Beyond it, the soft tropical darkness chirruped with night creatures, and an owl made mournful calls to its mate.

The white-bearded Swahili shook his head, sighed, and began counting again.

Freeman had arrived in Mombasa earlier that day, and since then he'd seen, or imagined he'd seen, nefarious characters eyeing him suspiciously. Now he understood the warning of his fellow hunter, Jack Ryder, who told him it was better to accept a little less from the shipping agent in Nairobi than lose the lot in the notorious dark alleys of Mombasa's old town.

But Freeman was greedy. He wanted every possible penny from the sale. Even then he knew the funds from his tusks would be stretched extremely thin when he started his safari business.

He'd tried to complete the dealings at the agent's office during the afternoon, but he spent so much time haggling that it was now quite dark. And it was all for little gain. The wily trader bargained hard. Freeman now faced a long walk to his hotel in the dark, with all his money in a flimsy cotton sack.

The Swahili finished his counting. He thrust the docket at Freeman as a large moth attacked the lantern cover in a frenzy, sending demonic figures flying around the warehouse. Freeman felt ill as he quickly counted the money and nodded.

'It's all correct,' he said, his mouth as dry as wood chips.

The Swahili trader smiled. 'Very fine, Mr Freeman,' he said. 'Thank you for your business. We hope to see you again. Soon.'

'Yes,' he mumbled while stuffing his money into the cotton bag. He then slipped the bag out of sight under his shirt.

The Swahili followed him to the alley. He wished him good night as he closed the large warehouse door behind him with a thud. The sound reverberated down the dark alley.

Freeman looked quickly in each direction, then hurried down the alley towards his hotel.

* * *

Dan had no plans and no idea what to do next. He was a deserter from the empire's forces, taking refuge in a British protectorate where he might easily be discovered and taken to trial by court martial. It wasn't ideal. He thought he might find work in Mombasa and keep low for a year or so before attempting to return home. The word *home* made his heart sink. It invoked an image of an impossibly distant place.

The dry backblocks of the Darling Downs were a world apart from the steaming, spice-filled atmosphere of Mombasa. The Swahili women wore bright *kangas* of many designs, often with a second *kanga* to make a shoulder covering. They matched in neither colour nor design so that a yellow *kanga* wrap overlaid a red *kanga* skirt. A third, perhaps green or blue, might form a carrying sling for an infant. Large gemstones flashed from nostrils and ears. In the lamplight they glittered enough to challenge the radiance of the women's smiles. Many of the men wore a long white *kanzu* tunic and embroidered cylindrical *kofia* perched on the top of the head. Indian men were dressed in *dhotis* and the women *saris*.

A Somali moneychanger traded Dan's remaining pound for a handful of rupees, and at a hawker's stall he bought some curried plantains and rice wrapped in a banana leaf. He ate while walking along the market alley, where many stalls were now closing for the night. Soon he found himself in an empty laneway with a single lantern hanging from a pole at a distant corner.

A muffled profanity came from the darkness. Dan casually finished his plantain, licked the curry from his fingers and just as casually searched the gloom to find the cause of the outcry. He could hear the sounds of a scuffle but had no inclination to interfere. It was not his fight, and becoming involved could only attract the attention of the local Mombasa constabulary, should they be around.

He turned to retrace his path to the market when he heard: 'Get orf me, ya *bastards*!'

Which could only have been uttered by an Australian.

Dan hesitated a moment before hurrying towards the voices.

As he drew nearer, he could make out three figures clad in long robes. Swahilis or Arabs. They had a man wearing a brimmed hat — the Australian, he guessed — surrounded. One of the attackers grabbed the Australian from behind. Dan pulled him off, dodged a few wild swings, then landed a couple of good punches to the attacker's torso. Another came at him with a wicked-looking knife and swung it at his face. He ducked, then stepped inside the next swing, giving the Arab a rip to the solar plexus and a knee to the groin. The robed one doubled up with an anguished grunt, dropping his weapon. Dan kicked it into the drain.

The attackers seemed to lose enthusiasm with the change in numbers. The man who had first challenged him took a few more punches before he ran off down the alley. Dan then joined the Australian dealing with the remaining two and after a short while all the attackers had scampered off into the night.

'Go to hell,' the Australian flung after them. 'The bastards,' he muttered for good measure.

Wiping his hand across his lips, he turned to Dan. 'Ha!' he said, slapping him on the back. 'We gave them what-for, my boy. Taught 'em a lesson or two, I reckon.' He extended his hand. 'Bill Freeman.'

Dan nodded. 'Dan Sulli— Sutherland. Dan Sutherland. Pleased to meet you.'

Freeman was unlikely to have much to do with those in authority, but Dan was happier safe than sorry.

'Not as pleased as me,' Freeman added, wryly. 'I reckon I'd'a been done-for in a few more minutes.'

'What happened?'

'After my money,' he said, patting his chest. 'Would've got it too if you hadn't come along.'

'My pleasure,' Dan said. 'Well … I'll be off then.' He turned to go.

Freeman placed his hand on Dan's shoulder. 'Hold on, Danny boy. You're an Aussie. Let me buy you a drink.'

'No thanks. I'm not thirsty.'

'If someone does old Bill Freeman a good turn, he at least gets a drink for his troubles.'

'Really, it was nothing.'

'A meal then? You look like you could do with some tucker.'

Dan's stomach rumbled at the mention of food. He hesitated.

'It's agreed then. Come along to my hotel. They have the best curried chicken on the coast.' He put his arm around Dan's shoulders, drawing him towards him. 'And we might sink a jar or two while we're at it, eh?'

* * *

Dan agreed. The curried chicken was delicious. He finished it off and accepted a pudding as well. After the meal and the three large porters, he sat contentedly while Freeman, who'd put away twice as many beers, elaborated on the opportunities available in British East Africa.

'Ivory's bringing in top prices at the moment, but the real money is in safaris. The Americans love to shoot. Englishmen too, but the Yanks have it in their blood. And they're willing to pay plenty of pretty Yankee dollars for a pot-shot at a lion or a buff.'

Freeman took a large draught of his beer, leaving a white line of froth on his upper lip. 'Believe me, there's *plenty* of money in it,' he said, as if Dan was in any position to doubt him.

Freeman wiped his mouth and pulled a pipe from his vest; he spent some time cleaning it with a penknife. He filled it and, when he had it alight, took a long thoughtful puff as he studied Dan.

'I was goin' to go into farming with my boy,' he said. 'He's on his way over here with his family. But I've changed my mind. Safari's the way to go. I'm in need of a junior partner.'

'What about your son?'

'Nah, Walter's a city boy. Adelaide. Raised mostly by his mother. Probably make a good farmer. Maybe. A young buck like you — able to handle himself — that's the type I'm lookin' for.'

'Me? I know nothing about big-game hunting.'

'You're from the bush. Like me. Bush kids are raised around guns. I knew how to handle a rifle when I was knee-high to a grasshopper. I bet you did too.'

Dan had always owned a rifle, and could indeed handle one reasonably well.

'All I've ever shot are rabbits, roos and foxes.'

'Doesn't matter the size of the target, so long as you hit the mark. You've used a 303, haven't you?'

'Why do you say that?'

'Just askin'. Thought you might have come up from South Africa after a term in the forces. I know of a few who have.'

'No. I ... I was a crewman on a British merchantman, and just decided not to renew my brief. I don't have a gun.'

'I see. Well, I have an old three-oh you can borrow. I'm offerin' you a job in a growing business. Full of excitement. A chance to see the country. What do you say?'

Dan considered it. The job might solve his immediate problem — a desperate need for money. Freeman seemed to be a man reluctant to let a few facts stand in the way of a good story, but Dan had met plenty like him. He knew that as long as he didn't take him too seriously and discounted almost everything he said, he might be able to tolerate him for a while. He also needed to lie low for a period before attempting to make his way back home. Accepting a position in Freeman's safari company could offer both.

Dan asked what he would be paid. He had no idea what a reasonable rate might be, but he guessed Freeman would understate it. He haggled half-heartedly, and Freeman told him the job included his keep.

Dan bargained a moment longer to show he wasn't an easy mark, then said, 'I'll take it.'

'Hah!' Freeman said, extending his hand. 'And you won't regret it, Danny my boy.'

Dan Sullivan, now known as Sutherland, hoped he was right.

* * *

Freeman took another mouthful of his beer and watched Dan climb the stairs to his room — a room, Freeman guessed, that he would not have been able to afford had he not received an advance on his first month's wages.

He was pleased young Dan Sutherland had taken up his offer. It meant he wasn't required to employ his son.

It was true Walter had been born and raised in the city, but that wasn't the reason he didn't want him in the safari business. He had a wife and child to support and the safari business was dangerous. He also knew that he'd have to offer Walter a proper wage and even a share of the business.

He took a sip of his beer and conceded it would be difficult to explain the changed circumstances when Walter arrived, but he would help them find a plot that met their new financial constraints. Walter would understand. And he was confident his son would make a good living from farming because he had the right temperament. He was dependable, steady and careful — whereas Bill was none of those things. That's why he was better off living his dream of being a white hunter.

He felt a twinge of guilt that the new situation might cause a ruction between Walter and his wife, Vivian, whose family assets would fund the majority of the farm purchase now that Bill wasn't planning to contribute. She was a formidable woman, and he was relieved not to be entangling himself with her financially.

He drank his beer with a deep feeling of satisfaction. All was progressing well. The family complications were small matters that Bill would deal with at the appropriate time, and his discussions with Dan concluded quite nicely.

He did have something of an advantage though. He knew Dan was broke when he made his offer. He also knew he was a deserter from the Boer War. Merchant sailors didn't wear those boots.

Poor bugger, he thought. *Must have done a scarper just before the whole show ended.*

Freeman didn't care if Dan Sutherland was a deserter. He could be pragmatic about such matters when it suited his purposes. What was important was that he was a strong young fellow, with plenty of pluck. It was just the combination that Freeman Safaris needed in its first employee.

* * *

The train journey to Nairobi provided Dan with his first view of British East Africa, and for the first hundred miles he watched the sansevieria wasteland that surrounded the track roll by with mounting dismay. It wasn't the lush garden he'd imagined tropical Africa to be. As they approached the town of Voi, the matted spiny scrub dispersed, but the red, rock-hard earth with its bleak grassland, peppered by only a few gnarled and knotted trees, persisted. He bedded down in the dak bungalow at Voi regretting his decision and wondering how long his run of bad luck would continue.

The following morning was crisp and moist, giving a lie to the almost unendurable dry heat of the previous day. As they steamed northwest, and the sun climbed, it again became very hot, but there were some signs of improvement in the countryside as they made several river crossings.

An impressive stone construction bridged the Tsavo River, where a large herd of buffalo were bathing in the muddy brown waters.

Freeman had been able to answer his many questions during the journey and Dan asked him what he knew about buffalos.

'Big trouble,' he answered. 'Some say they kill more people than lions.'

'I've spent plenty of time around cattle,' Dan said. 'In western Queensland once I was sent out to find a small herd of strays. They'd been stuck in the backblocks for more than a year following a long wet spell. When I found them they were really wild. A couple of times a bull would charge me, but a few cracks of the stockwhip got him into line. I wondered how bad buffalos might be.'

'I think the only thing that will stop a buffalo is a 450 Rigby, or something similar. Even then, you have to hit them just right. Most amateurs make the mistake of taking a front-on brain shot.'

'What's wrong with that?'

'There's so much bone and horn in that skull that the bullet can easily be deflected. And you don't get a second chance.'

Dan looked down at the herd, remembering the bull he'd faced in the Transvaal. Maybe his luck was not so bad after all.

As the second evening approached, the track crossed several deep ravines in the densely wooded hills around Kibwezi. This was more as he imagined East Africa to be. They slept that night at Makindu, in another dak bungalow, surrounded by dense bush. At more than three thousand feet above sea level, Makindu's air was tangy and cool. Dan was starting to feel more and more positive about his new adventure, though he was reserving judgement until he saw how Freeman handled the new business.

They were en route again at daybreak.

Dan was facing the north side of the track. Freeman, sitting opposite him, indicated to the view out the window behind him.

'Mt Kilimanjaro,' he said.

Dan turned, but at first couldn't see what Freeman was referring to. He was looking for something in scale with the landscape. Then he saw it. The mountain rose from the plain like a colossus — a shining, breathtaking mirage.

'Is that snow?' he asked.

'It is. We're lucky today. Once the sun gets up, the cloud or heat haze hides the mountain.'

'How far is it?'

'Well, it's in German East. Must be about eighty miles away.'

Dan couldn't take his eyes from it. The mountain seemed to have gathered all the surrounding hills into its embrace so that the eye raced across the flat land to its wooded foothills. Then it rose, etched against the sky, to overshadow the entire horizon to the south. He could see the ravages caused by ancient lava flows. The mountain stole shades of pink and green from the early sun to colour its glaciers.

'What a beautiful mountain,' he said, almost to himself.

'We have another one,' Freeman said.

'Another what?'

33

'Another snowy mountain. To the north. Mt Kenya. Sometimes you can see both from the hills outside Nairobi.'

Dan's mood lifted further and his earlier optimism went up with it.

Then the train arrived in Nairobi.

'How far is it to town?' Dan asked as they alighted at the station.

'You're looking at it,' Freeman said, nodding towards a wide, pot-holed track and a collection of odd buildings strung the length of it, many no more than hovels. Vacant lots between the structures were littered with rubbish and partially submerged in large pools of evil-looking water — likely the remnants of a recent downpour. Beyond the buildings, such as they were, the black mud surrounded drab canvas tents, many with stained bedding strung on lines to dry out.

Nearest the station was a double-storey timber building with a corrugated-iron roof: *Victoria Hotel*. Beneath the main sign was another with *Tommie Woods* in parentheses. A goat sauntered through the open door.

Various conveyances ferried people and their possessions down the road. Freeman chose one of the many natives touting their services outside the station. He and Dan followed him to his rickshaw and, with their bags loaded behind, they bobbed along the rutted road with one boy pulling the contraption, and another pushing.

Bill directed the boys down a track even worse than the rutted mess they'd bounced along from the station. He pointed at a weatherboard and iron-roofed house and told them to stop at the steps. A woman came onto the veranda, folded her arms across her buxom breasts, and fixed Freeman with a withering look.

'That fob-watch you left me stopped the minute you walked out the door.'

'Ah, Mrs Cobb,' Freeman said. 'This is Dan Sutherland.' Turning to Dan, he added needlessly, 'Mrs Cobb is the keeper of the boarding house.'

'If you don't have the back rent, you can just get back on that rickshaw and go to hell.'

Freeman was busying himself with his luggage — a single leather Gladstone bag.

'Mrs Cobb, Mrs Cobb ... I have your rent and ...' He swept an arm towards Dan in a charade of cordiality. 'A new customer. Mr Sutherland is interested in a room in your excellent guesthouse. Surely that calls for a smile?'

'Hmmph,' she said, and turned on her heel.

Freeman shrugged. 'Come along, Dan. I'll show you to your room.'

Dan collected his bag and followed Freeman into the hall.

He'd given little thought to the security of his tenure with Freeman Safaris. If he had, he might have wished for better prospects. But it would have made no difference. It was either Freeman or, if he was to avoid starvation, turning himself over to the authorities.

Somehow, the fact that he had no choice was, perversely, a comfort to him.

CHAPTER 4

Gentleman's Safari Outfitter. White hunter for hire. William Freeman Prop'r.
Fully equipped for your convenience and comfort. Contact prop'r c/- Nairobi PO.

The train rolled into Nairobi station, gave a final exhausted huff of steam, and came to a rattling, shuddering stop.

The usual clamour of activity erupted, with vendors and their assistants vying with the arriving passengers' friends and relatives for space on the packed platform.

As the train emptied, Dan craned his neck over the heads of the crowd. An Englishman had responded to Freeman's advertisement in the *Mombasa Mail* and was expected from the coast. Dan had been given the task of finding the client and ferrying him safely to the guesthouse. Freeman was unavailable for the welcoming as he had by now realised he needed to find porters if he was to deliver the promise of his advertisement. He'd gone off to the Kikuyu village on the outskirts of the town to negotiate with the chief, promising to return with the essential manpower before Dan delivered the client into the gentle hands of Mrs Cobb.

A heavily built fellow wearing a broad-brimmed grey hat and blue serge suit stepped down from the train. He paused, perusing the crowd, and then offered his hand up to the most eye-catching woman, who appeared at the top of the steps. She lifted the hem of her brown linen skirt, stepped daintily down to the platform and immediately unfurled a pretty lace parasol and twirled it, causing the delicate fringes on its rim to spread and the long ostrich plumes of her wide-brimmed silk hat to flutter like startled birds. Under her brown linen travelling coat was a striped cotton twill blouse of many colours. Her gloves and silk hat matched the tobacco brown of her coat. She smiled at no one in particular, and Dan took an intake of breath.

The train seemed to have disgorged all its passengers by then, and Dan guessed that this well-dressed pair were his clients, although he was almost certain Freeman was not expecting the Englishman to have a female companion. If she intended to accompany the client on safari, it would make life infinitely more complicated.

Dan approached, intending to catch the man's eye, but his gaze was drawn to the woman. She was not quite as attractive as she had appeared from a distance, but she had fine features and her figure filled her many-coloured blouse quite comprehensively. She caught him staring at her and for a breathless moment Dan felt she held his eyes with hers before they moved on to witness the goings-on around her.

'Good morning,' Dan said, addressing the man. 'Mr Basil Rifkin?'

The man looked Dan up and down before answering that he was.

'I'm from Freeman Safaris.'

'Mr Freeman?' the man asked.

'No. Sutherland. Dan Sutherland. I'm Mr Freeman's associate.'

'Thank God,' Rifkin replied in a refined English accent. 'No offence, Sutherland, but I thought you were our safari leader. I was expecting an older man.'

'There's no need to concern yourself on that score. Mr Freeman is unavoidably detained and apologises. He'll greet you personally as soon as he's able.'

'Oh, and this is my wife, Ruth.'

She turned towards him and gave him a generous smile as she raised her gloved hand. 'Charmed,' she said.

He took her hand in his and replied that he was pleased to meet her, which he thought inadequate. As he searched for a more convivial salutation, she raised her eyebrows at him, and he realised he still had hold of her hand. He released his grip.

'So ...' he said, businesslike again. 'May I show you to your accommodation?'

* * *

37

'I do hope this isn't an inconvenience, Mr Freeman,' Ruth Rifkin said in her east-coast American accent. 'It's just that I felt it would be so awfully boring in Mombasa while Basil was out with you, having all the fun.'

'Absolutely no trouble at all, Mrs Rifkin,' Freeman said. 'I'll just make a few small adjustments to our inventory, and everything will be bonzer. We still have plenty of time before we leave.'

'I'm such a bother.'

'Not at all, darling,' Rifkin said. 'I'm just thrilled you could come.'

'I hope you understand, Mr Freeman,' Ruth added. 'I wasn't planning to come to Africa at all. We weren't sure if we could find a suitable nanny, and then ...'

'Delighted,' Freeman insisted. 'Leave it to us.'

Suitably assuaged, the Rifkins returned indoors to Mrs Cobb's guesthouse.

'Bloody hell,' Freeman muttered after the Rifkins were out of earshot. 'That buggers it.'

'"Absolutely no trouble at all, Mrs Rifkin",' Dan said, mimicking Freeman's nasally twang.

'You won't find it so funny when I tell you it's your job to take care of her.'

'Me? But I'm not going with you.'

'Well, you are now. We're off to Baringo with the Rifkins.'

Dan groaned in protest, but to himself he rejoiced at the prospect of having Ruth Rifkin under his care.

The idea continued to occupy his thoughts over the following days.

* * *

'Next, we find you a decent rifle,' Freeman said after they'd completed their order for safari supplies.

'What's wrong with the 303?' Dan asked as he followed Freeman down dusty Government Road.

'It's no good for the new cordite cartridges.'

'What do you use?'

38

'I use 450 Rigbys in a Holland and Holland, but folk around here use all manner of things. There's this bloke, an English lord, who went hunting up around Lake Baringo before the railway came through. Made a fortune shooting elephant with a Maxim gun.'

'A Maxim gun?' Dan had seen them in operation against the Boers.

'It was before the commissioner declared Baringo a game reserve — damn him. A man could make a tidy sum from ivory back then. They say that Delamere — the English bloke — made fourteen thousand pounds! Can you imagine? Now it's off-limits without a licence for the likes of us. If you don't want to buy a licence, you have to go to the godforsaken Sudan these days. Anyway, here we are.'

Freeman had stopped outside a shop with a shiny bicycle propped against the veranda post. On its seat was a sign: *Brand New from Manchester.* The shop was a weatherboard, single-storey building, and appeared as if it had been built before the road was aligned: it was set back a few paces from the line of adjoining shops. *Murdock's Merchandise*, proclaimed the sign above the door.

Inside was a motley assortment of hardware, camping equipment, bicycles and a variety of trade goods, like *mericani* cloth and red beads typical of those used to barter with the natives.

The storekeeper came from behind his counter, wearing a stiff calico apron.

'Gentlemen, good morning. John Murdock at your service. May I be of assistance?'

'Good morning,' Freeman said, answering for both of them. 'Mr Sutherland here needs a rifle.'

'Does he indeed?' he said, turning his attention to Dan and giving him a broad smile. 'May I ask what you have in mind for it, sir?'

'Big game,' Freeman answered before Dan could respond.

'And not too expensive,' Dan added.

Before the shopkeeper could begin his spiel, Freeman headed for the door. 'I'll leave you to it, Dan. I've got some business to do. See you back at the house shortly.'

As Freeman walked out the door, Murdock moved into Dan's line of sight, his smile unchanged.

'So you want a piece for big-game hunting?' Murdock said.

'Yes, and not too expensive,' Dan repeated.

'Ah … but you may reconsider your opinion of what's expensive when you're staring down the barrel at a charging rhino, eh?'

He went behind his counter and moved some boxes aside. 'Now here's my recommendation,' he said, reverently opening the case to reveal a beautiful piece of gleaming steel and polished wood lying on red baize. Even the case with its leather binding and brass corners conveyed extravagance.

'The 450 Rigby,' he said in the hushed tones one might use in the presence of royalty. 'A double rifle for the discerning sportsman.'

Dan took the Rigby and hefted it in his hands. 'It's beautiful,' he said. 'And heavy.'

'As it should be,' Murdock remarked, gently lifting it from Dan's hands and returning it to its case. 'It takes the 450 Nitro Express three-and-a-quarter-inch cordite cartridges. Designed to stop dangerous game in its tracks.'

'Hmmm …' Dan said.

'Elephant. Rhino. Buffalo,' Murdock said, reaching to gently stroke the rifle. 'This is your friend. Muzzle velocity of over two thousand feet per second.'

'I see … How much?'

'The rifle was, of course, calibrated for the 450 Nitro Express cordite cartridge at the factory.'

'Of course.'

Murdock rambled on for a further ten minutes, expounding the virtues of John Rigby and his excellent double-barrel rifle, all the while smiling in the manner of a proud parent presenting his new offspring.

Dan was becoming emotionally attached to this exquisite piece of workmanship, and he reached out his hand to gently touch the barrel.

'So … ahem … How much?'

'Fifteen pounds, sir.'

Murdock's expression didn't change, but Dan's did. He swallowed hard and removed his hand from the Rigby as if he'd been scalded. It was more than he'd earn with Freeman in three months.

'Hmmm ...' he said again, regaining his composure. 'What else do you have?'

An hour later, Dan handed over the remainder of his cash, which included most of what Freeman had paid him in advance of wages. He walked out of the shop with his second-hand 404 Jeffery. It was a bolt-action rifle, which was not his first choice, but an affordable one. He had to admit that Murdock's praise for the name 'Jeffery' restored a degree of confidence that the second-hand status of the rifle had shaken.

It was a couple of days later, when Dan was firing a few rounds to familiarise himself with the action, that Freeman saw the Jeffery for the first time.

'What's that?' he asked.

'It's my new rifle.'

'I can see that, but it's a bolt action.'

'Yes, a 404 Jeffery.'

'A bolt action! Why in blazes did you buy a bolt action? I told you to get a Holland and Holland double.'

'No you didn't. Anyway, Murdock said it's the best available. And I got it at a good price.'

'No doubt,' Freeman said, and turned away.

There was something in Freeman's tone that unsettled him.

'What do you mean?'

Freeman sighed. 'The 404 Jeffery is all right ... I suppose ... only ...'

'Only what?'

'I don't trust a magazine. They can jam, and if the cartridge gets stuck in the only barrel you have, well ... you're left with just a club against an oncoming elephant. Still, if you're good enough, you'll drop it with your first shot, won't you?'

'You mean it can jam?'

'Pretty much. Particularly if it's not been cared for.' He squinted at the rifle. 'Yours is second-hand, right?'

'It is.'

And it was Freeman's turn to say, 'Hmmm ...'

CHAPTER 5

Dan was at the site Bill had selected for their first camp, trimming the tree he'd felled for the ridge pole of the clients' tent, when he heard voices singing in the distance. The songs grew stronger and finally a column of about ten porters came into view with Freeman at its head. Beside him was a small, nearly naked native carrying a long throwing spear.

When Freeman was almost up to Dan he raised his arm, bringing the column, and the singing, to a halt.

'G'day, Dan,' he said, taking his bandana from around his neck and running it over his sweating face. 'How's the camp coming along?'

'Well enough. Where're your clients?' he asked, looking down the line of men, now sitting beside or on their loads.

'They're not joining us yet. I'm spending a few days raising more porters and getting some supplies first.'

'And who's this?' Dan asked, nodding in the direction of the man at his side.

'This is Korok,' Freeman said.

The little man thrust his long throwing spear haft-first into the ground beside his foot, and took Dan's hand from his side, pumping it vigorously with both of his. The ivory lip plug bobbled as he made a grimace that was intended to be a smile, revealing his small teeth, filed to points.

He had an elaborate *siliot* — the small circle of hair, matted with mud into a long pigtail — sprouting from his otherwise shaved scalp and swinging like a pendulum whenever he moved his head. A hunting bow was slung over his shoulder and a handful of arrows hung from a plaited and beaded waistband, which also supported a strip of woven and beaded cloth, front and back, meant to afford him a semblance of decency. Tight strands of red and yellow beads ringed his thin throat.

'He's a Pokot,' Freeman added, as if that simple point would explain everything.

'Does he speak?' Dan asked, as the Pokot's gaze roamed the surroundings.

'Not much. But he understands. And he's the best tracker in British East Africa.'

'You know him?'

Freeman shrugged. 'I'm not sure anyone could know this little bugger, but he worked for the most successful hunter on the railway. Inseparable, they were. Turk and his Pokot. If you found one, you found the other. Then Turk disappeared and Korok too, until I spied him passing through Nairobi. He knows animals like nobody else. When do you expect to finish the camp?'

'I should have it done in another couple of days. It would help if I had some labourers,' Dan said, nodding towards the group of porters.

'Can't afford 'em. I'll be bringing the clients and the safari here the day after tomorrow. Then we're off hunting up near Mt Kenya.'

'What are we hunting?'

'Anything and everything.'

* * *

Dan made a final inspection of the camp. The kitchen, with its rack of pot-rails made from stripped saplings, was set in a clearing he'd made in the bush. At the back of the kitchen was the cooking fire, surrounded by flat round stones he'd hauled up from the creek. The clients' tent, with lines as sharp as sabres, faced the campfire. The supply tent was pitched close to his and Bill's and far enough from where the porters would spread their bedrolls to be safe.

Satisfied, Dan sat on one of the seating logs he'd put under an awning that he'd pitched in case of rain, and relaxed. Within minutes, he heard the lilting voices of a column of porters.

'Right on time,' Dan said, as a hundred or more porters appeared through the bush with Freeman and the Rifkins at the head of the line. Ruth looked stunning in a close-fitting, leopard-skin shirt, tan

43

jodhpurs and high leather boots. A natty slouch hat with a bold yellow feather sticking from its leopard-skin band completed her outfit. Her husband, Basil, was also in jodhpurs, with a many-pocketed tan shirt, wide-brimmed hat and a bandolier of cartridges circling his midriff. There was another over his shoulder.

Freeman came ahead of them.

'Is the camp ready?' he asked quietly.

'It is.'

'Good.'

Looking back to ensure the Rifkins were still out of earshot, Freeman whispered to Dan. 'He's a ripe one, this Basil Rifkin. A right proper toff at times, but as soon as he gets a few ales in him, he's all hellfire and brimstone. He wants to make a trophy of everything that's out there. Lion, rhino, elephant. He said that he and his father went shooting in North America year after year. Never worried about a bag limit. I explained the licensing system, but I don't think he wants to hear it. Says it's just a load of nonsense cobbled together for the sake of local revenue.'

'What are we going to do?'

'I'll have to watch him like a hawk. Can't have my licence cancelled on my first safari, can I?'

The Rifkins joined them.

'Basil. Mrs Rifkin … you remember Dan, my associate?'

Rifkin greeted him and shook his hand. Ruth nodded and smiled.

'Dan will show you to your quarters for tonight. I'll see you at dinner.'

The Rifkins began to follow Dan, but Basil turned back to Freeman.

'Oh, Bill,' he said. 'Can I speak to you about this Winchester of mine? I have a few questions.'

Freeman agreed and Basil waved Dan and Ruth to go.

In the walk to the clients' tent Dan struggled to make conversation. Ruth Rifkin made him nervous — he'd hardly met a woman like her before. Poised, self-confident; he didn't know what might interest her.

'Your husband is a keen sportsman,' he said.

'Mmm,' was her reply.

'Has he … have you, done a lot of hunting?'

'Oh, Basil is always hunting. Borneo. India. America these days. Both North and South. Mind you, I shouldn't complain. I knew he was obsessed with hunting. I met him in Chicago when he was on a hunting trip with his father.'

'And you? Do you hunt?'

'Good heavens, no. It's an appalling pastime.' She quickly glanced at Dan, and added, apologetically, 'Sorry, I'm sure it has some redeeming aspects.'

'Oh, I don't mind you saying,' he lied. 'I've only just started in the business with Bill. Here we are.'

He stood with her at the door of her tent.

'You're an Australian?' she asked.

He nodded. 'I am.'

'Then … what brings you so far from home if you don't like hunting?'

He was momentarily stumped for an answer. It had been some time since he needed an explanation for his presence in East Africa. 'Travel,' he pronounced abruptly.

She nodded and paused, seemingly lost in thought.

'Yes, you're wise to do so when you're young. I wish … Oh, well, I'd better go in.'

She reached out her hand and he shook it.

'Thank you, Dan.' She pushed open the tent flap, then turned back, eyeing him thoughtfully for a moment. 'Would you do something for me, Dan?' she asked.

'Yes,' he replied too swiftly.

'Would you ask one of the boys to fetch me some water so that I might take a bath before dinner?'

He nodded, the image of Ruth Rifkin disrobing and stepping delicately into her tin bathtub forming in his mind. 'My pleasure, Mrs Rifkin.'

* * *

45

After dinner that night, Freeman, Dan and the Rifkins sat around the fire together, discussing the arrangements for the start of their safari. Ruth Rifkin had changed into buff-coloured slacks and soft canvas mosquito boots. Her matching jacket sported fake leopard-skin lapels, and it was open at the neck, giving the skin of her long slender neck a delicate glow in the flickering firelight.

'I'd like to be out beyond the Kikuyu reserve by next Saturday,' Freeman said. 'That's where we'll start to see some big game.'

'Excellent,' Basil said in his fine British accent. 'You've been painting a jolly fine picture of your successes up there, and I can't wait to get one of those big trophies in the sights of my 275.'

'Not all of them will make it into Ward's, but I've had a couple of opportunities up in that part of the country. Mind you, I'm not one to worry about records and such.'

Dan tried not to groan. He'd already been at enough fireside chats with Bill Freeman to know that although he was an excellent hunter, he was loose with the truth. When an opportunity arose to paint himself as the best of the white hunters, he was not afraid to gild the lily.

'Yeah,' Bill continued, staring into the fire as if he could see it all again. 'There was this big bull elephant up at Lake Rudolph. He was a world record if ever I saw one.'

'Really?'

'My oath. A hundred pound of ivory a side, he was. At least.'

'Did you bag him?'

'I did. But not until I'd spent a day stalking him on my belly, crawling over razor-sharp lava rubble. You should have seen the toes of my boots. Completely gone by the time I got into range. Wore my metal belt buckle clean off. But I had to take my time. Hiding behind boulders. Over the lava. Hands and elbows worn raw and bloody. You can't be too careful when a world record is within your grasp.'

'Did you get it entered into Ward's?'

'Nah. As I say, I'm not one for records, so I've never bothered to inform old Rowland about him.'

'My father got an entry in Ward's for his Mule Deer in 1890,' Basil said. 'It was a beauty. Twenty-nine and a half inches tip to tip.'

'What's Ward's, dear?' Ruth asked.

'Rowland Ward's *Records of Big Game*. It's the hunter's bible, darling. It contains a list of all the record big-game trophies from all over the world. Elephant tusks, antelope horns, the nose to tail of a lion. They're all there.'

'Is that what you want, Basil? To get your name in the record book?'

Basil chuckled wryly. 'There's not a hunter on this earth who wouldn't give his eye teeth to have his trophy entered in Ward's. But to be honest, you have to be very lucky to even catch sight of a trophy animal. It's quite another thing to bring it down.'

Dan glanced at Freeman, knowing that he too would be happy to have a client of Freeman Safaris appear in Ward's. Freeman Safaris' reputation would soar. And hunting fees, likewise.

* * *

It took the safari and its one hundred and twenty-five porters, sixteen pack animals and two wagons three days to reach Fort Hall and a view of the jagged white peaks of Mt Kenya, rearing before them like two broken fangs. They then skirted the foothills, and entered the fertile valleys undulating between the mountain and the Aberdare Range to the west.

Although the safari was self-sufficient in food, including caviar, tinned fruit and ham from Fortnum and Masons, French champagne and even ice, wrapped securely in folds of burlap, Freeman kept a lookout for fresh meat. When a herd of impala, or Grant's or Thomson's gazelle, appeared in the distance, the Pokot would materialise at Freeman's side, bobbing along in his curious gait, ready to lead the stalk.

Much to his annoyance, Dan was excluded from these excursions, remaining in camp to ensure that the clients' every wish was heeded.

On day seven the safari set off shortly after dawn, and by mid-morning Freeman led them along the Naro Moru River, where the umbrella trees threw shade so deep and in such stark contrast to the sight-searing brilliance of the whitened grassland that they often passed from one to the other in temporary blindness. Ahead of them loomed the mountain, with its lure of even cooler, more shaded, retreats.

At noon, they paused to rest in a grove of acacias and scattered doum palms. Dan slumped down beside Freeman, his back resting against the yellow bark of a fever tree.

'Oh, gawd,' Freeman muttered as Abubakar, the Swahili headman, approached. He stood to attention until Freeman acknowledged him.

'What is it, Abubakar?'

'The men are unhappy, sahib.'

'What is it this time?'

'They say that if the *bwana* must make such haste to Kirinyaga they should have food or they will surely die on its sacred slopes.'

Kirinyaga — the mountain of brightness — was the name the Kikuyu gave to their sacred mountain.

'They have their *posho*. Two pound a day. It's regulation.'

'The men say it is meat not maize meal that gives strength to the leg, *Bwana* Bill.'

Freeman turned to Dan. 'Do you see what a bloke has to put up with?'

The question was rhetorical. Dan remained silent.

'It's not enough that a man must suffer a woman on his first safari, to keep an eye on his Ps and Qs at dinner and mind his language, but I have to pander to a hundred and twenty or more whingeing Kikuyu porters.'

Turning back to Abubakar, he said, 'They'll get their meat presently. In the meantime, tell them to keep up the pace or they'll have the taste of my *koboko* on their backs.'

Abubakar knew as well as Dan that Freeman's threat of the hippo-hide whip was merely bluff, but he snapped to attention and returned to the line of porters.

Dan knew the porters' complaints were well founded. Freeman had been unable to shoot enough fresh meat for the men and, whether it was in response to the porters' protests, or that he simply wanted the sport, they made early camp that day so that Freeman could hunt for the pot.

Basil Rifkin decided to add his rifle to the task and, with Korok leading the way, the two men and their gun-bearers headed out, leaving Dan in charge of setting up camp and making it safe for the night.

He formed a team to cut down some thorny acacia branches to safely corral the livestock from any predators. When the *boma* was completed and the oxen enclosed, he gave the men leave to take refuge from the heat of the day, and to a man they retired to their shelters to sleep.

Dan made one last round of the camp. All was quiet. Ruth had apparently taken to her tent for a nap. He was dripping with sweat and the river seemed a good idea.

In his tent, he pulled off his socks and boots and removed his shirt before heading to the water with a bar of soap in his pocket.

As he approached the river, he heard a scream. It was Ruth.

Charging through the long grass, he arrived on the sandy riverbank to find Ruth, wrapped in a cotton *kanga*, dancing around a ball of black-and-white fury that was determined to investigate her pile of clothing, regardless of the commotion.

Ruth was making breathy distress sounds as she tried to rescue her clothes while the animal responded with snuffling guttural growls, and bared fangs.

'Oh ... oh ...' she said. The animal turned on her each time she approached.

'Ruth,' he called. 'Leave it.'

She ran to him, flinging her arms around his neck, and almost knocking them both to the ground.

'Dan! My clothes! Make it go away.'

'Calm down,' he said. 'It won't hurt your clothes. It's just ... curious.'

'But what *is* it? It's so ... vicious.'

'Just nosey. It's a honey badger.'

He now knew the animal well, unlike at his first encounter, while hiding from the Boers in a burrow in the Transvaal.

'Oh, but look ... my new blouse!'

The badger had its nose buried in the material and was swinging it about in an obvious attempt to be free of it. He succeeded, and with a final snort scurried off in search of more nourishing items.

Ruth took a deep breath, and Dan became acutely conscious of the press of her breasts, which had nothing but a thin film of damp cotton between them and his bare chest. His hands slid down her back and she stiffened for a moment. Then she sighed, and relaxed. He could feel the undulations of her spine as his fingers glided lower until he reached her firm and well-rounded bottom. For a long moment, neither of them moved.

Something changed in Ruth's posture, and as she raised her face and met his lips, her body moulded to his.

Dan felt the same rush of adrenalin he'd had when facing the Cape buffalo. His breath caught in his chest and he felt the pump of blood through his veins.

Ruth responded to his excitement, locking her fingers in his hair and holding him to her mouth while her tongue engaged his.

Her hands fell to his belt buckle and her colourful *kanga* dropped to the ground, revealing a starkly white body in contrast to the nut-brown colouring of her arms, neck and face.

She drew him to the ground and opened to him.

CHAPTER 6

For days, Dan watched Ruth surreptitiously, hoping to catch a glimpse of acknowledgement of their new relationship, but she was a marvel of discretion. When others were in the vicinity, it was understandable that she took care to keep their conversations as they always had been: informal, but polite and cordial. Dan reciprocated, and additionally, was mindful to follow a correct professional client–employee relationship.

However, when it was clear there was no one around, Dan found it more difficult to understand Ruth's detachment. On the first such opportunity, when he saw Ruth wander away from the camp towards a small waterhole concealed in the bush, he followed her, feeling sure she intended him to do so. She was standing at the waterhole quite alone. When he reached out to her, she drew away.

'Dan,' she said. 'This isn't wise.'

She turned from him and returned to camp, leaving him feeling confused.

He decided Ruth was simply being extra cautious. Of course she must be careful. She had a marriage to consider.

There would be other times when they could be themselves without fearing intrusion.

* * *

Old Tom Worral had been farming the fertile lower slopes of Mt Kenya for ten years. In the stretch of land between the dry East African plateau through which the Naro Moru and several other rivers flowed, and the heavily forested higher slopes where towering podocarpus, stinkwoods, camphors and juniper trees lived in a cloud forest, Tom had built a large shack, where he lived alone with his small pack of Irish wolfhounds.

He'd tried his hand farming potatoes, cassava, millet, wheat, sugar, flax, beans, aloes, sisal, ground nuts and many forms of fruit trees.

'I tried brussels sprouts,' he said to the four visitors sitting around his fire. 'They grew six feet high. Six feet!'

Freeman told Dan he'd met Tom Worral years before when he was the hunter for a survey party of railway engineers investigating the possibility of a railway line to Nanyuki. Worral's farm was the reason Freeman had now decided to make camp nearby. He'd hoped that Worral could restock their dwindling fresh vegetable supplies, but on the walk to the farm that evening they could see he wouldn't be able to help. The fields were a graveyard of dead or dying crops.

Dan asked the obvious question: 'What happened to the brussels sprouts, and the other crops?'

'Blight, droughts, floods. Sometimes the damn things just wither for no reason. Like the livestock. I've tried sheep. They started well, then they just grew thin and died. The native goats and fat-tail sheep are about the only ones that seem to last. I've held onto a few cattle, but it's a constant battle. It's the leopards, the wild dogs, the lions. One way or another, you have to fight to hold onto what you have up here.'

A dog howled somewhere out in the darkness and the call was carried by others. Soon there was a dissonance of yelping and yowling animals.

'They've probably scented a leopard,' Tom said by way of explanation.

'Is that why you keep them, to protect the cattle against the leopards?' It was Ruth who spoke. She sat close to the fire in an effort to keep the chill night air at bay.

'Nah, the dogs were another experiment that failed.'

'What was it?' she asked.

'There's an antelope in these mountain ranges, the most beautiful animal you'll ever see,' he said wistfully. 'It's called a bongo. I've had a few quick glimpses of the creature but nobody has ever shot one here in British East. It has a rich red coat with white stripes and horns shaped like a spiral staircase. Just beautiful.

Well, someone told me about Irish wolfhounds. How they could run like greyhounds, but had the killing power of mastiffs. They must have done the trick in Ireland. The last wolf sighted there was over a hundred years ago. The breed's been kept going by only a few families since. A friend of mine knew of one such family and arranged for a few pups to be sent over here.'

'Surely there's a world of difference between a wolf and an antelope,' Freeman said.

'Aye, but the wolfhound is closely related to the Scottish deerhound, which have been used for centuries coursing for red deer.'

'How did it go?'

'A total failure,' he said with a nod of resignation. 'The bongo are too shy, too smart and too quick.'

Silence descended on the group until Basil Rifkin, who had sat enthralled during the telling of the story, spoke for the first time.

'That's it,' he said.

The others looked at him.

'That's my quarry. A bongo. A creature that's never been shot in British East Africa. That's the trophy animal I need to get my name into Ward's *Record*.'

* * *

'Forest hogs,' Bill Freeman said. 'They're big brutes, three hundred pound or more, with nasty little tusks that can slit a man's gut or carve the meat from his shin bone as quick as a wink.'

Freeman had the habit of gleefully reciting to Dan the most dreadful possibilities that could arise from any hunting excursion. He said it was part of his education, but Dan suspected it was Freeman's way of impressing upon his young protégé how learned and skilled he was in the art of hunting.

'Even a full-grown leopard will think twice before tackling one of them,' Freeman added.

On this occasion his audience included not only Dan but the Rifkins as well. It was the night after they'd left Tom Worral's farm and in the morning they would enter the misty forest on the side of the mountain to hunt. Dan wondered if the wily Freeman was trying to dissuade his clients from the folly of pursuing the elusive bongo in the almost impenetrable jungles that awaited them.

Later, when Dan found Freeman alone, checking the *boma* fence surrounding the camp, he asked him how he expected to satisfy Rifkin's request to bag an animal that few had seen, and none had shot.

'Are you hoping he'll change his mind?' Dan asked.

'Not at all.'

'Then why make the whole expedition sound so difficult and dangerous?'

Freeman tapped his index finger on the side of his head. 'So's he knows what a clever chap Bill Freeman is. I want him to know that when we find a bongo for him it's no small thing. I want him to rave about it when he gets home. I want him to tell all his hunting friends in England and America about Freeman Safaris.'

Dan had some considerable reservations about this strategy. It was true that the skill demanded of the white hunter by his client was to locate the desired quarry. It was then entirely in the hands of the client to complete the contract by shooting it. But, since none of the considerably more skilled white hunters had managed to find a bongo let alone shoot one, he imagined that Bill Freeman was unlikely to be the first. In which case the plan would backfire, Rifkin would consider the safari a failure and the fault would lie with Freeman Safaris.

'But Bill, what makes you think we can find a bongo?'

Freeman smiled.

'The Pokot,' he said.

* * *

Korok's Nilo-Hamitic ancestors had lived in the Great Rift Valley with its sweeping grasslands and occasional acacias for seven hundred years. Like their cousins the Maasai, the Pokot raised cattle and, whenever possible, stole them from their traditional enemies, the Marakwet.

Korok's mother had died soon after he was born and he was raised by one of his father's other wives, a kindly woman who loved to sing to him. With her encouragement, Korok learned to compose poems that she would put to music of her own creation.

He was much younger than his half-siblings, but was quite close in age to his uncle's son, Tobeya. When not attending to their herding duties, the boys would spend hours together, battling imaginary enemies to save their village from death and destruction. They also loved to hunt.

The Pokot were not jungle dwellers and therefore Korok was not familiar with the creatures of the forest, nor was he experienced in jungle tracking, but he could follow a trail anywhere, and he had an uncanny understanding of animal behaviour. He could enter the mind of any animal, reptile or amphibian and feel what they felt, hear what they heard, and see what they saw. There was no animal activity that took him unawares. He could anticipate a creature's every move, feeling it as his own. If anyone had thought to ask him how he developed such a skill, he would have been unable to answer. Perhaps he'd been born with a gift that had lain dormant during his early life as a cattle-herder. Had it not been for the great catastrophe that swept his homeland when he was a young man, causing him to leave what remained of his village and his people, he may never in fact have realised he had such a talent at all.

The great Rinderpest panzootic of the 1880s and '90s swept south from the Horn of Africa with the inevitability of a flood, killing cattle and almost all the buffalo, antelope, giraffe, wildebeest, warthog and other even-toed ungulates in its path. Many thousands of Pokot starved to death, as did countless others in eastern Africa who depended upon cattle or hunting for their livelihood at that time.

Korok survived the famine, but it was a later, far more devastating disaster, which caused him to leave his ancient lands and find a place on the railway where his skills were found to be useful.

The white man, Robert Turk, had been a man of his own heart. Detached, proficient, practical, methodical. Unencumbered by pointless emotions. They worked well together, hunting for days with not a spoken word and although seldom sighting another human neither suffered the loss.

Freeman wasn't the hunter Turk had been, but Korok had known the Australian during his time with Turk and knew that, despite his bluster, he had the necessary qualities of courage and determination needed to be a good hunter. If he hadn't, Korok would not have agreed to be his tracker.

Now, as they entered the forested slopes and mist-shrouded valleys of Mt Kenya, Korok was prepared for the unknown. Freeman said the white client wanted a bongo. Korok had never seen such an animal, but had learned from the Ndio forest hunters how to find and identify one.

He was excited by the prospect of a new and challenging quarry. His entire body drew tense at the opportunity to test his wits against such an exceptional animal.

* * *

It had been three days since they entered the jungle, and Dan felt there was something intangibly different about it. Around the Transvaal and in the Free State, the countryside was much like that part of Queensland where he'd lived and worked — scattered scrub in waving grasslands that would take days to cross. In the distance would rise the smudged blue of distant hills. The coast, on the other hand, wore palm trees amid blue, coral-studded lagoons. Kikuyuland had forests surrounding large areas of cultivation, but those forests were nothing like the almost impenetrable mass in which they now trekked. It was truly jungle.

The understorey dripped with lianas, mosses and strangulating vines. He had read somewhere about poisonous plants, but couldn't recall if they were African or from some other exotic place. At the time it was of no consequence. Now it felt important that he know.

Every living thing had a strangeness about it that was intimidating. He knew nothing of the insects that jumped, flew or crawled around him or if any or all of them might inflict a poisonous sting. Flamboyant butterflies flopped about in the moist air, heavy with the scent of decaying vegetation. In his ignorance it was both exhilarating and daunting.

With darkness came sounds of a multitude of creatures large and small, calling, feeding, doing battle or mating.

Sometimes, when Freeman called a halt for rest or water, the porters remained strangely quiet and only the tweet or whistle of invisible birds punctuated the silence. It was as if these men too, familiar with the bustle of village life and only the occasional intrusion of wildlife into their existence, sensed the difference.

Somewhere above the dense undergrowth soared enormous trees whose crowns could not be seen except in places where an ancient tower of timber had finally succumbed to age and gravity, fallen to earth, and in so doing cleared a corridor to the sky. The hole in the foliage opened a view to the upper echelons, where grey mists floated on warm eddies.

In such dappled clearings, where the sun had not fallen for many decades, a furious new battle raged as thousands of plants fought their way towards the light. The growth spurt was so vigorous that it was impossible to pass through the dense foliage. It was in these spaces that he could finally see the birds whose calls high in the canopy had previously been the only evidence of their presence. Parrots, turacos, various chats, sunbirds and francolins appeared. High above all soared eagles and hawks.

At the head of the safari Dan caught glimpses of bushbucks, duikers and mongooses as they scattered into cover. Overhead, an occasional flash of black and white suggested a troop of colobus monkeys were aloft among the branches, and the muffled bellow of unseen elephants was a constant reminder to be on guard. But there were few opportunities to test his skills with his new 404 Jeffery.

There was no chance of finding game during their tramp around the mountain. Although Freeman had split the porters into two groups with the majority remaining at their base camp, the sound of a hundred bare feet was enough to set to flight most of the shy forest creatures within a mile of their march.

That night, it began to rain. After dinner, the Rifkins joined Dan and Freeman under a canvas fly, and they watched the cooking fire sputter in a fusillade of raindrops that fell from the foliage in large dollops.

'The Pokot spotted fresh spoor this afternoon,' Freeman said.

'Wonderful,' Basil said. 'Then we can go on the stalk in the morning.'

Dan watched Freeman stiffen. He didn't like to be upstaged on his own podium.

'Quite right, Basil,' he said tersely, 'but not before we get another positive sighting. With this rain, all trace of the spoor may be gone by morning.'

'I thought your little man was the best,' Basil taunted.

'He is, but he's not God Almighty. We'll see, and if he can pick it up again, we'll strip down for a fast, light stalk. Provisions for a day or so and only the absolute essentials. It'll be just us two, Korok and two bearers.'

Dan was about to take umbrage, but Ruth beat him to it.

'What about me?' she asked.

Freeman looked aghast. 'You?'

'Yes, me. I've decided I want to see a bongo too.'

'But darling ...' her husband protested. 'Is that wise?'

Even he appeared nonplussed at the prospect of his wife trudging through dense jungle on what was effectively a forced march.

'You said you were glad I could come, so I'm here and I want to go too.'

She folded her arms and glared into the rain.

'Um ... very well, dear. I'm sure Bill can arrange it all for us.'

Even in the feeble light of a flickering campfire, Dan could see Freeman's complexion redden.

'Of course,' he said with great restraint. After a tense silence, he turned to Dan and said, 'That means you'd better come too so you can ... so you can be an extra rifle in case we need it.'

* * *

Korok arose while the dawn was still an hour away, and slipped into the jungle, where the light of neither moon nor stars made an impression on the profound darkness surrounding him.

He relied on his inner eye to guide him, sensing the bulk of trees in his path and using his delicate fingers to find the lacy ends of spindly foliage. His toes found and avoided the brittle dead-drop that would snap upon the smallest added weight, and his small feet occupied spaces between rocks and logs.

He moved into a clearing where the starlight momentarily removed his night vision, and almost collided with a sleeping elephant. The weight of the giant's head rested on two enormous curving tusks, and the steam from his deep rumbling breath rose from the tip of his trunk like vapour from a genie's bottle. Korok stopped for a moment and studied the animal. He'd stalked hundreds and been involved in the slaughter of scores, but the elephants were not his hated enemies; they were his noble adversaries, with whom he engaged in a game of tactics, where either side might succumb, leading ultimately to death. So far, he'd been the victor. How long that continued depended upon luck, skill and god Asis's will. He stepped around the giant and again melted into the thick undergrowth.

After half an hour, the imperceptible light of dawn allowed him to find his bearings and shortly thereafter, the spoor he'd found the day before.

He came upon the bongo quite abruptly as a cacophony of birdcalls welcomed the golden beginning of the day. It lowered its muzzle to hover above the water of a burbling stream and its chestnut coat, boldly striped in white, quivered. Its spiralling horns, tipped with ivory, curved three feet above its head. It was almost the size of a cow, and perhaps because of the tranquillity revealed in its dark moist eyes, appeared harmless. The birdcalls distracted it, and were probably the reason Korok had been able to stalk it so closely, for it remained frozen in its handsome pose for some time.

Korok already knew that this animal was very shy, and not one to linger if there was the slightest suggestion of threat. A sound, an unfamiliar scent, and he would be gone like the wind. The Pokot wanted to whisper sweet words of reassurance to coax it to linger longer, for he wanted to touch it and know all its secrets.

The bongo's long ears swivelled and its large brown eyes, between which flashed a bold white chevron, suggested it had an instinct that something had invaded its secluded, verdant world, but was uncertain.

He watched it drink daintily from the stream and then casually move off, now satisfied that it was safe. Korok knew he could stalk this creature with confidence. He had learned all he needed to know about it in the few minutes it had been his to know.

It was a noble creature, and Korok, who had often been perplexed by the habits of the white man, understood why they would value the bongo as a trophy. He would help them find this elusive creature, and perhaps kill it. That was his job.

But should the bongo escape death, Korok would not be displeased.

Korok felt moved to compose a song for the bongo. The words came easily to him.

Beast of green jungle, be careful
A hunter lies waiting for dawn
Take care, my brown curl-horned beauty
A whisper at dawn will forewarn
The hunter will come. He will kill you
Go softly, your whisper dies too.

CHAPTER 7

The morning arrived dry, and soon after dawn, when everyone was rising, the Pokot returned. Dan saw him jogging in, his head bobbing and his long pigtail swinging.

'Korok's confirmed the bongo's tracks,' Freeman told him. 'He's about an hour or two into the forest. We need to get a wriggle on if we're to reach him today. You see to the clients while I organise the safari.'

The Rifkins were already prepared, even Ruth, who wore a floppy-brimmed hat, jodhpurs and cotton khaki shooting jacket. Dan thought she looked particularly beautiful but also very practical, dressed for the bush with sturdy boots and knee-high gaiters.

He still hadn't had a chance to steal some time with her, and had difficulty controlling the surge of emotions that coursed through him each time she appeared. Every day that passed without her touch was a torment. He spent his idle hours planning their next rendezvous, and how they would make love. He had never felt such emotion, and was impatient to speak to her to confirm it was something special to her too.

He tried to catch her eye as she loosely knotted a red scarf around her neck, but Bill returned before he could do so.

Freeman said he had three porters whom he'd conscripted to carry the extra provisions needed for their expanded numbers.

'Ten of us!' he said under his breath to Dan. 'We're looking more like a caravan than a bloody hunting party.'

Korok led them along a game track, at times disappearing through the dense green curtain to reconnoitre ahead, and then returning to ensure the hunting party was still on course. Freeman and Basil led the main body with their respective gun-bearers in tow. Dan followed Ruth, and the porters brought up the rear.

Freeman had told Dan he didn't need a gun-bearer as it was only he and the client who would make the final stalk.

Although Freeman was concerned about the size of their party because of the noise they would make, they still came upon far more game than previously. During the morning, Dan spotted a giant bush pig family as they dashed along a creek bed. The big boar was every bit as formidable as Freeman had described it. There was the usual clamorous troop of monkeys above, chattering vacuous threats, and several times he caught a glimpse of fleeing duikers and bushbucks as they scampered to safety.

But there was no shooting allowed. Freeman had the clients' agreement that the hunting safari had only one objective, which was to claim a bongo. Until that objective was reached or abandoned, everyone understood there would be no pot-shots taken at other game.

As the morning progressed, the safari line became extended so that Freeman and Basil were a hundred yards ahead of Dan and Ruth. The porters, with their sixty-pound packs, were straggling along the narrow track some distance behind. Although they were alone, Dan kept to himself. It was difficult to walk abreast on the narrow track, and he would not attempt to make conversation to Ruth's back.

About an hour or so after starting, Freeman came trudging back to meet them.

'Where's our porters?' he asked.

Dan told him they hadn't sighted them for a while.

'Why don't you take a rest, Mrs Rifkin,' Freeman said, 'while I go back and give them a bit of a hurry-up?'

'I'll come with you,' Dan offered, hoping Bill would tell him to stay.

'No, you stay here with Mrs Rifkin. The Pokot's up ahead with Basil.'

They sat on a fallen tree beside the track and watched Bill disappear into the bush.

Dan waited for a moment, hoping that Ruth would seize the opportunity denied them for so long. But she sat with him in silence.

He could wait no longer. He turned to her and placed his hand over hers on the log.

'Ruth, I've missed you. When can we be together again?'

She lifted her head and tossed her long dark hair from her face before facing him. 'If you mean as we were the other day by the river ... we can't.'

It wasn't the words so much as the tone of her voice that caused a hard cold knot to form in his stomach. She sounded so clinical that he was cut to the core. 'I don't understand, Ruth. I thought something special happened between us. I certainly felt that way.'

She glanced up the path before speaking. 'I'm sorry you took it so seriously.'

'Of course I took it seriously. How else should I take it? I thought ... hoped ... you felt the same way.'

'You're young, Dan. And I suspect you have a lot to learn about such things.'

'I'm not a child, Ruth. You have no cause to lecture me.'

'Then we'll just leave it, shall we?' She stood, and marched off towards the head of the caravan.

Dan rose and stepped quickly towards her. He grabbed her arm.

She swung to face him with a look of such venom that Dan was stunned. 'Don't you dare lay a hand on me,' she hissed.

Dan's mood swung from wounded to resentment. She had no reason to react as she did, and he felt naive and stupid to have thought she had feelings towards him. He was about to make an angry retort, when from behind him came a loud yell.

'Bill,' he muttered, and ran back along the track. He'd gone about a hundred paces when he came upon the porters dashing towards him.

'*Chui! Chui!*' they shouted.

Leopard.

He heard Bill screaming.

He ran on and found the spot in seconds. Freeman was on the ground, the leopard over him — a snarling yellow fury. It had hold of Bill's arm and was shaking him like a dog with a rat.

Dan had his rifle in his hands and started manoeuvring into position for a shot.

'My God!' It was Ruth, now beside him.

'Ruth! Get back!'

He had his finger on the trigger and all his attention concentrated upon the leopard in his rifle's sights. He was unable to shoot because the animal was crouched too close to Bill. Freeman was roaring obscenities and fighting back, fending off the leopard's strikes and punching it with his free hand when he had the chance.

Dan aimed as low as he dared, but his shot hit the leopard high on a rear flank, spinning it around. It snarled in pain and anger and, as Freeman rolled away, it turned its wild-eyed attention to Dan, glaring at him for an instant before charging down the path at him.

Dan pushed Ruth into the bush beside the track.

He'd expected the leopard to flee, but now quickly levered the magazine, regained his firing position, and squeezed off the shot.

There was a heart-stopping *click* as the pin struck the cartridge that had failed to eject.

The leopard was almost on him. He raised his now useless rifle across his body against the leopard's charge. The animal hit him full on the chest, sending him to the dirt, the leopard with him.

The cat's jaws closed over Dan's arm, but it was unable to get a good grip because its fangs had also grabbed the rifle's stock. Dan's immediate problem was to avoid the leopard's raking rear claws. It growled in rage and frustration as he continued to kick and wriggle out of reach of its attack.

'Oh, God!' Dan muttered, knowing he couldn't continue to hold off the power of the leopard for much longer.

A black blur flew from the bush at the side of the track.

Dan felt an impact on the leopard's body and a heavy weight fell on him.

When he opened his eyes, the leopard lay dead across his chest. A spear wobbled back and forth in its pierced rib cage.

Above him was the Pokot, his chest rising and falling with his laboured breathing, and his hunter's eyes gleaming in deadly delight.

Dan climbed unsteadily to his feet, and looked at his shirt, bloodied by the leopard. He felt slightly stunned and his heart was racing. He made an effort to stop his hand from shaking as he peeled back his torn sleeve. The damage wasn't as bad as he imagined it might have been. His Jeffery had taken the brunt of the leopard's potent upper fangs.

He turned his attention to Bill, who was rolling about in agony. Dan kneeled beside him. Freeman's arm was a mass of gore and his thigh had been severely torn by the leopard's back claws. He was ashen and moaning in pain.

Basil Rifkin joined Ruth, who kneeled beside Dan and began to dab at Bill's wounds with her scarf.

'Ruth,' Dan said. 'Not here. Not now. We need to get him away from here before we can clean him up.'

She started to make a reply, but Dan had turned and called the Pokot to him.

'Korok,' he said. 'We make camp. A fire. Find a place.'

He turned immediately and trotted up the track.

'You,' he said, pointing to the three porters. 'Go with him.'

He turned back to Freeman and helped him to sit against a tree. He had no colour in his face. 'How are you, Bill?'

He looked up at him, and shook his head. 'Buggered,' he said.

'Can you walk? I don't want to try to patch you up here.'

'You're right,' he said, and tried to stand.

Basil took one arm and Dan, using his good arm, took the other. Bill moaned as he got to his feet.

'At least let me help with moving him,' Ruth said, and without waiting, took Dan's place at Freeman's side.

Dan conceded the issue, and the party made their way slowly up the track. He turned his attention back to the leopard, lying almost at his feet. It was a male, about eight feet long from velvet nose to the black tip of its very long tail. In death it had a dignified beauty. The golden coat with its dark rosettes invited his touch, and Dan crouched beside it to feel the soft press of the longer filaments before reaching the thicker undercoat covering the leopard's iron muscle and bone, still warm. He moved his finger to tentatively touch the hole in its chest where the Pokot had removed his spear. A final trickle of blood rolled down the fur on its ribs to a dark pool now coagulating on a broad leaf beneath it. He stared into its vacant eyes. It was handsome in death, but it was the leopard's courage, the sheer audacity to charge at this man with his killing weapon, that had elevated mere beauty and courage into magnificence. This animal, weighing less than him, had very nearly killed two hunters. It was now inanimate flesh. A meal for the scavengers.

He'd been lucky. If the Pokot hadn't arrived, the outcome would have been grim. He'd been lucky, twice. On the South African veld, he'd taken a head shot at a buffalo. He now knew the heart shot was safer, because it took some luck to hit the brain. He realised that if he was to survive in this profession he needed to know more than he presently did about hunting dangerous game.

He stood and opened the breach of his rifle. The spent cartridge came loose when he jiggled it, and in so doing dislodged a small twig splinter that had somehow found its way into the chamber. It must have entered when he placed his rifle on the ground with the breach open. He should have taken more care. Again, it was a salutary lesson.

He went through the sequence of events. Could he have done better?

His aim was deliberately high to avoid hitting Bill and he still believed it was the right shot, but he'd had the 300gn ammunition in the magazine that he used days before to hunt plains game for the pot. A heavier charge behind the soft nose might have crippled the leopard, preventing its rush.

He should have given more thought to what he might need in the forest. It appeared he had not only a lot to learn about animals, he needed to know more about rifles, cartridges and the right choice of both for dangerous game. And he had to learn quickly, or else the next error of judgement might be his last.

He gave the dead leopard a final glance, and headed up the track.

* * *

It took them less than an hour to have a fire going and a shelter constructed, under which Freeman was laid out on his ground sheet.

66

Ruth proved to be a proficient nurse and set to work with hot water and iodine to clean Bill's wounds.

It was late afternoon when she came to Dan, who was supervising the small supplies tent. 'Let me look at you,' she said.

'Thank you, but I need to set the camp before dark.'

She looked at him sternly. 'If you don't let me clean up those gashes, your arm will become gangrenous and you'll lose it.' She took his arm when she saw he'd acquiesced and lifted the shredded sleeve. 'You see? It's a mess. Come, sit over here, and I'll clean you up. It won't take a minute and then you can get back to your work.'

They sat on a large boulder at the edge of the clearing. He dropped his hat on the ground and she carefully rolled back his sleeve. 'I want to thank you for what you did today,' she said as she dipped a cloth into a basin of warm water.

He shrugged.

'You might have been killed.'

He remained silent.

'You were very brave.'

'I was lucky.'

'Bill said you handled everything quite well indeed.'

'He did? He must be delirious.'

She smiled with him, and started to bathe his wounds with the warm water. 'Is that painful?'

'No.'

He could feel her eyes on him as she rinsed the cloth.

'Ouch,' he said, the iodine biting when she applied the cloth to his arm.

'Sorry.'

She rinsed and squeezed the cloth several times, then patted around his wound before rolling a clean gauze bandage onto it. She tied it off with a neat bow. 'We can still be friends, can't we?'

He turned to her then and studied her dark brown eyes. He'd peered into them in passion, but now realised there'd never been anything more. He'd overlaid their relationship with a fantasy of his own making. If not love, it was certainly more than a tumble in the hot river sand. She appeared contrite, but if he'd imagined there was anything of importance between them, it was totally gone. She was an attractive woman, but things would be different between them.

'No we can't, Ruth.'

'Why not?'

'Because it's business.' He stood and buttoned up his shirt. 'I'm the hunter and you're the client.'

He stooped to retrieve his hat.

'Thanks for fixing my arm.'

He left her seated on the rock, staring after him, and headed to Bill's shelter.

He was sitting on his bedding, his back propped up against a chop box, and an empty shot glass in his hand.

'You're looking better,' Dan said. 'As white as a ghost when we got you onto your bed.'

'I'll live,' he said in a gravelly voice. 'Could use another drop of brandy, though.' He raised his glass to him.

'In a minute,' Dan countered. His boss wasn't looking quite as good as Dan had made out, and his voice, a little breathless, indicated he might be suffering from shock.

'That's the second leopard that's taken a dislike to me.'

'Maybe you should stop annoying them. What made him attack you?'

'Obviously knows good tucker when he sees it.'

'Nah. Tough as old boots.' Dan's smile faded as he gathered his thoughts. It was never going to be easy. 'We've got to turn back, Bill,' he said at last.

'Ah, geez, I knew you were going to say something like that. You came over here with a long face like a preacher at a funeral.'

'I mean it. We can't risk an infection. We need to get you to the hospital in Nairobi and have those wounds seen to.'

'Nurse Rifkin has done me just fine, thank you, Reverend.'

'You need real medical treatment, not just a dash of iodine.'

'You haven't seen Nairobi Hospital, have you? No. Well, it might be new, but a dash of iodine is about all I'd get there, *and* it'd cost me three or four weeks of client fees.'

'Then we'll take you down to Mombasa.'

'No you won't.'

'Bill —'

'Listen, Dan. We need the money. The fees we'll lose if Rifkin goes back without his trophy will kill us. This's not the first time I've got into a bit of trouble in the bush. Won't be the last. What we'll do is this: I'll rest here a day or so, get some strength, then we get back on the track of that bongo.'

'Sorry, Bill. I can't do that.'

'What? But that's a bloody order!'

'Don't give me that. I'm taking over. You're going to rest here, just like you say. But what I'll do is take the Pokot and the client. We bag that bongo, and *then* we'll take you home.'

Freeman was still spluttering as Dan walked off.

* * *

Dan found the Pokot squatting on his heels on a log where the rise gave a view over the whole clearing. It was his custom to find such a position before the late afternoon light disappeared. He had his spear across his folded arms. From Dan's previous observations, Korok would sit there all night, sleeping and keeping guard. He had no idea how he could do both. He imagined he could pick up threatening sounds while in his sleep.

Dan stood beside him for a moment, watching the porters working. They had pitched all the tents and were now preparing the meals. Preparations were proceeding slowly. They would eat under lantern light that night.

Ruth came from her tent carrying a set of clean clothes. Another porter went before her with a basin of water to a small square surrounded by a six-foot canvas screen. Once inside, she hung her clean clothes over the top of the canvas and began throwing the clothes she'd been wearing, one by one, onto a bush.

Dan sighed and lowered himself onto the log beside Korok, who sat quietly in his usual mute contentment. He watched him, but he seemed oblivious of the attention.

'I thank you, Korok,' Dan said.

The Pokot made no move for some time, then he turned to Dan with a quizzical expression.

'I said I thank you for killing the *chui*.'

When he still showed no indication that he knew what he meant, Dan added, 'Very good, Korok. Kill *chui*. Very good.'

The little man's lip plug bobbled as he arranged his face into what Dan suspected was the Pokot's notion of a smile.

CHAPTER 8

Ruth stamped her foot and marched up and down outside her tent, glaring first at Dan and then at her husband, who looked decidedly abashed.

'Well, are you just going to stand there, Basil? For God's sake, say something.'

'I'm sorry, darling. I've spoken to Bill, and to Dan of course. Bill says it's entirely up to Dan, and well ... Dan has a good point.'

She stopped her pacing, and folded her arms across her heaving chest. 'And what, may I ask, is that?' she demanded of Dan. Her eyes were brimming with angry tears. It was obvious she'd seldom been denied anything she wanted.

Dan shook his head. 'We're after a bongo, Ruth — an animal so difficult to hunt that very few people have seen one and nobody has even been able to take a shot at it. It's a stalking expedition. We have to keep our numbers down. I'm not even taking gun-bearers.'

Ruth dropped her aggressive stance, and blinked the tears from her eyes. 'But I promise I won't be in the way,' she said in a soft voice. 'I'll be very quiet and you won't know I'm there.'

Dan remembered how Ruth Rifkin could be a very persuasive person when she turned her soft brown eyes on her target. With some relief he was comforted to find it easier to remain resolute, which softened the pain of the previous twenty-four hours. 'Sorry,' he said. 'I've made my decision on the matter.'

'Oh, fiddle-faddle,' she said and stormed off to her tent.

* * *

Dan followed closely behind Korok through the dense forest — he continued to think of it as *jungle* — and was careful to place his feet to avoid any unnecessary sound. As leader of the shooting expedition, it was now purely upon him to make it a success. The future of Freeman Safaris may well rest upon his ability to do so. He immediately thought it laughable that he, an entirely untried white hunter, was in charge of surely the most testing debut ever attempted by a safari company: to find and shoot the most elusive animal of the forest. He shook his head. He couldn't afford to think that way.

He also knew that his success depended upon his relationship with Korok, the enigmatic little Pokot who even Bill admitted was almost impossible to fathom. Unless the tracker was at his best, they might wander the jungles for many days, possibly weeks, and not find the quarry.

And he didn't have days or weeks. Even if the hospital had, as Bill proclaimed, only a semblance of medical care, he must get the old man back to Nairobi quickly. He'd seen enough young soldiers die in South Africa from minor wounds to know how fast they could become lethally septic. Time was against him.

Having found the bongo, the next task would be to place the client in the position to exercise his indifferent shooting skills. So far, Basil had not inspired confidence in his abilities. While shooting for the table on the plains around Naro Moru, Basil and the very handsome 303 Lee-Enfield he used for light game seldom brought down the target with a clean shot.

For hours, the Pokot carried his head low, studying the ground beneath the heavy covering of vines and undergrowth. The short tunic covering his skinny bottom often disappeared in the foliage although he was merely a few paces ahead of them.

By the end of the day the Pokot had nothing to report, and Dan went to bed agonising over how long he could continue to hunt while his partner was back at camp, enduring pain and possibly developing a fatal fever.

* * *

When Dan arose before dawn the following morning, he went searching for Korok but couldn't find him. After breakfast, Dan supervised the porters in their packing, not knowing how to proceed without the Pokot. Luckily Korok soon appeared.

As he danced from one foot to the other, he told Dan with words and much gesticulation what he'd found.

'The tracker has spotted the spoor of a bongo not far away,' Dan said to Basil Rifkin. 'I'll keep close to Korok until we spot the target. When we come up on him, I'll get you to take first shot with your Lee-Enfield, right? But remember, we'll be in deep bush and one shot is probably all we'll get.'

Dan ordered the porters to remain in camp and with Basil in tow slipped quickly into step behind Korok.

An hour later the Pokot held up his hand and, as the hunters paused, turned his head, listening, and was apparently pleased with what he'd heard. He pointed an index finger at his ear, and then waggled it in the direction they were headed.

Dan listened intently. There was a conglomeration of sounds emanating from all points of the surrounding green mass, but he heard nothing that might indicate their bongo was at hand.

Korok searched Dan's expression for a sign of acknowledgement, and when he found none, wobbled his head, and motioned them forwards again. After a further five minutes of careful stalking, Dan followed the pointing finger at the end of Korok's outstretched arm and saw the bongo.

At first, he didn't realise he was looking at an animal. A shaft of sunlight had found an unlikely path through the treetop canopy, the dense understorey and the mass of vines to highlight a vividly striped, russet patch of bark on a wide tree-base. It was only when it flicked away an insect with one paddle-like ear that the flat, shapeless collection of patterned bark and swaying golden grass assumed the form of a beautiful antelope. It was less than forty yards away.

Dan took a sharp intake of breath and held it while he slowly unhitched his 404 from his shoulder and waved Basil forwards. With a patting motion of his hand, he stressed the need for silence, but a tiny twig fractured under Basil's boot, and the bongo's head rose sharply. Its nostrils flared, but the breath of air, if it was there at all, came rolling down from the high ground beyond the animal into their faces. The bongo hadn't taken their scent.

The hunters were almost completely concealed behind a large-leafed tuberous plant, but they both raised their rifles very slowly and carefully.

Dan held the place behind the crease in the bongo's front leg in the centre of his sights. Basil took his time — a long time — and Dan was becoming fearful that the bongo would move off, when there was the crack of the 303.

Dan saw the impact, a little high on the flank. The bongo's reflexes were lightning fast, and he raised his sight in anticipation of the explosive power of its bound. He pulled off a shot.

The bongo was dead before it completed its leap.

* * *

Korok kneeled over the fallen bongo, his long sharp cutting knife in one hand and the other holding the horns to expose the neck.

The animal's eyes, glazed and frozen in shock, stared at him. He had never before felt such an affinity with a creature that he'd set out to either kill or assist others to kill. It was such a waste. They were alone in the forest. None of the hunter tribes were anywhere near, and their small safari did not have the manpower to get the meat back to camp, though the white hunters, having removed themselves from the killing field, would send back two porters to carry out the trophy sections. When he skinned it and removed the neck and head from the beast, the carcass would be left to rot or to feed the pigs and leopards.

Korok ran his hand along the corded muscles of the bongo's flanks. They were still warm. The Ndio forest hunters, in describing the bongo to him, had alluded to its magical beauty, especially in death. It was said that a young man of their tribe, who had been driven by hunger almost to death, had killed a bongo. When he approached it after shooting it with his arrow, the bongo looked so beautiful he wept and lay beside it, there to die of hunger. His father, upon finding his son dead beside the beautiful bongo, decreed that the Ndio should not take the life of such a creature. And they never again hunted bongo.

Korok had listened to their story and discarded it. They were such a simple people, he'd given no credence to their story — until now. Kneeling beside the dead bongo he felt wearied to exhaustion by its killing. He could barely lift his knife to the chestnut throat.

Here was a waste of life; a waste of beauty.

Beast of green jungle, be careful
A hunter lies waiting for dawn
Take care, my brown curl-horned beauty
A whisper at dawn will forewarn
The hunter will come. He will kill you
Go softly, your whisper dies too.

As his knife sliced the hide from the warm flesh, tears rolled down his cheeks.

* * *

The return to camp was completed in a full day's march since there was now no need for stealth. They arrived triumphant. Even Bill stirred from his camp bed to congratulate them.

'So this is the famous bongo,' he said, admiring the severed head and neck. 'Better get it salted.'

Ruth came truculently from her tent to see what all the bother was about. 'It doesn't look much,' she said.

But her manner couldn't dampen Basil's exuberance. 'Just wait until you see what the taxidermist in Nairobi can do with it.'

'I'm sure it'll be perfectly fabulous, darling.'

He chose to ignore her sarcasm.

Dan called on the porters to salt the trophy piece, before drawing Bill away from the others. 'How are you?' he asked.

'How am I?' he exploded. 'How do you think I am? I could've been there with you, if you hadn't been such a bloody old fuss-box.'

Dan remained silent to let Freeman's anger run its course. When it finally petered out he asked him again, 'How are you?'

'Oh, I'm not bad. A bit of a fever, but last night I slept pretty well.'

'Will you be able to travel tomorrow?'

'Yeah, I reckon. How was the shoot?'

Dan shrugged. 'The client's happy.'

'I can see that, but how did it go?'

Dan explained the details of the final minutes of the stalk and the kill.

'So he went high and you dropped it, is what you're saying. Does he know this?'

'If he does, he's not letting on.'

'In that case, we'll just let it lie.' He raised his eyes to Dan. 'Remember this, my boy. A client always wants to take the credit for the kill no matter which way it goes.'

CHAPTER 9

The carriage was oppressively hot, and Vivian was annoyed. She glanced at her husband, Walter, who seemed blissfully unaware of her discomfort and was idly staring out the window at the bleak expanse of the Taru Desert. There was nothing in sight to excuse his neglect of her. No animal or reptile. Nothing, so far as she could determine. Just the red dust and drab grey scrub that spread as far as the eye could see on both sides of the railway line.

The outlook was even worse than their home in South Australia, which she had learned to despise from her mother, who never liked any of it — not even the greener parts of Adelaide.

The family had fallen on hard times and moved from England to Australia, where her father found work in the bank. It wasn't until five years later, when Vivian was eighteen and recently married to Walter, that her parents were able to return to England, and civilisation. Her mother became distant and lost interest in Vivian and her life in the ex-colony, not even becoming engaged by the birth of her first grandchild, Elizabeth.

Vivian pulled her embroidered handkerchief from under her sleeve and irritably flicked a cinder from her blouse. 'Elizabeth,' she said, 'will you please close that window? You're letting all the dirt fly in.'

'Yes, Mother,' the child said.

She should have insisted that they move to England when they were first married, but Walter had felt obliged to keep an eye on his mother until his father returned home. It was quite ironic. After more than ten years of waiting, they were now joining him, rather than the reverse.

Vivian looked at her daughter kneeling on the bench seat, her elbows on the windowsill and her plaits touching her shoulders. Elizabeth needed a proper education among people of her own class. While Vivian's parents were themselves not wealthy, on her mother's side there was a distant cousin who was a peer of the realm.

At nine, Elizabeth was of an age where she should be learning the finer aspects of life. Provincial living was turning her into a tomboy, utterly without grace. How much worse would it be in this godforsaken land? But Walter insisted they seize the opportunity suggested by his father.

Land for the taking, Bill had said in his letters. *I have all the necessary connections here. Come and we'll start a farm.*

'How much longer is it to the place where we stop for dinner?' she asked Walter.

'Voi,' he said. 'They expect we'll be there around five.'

'*Hmmph.*'

'And Vivian, please let her be,' he said under his breath, nodding in their daughter's direction. 'The child's hot and bored.'

'And do you think I'm not?'

She turned from him, fanning herself vigorously.

Outside the carriage the countryside had gained a semblance of colour. A tree with an enormous girth and very little foliage came into view at a distance. Then another flashed by the window. Clusters of trees with spreading tops, like umbrellas, appeared.

'Look!' Elizabeth said, pointing out the window. 'A giraffe!'

Walter moved across the carriage to join his daughter.

'You're right, darling. They are giraffes. Five of them. I promised you we'd see wild animals here in Africa. And here they are already.'

It wasn't the only promise her husband had made the family. He promised her that if it didn't work out, they would abandon his folly and travel on to England, where Vivian was hopeful that her mother would take an interest in them, and through her influence find them a suitable place in society.

She was somewhat reassured that in British East Africa, she was at least halfway home.

Vivian was determined to keep Walter to his promise. She would watch the farm for the first sign of failure, then demand a return to the England that had been her dream for fifteen years.

Bill spotted his son and daughter-in-law the moment they stepped down from the train. Walter was thirty-two and looked it. His full moustache didn't quite hide the slight puffiness of his cheeks nor did his jacket conceal his ample girth. Vivian, a few years younger, had barely changed. She'd always been a glamorous young thing, a cut above the Freeman's class, he'd thought at the time. But Walter had been obsessed with her and his mother rather liked the idea of having a daughter-in-law from the old country.

At their heels was a gangly slip of a girl. It had been some time since Freeman had received a photograph of the family, and his granddaughter did not look as he'd expected. She had a straw bonnet plonked on her fair hair, which was in two long plaits. Her pale blue tunic was smudged with smoke soot and her eyes darted everywhere, not in fear — as might be expected of a nine-year-old surrounded by half-naked, gawping savages, and a melee of land brokers, commission agents and gharry men in jodhpurs spruiking for fares — but with curiosity.

Bill pushed through the crowd and was almost within handshaking distance before Walter recognised him. Even then it took him a moment to speak.

'Dad!' he finally said, reaching towards him.

'Hello, Walter,' Bill said.

There was an awkward moment when Bill made an attempt at a handshake while Walter lifted his arms for an embrace. Finally, Freeman wrapped an arm around his son's shoulders and gave him a brief hug.

'Daddy Freeman,' Vivian said.

Freeman winced. He'd forgotten the title she'd invented for him. 'Vivian. You look lovely.' He pecked her on the cheek. 'And who is this?' he asked, looking down at the little girl watching him with quiet fascination.

'Elizabeth,' she said.

'Your granddaughter,' Walter added, somewhat superfluously.

'Of course you are,' Freeman said. 'And I love your hat.'

'Do you?'

'Well, it's very practical for the tropics.'

'I told mother I should wear a double terai.'

'How do you know about a double terai?'

'I read about it in the *'Cyclopaedia Britannica.'*

'Really? And what did it have to say?'

'It said that most people wear a double terai to protect them against the actinic rays of the sun.'

'Hmm ... that sounds serious. What does *actinic* mean?'

'I don't know, but it sounds bad. And also spine pads.'

'Spine pads?'

'Yes, they're red and thick and they run down the middle of your back. They keep the sun from your spine.'

'What do you think?'

'I'm not sure ... None of the black people wear them,' she said, looking around the crowded platform. 'See?' She pointed to a haughty group of Maasai warriors watching the crowd with detached interest. They were bareheaded and bare-chested, wearing only short red *shukas* that barely covered their vitals.

'Maybe they didn't read the *Encyclopaedia Britannica*,' Freeman suggested.

She smiled at him. 'Silly. But I *have* been wondering about it, and now I know.'

'And ...?'

'And I've decided that since they've been here longer than anyone else, they probably know best.'

Walter put a hand on his daughter's shoulder. 'Take no notice of her, Dad. She never has her head out of a book. She's such a know-it-all at times. You'll get used to her.'

* * *

After breakfast in the dining room of the Valley Guesthouse — a slightly more stylish establishment than Mrs Cobb's — Vivian took Elizabeth for a walk around the town. She needed time to compose herself. Walter had announced at breakfast that he and his father were travelling upcountry that morning to inspect the land they intended to purchase for their farm.

The news didn't surprise her but she'd maintained hope that common sense would prevail and he would forget setting up a farm in such a godforsaken country and continue their travels to England. She felt sure her father could find a place for Walter in the bank. They could enjoy a life of relative comfort in the English countryside. Now it appeared that her husband had heeded none of her pleas and was determined to press ahead.

She led Elizabeth past the paltry shops at a brisk pace. Her impressions of the town had not altered since the day of her arrival. She thought it a dismal place, dumped on a featureless expanse of swampy ground, strewn with grassy clumps and foul-smelling bogs. The stench coming from the open drains, which carried the effluent of the town, was quite abominable.

The town buildings consisted of a haberdashery, with a sizeable proportion of the small shop given over to a land agency office — one of several in the town. It appeared to her to be the only commercial venture enjoying any success. There were a butchery, a general store that also sold bicycles and a frightening array of firearms and bullets, an ironmonger, a stock agency, a post office, two dubious hotels and a tailor. The other premises in the town accommodated a variety of administrative and railway offices.

Beyond Wood's hotel, on the other side of the river, was the foul-smelling native bazaar. Walter escorted her there on their first excursion, but upon approach, she had insisted she be taken back to the guesthouse. In spite of her obvious distress, he took little Elizabeth the next day. She returned full of excitement and dreadful stories of meat hanging in the open air surrounded by flies, rats scuttling along open drains and what sounded like a general and pervading filth.

As she picked her way between the puddles, her anger brewed. She'd told Walter from the outset that she had doubts about the wisdom of the venture, but without apparent effect. It still rankled that he'd become so determined to proceed. He said he was glad that his father had belatedly shown an interest in him — his only child — and could not refuse him. He had disregarded her reservations on the matter, and even when she said she had concerns about their daughter's education — a matter normally important to him — he remained unmoved.

'I can't disappoint him, Vivian,' he'd said. 'He seems to have his heart set on it. And frankly, I'm quite happy he had me in mind when he decided to start a farming business. In any case, if it is as profitable as Dad says, it's our big chance.'

Memories of the conversation still chafed, and as she took Elizabeth by the arm and hurried across the puddled road, she caught her foot on a rock and in regaining her balance, stepped into a muddy pothole.

'*Oh!*' she exclaimed, now even more upset.

'Ooh-la-la, madame,' came a voice from the boardwalk outside the post office. A well-dressed man in a suit and pinstriped vest stepped onto the unpaved road and offered his hand. 'Allow me, *s'il vous plaît.*'

She hesitated a moment. He had a pleasant smile and his expression was one of genuine concern. She took his hand, which was soft although his grip was firm. He led her to the safety of the boarded walk.

'And the mademoiselle too,' he said, tut-tutting at the muddied fringe of Elizabeth's dress. 'It is just *too* impossible, no?'

'Thank you,' Vivian said. 'I don't know what I was thinking. I just wasn't looking where I was stepping. You're so kind, monsieur ...'

'Marcel de Clemenceau, madame.' He swept his grey homburg from his head and gave her a slight bow. 'At your service.' He had a full head of dark wavy hair, greying slightly at the temples.

Vivian was charmed by the Frenchman's chivalry; and she had not forgotten the manners she'd learned growing up in her parents' house. 'Monsieur de Clemenceau,' she said, extending her hand. 'I am most grateful. I am Vivian Freeman ... Mrs Vivian Freeman. And this is my daughter, Elizabeth.'

De Clemenceau raised her hand and kissed it, then gently took Elizabeth's hand in his and shook it. 'Such a pity the weather hasn't favoured your stroll with a dry pathway. I am afraid it has muddied your shoes and the little mademoiselle's pretty dress as well.'

'We're becoming used to it,' Vivian said.

'Ah, and so we must, I am afraid.'

'Yes ... I suppose so ... But thank you, you've been very kind and, if I may add, very gallant, Monsieur de Clemenceau.'

'Ah, but if I were truly gallant, I should have thrown my cape on the muddy waters so you would not wet your feet, like your English knight, Sir ... Sir ...?'

Vivian laughed. 'I think you may be thinking of Sir Walter Raleigh?'

'Ah, *oui*. Sir Walter Raleigh.'

'But I'm afraid I am not a queen.'

'Perhaps merely a beautiful princess?'

Vivian flushed, but couldn't hide her smile. 'Gallant, indeed, monsieur. But now we must away. Good day to you.'

'May I offer to take you to your hotel in my carriage?'

'I think not, Monsieur de Clemenceau.'

'I do beg your pardon if my offer offends, madame. I meant no offence ...'

'Not at all, monsieur. No offence taken. Good day to you.'

'And a good day to you too, madame; mademoiselle. *Au revoir.*'

When Vivian and Elizabeth returned to the guesthouse, Vivian's initial mood had improved and she found Walter talking to her father-in-law on the veranda.

'Morning, my dear,' Freeman said, without rising from his chair.

'Good morning, Daddy Freeman.'

Walter sat with his elbows on the table, drumming his fingers together in the manner he adopted when distracted or thinking seriously.

'Lovely morning for a walk,' Freeman added.

'Indeed,' Vivian answered, looking again at her husband. What had happened in her absence?

Walter finally looked up. He covered his mouth with his hand and gently cleared his throat. 'Dad and I have been talking,' he said, unable to hold her gaze. 'We've ... That is, he's advised me of some changes to our plans.'

'Oh ... Really?'

'Yes, he's decided to start up a safari business.'

'What's that?'

'It's wild-game hunting,' Freeman said, interjecting. 'Safari people are sometimes called white hunters. Very popular these days.'

She turned from her father-in-law to her husband. 'But Walter, what do you know of hunting?'

'Hunting? Nothing. No, I'm not involved, dear. It's just Dad. And his assistant. We will still have our farm, only Dad isn't going to be part of it.'

'I see,' she said.

Walter wore a brave face, but she knew he was very disappointed. It mattered not to Vivian whether her father-in-law was involved in the farm. In fact, it pleased her that they now would likely not be going ahead at all. 'Then I don't suppose you'll need to go to Limuru to see the land,' she suggested.

'Farming is still a very profitable business,' Freeman said. 'And Walter will do very well, you'll see. So, it's all arranged. Train tickets. Provisions for a couple of days. We're ready to go. Just waiting for my man to arrive.'

Vivian tried to send a signal to Walter that she was unhappy about proceeding, but he avoided her gaze.

'Ah, speak of the devil,' Freeman said.

The young man walking up the path was tall and square-shouldered, and when he pulled his hat off, his brown hair fell over his forehead. He nodded and smiled a little self-consciously.

'This is Dan,' Freeman said.

The young man shook Walter's hand and nodded to Vivian with a mumbled, 'Ma'am.'

'Oh, and this, of course, is my granddaughter, Elizabeth.'

'Hello, Elizabeth,' Dan said, taking her outstretched hand in his.

'Pleased to meet you,' she replied, giving his hand a shake.

'Come along, Dan,' Freeman said. 'Let's find something to get the baggage to the station.'

When they'd gone, Vivian told Elizabeth to go into the parlour. 'Walter,' she hissed when the child was safely out of earshot, 'I don't think we should go into this farming business alone. We know nothing about farming.'

'We can manage. You should see the farms up on the hills around here. You can grow anything. And we won't miss Dad's involvement — he's not a farmer either.'

'Well, the situation is definitely different now. I think we should discuss it further.'

'Don't worry, dear. Nothing will be decided on this trip. We're just going to take a look at what's available. When I get back in a couple of days, we'll talk.'

Freeman and Dan returned in a donkey trap driven by an Indian Sikh. Dan began to carry their provisions to it.

'Can I come too, Daddy?' Elizabeth asked.

Walter kneeled beside her. 'I thought you were going to stay here and look after Mother,' he said.

'I know. But I changed my mind. I'd like to come with you on the train.'

Walter looked at Vivian, who shrugged.

'Won't you change your mind and come with us too, dear?' he asked.

'Another train journey? I think not, Walter.' She headed towards the door. 'I'll pack a few items for Elizabeth.'

Elizabeth squealed her excitement and ran to join Dan and her grandfather.

CHAPTER 10

Elizabeth sat on the chop box swinging her legs in time with the *clop-clopping* of the donkey's hooves. The day was turning out to be just as thrilling as she'd hoped. There was the train journey ahead, with the chance to explore the bush when they arrived at Limuru, but the morning had already had its share of excitement.

The Sikh holding the reins in the driver's seat was a huge man in a large turban and knee-high leather gaiters. He looked so formidable when he arrived at the guesthouse, standing to attention while awaiting her father and grandfather, that she was afraid to approach the cart and the donkey she so wanted to touch. When she finally mustered the courage, he clicked his heels and saluted impressively. She giggled, and he raised his eyebrows in surprise, but she spotted the smile hidden in his bushy beard. He held the donkey and she patted the grey bristly coat that jerked and shivered under her touch. It was another first-time experience for Elizabeth, one of many since arriving in Africa.

After initially feeling sad to have left her friends behind in Adelaide, she was happy to be in Nairobi. She had felt some very anxious moments during the long sea voyage. The waves that crashed over the bow of their ship as they steamed around the southwestern point of Australia frightened her, but there were sunny days too, when she was able to play shuffleboard on deck with her father.

Since arriving in Nairobi she'd made friends with the Kikuyu cook's son, Tanu, a boy about two or three years older than Elizabeth, although he told her he didn't know the date of his birthday.

'But you must,' she had insisted. 'Everyone has a birthday.'

The boy stuck out his bottom lip and shrugged.

Tanu introduced her to the wonders of a Nairobi garden, like the very strange lizard he showed her among the purple bougainvillea bracts in the guesthouse's garden. It had eyes like inverted saucers that could rotate in all directions and independently of each other. It crept along the most slender twigs using its toes like a pair of tongs. Tanu told her they were *bahati mbaya* — bad luck — and refused to go near it. When she overcame her fear, she allowed the sleepy creature to make its hesitating climb onto her hand. As it made its way towards her shoulder, with its sticky toes grasping her skin and scaly tail curling around her arm, Tanu could stand it no more, and ran away, muttering Kikuyu words meant to ward off evil.

Her father came into the garden to investigate the commotion and was shocked to find the lizard sitting on his daughter's head. He wanted to kill it, but Elizabeth said it was her pet. Later they found the animal in the encyclopaedia. It was called a chameleon, and she'd since found two more of different varieties that she kept in an empty soapbox on the guesthouse's veranda and fed with crickets, caterpillars and beetles.

The Sikh helped the men carry the bags, tents and provisions from the cart to the railway platform, and stood at attention while Bill fumbled around in his coat pocket.

'Do you have a rupee?' he asked Walter, who obliged.

The Sikh gave a brief nod, clicked his heels and returned to his cart.

As they waited for the train to arrive, Elizabeth amused herself by annoying a line of driver ants with a stick. Unseen by her, the ants sent out a column to make a flanking attack, and one gave her an agonising sting on her ankle. She danced about and fought back her tears. Fortunately, the train arrived and she was distracted as they loaded their luggage into their carriage.

On the train in a compartment with Walter and Bill she discreetly licked her finger and dabbed the spit onto the sting, but as soon as she heard the shriek of the steam whistle and felt the jerk of the carriage, she had her nose pressed to the window glass.

She watched the muddy flats around Nairobi give way to food gardens and greenery on the sloping hills, then to a profusion of vines, flowering shrubs and flashes of colour as mysterious birds took startled flight into the towering jungle at the sound of the approaching train.

She looked back into the carriage to her father, who was in conversation with her grandfather: neither of them seemed aware of the splendour they were passing. Didn't they know they should be *keen of eye*, as the encyclopaedia advised? Didn't they know that to learn from nature required attention to the fascinating world outside the railway carriage? Only Dan, the tall, slender, handsome young man with the mop of hair protruding from under his broad-brimmed hat, seemed to be interested in it.

She caught his eye and he grinned at her.

It somehow made her happy to know that he felt the same way she did.

* * *

As the dawn's light brightened the canvas of his tent, Dan awoke to a cacophony of birdcalls. It took him a moment to remember he was in the Kikuyuland forest; he was cold — surprisingly cold.

Freeman was across the tent from him, asleep on his back, snoring.

He poked his head through the tent flap. The air was crisp and cold and his breath became a stream of vapour. He pulled on his trousers and stepped out. Immediately the chill attacked him and he reached inside the tent for his blanket, which he threw around his shoulders.

The previous night's campfire was a cold pile of black embers. He poked at them with a stick, and decided to leave the tea-making to one of the porters Freeman had hired at the station to carry their gear.

He moved towards the ridge to the east of the camp, where a cloud spread below his line of sight like a fluffy, white eiderdown, and filled the hollows between the hills so that only their black tops protruded. The sun rose from this sea of white into a crystal-clear blue sky. Even the birds were hushed by the beauty of it.

'Do you think we're on the top of the world?' came a soft voice beside him. It was Elizabeth, who was sitting on a log, staring down onto the bobbing sea of mist.

'I didn't see you there,' he said.

'If we're not on the top of the world, how come the clouds are below us?'

'Maybe we *are* on the top of the world.'

'Do you think?'

'No. Mt Kilimanjaro is higher than us.'

'That's what I thought.'

Her face was lost in concentration. She was an odd child. Elizabeth — the name didn't suit her at all. He felt sure an Elizabeth, even a very young Elizabeth, should be reserved, cultured and completely predictable. She was none of those things.

'I think I'll call you Lizzie,' he said.

'Do I call you Mister Dan?'

'No, you call me Dan.'

She nodded, pleased. 'Are you going to buy a farm, Dan?'

'No. I'm just here to help your grandfather.'

'Will you be living with us?'

'No.'

'Where will you live, then?'

He thought about it. 'Probably in a tent. Aren't you cold?'

She shivered, as if the thought of it made it so.

'Here,' he said. 'Let me put my blanket around you.'

He sat beside her and wrapped half his blanket around her. They watched the sun rise, and as it did, the misty eiderdown frothed and eddied under the influence of the warming air. It came sweeping up the ridge and when it reached them they were drenched in a fine spray.

Dan pulled the blanket up to make a canopy over their heads. When he lowered it, five minutes later, the clouds had disappeared without trace, but the droplets on the grass sparkled like diamonds. The sun speared golden rays into the valley below, illuminating the treetops and the rows of crops, which were like brightly coloured bunting strung around the cherry red of the turned earth.

'This is the most beautiful place in the whole world,' she whispered.

'It's wonderful, isn't it?'

'Do you think we'll ever see anything as lovely as this again, Dan?'

He turned to look at the girl. It was such a serious thing for one so young to say, he couldn't immediately form a reply.

A bright blue butterfly fluttered by and Elizabeth threw off the blanket and went scampering after it.

* * *

'How did you find this place?' Walter asked.

'A missionary fella put me onto it,' Freeman answered, hands on his hips and clearly proud of his discovery.

Dan followed Walter's eyes around the valley, which was demarcated at each end by steep rises. It was sparsely wooded in parts with patches of thin scrub that could be easily cleared. The land gently sloped up from a distant stream and came to an abrupt end at a heavily forested section, but there were at least fifteen acres on the flat that were ready for the plough, and a further seventy or more along the stream and on the rises that required modest clearing.

'Rainfall about fifty, sixty inches. You have running water down there in the little stream. Further up there's a waterfall. You could generate your own electricity.' He made a loud sniffing sound as he filled his lungs and then exhaled. 'Ahh ... Smell that. All the fresh air in the world and not a mosquito within cooee.'

Walter lifted his hat and scratched his head. 'How much is this going to cost?'

'You could put in pigsties, chook runs, beehives. You might even run a few head of dairy cows.'

'Dad ... who do we need to see to discuss the price? I mean, assuming we're interested.'

'Aren't you interested? Surely I haven't brought you all the way up here for the sight-seeing. I'm off on safari shortly and I can't be running all over Limuru while you make up your mind.'

'No, but I mean, this is the first property I've seen. It's lovely, but —'

'Lovely? It's perfect. Plenty of flat ground for a nice house, or at least a *banda* until you and Vivian get organised. Dan'll help.'

Dan glanced at Freeman but he diligently avoided his eye.

Walter persisted. 'But how much?'

'We can make an offer to the local chief of a few cows and a handful of rupees, and it's yours. The missionary chap reckons the natives need the rupees for their hut tax. Otherwise they get into trouble with the collector.'

'Well ...' Walter said, his smile broadening, 'if it's so cheap ...'

He wandered towards the stream, plucking grass stems and kicking at the rich red soil.

'Bill,' Dan whispered. 'What's this about me helping him build his house? I don't know how —'

'Nonsense! You're a Queenslander. You blokes can do anything you put your mind to. Anyway, the natives will know how to build the bloody thing. All you need do is keep their backs bent to it.'

Dan opened his mouth to protest, but Walter came striding back, his face alight with enthusiasm.

'And you say the natives are available to do the heavy work?' he asked.

'For a handful of rupees a month.'

'I should talk it over with Vivian.'

'Really? What for?'

'You know ... it's partly her money, and —'

'Nonsense. Her money. Your money. It doesn't matter a damn. I've been all over these hills and I can tell you this is the best land you'll find.'

Dan could see that Walter was wavering.

'It's an excellent place for a farm,' Freeman added. 'For you and Vivian and little Elizabeth.'

Walter nodded. 'You're right! Let's see what the chief would want for this place,' he said, then hastily added: 'If we decide to buy.'

* * *

91

'This *mzungu* wants to buy the land on the stream, between the hills,' Freeman said to the chief's interpreter while waving his hand in the general direction of the valley. 'And if he buys, he will give five rupees to the chief for each person who works on this land for a month.'

As the interpreter began to convey the request to the chief, Walter took his father's arm and whispered into his ear: 'Dad, I don't want to make any commitments until I speak to Vivian.'

Freeman shushed him, saying there was no point in asking hypothetical questions of the chief. He said they were simple people and the higher points of business were concepts unfamiliar to them.

'We have to strike a bargaining position otherwise we'll be here all day arguing the toss.'

As this conversation between Walter and Bill was taking place, the interpreter and the chief were in deep discussion. Dan noticed the chief raise his eyebrows ever so slightly to what the interpreter was saying. The old man stroked his chin thoughtfully. Dan guessed he was a past master at business negotiations of this kind. He made his response, which the interpreter passed on.

'The chief says, *And what of the land?* What can the *mzungu* offer for the land?'

Freeman entered into the discussion with gusto. Numbers of cows, sheep and even goats were mentioned in a long-winded negotiation that flowed back and forth for some time. Finally, Freeman turned to Walter and said, 'Seven cows and it's yours.'

'Is that all?' Walter asked in a hushed voice.

'Didn't I tell you this was the land of opportunity? Seven cows for eighty or ninety acres.'

Walter paused. 'Tell him I'll take it,' he said at last.

CHAPTER 11

The short-rain clouds had not materialised that morning, and Vivian stepped into the intense sunlight with her parasol jauntily tilted over her shoulder and her fine pale yellow summer dress swishing the dust of Government Road. The sky was more than blue: she imagined it was the colour of sea ice — crystal-like with a bluish tinge. She'd come to accept it as part of the curious aberrations of living high up, close to the equator.

With Walter and Elizabeth upcountry, she had no one to bother about but herself. It was a luxurious feeling and it was that sense of freedom that made her decide to defy convention and take a stroll to see the latest talk of the town: the new Norfolk Hotel.

Before long, she found she was part of a leisurely procession of well-dressed Nairobians heading down Government Road in all manner of horse- and donkey-drawn contraptions, rickshaws and on foot. There was even one bearded gentleman wearing a three-piece suit and sitting in a trap drawn by a zebra.

The advertisement printed in *The African Standard* described the new hotel as *the only stone-built and tile-roofed hotel in East Africa*. It had thirty-four bedrooms and two cottages for married couples and was described as *a fashionable rendezvous with hot and cold baths and a billiard room*. The French chef, it was said, had been recruited from the Waldorf Astoria in New York. Many thought the owners had taken leave of their senses and put themselves at enormous financial risk. Who would come to such a squalid, dirty little town to stay in such splendour? Vivian certainly couldn't say.

Upon arriving at the Norfolk, she joined scores of curious townspeople, including prominent members of the administration, senior railway people and, by the look of them, upland farmers and their wives who had made the long journey to witness the opening.

Assembled on the other side of the wide, dusty road, with eyes that missed nothing in the comings and goings of the white folk, were a further hundred or so near-naked natives.

A six-piece brass band provided an odd medley of marches and waltzes. Nobody seemed to mind. Formally dressed waiters bearing tankards of beer made a steady line between the bar and the predominantly male gathering. There was merriment throughout the crowd, including one group of young men who were taking pot-shots at the porcelain insulators on the telegraph poles.

It had become stiflingly hot and the crowd pressed around her. A new spate of gunfire caused a pair of highly strung horses to rear in their traces. A ripple of alarm spread rapidly through the section of the crowd where Vivian stood. The press of bodies became unbearable and, as the crowd retreated from the horses, it threatened to overwhelm her. She stumbled on the hem of her dress, but before she fell beneath the feet of the onlookers, a strong hand caught her elbow. It was Marcel de Clemenceau: he drew her up the steps to the hotel veranda, and safety.

'*Sacre bleu*, madame, I have caught you yet again!'

'Oh, Monsieur de Clemenceau. Thank you. The crowd —'

'Behaving very badly, I am afraid. We can never be too careful.'

'Indeed, never too careful.'

A series of loud tweets on a police whistle sent the shooters scampering down Government Road, laughing. The crowd hooted, some in favour of the larrikins, others in support of the police.

'Please, won't you sit here while I get you a brandy?' he said.

'A brandy! At this time of day? Good heavens, no.' She sat at the table he indicated.

'Quite right. A champagne then.'

'Monsieur de Clemenceau, I couldn't possibly —'

'Please, Madame Freeman, won't you call me Marcel? Although we have not been formally introduced, you have the habit of falling into my arms, no?'

She laughed. 'Well, I must admit, you have shown remarkable timing.'

'And remarkable good fortune, if I may say so.'

She smiled and dropped her gaze from his twinkling eyes. 'May I have just a glass of water please?'

'*Certainement,*' he said, and raised his arm to catch a waiter's attention. 'A glass of ice water for madame,' he said with a theatrical flourish of his hand. 'And another bottle of the 1898 for me.'

The waiter turned to leave.

'Oh ...' he said, calling him back. 'You had better bring two glasses.'

The waiter nodded and disappeared among the crowd.

Winking at Vivian, he smiled and said, 'As we have already agreed, you can never be too careful, no?'

Marcel was dressed less formally than he had been when they first met. He wore a bushman's khaki shirt, though it was finely tailored. His trousers were crisply pleated and his boots had the deep shine that only a well-trained English gentleman's man could achieve. Everything about him indicated that he took care with his appearance and most probably had a string of servants to help him create it.

The waiter returned with the drinks. As she sipped her water, and Marcel the Veuve Clicquot, he chatted amiably about his farm in the Athi Plains, east of Nairobi.

'My husband is at this moment surveying a farm somewhere in the hills,' she said. 'He believes we can make a fortune on the land. What is your view?'

'Ah, this country, it offers so many opportunities. Myself, I am raising feathers.'

'Feathers!'

'*Oui*, ostrich feathers. The finest available. For ladies such as yourself, madame, who must have fine feathers adorning their hats, boas and fascinators in a manner that complements their beauty.'

He explained his program to cross-breed Barbary ostriches with the local Maasai ostrich to produce a more robust feather product. She said she'd seen flocks of the great birds on the plains as she travelled up from Mombasa on the train, but had no idea what variety they were.

'I thought all ostriches were the same,' she admitted.

'Oh, no, no, no. Here in British East Africa we have the Somali ostrich, which has a blue-grey neck and thighs, and also the Maasai race with pink necks and thighs. But the Barbary, from north Africa, has double-fluff feathers, and there lies the key to my fortune.'

He told her he had imported four Barbary ostrich cocks to put to his Maasai hens and had already produced forty healthy chicks, the older ones showing signs of thicker feathers.

'The Boer War has put many of the South African Jewish breeders out of business, so now is the time. I am investing all I have in feathers.'

Vivian thought the Frenchman was rather full of himself, but it fascinated her to listen to him — a big, masculine man — talking so passionately about such a frivolous topic.

'Is it hard work?' she asked.

'No, but one must be careful. I am on constant watch for lions. *Sacre bleu*, they are such vermin, no?'

'Do you shoot them?' She thought of her father-in-law, wondering if this might be an opportunity for him.

'I did in the beginning, but it demands my constant attention. I could not even come to Nairobi for Saturday night and the dancing. But now, I have found a much better way to control them.'

'And how might that be, monsieur?'

'Strychnine. They die like the rats that they are. And it allows me to come to Nairobi and enjoy the good life.' He raised his glass and saluted her. 'And to sometimes meet a delightful mademoiselle.'

She felt the Frenchman was going too far and showed her displeasure by refusing to be drawn by his bold smile.

He did, however, cause her to think about her husband's recent obsession with running a farm. In his tacky efforts to impress, Marcel de Clemenceau had revealed much about ostrich farming which she now realised was a big business, ideally suited to the high dry plateau through which she'd passed en route to Nairobi. Instead of looking for farmland in the wet rainforest to the west of Nairobi, they should buy the cheaper land on the dry eastern plateau, or anywhere suitable for ostrich farming. She could imagine herself doing business with aristocrats and the well-to-do in the fashion circles and feather markets of the world.

It was midday, and de Clemenceau ordered some light refreshments, which was all the hotel could offer due to the number of people making demands on the kitchen. When the food arrived he again offered her a glass of champagne.

'Maybe the passing of noon means it is permissible to try the wine?' he said. 'Or perhaps you do not enjoy the fruit of the grape as I do.'

'I do enjoy wine. In fact, my husband's home town, Adelaide, is known for its wine, but ... I can't say I'm familiar with champagne.'

'Ah, then you simply must try a drop.'

She agreed to taste a little. He took the bottle from the ice bucket, tilted her glass, and reverently poured the effervescent liquid down the side to, as he explained, 'not disturb the little bubbles'.

He waited expectantly for her declaration.

'It is perhaps a little dry for you, no?'

She took a second sip. 'Mmm,' she said, nodding. 'Quite pleasant.'

He beamed. 'Voilà!'

'Why is it so ... different?'

'You mean the bubbles? Ah, the bubbles are the magic bestowed on the wine.'

He explained how the wine was allowed to ferment a second time in the bottle, adding the sparkle that gave its distinctive qualities. He described the differences between the varietal styles of the cuvée, blanc de blanc, blanc de noir and many others.

'We are drinking the Veuve Clicquot's so-called brut variety. It has not so much sugar in the second fermentation, and so, not so sweet.'

'You seem to know a great deal about champagne, monsieur.'

'Because of our family history, a bottle of champagne on the table before meals was de rigueur.'

'What do you mean by family history?' She wasn't particularly interested, but felt obliged to appear so, since he'd generously shared his wine with her.

'The Baron Ponsardin was a very good friend of my father, the Marquis. It was he who asked Madame Ponsardin to be my godmother, and ...'

Vivian only heard a fraction of the details that followed the mention of his nobility. The son of a French Marquis! She studied Marcel de Clemenceau a lot more carefully. She imagined she could see aristocracy in his finely honed features, the squareness of his jaw, and his dark, green-grey eyes. From her own personal observations, these were the characteristics of the upper classes.

When he paused in his explanation of the connection between his family and the vintner, she felt compelled to clarify. 'Did you say your father was a Marquis?'

He appeared a little surprised by the question. '*Oui*,' he said. 'But that was before the second republic. Things must change in this world.' He shrugged. '*C'est la vie*, eh?'

Vivian composed herself and said, 'Quite. I'm sorry, you were saying ...?'

'The *veuve*, yes ... She was a remarkable woman. She married Francois Clicquot quite young, but was widowed only a few years later. But the widow Clicquot was not content to live the sheltered life of the French aristocracy: she continued her husband's art of wine-making and in the process, discovered the way to improve the champagne.'

'How?'

'The bubbles were pretty, yes, but the yeast made the champagne cloudy. She discovered a way to remove the cloud and replace it with a sparkle that also added sunshine to the bubbles.'

She enjoyed the way he expressed himself, and his accent. He made the mundane task of wine-making seem so romantic.

'It sounds very complicated.'

'Maybe it seems so because of my very poor English.'

'Oh, no, Monsieur de Clemenceau. Your English is excellent.'

'You are too kind, madame.'

He took a sip of his wine, but his smiling eyes held hers over the rim of his glass. This time she didn't drop her gaze.

'But you have nearly emptied your glass, madame. Please, may I offer you a little more?'

Vivian glanced around the tables surrounding theirs. One of the advantages of being a new arrival was that she was virtually incognito and had no need for undue concern about town gossip.

'I think that would be delightful, Monsieur de Clemenceau.'

'Please, madame, I beg of you, call me Marcel.'

He handed her his card. It read:

M Marcel de Clemenceau
Fashion Accessories
Athi River c/- Norfolk Hotel

'Very well,' she said, smiling. 'Marcel it is.'

* * *

Dan and the others alighted at the Nairobi station to the usual clamour of activity. He slung his pack over his shoulder and held Lizzie's hand while Bill and her father thrust their luggage into the hands of the waiting porters.

'You help Walter and Elizabeth back to their guesthouse,' he told Dan.

'Where are you going?' he asked him.

'Business to do,' he muttered.

'Really, Dad,' Walter said. 'Won't you come back with us for a bite to eat?'

'Busy, Walter. Sorry. I'll see you tomorrow to make arrangements for the move to Limuru.'

Dan sensed that Walter was hoping for his father's moral support when he broke the news of the land purchase to his wife, because as they'd hiked to the Limuru train station, Walter had told his father he thought he might have been a little hasty in his decision to buy the land without consulting Vivian. Bill had dismissed this with his usual alacrity.

At the guesthouse, Walter stood at the bottom of the short flight of steps.

Dan squatted on his haunches beside Elizabeth.

'Would you like me to help you find some insects for your new lizard before you go in?'

'Oh, yes, please,' she said. 'He hasn't eaten all day.'

'That's a good idea,' her father said, patting her on the head. 'You and Dan find some food for your pet while I find your mother.'

Lizzie put the box on the bottom step and ran into the vacant plot next door.

Dan joined her, pulling grass clumps out of the thick black soil and shaking them to release earthworms and other insects.

It wasn't long before he heard Vivian's voice rising from inside the guesthouse walls.

* * *

'For God's sake, Walter,' Vivian said through gritted teeth. 'We hadn't even discussed what manner of farming we would try, let alone the choice of the actual farm. Now you tell me that we are proud owners of a patch of dirt and bush in the mountains.'

'Vivian, please. Keep your voice down —'

'I am *trying* to keep my voice down, but honestly, Walter, what am I to think? We were supposed to discuss the situation before we bought anything. There are so many different ways to farm in this country.'

'What are you talking about? What do you know about farming?'

'I know that not all farms involve digging dirt or feeding cows. I'm told that many other forms of farming are quite profitable.'

'You don't know what you're talking about.'

'I am not as stupid as you may imagine, Walter Freeman. And I am fully aware that you know nothing about farming, or anything else for that matter.'

'There is never a time when I am not aware of my occasional shortcomings, my darling. You never fail to remind me.'

'Walter, I swear, sometimes ...'

She stormed out of the room and slammed the door.

* * *

In the plot next to the guesthouse, Dan made much of the search for grubs and insects, drawing Lizzie further and further away from the vicinity of her parents' argument, which could be plainly heard through the thin weatherboard walls.

'Look, Lizzie! Look at the size of this worm. I reckon your lizard will just love it.'

She came over to him and peered at the earthworm before picking it up and depositing it into an empty jam tin she'd found amid the grass and assorted refuse on the lot.

'By the way, Lizzie, what kind of lizard is it?'

She shrugged, continuing to search.

'I bet you'll find out soon enough from your *Encyclopaedia Britannica*.'

Again she indicated a reluctance to engage in conversation, even though it was about her animals — a topic usually guaranteed to bring forth a rush of animated discussion.

He knew she could hear her parents arguing, and although she might not comprehend the issues, and maybe not even care about the merits of the respective cases, he also guessed that it saddened her.

And by her quiet acceptance of the situation, he also knew the argument was not the first that she'd heard between them.

CHAPTER 12

Vivian crossed her arms and ran her eyes over the gentle slopes of the Limuru uplands to the mottled patches of last season's maize crop and remnant scrub to the forested ridges to the east and west and then down to the stream below.

Walter watched his wife's expression carefully. It had taken him ages to overcome her stubborn refusal to visit the farm. In the meantime, she had dragged him off to several tracts of savannah land, lost in her own obsession to buy an ostrich farm.

Vivian shrugged. It was as close as he'd get to an acknowledgement that she was prepared to concede Walter's point: the Limuru farm was as much as they could afford.

'And how much of it is ours?' she asked.

'Eighty acres of prime farmland,' Walter said, trying to keep the pride out of his voice.

'For seven cows.'

'Exactly.'

She took a deep breath and let it escape in a long sigh. 'And how are we going to work it, Walter?'

'The chief said he'd supply labourers for five rupees per month.'

'Five rupees?'

'Yes. I've hired a few each time I've come up to clear the first sections.' His smile broadened. He had taken the moral high ground, acknowledging to her that he might have made a hasty verdict, but insisting the purchase of the land had been a good decision. He knew that Vivian was trying to find fault in it, but was struggling to do so. He was pleased he had held his ground; a man had to exert his position within the household once in a while, otherwise it would be lost.

'Prime farmland,' he repeated. 'Look at it.' He scuffed the dirt with his boot. 'Look at the lovely rich red soil. We can grow anything we want here, Vivian. We can grow our own vegetables. We'll keep some chickens and ducks. A few cows for milk and a flock of sheep. We can butcher what we need and sell the rest. And then there are the cash crops: millet, maize, wattle. Maybe tea and coffee.'

Vivian looked down at Elizabeth. She had a stick and was attempting to coax a large black beetle onto it.

'What about Elizabeth? Where will she go to school?'

'Darling, she's barely nine years old. You can tutor her until we get settled, then we can send her into Nairobi to one of the church schools.'

Vivian fell silent — the ultimate endorsement, and a great relief. He'd had many opportunities to reflect upon his impetuous decision. It was good land, but as he wrestled with his guilt about not including Vivian in the decision, he'd been aware of the subtle pressure his father had exerted from the time they set out to see the place. It was almost as though he was daring Walter to say he couldn't decide before speaking to his wife. He knew his father would have said nothing, but Walter was in no doubt of what his thoughts would have been. *Apron strings!*

Now that Vivian was won over, he enthusiastically related the arrangements he'd made with the chief.

Vivian listened and nodded from time to time. 'When do you get the title?' she asked.

'The title?'

'Yes, the title deed to the land.'

'Oh, any day now. I'll go down to Nairobi and get it from the commissioner's office.'

'I suggest you don't leave it too long.'

'Of course not.'

His response was a little abrupt, but he was annoyed with himself for forgetting such a detail. It would have been far better to have been able to hand her the title with a flourish. In fact, he had no idea what administrative processes there were in British East Africa. He decided to raise the matter of title with his father as soon as possible.

A month later, when Dan and Freeman returned to their camp site on the future farm, they found that Walter had moved his family into a tent he'd pitched beside theirs on the flat ground a hundred yards above the stream.

After greeting Walter and Vivian, Freeman told his headman to order the porters to make camp. They then joined Walter and Vivian for tea.

'I see you're all settled in,' Freeman said.

After a brief glance at Vivian, Walter replied that things were going reasonably well. 'We've had a few difficulties getting established,' he said.

'Quite a few,' Vivian added.

'But much improved now.'

'What's been the problem?' Freeman asked.

Dan sensed that Walter didn't want to continue that particular line of conversation, but Freeman, as always, was oblivious to the tension simmering between Walter and his wife.

'The chief's been a little tardy in providing us with the workers we need,' Walter said.

'Obstinate, to be more precise,' Vivian said. 'We had a couple of lazy good-for-nothings for a few days, and then they were not to be seen again. We even have to haul our own water from the stream.'

'Did you pay him the five rupees for each man?' Freeman asked.

'I gave him half and said I'd pay the remainder at the end of the month.'

'Hmm, seems reasonable. What about the payment for the land?'

'I've sent him two cows on deposit.'

'Until Walter registers the title,' Vivian added.

'The chief's been a little annoyed about the delay,' Walter said by way of explanation.

'And not another penny until it's done,' she said, glaring at her husband.

Freeman was about to speak, but raised an eyebrow and closed his mouth without saying a word. It gave Dan his first inkling that Freeman had finally picked up on the friction between the two.

Turning to Dan, he said, 'Danny, why don't you go find little Elizabeth while Walter and Vivian and I sort out some details?'

* * *

Dan found the girl playing in the stream with a little African boy. She came running to him, dripping wet.

'Dan! Dan!' she cried. 'Where have you been?'

'Hello, Lizzie,' he said. 'I've been away for a few weeks, with your grandpa. Who's your friend? Isn't he the boy from Valley Guesthouse?'

'Yes, it's Tanu. Mother hired his father to cook for us. And we're living here on our farm with you and Grandpa now.'

'So I see.'

'What have you been doing?'

'Hunting. In the Aberdare Range.'

'Hunting for what?'

'Skins. We bagged a couple of eland and a leopard.'

'Why?'

'Well … until your grandpa gets some safari clients we have to make some money with the skins. We've also salted some gazelle. It'll keep us in meat for a few weeks.'

'I don't know what an eland is, but I know about leopards. I saw one just last week. And they're so-o-o beautiful.'

'They are. That's why people will pay for their skins.'

Elizabeth's brow furrowed. 'Can't you do something else to make money?' she asked. 'Why don't you start a zoo?'

Dan scratched his head. 'I'm not sure if that's a good business to start in Africa.'

'Why not? I have some animals you could use.'

'Do you mean Lottie?' he asked, pointing to a tiny Thomson's gazelle fawn tethered to a nearby tree. Dan continued to be surprised that the little girl had managed to keep the little orphan alive for so long. It had been the first of her larger acquisitions.

'How's your baby coming along?'

'She's getting very fat and heavy.'

'Maybe she was too thin when you found her and now she's how she'd look if her mother hadn't been killed by the leopard.'

'She's not as fat as Oscar.'

'Who's Oscar?'

'My new baby warthog.'

'If you don't stop adopting animals, there'll be none left in the jungle.'

'I have to. They'll die on their own.'

'Well, sometimes we have to ...' But he stopped short on his lecture about nature and its way. Time enough for Lizzie to discover that painful fact.

'Anyway,' she said, 'I'll show you some others you can use in your zoo.'

She took him by the hand and led him a short distance.

'I have three chameleons in there that you can use,' she said, pointing at a box set among the low tree branches. 'And there's a mole rat down in that hole on the bank of the stream. And over there is where I feed the dik-diks, and duikers — there's five of them.'

'It seems you already have a zoo.'

Her face brightened. 'Maybe I do.'

'But no lions.'

She sighed, 'No. I've never even seen a lion. Grandpa said he'd take me on safari one day, but he's always too busy.' She turned to him. 'Will you take me on safari, Dan?'

'One day.'

'Do you promise?'

'I do.'

'Do you really, really promise?'

'Of course.'

'But no guns.'

'What kind of safari will it be without guns?'

'Dan, it would be just awful to see a beautiful lion get shot. So, no guns.'

'If you say so, Lizzie,' he said with a shrug of resignation. 'No guns.'

* * *

Walter followed the men from the produce store and watched as they loaded his wagon with the potatoes, flour, salt, tinned meat and various items that Vivian had forgotten to order on his last visit. The new house was now completed, and it seemed the expenses were only just beginning. A broom, fire tongs, a small axe for chopping the kindling. There were so many items that were required only once in the lifetime of a household and it appeared that Vivian had decided to buy them all in the first month.

With his wagon loaded, he drove to Government Road to seek assistance from the provincial commissioner in registering his landholding at Limuru.

The feisty commissioner of the Ukambani Province, which included Nairobi, was John Ainsworth, a man of little formal education, but a great deal of personal experience earned from his time as the transport officer for the Imperial British East Africa Company. When the IBEAC collapsed in 1896, the British Foreign Office wisely placed the administration of the protectorate in the hands of men like Ainsworth, who had brought order out of the chaos of pre-colonial times.

Ainsworth had a good rapport with many African leaders, particularly the Kikuyu headmen, whom he'd educated into the ways of the British system of law and order. He held the strong personal opinion that white settlers had no place in British East Africa and the country should be left to the natives to develop in their own manner. These views were not supported by the British government, who were encouraging Europeans with sufficient funds to take up land. However, Ainsworth also held the position of lands officer, so Europeans hoping to settle in the country often found Ainsworth to be unaccommodating and uncooperative.

Walter knew nothing of Ainsworth's reputation so when he arrived at the provincial commissioner's office he expected to be given a formal if not friendly welcome.

Ainsworth was in the open office, shuffling through a pile of correspondence. Walter waited patiently, but when the PC turned on his heels and headed back to the inner office without a word, Walter coughed and said, 'Mr Ainsworth?'

The PC turned and peered over his glasses as if he was an intruder.

'Do I have the pleasure of addressing Mr John Ainsworth, provincial commissioner?'

'You're new,' Ainsworth said bluntly.

Nairobi's white population numbered no more than a thousand. Newcomers were immediately recognisable.

'I am, indeed,' Walter said cheerily. 'Quite new.'

'Here hoping to snap up land from some luckless native, I suppose.'

Walter, now a little abashed and defensive, said, 'Um ... not really. I already own land and I'm here to register for title.'

Ainsworth removed his spectacles and fixed his pale, watery blue eyes firmly on Walter, making him wonder if he'd said something gravely offensive.

'What land?'

'Why, the land I bought from Chief Karanja up in Limuru.'

'Chief Karanja up in Limuru,' he repeated almost in a whisper.

'Yes,' Walter replied, by now becoming a little indignant at the other's tone. 'About a hundred acres give or take.'

'Hmmph ... And you paid, what, a couple of cows for it?'

'Seven, actually,' he said, now irate at the PC's tone. Although he'd only made a down-payment of two, he fully intended to deliver the remainder when he was able, but he felt no obligation to reveal his private dealings with a public official, and would tolerate no cheek from him, regardless of rank. Walter was a British citizen and a loyal one.

'And you came here to register your title?'

'Quite so.'

'Well, Mr ...?'

'Freeman. Walter Freeman.'

'Well, Mr Freeman, Chief Karanja has no land to sell and therefore no title to transfer. He, like all the Kikuyu, indeed like all natives in British East Africa, merely occupies his land. The Crown owns it, or on occasion, leases it for ninety-nine years to people such as yourself, people who will pay too little, often leave it to others to work on their behalf, and ultimately snap up a considerable capital gain in a few years, leaving the land the poorer than when they arrived.'

'I intend to do nothing of the sort!'

'And I intend to see that you don't. There are strict conditions that you must adhere to regarding leasehold, but first, you must have it surveyed and pegged.'

Ainsworth opened a large, blue-lined book and began to scribble details into it.

'Certainly. I have no qualms about paying for government services.' Walter was becoming increasingly annoyed but was determined to show he could remain courteous regardless of Ainsworth's disrespectful manner.

'And to pay me four hundred rupees,' Ainsworth said.

'What for?'

'For the leasehold — subject to confirmation of the size of the claim.' He scribbled figures in the book. 'Plus one hundred and eighty rupees for the Crown survey.'

'What about my seven cows?'

'I am sure Chief Karanja is most appreciative.'

'But —'

'I am also required to inform you of the conditions of your lease, which are that you cultivate at least sixteen new acres per season and that you keep them in good condition.'

'What does that mean? Good condition?'

'It means you must continue to cultivate what you have, paying due regard to crop rotation, soil preservation, prevention of erosion, etcetera.' Ainsworth peered at him. 'You *are* a farmer, are you not?'

Walter walked from Ainsworth's office smouldering in rage. There was no cause for the provisional commissioner to behave so badly. It made him angry to be treated in such an offhand and disrespectful manner. He was furious at his father for letting him get into such a predicament. What would Vivian have to say? And he was angry with Chief Karanja: he'd taken payment for land that wasn't his to sell.

Walter could do nothing about Ainsworth's manner. It wasn't the first time he'd been enraged by petty officialdom. Nor could he avoid Vivian's ire when he revealed the situation to her. His wife seemed to exalt in his failures, and in this case she had a valid reason to lecture him. She had never been keen on the idea of a farm in Africa, and this would give her a host of opportunities to remind him of the wisdom of her opinion.

He blamed his father for encouraging him to haste, and for not informing him, if he knew, about the restrictions and conditions of a lease. If he didn't know, then he shouldn't have been so free with his advice.

But Bill's recklessness in either his belated abandonment of the original plan to share ownership and running of the farm, or his ignorance of the law, was yet another thing Walter could do nothing about.

Ever since his childhood, Walter had craved his father's approval, but seldom received it. It was not because Bill Freeman had been a negligent father — he'd merely been preoccupied by whatever was his latest plan to become wealthy. If by chance he discovered one of Walter's accomplishments, he would briefly acknowledge it before launching into a flowery description of his latest get-rich project.

His mother was more supportive, but being the practical parent, she invested most of her energies in making ends meet.

It was his father's praise that he craved.

No, he could not confront his father about the land-title debacle, but he could, and would, confront Chief Karanja about his duplicity. And the matter of the seven cows.

CHAPTER 13

Walter stewed on the matter of Chief Karanja's trickery, the more so when Vivian enquired about the title and he was obliged to reveal he'd not properly acquainted himself with the legalities involved. It was all a sorry mess.

'What were you thinking, Walter?' she demanded. 'Buying land without a title!'

'Dad said —'

'Surely you know by now that your father is a blatherer, free and loose with the truth at times. In this case he's cost us several hundred rupees and seven cows — seven cows that we don't have and precious little money to buy them.'

But it would not cost him seven cows. He'd paid two, and there'd be no more. In fact, the more he thought of it, the more indignant he felt, not to mention fully justified in marching to the chief's camp to demand a return of the two already paid.

'Vivian,' he said, drawing himself up to his full height. 'Over the next few days I will attend to these trivial issues. Rest assured, I will do what is necessary to rectify matters.'

'You may do as you please, Walter. Tomorrow, I am leaving for Nairobi for a day or so of shopping.'

* * *

Elizabeth was kneeling beside Tanu in the shade of the large mango tree, arguing with him over a game of jacks. In fact, the game they were playing was not actually jacks, but an amalgamation of jacks and a similar game played by Kikuyu children. In time, Elizabeth couldn't remember which rules were hers and which were Tanu's. Arguments were not uncommon, but the friendly rivalry that had begun at the Valley Guesthouse continued after both families moved to Limuru. Tanu's parents had been pleased to accept the offer of work in the area, where they had many relatives.

'No, 'Lizbeth,' he said, 'that is not correct. You must place the black stone beside the white stone before lifting any other stone.'

'Where is Daddy going?' she wondered aloud when she saw her father hurrying from the house.

Tanu followed her eyes. 'It seems he is going to the village.'

'Let's follow,' Elizabeth said, leaping up from the dust and scampering towards the track. She'd been admonished many times for going alone into the bush, but so long as her father was there, she felt it couldn't do any harm.

Long before they reached the village, Elizabeth could hear the thrumming of the drums. The sound came in waves like the clatter of train wheels — a syncopation produced by the combination of large and small instruments.

Elizabeth noticed the musicians as soon as they entered the village. They were seated in a circle at the edge of an open space where a number of warriors were dancing and prancing dressed in fine feathers and black-and-white monkey fur. Beside the drummers were others playing the *gicande* — the shell-encrusted gourd that produced a musical rattle. Other rattles, the *kegamba*, were attached below the knees of the dancers, so that each leap and stamp of their feet jangled in emphasis.

Elizabeth stood enthralled by the spectacle. Tanu, if he held a view, kept it to himself. The dancers, daubed in white ochre and carrying full battle regalia of feather-decorated spears and boldly painted shields, cavorted and leaped to the beat of drums and rattles.

'What's happening?' she asked Tanu.

'A wedding,' he said.

'Then why are the warriors carrying spears and fighting sticks?'

'They are there to prevent the groom's family from taking the bride away to join her sweetheart.'

'But it's a wedding!'

'Yes, it is a wedding.'

Elizabeth waited for further explanation. When it didn't come, she asked again. 'If it's a wedding, why are the families fighting?'

'They are not fighting. The bride's family are showing everyone how much they love and cherish her. And they are protesting that she is leaving them. The groom's family are insisting the marriage continues. Is this not how your mother and father were married?'

'No, of course not.'

The thought of her father reminded her of her original intention, which was to discover why he had come to the village in the first place. It was only when serious matters needed to be raised with the chief that he did so.

'Come, let's find my father,' she said.

With the sound of the wedding ceremony receding, they continued into the village and found Walter with the chief. They were in heated discussion, only tempered by the need for the translator to convey each person's arguments in turn.

'But you had no land to sell!' her father said.

'My people have owned this land since before the oldest elder can remember.'

'But Provincial Commissioner Ainsworth says the land is no longer yours.'

'If so, why did you come to ask me to sell it to you?'

'Because ...' spluttered her father, 'my father said you owned the land!'

When this was conveyed, the chief merely shrugged and turned to leave.

'Wait!' her father said. 'Just you wait. I want my two cows back.'

This recaptured the chief's attention, saying through the interpreter that the cows were his as were the further five cows promised when he agreed to let the whites build their house and plant their gardens.

'There will be no more cows for land you don't own, and ... what's more ...'

He'd spotted the offending cows in the chief's compound and stormed off towards them. Snatching up their halters he dragged them from their fodder bin, past the chief, and headed towards the track. Elizabeth retreated into the bushes beside it. If she'd initially imagined her father might not mind her following him to the village, considering his present mood she thought it was most likely that he would be cross with her.

Walter stormed past her hiding place as the chief let out a shout of rage. It was only then, with the chief's voice shrieking into the silence, she noticed that the music from further down the village had ceased. Not only that, but the entire troupe — musicians, dancers and revellers — were gathered in her father's path. At the head were the warriors, their body painting and zebra-skin vests giving them a ghostlike visage and their long spears no longer appearing merely decorative.

Walter stopped short, his scowl of anger melting under the cumulative gaze of the formidable gathering. Even Elizabeth, who had become so familiar with their friendly Kikuyu neighbours that she could walk fearlessly among them at any time of day or night, gasped.

The line of warriors moved towards Walter, who stood frozen in the middle of the clearing.

When they attempted to rudely remove the cows' halters from him, Elizabeth saw his expression slowly turn from apprehension to near apoplectic fury. He lashed out at them with fists and feet. The warriors reacted by immediately grabbing him and throwing him roughly to the ground.

Her father's face was red with rage, but a rage kept severely in check as the warriors led the cows away. He climbed to his feet, fists clenched, looking wildly from side to side at the crowd, now united in their animosity.

'All *right*!' he shouted, his voice rising to an unseemly shriek. 'All right, Chief Karanja! But you've not heard the end of it. You will regret the day you tried to hoodwink Walter Freeman. And I promise you this: you'll get no more cows from me!'

* * *

Vivian stood to one side as the liveried doorman collected her bag from the mule cart, and led her into the cool interior of the Norfolk Hotel.

The manager swept up to her while she was at the reception desk.

'Mrs Freeman, I presume?' he said, beaming.

She acknowledged she was, and took his extended hand.

He bowed, and introduced himself. 'Welcome to the Norfolk. I trust your train journey from upcountry was pleasant this afternoon?'

'Thank you. It was quite comfortable.'

'Excellent. Thomas will see you to your garden suite.' He indicated a young black man, now in charge of her bag, who nodded respectfully when she glanced in his direction. 'May I ask whether you and Mr Freeman will be joining us for dinner this evening?'

'Mr Freeman has been unavoidably detained at our property. I shall be dining alone.'

He bowed and offered to arrange a suitable table.

'Thank you, but that won't be necessary.'

Following the porter to her room, Vivian admired the aviary they passed on the way, where dozens of brilliantly plumaged birds fluttered about, twittering and squawking. The gardens and lawns were immaculately manicured. There wasn't a stick or a blade of grass out of place.

The Norfolk appeared to be living up to everyone's expectations. If the reception she received at the front desk was an indication, guests were greeted as if they were visiting royalty, with much bowing and smiling. It reminded her of her single season as a debutante, when her mother introduced her to Adelaide society — such as it was. In those days it meant something to have a station in life — something she realised she had relinquished soon after she married Walter.

When she reached her room, she sent for hot water to take a bath. While she waited, she removed her white lawn dress from her suitcase and spread it on the bed. It would be perfect for the mild evening; although it was a few years old, the handsome drawn work was still in good condition. It was the best — the only — bespoke dress she owned. She had ordered it when she and Walter were invited by the bank to Victoria Park for the opening of the racing season. There had seldom been an occasion to wear it since.

It had been something of an indulgence to take a room at this, the most sumptuous hotel in all of East Africa, but after all it was her money, as distinct from the household funds she shared with Walter. Keeping her finances separate from her husband's was an arrangement her mother, who had come to her own marriage in much more comfortable circumstances than Vivian's father enjoyed, had taught her.

A procession of water carriers filled the large tin tub, and Vivian undressed before settling into the warm water with a sigh. It was an ordeal to arrange a hot bath on the farm, which was such a pity; it would be so helpful relieving the stress of life in the Limuru hills.

This brought to mind her husband, and his ill-conceived land purchase. She might have been satisfied with the Limuru land — title 'misunderstanding' aside — if she'd never met Marcel de Clemenceau. His plan to raise ostrich feathers was such a brilliant idea and one ideally suited to someone like herself, who had an interest in, and if she did say so herself, a skill in assessing ladies' fashion. Why didn't Walter see such possibilities?

In her correspondence with Marcel de Clemenceau, she'd learned a lot about the many options available to people with small funds, but good judgement. Instead of living in the oppressive confines of the steaming forest, she could be in the much drier air of the savannah, raising beautiful prancing birds and mixing with people who had time to enjoy the better things in life, rather than living hand-to-mouth in a hut on a highland farm. She'd not yet experienced the social life in Limuru, and doubted there was any to be had, but if there were she felt sure it would demand no more conversational skills than the ability to discuss baking recipes and ways and means to keep pythons out of the chicken coop.

She climbed from the bath and wrapped herself in her robe. At the cheval mirror she paused to study her complexion. The harsh sun of Limuru was worse than Adelaide's and she would need more than her *Papier Poudre* to disguise her newly acquired washer-woman colouring.

She dressed at her leisure, applied her powder and, before leaving the room, appraised her appearance in the mirror. She was satisfied.

The high neck of the gown reached just beneath her chin and the small train covered her shoes. Her hair was piled in a chignon of soft curls.

She strolled up the garden pathway with the hum of conversation growing as she neared the main building. Now and then came the lilt of laughter. She plucked a pink hibiscus and tucked it in her hair before climbing the steps to the main building.

At the entrance to the Norfolk's dining room, she paused. It was elegant, and had an ambience reminiscent of her early memories of home in England with her family. The dining room was high-ceilinged, with ornate cornices and dangling candelabra. The plush royal blue squabs of the redwood chairs matched the stylish blue-and-burgundy Regency wallpaper with its gold frieze.

Four long redwood dining tables enclosed the geometrical centre of the room and were laden with silverware and fine crockery. Everyone was dressed properly for dinner. Outside the perimeter of long tables were similar settings for four, and in each corner of the rectangular room was a table for two.

At the one furthest from the door sat Marcel de Clemenceau, his back to her. His fine pinstriped suit was perfectly tailored for his broad shoulders and his thick greying hair was parted on a knife-edge. As she neared his table, she could see his crisp white shirt cuffs protruding exactly the right length from his coat sleeves. He wore a large gold ring on the small finger of his right hand.

When she came abreast of his table he looked up and smiled.

He stood, kissed her hand, and then ignored the waiter to himself slide her chair out and in again as she took her seat.

When he sat again, he said, 'I'm so pleased you decided to come.'

CHAPTER 14

Early one morning, when Lizzie was walking Oscar and Lottie to the *banda* where she kept a few maize cobs for them, she noticed a number of Kikuyu men partly concealed in the foliage. The young gazelle and warthog became excited when she opened the door to the *banda* and it took all her strength and attention to keep them out while she scooped up some breakfast for them. When she looked for the men again, they'd gone.

Around mid-afternoon they reappeared when she was down at the stream, playing with Tanu.

The men remained furtively in the distance, prompting Elizabeth to ask, 'Why are those men snooping around here, Tanu?'

Tanu was absorbed in the dam they were building and barely glanced up in the direction Elizabeth was looking. 'Up to mischief, maybe,' he said.

Tanu's family had found religion while in Nairobi, courtesy of the Church of Scotland Mission. Tanu's brief interlude with Christianity left him with a belief that anyone acting strangely must be 'up to mischief'. His use of the term was not confined to people. Oscar was up to mischief when he chewed on her mother's washing as it hung on the clothesline, as was the huge python they'd discovered coiled in the hen house, awaiting darkness before taking a meal of fresh chicken.

'But they've been around here all day,' she persisted. 'Shouldn't they be out hunting or whatever else warriors are supposed to do?'

Tanu stood knee-deep in the water and stuffed a wad of moss into the hole in their dam. He stood back to admire his work. 'There,' he said. 'We have a very fine lake for our boats.'

But Elizabeth was no longer interested in the dam or the toy boats they'd made out of sticks. She pondered the appearance of the men — perhaps five or six of them, although she never saw all of them at once, so there may have been more. When she thought back on it, she realised she'd spotted the men, or others like them from the Kikuyu village, on several occasions over recent days.

'They've been hanging around more and more often,' she said to herself. She'd given up on eliciting Tanu's input.

But Tanu finally joined her in her study of the men. 'Yes,' he said. 'They have, ever since ...'

'Ever since my father went to complain to the chief about the land he bought from him.'

'And the payment of his cows,' Tanu added.

* * *

Walter came up from the bottom of the land to find a handful of men on the edge of the wheat crop.

'*Hoi!*' he yelled at them. 'Hoi. What are you men up to?'

They stared at him in silence.

'I said what are you doing here? Go on! Be off with you!'

Again they simply stared.

He strode to the house, where Elizabeth was helping her mother separate some freshly baked scones, hoping to win one as a reward.

Walter took the shotgun down from the wall.

'Walter,' her mother said. 'What are you doing?'

'I've had enough of them,' he said, 'standing around like they own the place.'

'What are you going to do with the gun, Walter?'

'I'll say who comes onto my land and who doesn't.'

'Walter ...?'

He was outside again in a moment.

Vivian calmly wiped her hands on her apron before removing it. Then she folded it and placed it on the table.

As they reached the door, there was a loud explosion.

Before her mother could stop her, Elizabeth ran outside to find a shower of shredded leaves falling from the tree above the wheat field, and four or five men heading into the bush.

'*Hah!*' her father yelled. 'That'll teach you to stay out of here!'

* * *

Elizabeth sat on a log with Tanu, looking over the vacant fields. At that time of day there should have been a dozen men and women from the village on the farm, clearing, hoeing or cleaning up, but none had arrived that day.

'This is very strange,' Elizabeth said. 'I wonder where everyone is.'

'Your father will be very angry.'

'He's not. Or at least, I don't think he's angry. He's going about his business as if nothing were different. Does your father know anything about this?' Elizabeth thought to ask.

'No. He says it is business belonging to the *bwana kubwa* and the chief. He stays away from the village.'

'But who's right?'

Tanu was silent for a moment. 'My father said if the *bwana kubwa* could sit with the chief and *shauri* then maybe the troubles would end.'

Elizabeth knew enough Kiswahili to understand, but couldn't say whether or not her father, the big boss, would agree to discuss the issue again with Chief Karanja. And she suspected that as her father had fired a warning shot over the heads of his warriors, the chief might also be in no mood for further discussions ... unless he understood why her father was so annoyed.

'Why don't I go to see the chief?' Elizabeth said. 'Maybe he'll listen to me.'

'You?'

'Yes. I will speak nicely to him and find out why he is so angry. And then I'll tell my father and the two of them can have a *shauri*.'

'But the chief —'

'We'll do it now before things get worse.'

She set out towards the village at a brisk pace. Tanu made it clear he was not at all sure if he should be joining her on this expedition, but Elizabeth ignored him.

They arrived a little out of breath at the outskirts of the village, where it was usual to find a bunch of children tending the lambs and kids. All was quiet.

They marched on to the village proper, but the same scene greeted them.

The village was empty.

* * *

A night bird called and another answered from the other side of the house. Elizabeth stirred in her bed, but it wasn't the birds that had awoken her: she'd been dozing for some time after something — a strange noise perhaps — had disturbed her earlier.

The rhythmic breathing coming from the other side of the woven room divider indicated that her parents were asleep. She lay there trying to recall the sound from earlier in the night. Maybe she'd only been dreaming.

She heard Oscar's soft high-pitched grunt come from the pen her father had built adjoining the house. Then he was silent again, and she drifted back to sleep.

A sharp snap brought her back to consciousness, and she recalled it was such a sound that had awoken her earlier. A leopard had terrorised her baby animals only a week before, but on that occasion she'd heard nothing until her father let loose a volley from his shotgun.

She slipped out from under her mosquito net, and padded across the dirt floor to the door.

The darkness inside the house was almost matched by the moonless night outside, but she sensed, rather than saw, movement.

From down the slope towards the wheat field there was the light of a campfire. It gathered in intensity and she soon realised she was watching the wheat field igniting. Silhouetted in its light were a number of figures that quickly approached the house. It was a scene she couldn't comprehend, and for several moments she watched them come, unable to move, until one appeared with a lighted torch.

'Daddy!' she screeched as the figure threw the torch onto the thatched roof of the house.

Now the silence was shattered by the sound of angry voices outside, her father's roar of rage and disbelief, and the crackle and crack of the fire as it consumed the dry grass roofing and took hold of the solid timber struts and crosspieces.

'Vivian! Get up! Elizabeth ... get out! Get out!'

The wheat was burning ferociously, sending shadows dancing into the surrounding bush. The night had been still, but now there was a strong hot breeze racing up the hill ahead of the fire front.

Her father dragged her mother from the house to join her in the clearing.

Elizabeth shrieked, 'Oscar! Lottie!' and dashed back towards the house.

Her father was on her in five paces, just before reaching the animals' night pen, and swept her away, as she screamed: 'No, Daddy, please! It's Oscar and Lottie. They'll die!'

The roof timbers were all but gone and the flames, fanned by the wind from the wheat fire, flapped like gold and red pennants.

Through the open door she saw the fire consume the inner walls and soon the front of the house slumped. The side wall, where Oscar and Lottie's pen was appended, fell outwards in a flurry of yellow sparks that rushed like night birds into the ink-black sky.

* * *

Walter's blood was up. After pulling Elizabeth back from the fire, he clenched his fists in frustration. He expected the perpetrators, under the cloak of darkness, were well into their cowardly retreat. He imagined their smiles of satisfaction in their victory over the white man who dared to stand up for his rights — a man who would rather risk mindless reprisals than retreat from them on a point of honour. If they thought they could frighten him into accepting their unscrupulous tactics, he would show them.

He gripped his rifle, the only item he'd had time to grab before rushing his family to safety, and walked quickly towards the bush, ignoring the calls of his wife. His shadow danced on the eerily bright green wall of bush ahead of him.

Once away from the fire his eyes grew accustomed to the darkness, and he saw sinister figures scuttling into the bush.

'You there!' he yelled. 'You! Hold fast!'

Muffled voices flew among the shadows.

Walter dashed blindly through the foliage, shouting at them to stop. In the clearing outside the Kikuyu village, he could see a man standing defiantly in his path.

Walter raised his rifle to his chest.

The warrior lifted his spear and Walter fired as he launched it.

There was an instant during which Walter felt sure the spear had fallen wide of him, but immediately following, he felt a thud and looked down to find its haft sticking out of his chest.

It was shock more than pain that caused him to gasp, and it was utter outrage that caused him to shoot again, blindly, before he dropped his rifle and grabbed the spear.

Blood pumped from a punctured artery and the darkness deepened as he fell.

* * *

Elizabeth and her mother had spent an hour calling for her father until Vivian decided they would spend the night in the tools *banda*.

Her mother held her close, reassuring her that her father had probably got lost chasing the men who set fire to their house and that he would find his way home in the morning.

Elizabeth slept fitfully during a night infused with nightmares. In the morning she awoke to realise that, although the nightmares were gone, her pets were still dead, and her father had not come home. They began calling for him until an old man came from the bush and beckoned them to follow him.

Vivian uttered a scream when she saw Walter lying on his back in the clearing before the village with a spear projecting from his body. An old woman stood over him, crossing herself, moaning, and rocking from side to side.

Elizabeth felt rooted to the ground. Tears streamed down her cheeks.

Her mother kneeled and sobbed over her dead husband.

The safari had been a particularly gruelling one, with a German client who had difficulty with the language and even more with the fundamentals of big-game hunting. More than once either Bill or Dan had to intervene as the client placed himself in perilous situations.

Now, as the men packed the last of the chop boxes and began to gather their few small possessions before commencing their final day's march to Nairobi, Dan handed Bill a steaming mug of tea.

Freeman sighed as he lowered himself to a canvas camp seat.

'I'm buggered, Dan. That German cove has aged me ten years. Can you believe what he did yesterday on the river?'

The German, a free-spirited type, had thrown off all his clothes as the safari leaders checked the river and its banks for signs of crocodile and hippo, and plunged in. As he was apparently unable to understand their shouted calls to come back, Dan had been obliged to go in after him.

'At least the water was refreshing,' he said, taking the chair next to Bill.

There was a spate of shouts and chatter among the porters as a runner came into camp carrying the customary cleft stick holding a waxed envelope.

Dan took it, then handed it to Bill, to whom it was addressed. He opened it and immediately stood before sagging at the knees. After Dan helped him down to his folding canvas seat, he took the note from his trembling hands. It was from Vivian.

Dan read it in disbelief. 'Walter ...' he gasped, and turned to Bill, who was ashen.

'What have I done to my son?' the old man whispered.

* * *

The Nairobi cemetery was not the place of silent contemplation that Elizabeth thought it should be. A great cacophony arose from the Asian quarter, where a number of funerals were in progress. Musicians blew horns, beat drums and plucked or scythed on stringed instruments. The bubonic plague had been raging through the Asian bazaar for weeks and, judging by the amount of music, its toll had been heavy.

Elizabeth stood at the graveside beside her mother, who was dressed in black and weeping softly into a white silk handkerchief. Behind her were Dan and her grandfather, who was red-eyed but held his mouth locked in a tight line. On the other side of the simple timber casket sitting on two planks over the open grave, was the man who should have been a clergyman, but wasn't. He wore a navy suit and read from the Bible with a raised voice so he could be heard above the clamour from the Asian corner.

'We should have a clergyman,' her mother had said to her grandfather earlier that morning.

'I did what I could, Vivian. For God's sake, don't you think I want the best for my son? But there's no one available. Funerals everywhere. The bloody plague. And not only the Pathans and Sikhs. There's plenty of dead white folk too. There's just not enough clergymen to go around.'

'Well, I want a dignified ceremony,' she insisted.

'Bert Milford is a decent man,' he'd sighed. 'A bit churchy, but a good man. And I just thank God he's in town. Otherwise we'd have no one.'

Elizabeth already knew, because she'd heard her mother and grandfather discussing the matter, that Bert Milford had been the chief surveyor on the Uganda Railway, and had conducted funeral services in remote places as the railway snaked its way from the Indian Ocean to Lake Victoria.

Elizabeth had recently overheard a lot of family business that would previously have been concealed from her, like things about her father's estate and new plans that would now have to be made for the family finances. Normally, she'd have been sent out to play at such times, but following her father's death she'd been rendered invisible. Only Dan seemed to notice her and tried to reassure her that all would be well.

Now at the graveside, the railway man in the navy suit droned on about the kingdom of heaven and God's chosen flock, then asked them all to take a few minutes for silent prayer. Elizabeth felt bad because she knew no prayers.

Her grandfather lost his battle to contain his tears and instead covered his distress by loudly blowing his nose into his large red handkerchief.

Elizabeth thought how different things would now be without her father and the tears that she had thought had all been cried out began to trickle down her cheeks again.

Dan reached out to her, placing his hand on her shoulder and giving it a squeeze.

She didn't want to need anybody, but she clung to him and he drew her closer to his side, where she stifled her sobs against his chest and wet his shirt with her tears.

CHAPTER 15

The year had passed quietly. Bill went to Limuru, where he stayed on the farm to help his daughter-in-law manage it. He rebuilt the house and animal enclosures, made peace with Chief Karanja, organised the Kikuyu labourers into field gangs and became involved in the mind-numbing multitude of trivialities to do with livestock.

He hated every moment of it.

There wasn't a day when he wasn't reminded of Walter and how he'd abandoned his son to deal with matters requiring a temperament and experience he so comprehensively lacked. If Bill had told the truth about the complicated nature of land ownership, if he'd prepared Walter properly to manage the natives — Lord, if he'd just been there when Walter finally snapped — they could all have avoided the tragedy that followed. At night he would stare at the thatched roof and count the many ways he had failed in his duty to his boy.

His three months in Limuru did have one benefit — they confirmed that he'd made the right decision to become a hunter rather than a farmer.

His safari business was doing very well in spite of his absence. It was sometimes hard for him to admit, but Dan had absorbed all that he could teach him and had become quite capable since the hunt on Mt Kenya. He was good at handling clients, and was now leading large, successful safaris on his own.

Bill's relationship with his daughter-in-law had not improved. On the farm he found Vivian difficult to work with. And although he didn't want to know her personal business, there were rumours around town about her and a farmer by the name of Marcel de Clemenceau. He ignored them until he saw her riding along Sixth Avenue with a well-dressed fellow in a very fine carriage. Fortunately, Elizabeth, who sat beside him on the mule cart, had not noticed her mother, who had said she would stay overnight in Nairobi to attend the early-morning stock sales.

He worried about his granddaughter. Apart from the Kikuyu son of their cook, Elizabeth had no friends her own age. She spent her days in the bush, either searching for new animals to add to her zoo, or hunting for food for the ones she already had. When Dan was not on safari she followed him around like a puppy. Their conversation was invariably about animals: it seemed the only topic that interested her. Although Vivian seemed to be a capable teacher, Bill thought the girl needed the discipline of a classroom if she was to be properly educated.

In any case, whenever Vivian was off in Nairobi, it fell to Bill to be Elizabeth's home teacher. This happened too often for his comfort: he struggled with elementary arithmetic and his reading had never been good.

He decided to raise the matter of Elizabeth's schooling for the coming year and was surprised to find that Vivian had already made a decision: a very surprising one.

'I've decided to send her to her grandmother's in Adelaide.'

'To Harriet's?'

The thought of his granddaughter under his wife's cool care troubled him.

'Why not to England and *your* parents' place?'

'The Australian school year starts in February. Anyway, my mother is too elderly and she's never been ... close, to Elizabeth. I've made a booking on a BI ship. We leave early in December.'

'But ... will you settle there?'

'Never. I'll be going home to England. Well, one day, but ...' She ran her eyes around the farm. 'I'll have to come back here for a time. Walter managed to sink quite a lot of our money into this place. I need to recover something from it.'

Freeman thought he heard an implied criticism in her voice. He let it go. 'So you'll lodge with Harriet?'

'Until we get Elizabeth settled into boarding school.'

He'd mentioned lodging with Harriet as a joke. Walter had confided in him that Vivian and his estranged wife could barely tolerate one another for the length of a dinner party. It was inconceivable she would consider staying in her house for more than a day or so.

'When were you going to tell me all this?' he asked.

'For goodness' sake, Daddy Freeman, I only made the decision the other day.'

'After discussing it first with Marcel de Clemenceau, I presume.'

Vivian flushed. 'My friendship with Monsieur de Clemenceau has nothing to do with this. Or with you for that matter. Need I remind you I am a widow, and thrown back on my own devices as to how to survive in this horrid country?'

Freeman bristled. If it was only her devices keeping the farm afloat, why did he bother to help her? Again, he held his tongue. 'How does Elizabeth feel about this? This is her home, and although I agree she needs schooling, Australia is a long way away and she seems content here.'

Vivian tightened her lip. 'I shall find an appropriate time to inform her of our new arrangements.'

* * *

It had been a long time coming, but three weeks before her departure for Australia, Dan finally took Lizzie on safari. Not before overcoming a number of hurdles.

Firstly, in view of their approaching departure date, Vivian — who had taken a deal of persuading to allow her daughter to go on safari at all — refused to allow her to be away for more than one night.

Dan protested, saying that it would be very difficult to find lions in such a short time.

The mention of lions caused the second major concern, made worse when Lizzie reminded Dan he was not allowed to take his rifle.

'No rifle? What sort of safari is this?' her grandfather protested.

'You'll not take my daughter anywhere near lions,' Vivian added.

After an hour's debate, they reached a compromise. They would travel with only light camping equipment and enough supplies for three days — the maximum period allowed by Vivian. Bill insisted Dan take his 404 Jeffery, and Lizzie agreed to relax her embargo on firearms so long as Dan promised to use it only in emergencies.

No one was completely satisfied, but everyone agreed the safari would be the best distraction Elizabeth could have considering her impending exile.

They set off with just Korok and three porters, taking the train to Mbaruk and then heading into the grassy foothills of the Aberdare Range, where they made camp.

Dan had promised lions, but it was Korok who found them on the second morning. Dan took his 404 and with the Pokot ahead of him, and Lizzie in the rear, they crept over a low rise to find a hide in the shade of a tree behind a tumble of rocks.

The pride was large — twelve adults and ten cubs of various ages. They had taken a zebra during the night. The older animals had eaten their fill and lay scattered in a wide circle about the carcass, dozing, while the smallest cubs gnawed half-heartedly on the bones or, having lost interest, tackled their siblings in playful skirmishes.

They watched them all morning; after returning to camp to rest through the heat of the day, the three returned and found the pride again in the afternoon as they were rousing from their naps.

Liz whispered to Dan that it was the best thing that had ever happened to her.

For Dan it was a strange experience. In all his time on safari he'd never seen a lion without unshouldering his rifle and drawing a bead on it.

On the train back to Limuru, Liz babbled excitedly about the experience with the lions.

Dan had accepted every settler's characterisation of lions as vermin without question, but sitting comfortably in the shade watching the cats indulge their young, play with them, quarrel and socialise had been a revelation. It made him contemplate how much of a creature's nature he missed while hunting it.

* * *

Dan took the bag from Mwangi, the cook, and placed it among the others in the back of the mule cart. Vivian, who a moment before had been impatient to be gone, had rushed back into the house to find something she'd forgotten.

Elizabeth was in earnest discussion with her grandfather and then reached up on her toes to kiss him on the cheek.

She looked different that morning. Her fair hair was brushed and a red ribbon held it back in a ponytail. Maybe it was the navy-and-white dress. She usually wore khaki overalls with pockets and cuffs and a floppy straw hat. He couldn't recall how old she was. She always appeared to be a child, playing childish games with Tanu or fussing over her animals. Now she came towards him wearing a serious expression.

'You'll take good care of my animals, won't you, Dan?'

'I will.'

'I worry about the leopards.'

'Don't worry. I'll keep them safe.'

'And don't forget Maggie.'

'Who's Maggie?'

'My flap-necked chameleon.'

'A chameleon! How do I look after a chameleon?'

'You're right. Sometimes I don't see her for days. Maybe you don't have to worry about Maggie.'

They stood together in silence.

'And Dan?'

'Yes?'

'Dan, will you —?'

'Come along, Elizabeth,' Vivian said, as she strode towards the cart. 'Mwangi! You too. I don't want to be on the road after dark.'

Lizzie glanced at her mother and began to join her at the cart, then threw herself into Dan's arms, hugging her cheek to his chest.

He was taken completely by surprise, and for a moment didn't know what to do with his hands, then placed them on her shoulders. He could feel the tension in them. 'Hey ... what's wrong?'

'Thank you, Dan.'

'What for?'

'You're the best friend I ever had.'

He tried to remember how he'd shown her any particular friendship, and couldn't recall doing so. Now he felt guilty for the times he'd been impatient when she followed him around, pestering him with questions. She'd been starved for company and affection. Perhaps he should have paid her more attention.

'Will you write to me?' she asked, taking her head from his chest and fixing him with an earnest gaze.

'Write to you?' He hated writing, and now here was this nine- or ten-year-old, asking him the impossible.

'How old are you, Lizzie?'

'I'll be twelve next month. Will you write, Dan?'

'I promise I'll answer every letter.'

This seemed to satisfy her. She sniffed and smiled and he bent to allow her to kiss him on the cheek, then she was gone, running to the mule cart.

Dan joined Freeman to watch them climb aboard the cart.

Tanu and his mother stood a few paces away with a small group of Kikuyu women. They were all howling in misery.

Vivian sat stiff-backed in her seat, eyes forwards, as Mwangi flicked the reins.

Lizzie hung over the back of the seat with tears in her eyes, waving.

'Oh, *lawd*,' Bill said. 'How will that poor child stand being with my Harriet?'

Part 2
ELIZABETH

CHAPTER 1

1914

Liz pedalled down Childers Street in cream linen bicycle bloomers that almost reached her canvas-and-leather lace-up shoes. She felt slightly daring — the bloomers gave a small glimpse of her calf-length cream cotton socks. She chose her outfit for comfort, though her white long-sleeved, high-necked cotton shirt and flowered straw bonnet tied with yellow ribbons were also to protect her skin from South Australia's summer sun.

As she turned into Jeffcott Street, she overtook a Crimp and Cartwright horse-drawn tram, and entered her favourite part of the journey — Wellington Square. The trees and the absence of smelly, noisy motor vehicles were the ideal way to prepare for her day in class.

The short bicycle ride from North Adelaide to the university was far preferable to the slow tram ride, although there had been occasions over the last two years when the freezing wind blew the rain sideways under the Childers Street veranda, making her gasp and scuttle back inside for her umbrella and tuppence for the fare. But she considered herself luckier than most students. There had been talk that the university would provide residential accommodation for the undergraduates as was done by the universities of Melbourne and Sydney, but it came to nothing. The grounds were simply too limited and the entire student population of four hundred had to live with their parents, or pay rent or board — neither of which were options for Liz.

She had therefore approached the end of her final year in boarding school with trepidation, waiting for Grandmother Freeman to make an offer of support, but afraid to ask when it didn't come.

Her grandmother had always been rather severe. She worked hard and her life seemed to revolve almost exclusively around her dressmaking business. As she had lived alone for many years, Liz suspected she was comfortable in her own routine; but if Liz could not room with her, she would be forced to return to Vivian in East Africa. The allowance she received from her mother was not enough to support her in any other accommodation.

Her grandmother had eventually offered her a room — reluctantly, Liz thought, though she was grateful nevertheless. After two years, although Grandmother was impatient with her if she studied long into the night, or was occasionally late for meals after lingering in the library and forgetting the time, they had reached an understanding, if not an intimacy.

Liz did, however, get the impression that Harriet grudgingly approved of her diligence, and she surprised her with her knowledge of Adelaide University.

'I do hope you're working hard,' she said one evening at dinner. She had scarcely shown any interest in Liz's studies, and her question took Liz by surprise. She said she was. 'Hmm, then it's just as well. You have a responsibility to maintain a certain standard. Do you know the University of Adelaide was the first Australian university to admit females into a science course?'

'I didn't know that, Grandmother.'

'Well, it was. It's a proud achievement for women and a burden as well. It would be useful to keep that in mind as you near your exams.'

'I will, Grandmother.'

Liz pedalled out of Jeffcott Street and coasted down Montefiore Road towards the river. As she crossed the bridge, she peered down into the Torrens, where flocks of waterbirds bobbed in sluggish waters. She often dismounted at that point and followed the dirt track along the river until she reached the path to the university, but she was running late and continued on to North Terrace. She could soon see the impressive spires and slate roofs of the university buildings.

As it was a relatively unknown tertiary institution in a distant ex-colony, it was difficult for the University of Adelaide's administration to attract experienced academics from Britain.

There were, however, quite a few younger ones who were prepared to take the chance to accelerate their careers.

Professor Cornwall in the mathematics department had been only twenty-seven when he was lured from England after graduating from Trinity College, Cambridge, in 1876. Much more recently, in her own department, Professor Osborn, who had been appointed some six months back, was even younger. At twenty-six he looked more like a student than a professor of botany. He told his class that shortly after he arrived he walked into the examination hall and asked the middle-aged woman supervising the Botany 1 exam if he could see a copy of the paper. She obliged, but when he asked to also see another exam paper, she told him he could do no such thing and that he was to take his seat immediately and complete his Botany 1 exam with the other students.

The students believed they benefited from having a majority of relatively young teachers. Most of the academics were not too far removed from being undergraduates themselves, and could identify with the challenges the students were facing. Of course youth didn't permit the lecturing staff to forget the formalities of staff–student relationships. The students addressed their lecturers formally, and the academics would always begin classes with, 'Good morning, ladies and gentlemen.'

Dress codes were strictly observed. Liz would not be permitted into class wearing her cycling outfit. The only items of her outer garments that were not immediately replaced upon arrival at the university were her cotton macramé gloves.

She felt her grandmother did not approve of her bicycle riding, or her cycling outfit.

'Far too like one of those Gibson Girls,' she'd huff under her breath.

But Liz had no such illusions. For one, she would never wear a swan-bill corset — the secret to the Gibson Girls' hourglass figures. She was far too active. And she didn't associate with rich socialites. But, should she feel the need, she could pile up her long hair and reveal her graceful neck, as did the women drawn by the famed American caricaturist, and she felt quite sure she was, like the

Gibson Girls, the intellectual equal of many of the men she met, with the possible exception of Professor Osborn, who was quite brilliant.

She parked her bicycle near the rear door of her lecture theatre and hurried into the cloakroom, where she changed into a long skirt, white shirt and navy tie and the long cloak that senior students were obliged to wear.

The academics set high standards in their personal appearance too. Professor Jacoby never appeared before his students in anything but his academic's gown and mortarboard, which he removed at the door. Under the gown he usually wore black trousers, a brown woollen cardigan or a grey vest, and a white shirt and plain blue tie. The younger professors were also conservatively attired, and in all cases, quite formal in their manner.

Then there was her science tutor, Mr Dinter. He was different.

* * *

Maximilian Dinter looked younger than his thirty-two years. Although he wasn't one to dwell upon personal appearances, he knew he looked even younger — too young to be a tutor — and suspected it was due to his blond hair and fair skin. He also suspected that his boyish face might prove disadvantageous in his pursuit of a career in academia, so before applying for his position at Adelaide University, he grew a beard.

The beard was slow to appear, and when it did, it turned out much darker than his hair. It added strength to his jawline and contributed to his overall *squareness* — a characteristic inherited from his German forebears.

In 1799, under King Friedrich Wilhelm III, a new Lutheran liturgy had been decreed as the Prussian state religion. Germans who wanted to adhere to the 'Old Lutherans' ways found it difficult to practise their religion in peace. George Fife Angas, a British philanthropist living in the new colony of South Australia, provided finance for this disenfranchised group to emigrate. The first arrived in 1838, and over the following decades, these new settlers encouraged others to follow so that by the time Max's forebears arrived, South Australia, more than any other colony, had a substantial minority of Germans, and Australians of German descent.

Maximilian — shortened to Max soon after he started school — was the grandson of one of three Dinter brothers who immigrated to Australia from the village of Martinstein on a tributary of the Rhine. Family folklore maintained that the Dinters had been farmers in Martinstein since the Archbishop of Mainz feuded over the location of his castle during the Middle Ages. However, since moving to Australia in the 1850s, no one could speak with authority because all ties with the Fatherland had been severed.

Grandfather Jorg, the oldest of the Dinter brothers, bought a town acre in Adelaide before leading his extended family into the wilderness of the Barossa Valley, where other German migrants had settled. The family combined their assets to buy one hundred and sixty acres in the area called Tanunda; they hoped to carry on the family tradition of tobacco production, but early crops produced a leaf that was far too rank for either smoking or snuff.

Short of cash, Jorg exchanged his town acre for a good horse and a reasonable harness and did what many other Germans had done in the Barossa — he planted a few acres of grapevines with the usual staples of potatoes and beans for home consumption.

While the Dinters waited for their vines to produce, they experimented with a crop of wheat, which proved to be a great success. The gold rush in the eastern states sent wheat prices soaring — though this was a mixed blessing. Gold attracted labourers like moths to the flame and one by one they abandoned South Australian farms for the promise of a quick fortune in the east. The Dinters managed the wheat with a horse and various implements but the vines were another matter. There were few mechanical aids to help them with the arduous tasks of pruning, weeding and harvesting, and when their produce was ready for market, it was the family who, unassisted, loaded the bullock drays and took the wines, cordials and liqueurs to the paddle-steamers on the Murray.

Nevertheless, Jorg expanded the business, doubling the size of the stone cellars in 1864, and doubling it again in 1875. He added a distillery and a vinegar plant and bought more land around Tanunda to meet the demands of their growing markets.

In the universal exhibition in Sydney in 1880, seventy of Dinterfield's ninety exhibits received awards. Dinter's wine casks now rolled onto ships and Dinter's wine was served at the tables in Albert Hall.

The Dinter family grew in number as did their vineyard holdings. Jorg gave Rainer, his third son, a wedding present of a small holding at Joseph's Creek, which was a few miles further up the Barossa Valley. It was there in 1881 that Rainer bottled his first vintage and named it *Maximilian's Claret* in honour of his firstborn boy.

Max's earliest memories were of large family gatherings where aunts would dance, uncles would argue and sometimes fight, and everyone drank too much wine. The day would end with the whole family singing German folk songs with gusto. Foot-treading the fruit with his cousins was an excuse for horseplay. He learned English at school and German at home and played soccer in *lederhosen* with the Seppelt, Gramp and Henschke children. Their opponents were often the Salters and the Hardys: Germany versus Australia or sometimes England. If their games were occasionally flavoured with a touch of the nationalism heard at their parents' dinner tables, it lacked conviction and was soon forgotten.

One way or another, Max's life with wine seemed predetermined.

As the younger generation of Dinters began to fill the shoes of their vintner parents, the families sent at least one child to be formally schooled in the art and science of oenology and viticulture. Max and, a year later, his younger brother Heinrich, studied science at Adelaide University.

It was around this time that Max experienced his first doubts about his future in the wine industry. Wine was only a part of the whole. He wanted to work in the larger field of agriculture and animal husbandry rather than dabble in the narrow study of germination, fermentation and soil acidification.

Rainer took the news very badly. He accused Max of turning

his back on the family. How would the business survive if his son abandoned his responsibilities?

Max pointed out that Heinrich was only a year behind him and there were more than enough cousins to share the load, but his father was appalled. Max was forced to make the choice between his father's approval and what he passionately wanted.

Max still attended family gatherings and was always given a warm welcome, but his relationship with his father remained strained. Away from the family home, he directed all his energies to his academic career in the broader sciences that connected him to his love of the land and animals.

* * *

Liz sat on the bench in the university's quadrangle with a half-eaten apple in one hand and her reference book in the other. As she took a hearty bite of the apple and flipped another page, a voice came from over her shoulder.

'Michael Foster.'

She turned to see Mr Dinter standing behind her bench seat, smiling down at her. He was wearing the blue suit he always wore to lectures, but with a straw boater against the autumn sunlight. He looked quite dashing.

'I do hope I'm not disturbing you,' he added.

Her mouth being full of apple, it was impossible to reply. She simply shook her head and felt the warm flush of embarrassment rise to her cheeks.

'Which of his treatises are you studying?' he asked, seemingly unaware of her predicament.

She made a mighty effort to force down her mouthful of apple and almost choked.

'*The tissues of chemical action with their respective mechanisms*,' she croaked.

He nodded, still smiling.

Her mind went into a spin. It appeared the conversation was more than just a polite aside before he went about his important business. He was obviously waiting for her to add something — something profound or witty.

'It's on nutrition,' she said, immediately regretting it. Mr Dinter taught the topic in one of her classes. 'But ... of course, you know that.'

'May I join you?' he asked, gallantly ignoring her gaffe.

'Yes ... Certainly. Please do.'

She quickly slid along the seat and suppressed her rising panic. How on earth could she make conversation with him? Her half-eaten apple loomed as a major embarrassment. She discreetly dropped it as he rounded the bench to take his place beside her.

'Oh, you've dropped your apple,' he said, and lifted it carefully by its tiny stalk. He handed the apple to her. It was tooth-marked, spotted with grit and already turning a faint shade of brown.

'Thank you,' she said. 'How did it get there, I wonder?'

He took his seat on the bench and slapped his hands on his knees. It startled her.

'Ahhh! What a beautiful day,' he said. 'Don't you agree?'

'Yes, beautiful indeed.'

'It's days like these that I miss my time in the vineyard.'

'Your ... vineyard?'

'Yes, well ... it's my family's vineyard. Up in the Barossa Valley. Do you know that part of the country?'

She said she didn't and admitted she knew very few places in South Australia, in fact none outside the city.

'You've not seen anything of our wonderful state except for Adelaide?'

'And not much of Adelaide, either.'

'But this is terrible!' he said in mock outrage. 'It will never do.'

After her initial surprise at the interest he was taking, Liz felt a little special.

Mr Dinter told her about his home in Tanunda, describing the sweep of the farmlands and vineyards that rose to the east, where gumtrees coloured the hills purple in the spring and turquoise in the heat of summer; how the Para River's horseshoe from its source at Mt McKenzie to the family's estate at Joseph's Creek and the surrounding farms and vineyards nurtured the land and gave his family confidence they could turn a profit from its dark brown earth; and how the air carried the heady scent of ripening grapes as the pickers unloaded their baskets into the hoppers.

He spoke with such passion of his home, the land and the wine that she was transported there with him, following the fruit from vine to press, from curing tanks to barrel, and from barrel to tasting room to bottle.

'My family's most popular label is Joseph's Creek. Have you heard of it?' he asked.

She shook her head. 'No, my grandmother says she's never touched a drop of wine. We don't have any alcohol in the house.'

'Ah, such a pity. A house without wine is a house without laughter.'

She wondered if a glass of wine *would* cheer her grandmother, and thought it most unlikely. Some people were simply dour by nature. Or else her grandmother's years of separation from her grandfather had made her more comfortable in her own company than in the company of others. Either way, Liz had early on decided to steer clear of discussions of a personal nature with her grandmother.

'Since you say you don't know much of Adelaide, what do you do of a weekend, or on term breaks?'

Although flattered by his interest in her, she was embarrassed by it too. She didn't want to go into personal details of her social life with her girlfriends, such as it was.

'Oh, I cycle a little along the river and around the town. Visit the botanical gardens. The library.'

'And the zoo?'

'Occasionally.' She enjoyed the zoo but the admission charge was an indulgence.

'I should have thought a person such as yourself, after your time in Africa, would be a regular visitor.'

His knowledge of her personal details intrigued her. He must have taken some interest in her to know of her background.

'I love the zoo, but I have to be careful with my budget.'

'Then you shall come as my guest.'

For a moment she thought she'd misunderstood him, but then he added, 'I mean, if you would like to. I'm an honorary adviser to the head keeper, and since you have an interest in animal physiology, what better place for you to have some practical experience.'

She was momentarily lost for words.

'Of course, there is always the matter of decorum. I believe you live with your grandmother. She's most welcome to join us.'

She thanked him, not bothering to tell him she had no intention of having her grandmother involved.

'Shall we say next Sunday then?'

She gulped and nodded.

'Excellent! I'll meet you and your grandmother outside the main gate at two.'

CHAPTER 2

After decades of enjoying vicarious adventure through books written by famous African explorers and fiction writers such as Henry Rider Haggard, who thrilled readers with Allan Quatermain's searches for dangerous game and lost treasure, as the twentieth century dawned, the public became enthralled by a new breed of adventurers — the white hunters.

Only the very rich could afford the time and expense of a hunting safari, but many of them made their way to Africa hoping to experience the excitement of the hunt as extolled in such books and magazines. East Africa was particularly popular because the British government had conveniently built a railway six hundred miles inland — nobody knew why — making it easier to launch hunting expeditions deep into the interior of the continent. The fledgling safari industry boomed, and Freeman Safaris, at least while bathing in the glory of its mention in the influential Rowland Ward's *Records* for the first bongo shot in British East Africa, surged. In the early days, serious hunters clamoured for their services, and were prepared to pay high fees for the privilege.

The cash-strapped British East African government saw an opportunity to bolster revenue and raised hunters' licence fees. They also noted with alarm that animal numbers were not replenished at the same rate as they were diminished by hunters, so they lowered bag limits. The large profits available from hunting disappeared, and many professional hunters, previously making a living from ivory, hides and horn, now entered the safari business. Freeman Safaris therefore not only faced increasing competition, but their early hunting successes such as the bongo had been matched, or bettered, by others in the decade they'd been operating.

'I tell you, Dan,' Freeman said, 'if we don't sign up another client pretty damn quick, we'll be broke.'

They were sitting on opposite sides of the single desk in their office — a room above Murdock's store on Government Road — with Freeman's shambolic financial records spread before them under the sputtering kerosene lantern.

'What about the Vandervold contract?'

'That's not for another month or two.'

'But Vandervold sent us an advance.'

'Gone.'

'Gone?'

'All gone.'

'But he'll expect to have his supplies waiting in store when he arrives.'

'Don't you think I know that?'

'Jesus, Bill ... Why don't you let me run the books?'

'I can handle it. Anyway, I have a plan.'

Dan nodded. Bill always had a plan. It was generally needed to overcome some earlier plan that had gone horribly wrong.

Many of Bill's problems arose from his inability to keep any semblance of useful financial records. Dan was no scholar, but even he could see that Bill's method of throwing all the invoices and chits onto the table and ignoring them until the debtor threatened legal action could use some refinement. Bill Freeman was an excellent white hunter, a fine marksman, and over the years had become a good friend, but he was not a competent businessman.

'Ivory,' Bill said with a grin.

'That means a safari to the Lado Enclave or the Sudan or wherever the hell else you think we're going to bag a decent tusker. If things are as bad as you say, how are we going to pay for supplies and porters for six months?'

'There's ivory enough not far from here.'

'We've talked about that Bill, and the figures don't work. The bag limit makes it hard to get enough to cover the licence and other costs.'

'You don't need a licence for old ivory.'

'What do you mean?'

'When the Arabs came through these parts years ago, they often buried their ivory on the way in, and collected it again on their way back to the coast. Sometimes the ivory's not collected. I don't know why. Maybe they forgot where they hid it, or maybe the caravan was wiped out by the Maasai. Who knows? But I've met blokes who have found some of these ivory dumps, and they've cashed 'em in, sweet as pie.'

'Are you saying you know where there's some old ivory?'

'No, what I'm sayin' is we don't need a *licence* for old ivory.'

'Bill, you're not making sense.'

The older man wrung his hands together as he often did when he was enthused. 'Then let me spell it out for you, my boy. This is how it works. We go elephant hunting — new ivory, right? — and by Bill Freeman's magic spell, we make it look old.'

Dan let the mention of Bill's magic pass, but the hunting question remained.

'And just where will we find this new ivory?'

'In one of the reserves.'

Dan sat back in his chair. A moth that had been circling the lantern for some minutes had found the opening in the glass chimney and plunged in. Tiny wings briefly erupted in flames and the carcass fell to the desk. He took a slow, deep breath. 'That's called poaching, Bill. It's illegal. We could lose our licence. We might even get gaol time.'

'Not if we don't get caught.'

Dan slowly shook his head. 'I don't like it.'

'Dan, my boy … Trust me. I know what I'm doin'.'

* * *

Dan climbed the stairs to his boarding-house room, still thinking about Bill's plan to turn new ivory into old. Ever since fleeing to East Africa from the bloody war with the Boers he'd been careful to avoid coming to the attention of the authorities. He had told Bill his plan risked losing his hunting licence or being gaoled, but what he didn't say — couldn't say — was that the crime might also cause the commissioner to enquire into Dan Sutherland's record and discover he was in fact Dan Sullivan — an absconder. A deserter.

He opened the door and flicked on the electric light switch. The bare bulb hanging above the bed-end struggled to fill the room with yellow light, flickered for a few moments, and then settled into a dull orange glow. The Nairobi Electric Lighting Company's service had again failed to meet the town's power demands.

He put a match to the lantern that he kept on the bedside table for just such occasions and noticed an old copy of *The Field* under it. He took it and the lantern to the old leather-bound chair under the window. This chair, the bed, bedside table and small writing desk upon which he placed the lamp were the only furniture items in the room.

He flicked through *The Field*'s pages: *The Gentleman Landowner's Responsibilities for the Upkeep of Salmon Stocks. Grouse Hunting in the Highlands. Gun Dogs of the American Mtains.* A folded page fell from the magazine to the floor and he recognised it immediately.

Dammit!

It was Liz's last letter, which he'd read when it arrived some months earlier, but which he'd completely forgotten after deferring his reply for too long. Feeling full of guilt — the poor girl was such a faithful correspondent, and he such a poor one — he unfolded it to again read it before, this time, replying forthwith.

Dear Dan,
 I hope this letter finds you as well as it leaves all here.
 Did you receive my letter of June last? I hope the post office has not misplaced it as it seems to do on occasions.

Dan winced. Another one completely forgotten.

Christmas was ever so hot. Grandmother says it can't be helped. It seems odd that a land so far south of the equator can be so much hotter than Nairobi, which is almost precisely on it. Maybe it's the hills around Nairobi that send cooler air or perhaps it's the position, which Grandpa told me was quite high.

*Adelaide has such scorching winds from the north at
Christmas time. There's simply no relief. Grandmother hangs
wet towels over the open windows. She says it cools the air
but I can't feel it. I remember that no matter how hot it got
in Limuru, there was always relief from the heat at night.*

*How did you spend your Christmas? Did you and
Grandpa Freeman visit Mother at her ostrich farm? Are the
ostriches very beautiful with their long white feathers?*

Dan smiled wryly. He couldn't remember what he and Bill had
done at Christmas, but he was sure that a visit to see Vivian was
never considered. Bill still couldn't stand the sight of his daughter-
in-law and neither he nor Dan had set eyes on her since she took up
residence at her new husband's farm.

*I've decided I want to help sick and injured animals and so
have decided to become a veterinarian. Adelaide University
does not have a veterinary science degree. I'm not sure
which university does, but I intend to find out. I hope that
by taking biology and science subjects I can qualify myself
for admittance to one somewhere or, if that's not possible,
equip myself to do the work anyway. Perhaps to work in
Africa I don't need a full vet. science degree. Who knows?
One day we may see Freeman Veterinary alongside Freeman
Safaris.*

*With very kind regards
Your friend
Elizabeth (Liz)*

Dan hunted for a suitable page to pen a reply, but found none. That
was only part of his problem. On all previous occasions he'd found
it very difficult to imagine items that might interest her. Young
women, especially those living in a city like Adelaide, were not
interested in the kind of life he led.

As he rummaged through a pile of papers to find a notepad, he
wondered what girls of Liz's age would find interesting — which

required him to first make a calculation. It came as quite a surprise. She was already twenty-one!

He began to scribble on the back of a print he'd had made at Pop Bink's photography shop, but realised, as he signed off, that he'd been writing to the eleven-year-old who had kissed him goodbye all those years before rather than the young woman she now was.

* * *

Dan had led a few safaris without Bill. Most were with clients who were not interested in large dangerous game. Many were merely after a magnificent pair of kudu or impala horns as mementos of their time in Africa. When handsomely mounted over the fireplace at home in their English or American mansions the trophy would provide opportunities to recount the stalk, the shot, the kill. There were other clients, more adventurous, who chose to go after one of the big cats. In all these situations, his 404 Jeffery was enough protection for his client, but he'd been postponing the purchase of an additional rifle for some time, and with Bill's determination to go after ivory, he decided to delay the decision no longer.

He raised the matter with Bill one day in their office. Dan had learned a great deal in the years since joining Freeman Safaris, but among the white hunter community there was much dispute about hunting weapons. Calibre — light or heavy. Make of cartridge. Soft nose or full metal jacket. Repeating or double rifle. The opinions were as varied as the men.

Bill had always argued that when hunting elephant, or any large dangerous game, the most important requirement was reliability. He had argued in favour of a double rifle.

'There's no need for a magazine full of bullets that can get stuck,' he said. 'If you don't stop a charging elephant with your first shot or, if you're extremely lucky, your second, you're dead anyway. Hunting a bull elephant is tricky. You're not hunting a big herd as you often are with the females. You don't need to drop four or five animals. As you probably know, the males travel in small bachelor groups, sometimes just a big fellow and one or two *askaris* — young bulls who want the company of an older animal. And you never know when you're going to come up on a bachelor group. They don't raise the dust or make a lot of noise. With bulls, you could walk right in on top of 'em. They might've stopped and you're not to know. Maybe they're tired. Maybe they know you're following them, and they wait to see what you're up to. Not too bad if they're in sight, but you might be hunting them in the bush. They're big, but you can sometimes miss one of 'em in the scrub, and while you're lining up on the big fellow, one of his *askaris* comes charging at you from out of nowhere.'

He did, however, concede it was not only reliability. Killing power was also very important. He thrust a thumb over his shoulder towards the gun rack and his Holland and Holland 450. 'Get yourself a double rifle for the big stuff, my boy. And while you're at it, better make it a decent calibre.'

The gunsmith, John Murdock, agreed and was also more than eager to educate him. He produced half a dozen fine hunting pieces and laid them out on the counter for Dan to admire as he ran through his spiel on each of the rifles and the options for ammunition.

The Nitro Express was the latest improvement in cartridges. It superseded black powder with cordite — a mixture of nitrocellulose, known as guncotton, and nitroglycerine. The suffix *Express* compared the velocity and power of the projectile to that of another new invention — the express train.

The other advantage of the Nitro Express was that it was a smokeless cartridge and, as Murdock had great joy in explaining to Dan, that meant that the hunter didn't have to 'run around the smoke' to take his second shot.

Dan's initial reluctance over a double rifle was due to the cost — they were more expensive because of the expert adjustment required during manufacture to align both barrels to one set of sights. Murdock had a familiar answer.

'Why not buy second-hand? Look at this Westley Richards 500NE,' Murdock said, whisking it from its case and assembling it with the touch of a magician. 'Isn't it simply beautiful?' he added, polishing an invisible blemish off the stock. 'I knew the previous owner. Seldom used it.'

He handed it reverently to Dan, who turned it from side to side, feeling its weight and balance. The metal plates were finely engraved, but discreetly so. The rosewood stock shone with a deep radiance.

'Try the stock weld,' Murdock said.

'Stock weld?'

'Put it to your shoulder as if you're going to shoot and feel how it settles against your cheek — stock weld.'

Dan did as he suggested and found he was looking straight down the gun sights.

'I thought so,' the gun dealer said, beaming. 'Perfect. He was your size and shape. This is the right Nitro Express for you, young man.'

He had never heard the term *stock weld* before, and Murdock was obviously trying to impress, but Dan knew how a rifle should feel in his hands and against his cheek and he liked this one. They entered into half-hearted haggling. Dan was still unsure if he should pay so much, and there was the matter of it being second-hand, so his negotiating lacked commitment.

Undaunted, Murdock pointed out more of the rifle's many attractive features, at the end of which he added, smugly, 'Extractors.'

Dan knew that an elephant had difficulty determining the direction of the gunshot, but it could pinpoint the *ping* of an ejected case, and therefore mount an unerring charge in the hunter's direction. Extractors allowed the shooter to tilt the rifle and let the spent cases drop silently to the dirt or into his hand.

'You said you knew the previous owner. Who was he?'

'A young chap, much like yourself.'

'And exactly why did he sell it?'

'Don't you love the stock carving? Look at those scrolls and twirls.'

Dan ran a finger along the rosewood stock. The detail was almost perfect. 'It doesn't look very old.'

'Oh, no, it's not. Like I said, he barely used it.'

'Then why did he sell it?'

Murdock reached for the rifle's case. 'It comes complete with this brass-cornered, oak and leather case, and all accessories.'

Dan grabbed his wrist. 'Why — did — he — sell?'

Murdock sighed. 'He was a nice young man. As I said, much like you in many ways, only ...'

'Only what?'

'A little impetuous.'

Pressed further, Murdock related the tale of the young Nitro Express owner.

'He was quite well-to-do. His family had a large holding in the Rift Valley. They were very good customers.' He said it as if that fact alone could excuse all else that was to follow. Then he returned his gaze fondly to the Westley Richards. 'He bought this beautiful piece from me to go hunting in the Lado Enclave.'

The Lado Enclave was a curious slice of territory along the Congo–Uganda–Sudanese border. Its administration seemed to be in constant flux, and at most times was unmanaged. Many hunters had made their fortune plundering ivory from the elephant herds of the Lado.

'It was there in the enclave where he met Karamojo Bell.'

Dan knew of the legendary Bell — everyone did — an ivory hunter famed for shooting hundreds of elephants with the relatively small calibre 275 Rigby Nitro Express. He'd heard jokes about Bell, a Scot, said to be too mean to invest in a large calibre rifle — a 275 cost a tenth as much as a 450 — and too miserly to use more than one bullet to kill each elephant.

'When he came back home I sold him a Rigby 275,' Murdock said, shaking his head. 'I didn't know he wanted to imitate Karamojo Bell and use it on elephants. Of course, people told him — I would have told him if I'd known — that Bell was an expert in the brain shot. He hardly ever missed. The young fellow wouldn't be warned. He barely took the time to get familiar with the sights or the feel of it. He went up north towards Marsabit and came upon a big bull. I heard he had a perfect line on a side brain shot and dropped the animal with his first cartridge. He ran to it, full of excitement. As I said ... impetuous. His bearer shouted to beware, but he took no notice, did he? The elephant was not mortally wounded, but only stunned. When the young fellow climbed onto what he thought was a dead elephant, it lifted its head, swung its trunk, and caught the lad a fearful blow, sending him flying. Then before he'd fully regained his senses, the bull staggered over to him and pressed his forehead onto his body, flattening him.' He shook his head yet again. 'Such a shame.'

Murdock had obviously wanted to avoid telling Dan the story, suspecting he'd lose the sale, but in fact, it was quite the opposite. Dan felt that knowing how the second-hand rifle came up for sale made it a better purchase for him. It was its provenance that sold it. If the young man had taken the Westley Richards 500NE instead of his new 275 Rigby, he might still be alive.

He only had one more question. 'What calibre would you use to hunt large dangerous game, Mr Murdock?'

Murdock paused before answering. 'For lion, rhino, buffalo — the 416 or the 450. They're both nice. And many use them for elephants. And it's true: you can bring down an ele with a 275 if you're sharp enough. But miss the brain with any of those lighter weights and, while you may cause the big fellow to stumble or falter, if you miss the brain you're in trouble.'

He paused, sensing he had almost clinched a sale and hence disinclined to say more and risk losing it.

'And for the big game?' Dan asked.

'You want a bullet that will stop an elephant's charge, even if you don't hit the brain. There are those like Mr Freeman, who swear by the 450 or the 470.' He shook his head. 'But this ...' he said, looking solemnly at Dan before lowering his eyes again to the Westley Richards 500NE '... this is an elephant gun, Mr Sutherland. A *real* elephant gun.'

CHAPTER 3

As she rode her bicycle through the wooded corridors of Wellington Square, Liz's thoughts about the coming weekend and her visit to the zoo with Max Dinter oscillated from eagerness and delight to fear and dread. She became very muddled and at times wasn't even sure if it was legal to fraternise with the lecturing staff, and considered cancelling the outing. Then she scolded herself. Of course it was legal. It was just unusual.

Daring was how one of her girlfriends described it. She didn't want it to be daring and laughed it off, but the word crept into her mind late at night, when she was trying to sleep. She'd had a number of outings with young men — friends or relatives of her girlfriends — but they were around her own age. Mr Dinter was at least thirty, maybe even thirty-five; very sophisticated and worldly. What would she do by way of conversation? How would she dress?

And there was her grandmother. She seldom took an interest in Liz's social life, but it seemed likely that she would have something to say about Mr Dinter's age. Although there was another, far more worrying aspect of the appointment that would concern her grandmother if she knew it.

Harriet Freeman, nee Robinson, was an aloof woman, a woman of sober demeanour and simple tastes, and Liz had a great deal of respect for her. She admired her grandmother's independence and the fact that she had supported herself — albeit in a modest way — with no assistance or even the presence of a husband. She also appreciated her grandmother's hospitality when on school holidays from boarding school, her generosity in providing her with food and lodgings as she completed her degree at university, and her support of the principle that girls could, and should, receive an education to the full extent of their abilities. Liz respected her grandmother for all these things, but she didn't love her. Even as a child, she had found Harriet unapproachable, and as a result she'd never been close to her. The relationship between her grandmother and her mother, which could range from cold formality to open hostility, hadn't helped either.

When she and her mother had arrived back in Adelaide, there had been no gushing welcome, and after barely a week the atmosphere had grown decidedly chilly. Although she'd been only twelve, Lizzie had sensed the acrimony. The two women managed to observe a form of truce during the day, but as soon as Lizzie went to bed, the bitterness came boiling forth.

Through the walls she could hear the arguments, the accusations and the counterclaims. 'I told Walter you would never be satisfied with what he could offer you,' from Harriet, and, 'You spoiled him. That's why he was useless as a man and a provider,' from Vivian.

Lizzie wasn't totally surprised when her mother told her that the arrangements with the boarding school were completed, and she would be going back to Africa earlier than planned. She left before Lizzie started at St Hilary's Boarding School for Girls. Lizzie cried, and her mother did too, but there was relief in Vivian's face, which had become taut and severe during that very trying month.

Term holidays at her grandmother's home in Childers Street were not enjoyable. Lizzie kept mostly to herself and was more homesick there than at school, where she was close to a number of the girls. They were fascinated by her time in Africa and encouraged her to relate her experiences while living there, which she did with commendable modesty.

Her grandmother never asked about her life in Africa, never enquired about the circumstances of her father's death, and never allowed her to raise any matters relating to it. She also made it known that she was not to mention her grandfather by name or inference, nor refer to any aspects of his life there.

Her bundle of books had come loose in her bicycle basket and she braked and slid from her seat to rearrange them. An Aboriginal man in a threadbare coat sat in a patch of shade surrounded by the sun-bleached lawn. It was too hot for a coat, she thought, but he appeared to be a vagrant and it was likely that, rather than carry them, he donned all the clothes he possessed. He ignored her, but she somehow knew he was aware of her presence. She shot him a glance as she resumed her ride, but he remained staring at the ground.

In the early days, as Lizzie lay in her boarding-school bed pondering the enigma that was her grandmother, she wondered if Harriet blamed her for her father's death. But that didn't explain why Lizzie couldn't mention her grandfather. The only theory she had was that her grandmother had lost both a husband and a son to Africa, and as a result, she would hear nothing of it.

Although Harriet had received only a basic education, she often surprised Liz with the breadth of her knowledge. She also had a strong interest in politics and world affairs. She knew all the facts about the two recent wars in the Balkan states. There had been a number of debates at Liz's university on the stance taken by the super powers with regard to the carve-up of the Ottoman Empire. She, like many of her friends, favoured peace at almost any cost. Her grandmother blamed Habsburg-ruled Austria-Hungary and Germany's encouragement of the Turks' fight and thought that Britain should exert her influence. She told Liz, with a touch of triumphalism in her tone, that she was pleased when Britain, France and Russia rejected Germany's offer to be mutually neutral in the Balkans. It was intended to reduce the risk of an accidental war, but she said it was Germany's way to divide and separate the allies.

'You can never trust a German,' she said with a vehemence that had surprised her granddaughter.

* * *

Liz agonised over her outfit for her engagement with Maximilian Dinter, and then, in the midst of all her deliberations, she had a very sobering thought. It hit her like a thunderbolt. She'd been very silly, treating the zoo outing as a social occasion. It was nothing of the sort. Mr Dinter was simply offering to assist her in her studies.

He had perhaps noticed her difficulties with some aspects of her animal physiology course and was kindly offering a practical road to improvement. Perhaps he thought her a dullard? The notion sent her into a downward spiral of self-doubt.

She became exhausted by the whole ordeal, and decided to be herself. The day was mild and bright, and she would simply try to enjoy her day at the zoo; she finally selected a pale pink cotton dress with a print of tiny black sprigs of forget-me-not flowers and a woven straw hat with a small corsage of pink and yellow flowers on the brim.

When she checked the time she gasped, pulled on her cream crocheted gloves and rushed out of the house, calling to her grandmother that she'd be out for the afternoon.

She took two trams, including one of the new electric ones down Hackney Road, but it was still a long walk to the zoo. Arriving at the main entrance, she folded her cream cotton parasol and searched for Mr Dinter without success. The clock above the turnstile said it was after a quarter to three. She was nearly an hour late, and Mr Dinter had gone, obviously annoyed and probably declaring he'd have nothing further to do with such an ungrateful and fickle girl.

'Ah! There you are,' he said, coming through the gate towards her. 'I hope I didn't keep you waiting.'

'Oh, Mr Dinter, I'm so sorry. I had to catch two trams and there was a delay waiting for the second and —'

'Don't trouble yourself, please. I was busy anyhow, attending to some tasks that I left over from my last visit, but I'm ready now, so if you'd — but where is your grandmother?'

'I don't have a grandmother, I mean ... she couldn't come.'

She was now worried that she'd created an enormous social blunder by not having a chaperone.

'Perhaps I should have brought her, but she dislikes going out on a Sunday. It's her housekeeping day and —'

'Miss Freeman,' he said, raising his hands. 'It is of no concern to me if you bring your mother, grandmother, second cousin on your father's side, or any other relative. I merely suggested you might like to bring someone to put you at your ease, but it seems I've achieved quite the opposite.'

She smiled with him. 'Not at all, Mr Dinter. I'm quite capable of getting out and about on my own.'

'Excellent, so let us begin, but before we do, would you mind terribly if we dispensed with titles and surnames? I find it difficult enough at the university.'

She smiled. 'Not at all.'

'Then it's Max and Elizabeth for today,' he said, extending his hand. 'Pleased to meet you, Elizabeth.'

'Liz is better,' she said. 'And pleased to meet you, Mr ... I mean, Max.'

He led her through the gates and into the gardens, where he pointed out his favourite exhibits. They started with the Asian elephants and as they walked he fed her pieces of the zoo's history. It was created by the South Australian Acclimatisation and Zoological Society in 1883, making it, after Melbourne, the second oldest zoo in Australia.

She found his voice easy to listen to, just as it was during lectures. He had a gentle, mature tone, but it could easily carry to the back rows of the lecture hall.

He pointed out the projects with which he'd had an involvement. At the waterbird pond he proudly told her that he'd provided recommendations on the appropriate plantings.

'Do you see that old brown bear down there?' he asked.

The bear was asleep in a concrete pit surrounded by a moat.

'Yes.'

'I removed his broken, decaying tooth.'

'A bear with a sore head?' she asked, and he laughed.

When they reached the lion's enclosure, Liz studied the animal. There was something odd in his appearance. 'What's wrong with him?' she asked.

'What do you mean?'

'He doesn't look well.'

'Why do you say that?'

'His coat is an unusual colour, don't you think?'

'Well, um ... actually, he's the only lion I've ever seen, so I can't speak with any authority on that.'

'It's quite dull. And his mane is thin.'

She walked to the other end of the barred enclosure. The lion lifted its head and yawned. 'His tongue's quite pale. Maybe he's hungry. But he doesn't look thin.'

Max's eye travelled over the animal as Liz made her points. He'd not noticed the lion's poor condition before she'd pointed it out. The animal was actually quite obese. 'You're right. He *is* fat.'

'And I think one of his front pads is split,' she added for good measure.

'That's quite remarkable, Elizabeth. Have you been making a special study of lions?'

'No. I'm not an expert, but I have seen lions in the wild and this one looks ... different.'

She stood back and studied the enclosure in more detail. It was a rectangular concrete box in a line of similar boxes. In the next identical cage was a hyena that ceaselessly paced the enclosure's perimeter, its drooling tongue dangling from its mouth while it emitted high staccato yelps.

She walked beyond it to where a cheetah paced the length of the bars, staring over her head to an invisible horizon.

She returned to Max, who was still studying the lion. 'This lion is quite unhealthy,' he said. 'And his tongue indicates his diet needs attention.'

'I can see why he's fat. He needs a larger space to exercise. Look at him — he's hardly got room to stretch. All the animals need more space. Even the smaller ones we saw earlier. And the antelope. They need to be able to run.'

'The authorities are quite proud of the zoo. It's been modelled on Regent's Park in London.'

'I don't care,' she said emphatically. 'It's not good enough.' She blushed. 'I'm sorry, Mr Dinter, I'm being impertinent. It's not for me to speak so boldly.'

'Ah, dear me,' he said. 'I've been demoted to Mr Dinter already.'

'I'm sorry ... Max. It's just that I've never seen a lion so sad.'

'Sad? I'm afraid that's an emotion I've never assigned to a lion, but I get your point, Elizabeth.'

He stroked his chin. 'The problem is, how do we fix it?'

* * *

When Max next attended the monthly meeting of the Acclimatisation and Zoological Society, he raised the matter of the size of the enclosures, especially for the larger carnivores. He described the condition of the zoo's only lion. 'He's quite unhealthy.'

'And quite old,' added one of the directors, himself a man of advanced years.

'And probably suffering some frustration,' added another. 'Especially since his lady wife passed away years ago.'

A number of directors chuckled at this.

'I know we have limited funds, gentlemen,' Max continued, 'but what I am proposing is the creation of a more natural environment — a place where the public can see the exhibits in as natural an environment as we can provide. Imagine it, gentlemen … lions in an enclosure of grasses, with fresh running water and pools where they can drink. Boulders they can recline on in the sun. A piece of the African savannah, if you will. And a leopard enclosure with natural foliage and trees they can climb.'

He glanced around the boardroom table. The chairman, John Goodwood, was a merchant banker. Henry Goss owned the flour mill and half the buildings in Rundle Street. George Squires was the principal in Gordon and Squires, a very successful accountancy firm. Nothing happened in Adelaide unless such men agreed it was worth doing.

'In short, gentlemen,' Max continued, 'I'm proposing that we establish a building program to progressively improve our animals' environments.'

He caught the chairman's eye. He had his answer even before anyone spoke.

* * *

At the end of his physiology lecture later that week Max closed the session and bid everyone good afternoon.

'Oh, Miss Freeman,' he said, as the classroom emptied. 'May I have a word?'

Liz joined him at the podium.

'I raised the rebuilding suggestion at the board meeting,' he said.

'And they declined,' she said.

'I'm afraid so. How did you guess?'

'Your face. I knew it was bad news when you called me back.'

'The trustees pointed out that the society established the zoo as a means of educating the public. They said if the exhibits are too large, the public will be unable to see the animals and the purpose would be lost.'

She nodded. 'In other words, they don't have the money.'

'I'm sorry, Elizabeth. The world's not ready to save the animals.'

'It won't stop me from trying,' she said, making an attempt to overcome her disappointment with a smile.

'Somehow I knew that.'

'Thank you anyway,' she said, gathering her books together under her arm. 'It was very sweet of you to try.'

He watched her climb the steps to the exit at the back of the classroom, her college garb unable to hide her shapely figure. Max smiled as he packed his lecture notes into his briefcase. Nobody had called him *very sweet* in quite some time.

* * *

The wind returned to Adelaide, blowing the plane trees' golden leaves down the city's wide streets, reminding Liz of how much she missed the warmth that was always a part of life in Africa.

Although Max always gave her a nod of acknowledgement when they passed, it had been a month since she had last spoken to him and she'd come to the realisation that the pleasant April day they'd shared at the zoo was no more than a tutor's interest in his student's chosen topic.

It was a surprise, therefore, when Max again approached her in the quadrangle at lunchtime. On this occasion she was sitting with Ann and Gregory — her biology classmates.

'Oh, Miss Freeman,' he said, after nodding hello to the other two. 'I need to see you when you have a moment. It's not urgent, but any time at your convenience.'

The remainder of lunchtime was consumed with discussion about what Mr Dinter could want.

It was curiosity touched with excitement that saw Liz heading to Max's office after the end of classes that day. She knocked on his door before opening it a crack to peep in. 'You wanted to see me, Mr Dinter?' she said.

Max leaped to his feet. 'Indeed I did. Please come in. Won't you take a seat?'

She sat uncomfortably on the edge of her chair while he fussed among things on his desk, moving them at random. She felt increasingly uncomfortable. It was obvious she was disturbing his organised day. He sat opposite her at last, but just as she thought he was about to speak, he picked up a book and moved it from one side of his desk to the other, before dropping it into a desk drawer and sliding it shut with a bang.

'Is it about my assignments?' she asked, unable to stand the tension any longer. 'I should have the last one to you in a week or so.'

'No, no. Your assignments are always on time, and the last isn't needed until ... Anyway, I'm glad you came by. I've been trying to catch your eye, but you're always with your friends, and I ...'

He straightened a stack of papers and began to fidget with a pencil before continuing. 'I wanted to tell you how much I enjoyed our outing to the zoo, Miss ... I mean, Elizabeth.'

He paused, making her think she needed to reply. 'So did I, Mr Dinter, it was a nice day.'

'Yes ... quite.' He returned to study his pencil. 'The fact is, I enjoyed it very much.'

This time she had nothing to add, and the silence extended.

'Is that ... all?' she asked, and made ready to rise.

'Yes, er, no. It was such a nice day I wondered if you would like to have another outing. That is, if you have nothing else to do. I mean, if you're free sometime.'

She breathed a sigh of relief.

'Oh, I imagine you must be very busy,' he said. 'Your friends, etcetera.'

'No. It's not that. I thought ... I thought there'd been some problem with my assignments and that —'

'No. Everything is quite ... adequate in that regard. In fact, quite good.'

'To the zoo again?' she asked, feeling a flutter of excitement inside as she realised that their outing wasn't an educational excursion.

It took him a moment to register that she was agreeing to his proposal. When he did he brightened. 'No, not the zoo again. I thought you'd like to see another aspect of life here in Adelaide.'

'Certainly.'

'I was thinking about seeing a game of football on the weekend. Would you care to join me?'

She had a vision of the boys at the neighbouring academy to her boarding school dashing through the mud after the ball. She knew little about the game, but in spite of her nervousness, felt quite flattered that Max Dinter wanted to spend more time with her. 'I would like that, but I must warn you, I know very little about soccer.'

'That's not a problem. It's not soccer, it's ... Well, it's probably best we wait until we're at the game.'

CHAPTER 4

Dan was forced to concede that Bill's planning for their hunt for illegal ivory was far more thorough than was his usual effort. They took the train from Nairobi, leaving no word of their final destination. In Nakuru, they put together a disparate group of porters rather than use their usual crew of Wakamba men from Machakos. They also raised most of their supplies in Nakuru before rejoining the train to Londiani.

The porters were poorly trained, but even so were more expensive than Bill had hoped to find, however the need for secrecy overrode the need for savings. They hunted sparingly for the pot and, when they met others on their travels, kept their plans to themselves.

By the time they reached the Laikipia Plateau and had made a sweeping arc towards the west, the last administrative post was days behind them, and the Pokot quickly picked up the spoor of a large herd of elephants.

* * *

Korok stepped past the steaming dung pile to examine some pad marks and scrapes in the ground. He touched a finger into a tiny wet patch of dirt, and took a sniff. It had the strong scent he expected. In his mind's eye he could see a large bull elephant, rocking from side to side as it ambled behind the main herd. There was also a set of overlapping, smaller pad prints.

Returning to the dung, he found the tiny green flies were taking their first tentative landings on the moist surface. He dropped to his knees and looked closer. As he sniffed it, he could feel the faint warmth from the large steaming mass on his face. He then patted the surface before plunging his hand into its depths. It confirmed his first assessment.

He shook the slimy muck from his fingers and trotted to the pad prints in the nearby soft earth to re-examine them. The fore-pads were deeply imprinted.

A bull was in musth and following the scent of a young female in oestrus. It was a very large bull. From its pad size he estimated it was the height of two men at its shoulder.

On further examination, he found two curving lines occasionally outlying the big bull's pads. They were not the spoor of any animal he could imagine; certainly not one that would so closely follow the tracks of an elephant.

He placed a hand on his forehead and closed his eyes, the better to see the towering animal lumbering along the track in pursuit of the females. It had beautiful outwardly curving ivory, which swung in an arc as the bull hastened onwards. But this was a big elephant and he made it grow in his mind's eye until it rolled like one of the Britishers' wooden ships on the angry waters of Victoria Nyanza.

Now he could see the bull's swinging gait, and now he could see the ivory tips that skimmed the dust, occasionally making curving lines in the dirt.

Freeman came to stand beside him, and began jabbering at him in the strange twang that Korok found difficult to understand, especially when he talked so fast. He waited, understanding nothing. When he'd finished, Korok told him in a mixture of poor Swahili and the few English words they shared — but mostly by using his signs — what Freeman must know if the hunt was to be successful.

He told him the herd was about twenty in number, led by a large matriarch. She and her herd had passed that place no more than an hour before, heading directly north.

The absence of any signs of browsing in the nearby trees, trees that elephants are known to favour, confirmed the herd was making haste. From the dung pile he found that they had grazed on the sweet grass of the valley through which their safari had trekked shortly after breaking camp that morning. But the elephants had taken little sustenance since. The herd was thirsty and travelling as fast as they could, this being the speed of the slowest members of the herd — the youngest calves. If they hurried, the white hunters could catch the herd within the day.

The herd was pursued by a very large bull. Two younger bulls were travelling with the big bull — what the white hunters would call his *askaris*, or guards. The first was also quite large, but his companion, possibly his brother, was somewhat smaller. Korok tried to convey the essence of all this information to the white hunter, Bill Freeman, but when he looked into the white man's dull grey eyes, he could find no sign of comprehension.

He sighed. It was difficult dealing with one so ignorant of the ways of elephants.

* * *

Dan watched Freeman and the Pokot discussing the spoor. There was much animation on the Pokot's part, which Bill seemed to ignore as he pressed for answers to his repeated questions. The Pokot continued to gesticulate and point, while injecting a rare decipherable English word like *elephant*, and an occasional Kiswahili word that Dan understood, like *upaci* — quick, and *maji* — water. But overall, he understood not a word of it, hoping his colleague coped better than he.

However, Freeman came away from the conversation with a perplexed expression. When he reached Dan he lifted his hat and scratched his head.

'What'd he say?' he asked Freeman as the little man rummaged in the leather pouch where he kept his few personal items.

'Not real sure,' Freeman said. 'But there're elephants up ahead all right.'

They both turned back to Korok, who was dipping the tip of one of his arrowheads into a very small earthen pot. It came out coated in a tar-like substance. He then withdrew his knife from his belt.

'What's that?' Dan asked.

'Some mumbo-jumbo potion he thinks he might need in case my Nitro Express fails.'

'For elephants?'

'Yeah. Watch.'

The Pokot drew his razor-sharp cutting knife across his wrist. It made a line that reddened and when he raised his hand, a thin trickle of blood ran down his forearm.

He touched the blackened tip of his arrowhead to the end of the stream. Immediately the blood turned black, and the darkness spread up the trickle towards the wound. As it was about to enter his bloodstream, he ran his thumb across his arm, breaking the flow. His lip plug wobbled in satisfaction.

'Bloody hell,' Dan said. 'What *is* that stuff?'

'Buggered if I know. He gets it from a tree. Anyhow, he reckons there's elephants up ahead.'

'How far?'

'Not a long way as far as I can make out. I think he said if we hurry we can catch them up before dark.'

It was Dan's turn to be puzzled. 'You've worked with this Pokot bloke for what, ten or more years? And you still don't understand him?'

'I can understand him all right, it's just … the details get a bit muddled.'

'Hopefully not when we're about to bag our tusker,' he said. 'Couldn't you find one that understands English, or at least, Swahili?'

Bill sighed. 'There's plenty of trackers who savvy English,' he said, shaking his head slowly. 'But none like this bloke. I wouldn't have hired him … but he's the best there is.'

* * *

Korok survived the famine that followed the Rinderpest, as did many of his tribe in the relatively isolated lowlands of the Great Rift Valley, but another disaster lay in store — one that would irrevocably change his world.

Korok's father was the tribe's spiritual leader, or *werkoyon*. He was a wise and kindly father, teaching him the Pokots' secret charms, potions and deadly poisons, and the skills needed to guard their livestock against invaders and predators. His father led the tribe through most of the famine, but finally succumbed during the worst of it, as did many older family members.

His father's brother took Korok into his family. He had only one other child — Tobeya — a boy of Korok's age.

Tobeya was not only a close family member; he was Korok's age-mate. This meant that the bond between them transcended even that between brothers. Age-mates progressed through a series of ceremonial initiations, from boyhood to manhood, learning the Pokots' ways together, and strengthening their bond. When they became warriors together, they swore an oath that if one of them should fall in battle, the survivor would exact full vengeance in his name.

The European powers had, years earlier in Berlin, agreed upon a set of rules by which they could divide the continent into so-called *spheres of influence*. Provided these rules were followed, the other imperialist nations made no objections. No one asked the Africans what they thought of the arrangement — the Gatling gun ensured that resistance was kept to a minimum.

Karl Peters, the German explorer, arrived in Korok's tribal land to find it rich in grasses, able to support herds of cattle. Peters wanted to sign treaties with the Pokot giving him and his German financiers virtual control over their traditional lands.

The Pokot knew nothing of Peters's African nickname: *Milkono wa Damu*, meaning the man with blood on his hands. They also knew nothing of the agreements made in Bismarck's Germany. They politely but firmly refused.

Such insolence could not be tolerated, and Peters led his men into the Pokot village. With ruthless efficiency they proceeded to destroy the Pokots' line of warriors. The Pokot fought bravely, but armed only with spears and hunting bows, they were no match for the Mauser repeating rifles.

Peters stood off to the side with his bodyguard, taking pot-shots at the villagers scurrying about in a panic.

Tobeya and Korok fought their way towards him, then made a rush, but Tobeya fell dead in the first steps — killed by Peters's bullet in the heart.

Korok dropped to his age-mate's side and for a brief moment stared into his glazed dead eyes. With a yell of pain and rage, Korok leaped to his feet and charged at the barrel end of Peters's raised rifle. He would have been dead in a further stride, had a bullet from a concealed rifle not hit Peters in the arm.

The rifleman was Robert Turk who, only two weeks earlier, had been Peters's assistant caravan master. The ruthless Peters had left Turk for dead beside the Tana River with nothing more than a handful of tea and a bottle of *duka* whisky.

Turk had tossed and turned in the agony of his malarial fever until it eventually broke. The whisky-tea gave him enough strength to set off up the Tana to kill the German. When he found him, he had barely the strength to aim his Holland and Holland, but mustered enough to wound Peters and save Korok from certain death.

Turk's shot distracted Korok in his charge forwards, and a German rifle butt dropped him senseless to the ground.

When Korok revived, Peters and his band were gone, and Robert Turk was standing over him. The battle was over, but most of Korok's people were dead.

Robert Turk had saved his life, and in so doing earned Korok's undying loyalty until, in 1901, Turk quit his job with the railway. He said he was going to an impossibly distant place called Mombasa, and that he couldn't follow. The Pokot watched him trudge eastwards on the railway tracks, his rifle over one shoulder. He never saw him again.

Korok was once more alone and without a tribe, his only sustenance the abiding hatred of Peters — the man who had killed his beloved cousin and age-mate, Tobeya.

When Freeman offered him the chance to again use his hunting skills, he accepted because his pride prevented him from begging for food as he'd seen many others do in Nairobi.

Korok had seen too much slaughter and was now tired of hunting. He was a pastoralist, and yearned to return to his life with what remained of his tribe. But because he had not honoured his vow and avenged his cousin's death, he could not do so.

CHAPTER 5

Harriet handed Liz a postcard of a lion stretched out in long grass without comment. Liz turned it over to discover it was from Dan. Her heart jumped. He hadn't forgotten this time.

In a carefully cursive hand, he told her he was well as was her grandfather and that the safari business was picking up quite nicely. He politely enquired of her studies and wondered if she had found any new friends. He made no reference to the contents of her letter. In particular, she was disappointed that he made no reference to her ambition to become a veterinarian. It had become a defining issue as she entered the final year of her degree.

He signed off, *Yours truly.*

Liz sighed and turned over to the lion photograph. On closer inspection the lion's head was propped up on two cleft sticks so that it appeared to be alert and alive. In fact it was quite dead, a fact confirmed by the man standing behind the deceased animal.

It was a rather grainy, amateurish composition and Liz had to strain her eyes, but there was no mistake. The hunter, grinning and holding a large rifle in the crook of his arm, was Dan.

It made her so annoyed. Dan had not changed one bit. He was still a thoughtless individual — no more than an overgrown adolescent in many ways — who could at one moment infuriate, and the next, completely charm her.

* * *

Liz didn't feel the cold although it was May and she and Max were sitting in open seats at the football ground. Before them were two groups of players who, as far as Liz could determine, were intent on inflicting violent assault on one another. Occasionally, a ball got in the way.

One team wore black-and-white guernseys and the other, whom Max supported, wore red, and called themselves The Roosters.

Max wore a red scarf and bought Liz a red Rooster's flag from the vendor at the main gate before leading her to stand about ten rows from the fence among many others wearing red. They chatted quietly until the match commenced, at which point Max became a quite different person, roaring encouragement to his team and condemning the umpire's decisions when they went against the Roosters. Liz thought it delightful that her normally polite tutor could become so boyishly boisterous.

Periodically, he attempted to explain the finer points of the game, but they eluded her.

'Why do they call it football?' she asked, as one man grabbed the ball and ran, bouncing it for thirty yards before being knocked to the ground.

'My dear Elizabeth,' he said, 'you're not meant to ask such logical questions at a football match. But since you have, all I can say is that here in Australia we play Australian rules — not to be confused with any other.'

During a break in the hostilities, Max bought them each a meat pie. It was a challenge to avoid spilling the sauce over her woollen coat.

She asked him how he became interested in such an unusual game.

'As a child, I'd played soccer with my cousins, but when I moved to Adelaide I joined my classmates to watch North Adelaide play the Roosters on the weekends. I've followed them ever since.'

'And you lost interest in soccer?'

'Oh, no. Every time I go home, I play soccer again. It's like having two homes; two cultures. When I go back to Tanunda, I have my family's German heritage surrounding me, but when I come back to Adelaide I'm an Australian again. Not that I have any choice. My father was born here, so I'm a second-generation Australian. In many ways I'm more Australian than many people in this football ground.'

'It must be confusing.'

'Not at all. In fact, I think it's invigorating.'

'What about others in your family, do they feel they have two competing sides?'

'It's not a question of competition. Australia is the only home we have. All our connections to Germany are long gone, but we can still enjoy what remains. You should see our family parties. My old uncles still bring in good black German beer for Christmas. And they shame us younger ones to get up and dance the *schuhplattler*.'

Someone blew a whistle and play recommenced in the centre of the field.

'Maybe one day you'll see what I mean,' he said, as a player in black and white grabbed the ball and ran towards their end. Max was smiling when he said it, but Liz felt his invitation was more than a joke.

She felt the colour rise to her cheeks and she could think of nothing to say so she asked if he had any other relatives in Adelaide.

'A few. In fact there's one right there.'

He pointed to the field where a tall, fair-haired man dashed from the goal mouth in front of them, leaped high over a crush of players and plucked the ball from the air.

The crowd roared.

'Who's that?' she asked.

'That's Klaus Mueller. My cousin.'

'But he's playing for the opposition.'

Max nodded. 'Sadly, yes. The Roosters couldn't afford him. He gets two shillings a week to play for the Magpies.'

Liz watched as Klaus Mueller was allowed to take his kick at goal, and scored full points. On the opposite side of the ground, the black-and-white contingent rose as one, waving their flags and cheering.

On their side, there were muted growls.

'You *mongrel*, Mueller!' the man standing immediately in front of them shouted. He was wearing a scarf identical to Max's.

Liz smiled. 'It seems he's not very popular with your Rooster supporters.'

Max shook his head. 'He's just too good.'

'Sauerkraut-mongrel-sausage-eater. Go back to where you belong,' the man added, winning the enthusiastic agreement of others around him.

Liz sensed Max stiffen. He was silent after the game recommenced in the centre of the field, and remained so until the Roosters made a resurgent attack, sending the ball towards the far end of the field. From a skirmish of players someone in red emerged, dodged his black-and-white opponent and sent the football sailing skywards for a Roosters' goal.

The crowd around them rose to their feet, roaring with delight. Max leaped in the air then claimed Liz in a bear-hug. His eyes were misted by excitement and pleasure and perhaps he held her for a moment longer than was spontaneous.

Liz was taken by surprise, but delighted by his genuine and unbridled joy. It was so uncharacteristic, but utterly charming. She cheered and clapped to his obvious delight, and the tension from the scurrilous attack on his cousin with the German-sounding name was forgotten.

* * *

Over the following weeks, Max found opportunities for chance meetings with Liz, but not so many that her friends would take note. Or so he hoped. Adelaide University was a small campus and, as in every village, gossip was a popular pastime.

During one of those encounters he raised the idea of a day on the river. They could rent a boat and have a picnic if the weather was fine. To his great delight, she agreed.

They met at the boat ramp. He was in a tweed jacket and navy twill trousers, while Liz wore a woollen skirt with a motif of gum leaves, a pink jacket, green scarf and white beret. He was relieved to find she was much more comfortable in his presence than she had been on previous outings. When she smiled it was warm and encompassing, just as on the occasions he'd spied her chatting and relaxing with her friends on campus. He dared to hope she enjoyed being with him as much as he did being with her.

The wind swept along the Torrens, buffeting the rowboat, and it wasn't long before they took refuge at a park where the river made a sharp bend behind the zoo.

He carried her hamper to a picnic shed, and Liz unloaded it while he went whistling to the refreshments kiosk to fill the teapot with boiling water.

When he returned, the table was spread with cutlery, paper plates and a bowl of salad. She unfolded a tea towel, and forked pieces of sliced lamb onto his plate.

'You've done wonderfully well with this roast lamb,' he said. 'You must be quite a cook.'

'Thank you. However, I hate to disappoint you, but my grandmother roasts a leg of lamb for us every Sunday. If I couldn't copy her technique after all this time, I'd be a failure as a scientist. In any case, I'd be tossed out of the female fraternity if I couldn't roast lamb. Or should that be sorority?'

'Either way, it would be a miscarriage of justice.' He took another mouthful of lamb. 'My compliments to you *and* your grandmother.'

She added the tea to the pot and he watched her move gracefully around the table to pour him a cup. She was about to return to her seat opposite, when he asked her to sit beside him.

'I ... I have something to say, Elizabeth,' he said, studying her expression.

Her shaped eyebrow rose, and she smiled at him. It gave him the courage to continue.

'I hope you know that I am very fond of you.' He took her hand in his. 'And I think, I hope, there is some fondness on your part.'

He waited a moment, holding his breath.

'Yes, Max. I am fond of you.'

He allowed his breath to escape.

'I dared hope. I can't tell you how happy that makes me feel. I know there's an issue about my age and being your tutor, which can make matters ... awkward. That's why I think I should, that is, we should ... normalise things. No, that's not what I meant. I've made it sound like a science experiment. What I mean to say is, I would like to see you more often, but to do so I feel obliged to meet your grandmother. I think it only proper that I introduce myself and assure her that I have complete respect for you, and ... Elizabeth, are you ... are you all right?'

She had stopped smiling. Had he misread her feelings? 'Elizabeth?'

She struggled to form a smile. 'Max, I don't know what to say.'

'Then say nothing at the moment. I'm sorry, I must have given you a shock. I could have, should have, expressed myself better. I'm such an oaf when it comes to this sort of thing.' He made an effort to raise a smile. 'It's what comes from spending half your life on a farm as a young man, and the remainder in a smelly laboratory.'

'Max, don't be worried about it. Yes, you did take me by surprise. But I ... I ...'

'Please, just forget I said anything. Maybe I'm rushing things too much.'

She placed her other hand on his and his heart thumped. 'Thank you for expressing yourself so ... honestly.'

Her smile returned and he felt a great sense of relief.

'As you say,' she said. 'Perhaps I need a little time to consider what you've said. I'm very flattered, and, well ... a little time would be kindly appreciated.'

'Yes. Yes, of course.' He took a deep breath. 'Now, may I have another serve of that excellent lamb, please?'

* * *

Liz put Max's wish to meet her grandmother aside for the remainder of Sunday afternoon, and was able to enjoy the picnic and his company. But as she rode her bicycle through the park home, it all came flooding back. How could she introduce a *Dinter* to her bigoted grandmother? Especially now that she knew why she had such a great dislike of Germans.

Harriet had occasionally mentioned she once had a thriving business making fashionable clothing for Adelaide's upper classes, but had lost it all through no fault of her own. Liz had learned the details at the dinner table one recent night, when she asked her about it.

At first, her grandmother was reluctant to say, but Liz was able to convince her of her interest.

As she began her story, it was obvious that she not only had pride in her achievements, but that they had given her a great deal of pleasure. She described her modest beginnings and the difficulties she had in establishing a foothold in the very competitive Adelaide clothing industry, made particularly so by the fact that she was effectively a single mother, what with Bill's mad schemes and lengthy absences.

Harriet was accomplished at sewing; however, it was her dressmaking designs that ultimately established her success. She could copy the latest fashions from Europe and did so with consummate ease, and more importantly her ability to add local touches gave her an edge over her rivals.

Liz had never seen her grandmother as happy as while she recounted those early times. She glowed with pleasure recalling the day she moved into the space above Gibson's grocery in Rundle Street and set up the cutting tables and six Singer sewing machines.

During the course of these happy reminiscences, her demeanour slowly changed as she began to relate what she had expected was to be her greatest commercial success.

She had been offered the chance to supply clothing to a chain of ladies' apparel stores. The orders would be quite large, so large that the owner of the chain made the proviso that she dedicate her whole operation to stocking him. Her grandmother closed her books to long-standing customers, who were forced to go elsewhere.

Shortly after she began supplying the chain stores the proprietor rejected a delivery, saying the workmanship was inferior. Harriet Freeman was proud of the quality of her designs and would never allow shoddy dressmaking to leave the shop, but she accepted his criticism and had the dresses redone at her cost.

Another large order was rejected. This time the store owner said he would accept the consignment, but only at a greatly reduced price. Her grandmother's face coloured in anger as she recalled the bitter haggling that followed.

Harriet felt an enormous sense of injustice and spent all of her remaining savings fighting the case through the courts, but to no avail. Her reputation was destroyed, her business was bankrupted, and she lost everything.

'I was stupid,' she said. 'But I worked hard to get to where I was. It's not easy being a woman in a man's world, but I wasn't going to give up without a fight. Not to a man, and certainly not when that man is a foreigner. It still makes my blood boil.'

All the pleasure in recalling her successes were now long gone. Her face was suffused in anger; her manner now caustic as she recalled the man who had destroyed her dream.

'That Klaus Hertzog was an unscrupulous … *bastard*!' she said in conclusion.

The language shocked Liz. Her grandmother had never before sworn within her hearing.

'He destroyed my business, and his German partner took what was left — the stock, the machines. Even the cutting tables.'

As Liz recalled that night, and the bitterness on her grandmother's face, she decided she would keep Max Dinter's German identity a secret when he was introduced.

But how could she ask him to be complicit in that deception?

* * *

Liz lay in bed on Sunday night, staring at the light fairies dancing above her. They had been her companions in that bedroom since spending her first night in her grandmother's house, nine years earlier. At first she kept secret their nightly appearance, finding comfort in the fairies' predictability in a world that was elsewhere changing at a frightening pace.

On the evening before her mother was to sail back to Africa, she told her about the fairies. Her mother glanced at the ceiling and saw nothing there. She said that fairies were for babies and that Elizabeth should just go to sleep. When she turned out the light and closed the door, the dancing fairies returned, defiant.

When Liz became overwhelmed by difficult decisions, such as was the case that Sunday night, the fairies were still a source of comfort to her. She let them carry her far away from her immediate surroundings. At a distance it was easier to evaluate any troubling situation. Invariably, her distant point of perspective was Africa, and the person she chose as her imaginary confidant was, curiously, Dan.

She knew that it was more usual for daughters to turn to their mothers for advice and consolation, but as a child Elizabeth had often had the feeling that her mother disapproved of her. In those days she turned to her father, who was always encouraging. When he died, Dan took his place, not as a father figure, but as her best friend.

Any chance that she could confide in her mother, either in her imagination or in reality, disappeared when she received a letter just three months after she deposited Liz in St Hilary's Boarding School for Girls. The tone of the letter was buoyant. Of course it should have been. It wasn't every day that a woman remarried. She described Athi River and the beautiful pink-legged, pink-necked ostriches that strutted the grassy fields. The house was beautiful, but they were seldom home, travelling the world instead to buy ostriches and sell feathers — in her mother's words, *Tons of beautiful feathers*. She reassured Liz that, should she decide to return to Africa, there would always be a place for her to stay. Somewhere. Between the lines she could read that a stepchild was not in Monsieur de Clemenceau's plans.

She wrote to Dan. He was a terrible correspondent, but had replied months later, saying nothing about the wedding — he obviously didn't know Liz knew — and that he seldom saw her mother. However, he said she had sold the farm in the Limuru hills and was living near Athi River.

It wasn't until her third school-term holidays that Liz made a concerted effort to uncover the mystery of the dancing fairies. Of course, at thirteen, and even when she first arrived at age twelve, she knew that fairies were — as her mother had reminded her — only for little children, but discovering their secret made her sad regardless.

The bedroom window only had curtains on the lower frame, allowing daylight to brighten the otherwise dull room. At night, the streetlight reflected off the goldfish pond, sending dappled patterns onto the ceiling that danced whenever the wind rippled the surface of the pond.

When the fairies existed, even as a mystery of light and shade, they were a comfort. Since learning the truth of them, she only had her own resolve to use when difficult situations arose, as one had now with her friendship with Max.

She had several options. Firstly, she could tell Max to present himself as something he wasn't. She could say that her grandmother was a woman set in her ways, with prejudices against people of certain backgrounds, and there was simply nothing to be done about it. They should therefore try to ignore it as best they could.

Alternatively, she could inform her grandmother about Max in advance of his visit and ask that she respect her choice of friends and that she be polite in his company.

Or she could take the principled stand and confront her grandmother's intolerance — also in advance — pointing out that her generalisations were unreasonable. Liz could compare them to the discrimination Harriet had suffered as a single woman in business and appeal to her sense of fair play.

None of these appealed. It would be disingenuous to ask Max to deny his heritage for her sake, to hide the truth because of her grandmother's warped ideas. It was one thing to ignore an insult at a football match, quite another to have it constantly hanging in the air while you spent time with friends.

The only way she thought she could avoid the unpleasantness was to tell Max he had misread her feelings and she wasn't prepared to take the friendship any further.

After tossing and turning for an hour, she was no closer to making a decision and another concern had emerged that made her feel even more uneasy.

She was flattered by Max's attention and knew he was quite taken with her. The question was, did she reciprocate those feelings? The budding relationship had great promise. She quite enjoyed Max's company. He was witty, charming and good looking. He was sophisticated, rendering all her previous boyfriends puerile in comparison. If the feelings she had for him were as strong as she thought they should be, how could she even consider ending their friendship rather than confront her grandmother?

She eventually fell asleep doubting that she had the courage to take any of the positive courses of action she had considered. Instead, she expected she would agonise over them for days — weeks — and do nothing until the last moment.

Without the dancing fairies she needed someone to confide in and fell asleep sending Dan dream messages listing all her troubles.

CHAPTER 6

They were in the Kerio Valley, between the dry riverbed and an escarpment that rose sharply above them. The valley was carpeted in thick yellowing grass, and on either side the dark, green hills rose to touch a sky as blue as coloured glass.

The Pokot gesticulated. Freeman nodded and asked in Swahili what lay ahead.

'He says the valley narrows to the north,' he said to Dan.

'I got that. What was the bit about the elephants?'

'I think he said he's worried that the big bull elephant will lead them into the hills beyond.'

Dan pulled a map from his jacket pocket. 'He's talking about this area here,' he said, pointing it out to Freeman. 'We're here, on the river. That's the Tugen Hills over there, and that's the Elgeyo Escarpment. He's worried about this area up ahead where the two lines of hills converge. Beyond the narrowing of the valley the gradient of the hills on both sides lessens, and the slopes are shown as dense forest.'

Freeman nodded. 'Well, he should know what he's talkin' about. This's part of his tribe's home territory. If anyone understands which way elephants travel around here, he does.'

Dan checked the sky. He had no doubt the Pokot could track the elephants — in the dark if necessary — but it was midday, and time was now an issue.

'We'd better hurry if we want to overtake them before losing the light.'

They pressed on into the heat of the day at pace, forgoing the usual noon rest period.

Dan carried his new Westley Richards cradled in the crook of his arm. He'd never forgotten the incident with the leopard on the Rifkin safari, and the tiny twig that nearly cost him his life when it jammed his cartridge case. Nowadays, he took far greater care with his rifles, and always carried his own weapon.

The Pokot was scampering ahead of them on spoor that was getting fresher by the hour, causing him to bob and grin each time he turned back to give Dan and Freeman an encouraging signal.

With about an hour of light remaining, they passed through the narrow point between the hills and shortly after that the Pokot indicated they were close enough for him to lead them on a close stalk.

Dan ordered the porters to make camp while he, Freeman and the Pokot went forwards alone.

As they feared and expected, the three bull elephants took the incline into the forest following, Dan imagined, some ancient path indelibly etched into the old bull's memory.

The spoor was obvious now: the small herd had begun to browse as they ambled through the forest. Young saplings were broken and the branches of quite large trees lay splintered on the forest floor.

The wind was fresher above the valley and into their faces. They were ideal conditions, except for the poor light.

The Pokot raised a hand to his ear, and indicated the two white hunters should pay heed.

Dan listened. In the distance he could hear the faint crack of splintering timber. He whispered to Freeman, 'Did you hear that?'

The older man shook his head. 'But I'll take your word for it.'

They crept forwards, keeping close behind the Pokot for a hundred yards, where he stopped. Pointing ahead, he moved to the side to be out of their field of vision.

Dan saw the first elephant through a break in the forest foliage. He was enormous, with tusks of at least a hundred pounds. He pointed it out to Freeman, who took some time to find it among the greenery, but when he did, his eyebrows lifted in surprise and delight.

Dan heard another sound and tried to find the source. For a time he thought he was staring at a part of the rock escarpment that had bulged from the wooded hillside. Then he realised it was an elephant the size of which he could not believe, with ivory that reached to the ground. When the bull stepped over a fallen tree trunk he had to tilt his head to lift his tusks over it.

He touched Freeman's arm and pointed. The older man shook his head in disbelief and awe.

Dan indicated he would take the smaller bull on his side, and Freeman should take the larger one, on the left.

In these situations, requiring synchronised firing, they followed the convention of allowing three seconds after they crouched or took their bead.

Just as Dan counted *three* in his head, his elephant moved behind a tree.

Freeman's Holland and Holland shattered the silence of the forest. The bigger bull stumbled and staggered sideways. Dan fired at the second bull as its head appeared past the tree. He knew immediately it was dead — a perfect side-on brain shot.

Freeman fired off his second cartridge and the enormous elephant fell like one of the towering podocarpus trees that surrounded them.

He broke the barrels, and the spent bullets *pinged* free.

From behind, Dan heard an ear-splitting shriek. They had both forgotten about the third elephant, which now came trumpeting towards them from Freeman's left.

Dan stood from his crouch, taking aim over Freeman's head. He had the only loaded weapon between them, and only one cartridge remaining in it.

He waited as the young *askari* bull came crashing through the undergrowth not more than ten yards from them. Then he waited again, firing when it was almost upon them.

The Westley Richards sent the 500 Nitro Express directly between the eyes at the top of the trunk and into the brain.

The third bull elephant crashed, dead, at Freeman's feet.

* * *

Bill seemed very pleased with himself.

'Should have done this years ago,' he told Dan as they sat around a smoky fire on the shores of Lake Baringo. Above it was suspended their ivory — six tusks, which they'd estimated to be close to seven hundred pounds.

'Here we have it. A small fortune for just a few days' work.'

Dan said he wouldn't rest easy until they received their clearance certificate from the game ranger's office. 'Then I'll believe it was a good idea.'

'Once they're all browned up, we'll shove 'em in the mud at the lake for a while. No one'll be the wiser.'

Dan had to admit the haul had solved all their financial worries for the immediate future. The last time he had checked, the price of first-class ivory was a pound a pound. The cost of the porters and supplies were small in comparison. They would clear six hundred pounds — a fortune.

'It was a good hunt,' Dan said, reflecting upon the day. 'I've never seen such ivory.'

'Nor I. Not together, at least.'

They sipped their tea in silence.

'That was a good shot of yours on the third of them,' Bill said.

Dan said nothing, but knew it had been the best shot of his life.

'Yeah, a good shot, all right, although you waited a little longer than necessary, I reckon.'

Dan smiled, arose from his seat at the fire, and stretched. 'Just taking your advice, Bill,' he said. 'Didn't you once tell me to hold fire until the elephant is about to take the rifle out of my hands?'

Bill took a stick and poked at the flames.

'Good night, Bill,' Dan said, walking towards his tent and denying Bill his chance to make a rude response.

* * *

Bill remained sitting at the fire long after Dan had gone to bed. The flames danced, sending flickering shadows out into the encircling bush. As often happened when Bill was in such a mood, shadowy thoughts gathered at the edge of his mind, threatening to awaken old and distasteful memories. Lately, they also brought new fears.

There was an unpleasant feeling lingering from that day's hunt. As the elephant had come crashing through the bush, towering massively above him, he'd been afraid. Not the healthy fear that the adrenalin-powered body uses to respond to imminent danger, but the mortal fear that causes a man to lose his nerve. He'd blamed Dan for causing him to rekindle those feelings by letting the bull elephant come too close, but in his heart he knew that Dan had made the correct judgement. He'd shot the third elephant at precisely the right moment.

The situation should never have arisen. If he'd not missed his first shot at his bull, he would have had the second barrel ready for the *askari*. And if Dan hadn't dropped his own bull with one shot, he and Dan would both be dead.

Even more worrying, this was not the first time he'd felt he had lost the essential self-assurance that kept every white hunter alive. He knew how important that first shot was, and instead of concentrating all his faculties on it, he thought about the consequences of missing it. Fear had become a greater part of his hunting than was healthy. It was the reason he'd allowed Dan to lead more than his share of safaris of late.

As much as he had resisted the notion for these last few months, and he would fight anyone who dared to suggest it, it was a sure sign that he was getting older. At sixty-eight he probably should be growing tomatoes, or watching cricket at Adelaide Oval, instead of pitting his failing eyesight, unsteady hand, and weak stomach against a six-ton killer.

He tried to imagine how his life in Australia might have progressed had he not chosen to seek his fortune in Africa. He would have been with Harriet all these years, living as many families did, working, saving, struggling to make ends meet. By now he would be retired, perhaps playing lawn bowls and sharing a beer with geriatric friends. The translocation of his soul from Africa to Adelaide brought on an involuntary shudder. No, it would never have worked.

Now he had a decision to make. He either retired from the safari business or contemplated the alternative, because it was said that white hunters without a steady hand were very soon dead.

As they came out of the hills on the easy walk down to Rumuruti, they saw a small caravan heading towards them. They made no attempt to avoid it, even after they noticed the administration's red-and-white pennant fluttering on the leading porter's staff. A ranger was at the head of the column.

As they drew nearer, Bill said, 'Gawd, it's Harold Bleasdale.'

'Who's Harold Bleasdale?' Dan asked.

'I knew Harold when we were hunting for the railway years ago. Haven't seen nor heard of him for ages. Now look at him — all decked out like a proper government toff.'

Freeman called a halt as they came abreast of the ranger's caravan.

'Harold Bleasdale,' he said. 'How in blazes are you? It must be, what, fifteen years?'

'Hello, Bill,' he replied, less than enthusiastically. 'Good to see you.' But his eyes were scanning the line of porters and had settled on the six tusks. 'I see you've had some luck in your hunting.'

Freeman followed his line of sight to the ivory. 'Oh,' he said, as if he'd forgotten he had it. 'Yes, not bad. Found them up beside Baringo.'

Bleasdale sauntered towards the ivory that the porters had laid on the ground as soon as the halt was called. '*Found them*, you say?'

'Yeah, found them in a shallow cave a bit back from the lake.'

'There must be six or seven hundred pound of ivory here, Freeman.'

'Not bad, eh?'

Bleasdale silently examined the browned ivory. After several minutes, he said, 'What were you doing up at Baringo?'

'Eh?'

He looked Freeman in the eye. 'I said, what were you doing up around Baringo?'

'Doing a recce,' Dan said.

Bleasdale turned to him, and Dan felt the interrogating eyes on him for the first time.

'A recce … For what, exactly?'

'Harold,' Bill said. 'This is my associate, Dan Sutherland.'

Bleasdale nodded; he had broken a simple rule of etiquette on the caravan routes by not greeting him at the outset. He knew he'd been rude and accepted Dan's outstretched hand.

Dan ignored the insult and forced a smile to his lips. 'Pleased to meet you, Mr Bleasdale.'

Bleasdale harrumphed a reply. 'A recce?' he repeated, returning his attention to Freeman.

'That's right, Harold, we were doing a bit of a look-see before bringing our next clients up this way,' he said, regaining his composure.

Bleasdale turned back to the ivory and studied it for some time while running his hands over the heavily soiled tusks. He seemed satisfied with what he'd found and wiped his hands on his trouser legs.

'Where were you planning to certify these?'

'Down at Rumuruti.'

'Hmm,' Bleasdale said. 'I'm the only one on duty at the moment. I suppose I can come back with you to give you your papers.'

'I'd be most obliged, Harold.'

'Very well. Follow me.'

He gave an order to his headman who shouted a command and the game ranger's column about-turned and headed down the slope.

Bill and Dan gave him a hundred yard's start before following.

'Did you say he was a friend of yours?' Dan asked.

'Hell, no. Bleasdale and I were never close. He reckons I did him in on something or other. There was a bit of a falling out, but I thought he got over it.'

'Apparently not.'

At the Rumuruti Game Department offices, Bleasdale, all officious and businesslike, supervised the weighing and tagging of the tusks. When he handed the papers to Freeman, Bill asked why he had chosen to work for the government.

'Times change. I got sick of the whole business.'

'It's tough at times.' Freeman nodded.

'No, I got sick of the numbers involved. Do you know, when I first came here, the game on the Laikipia Plateau was thick. I mean it was black with wildebeest from hill to hill. And lions everywhere.'

'I know what you mean. It's hard to fill your quota these days.'

'It wasn't that. I got sick of the slaughter.'

Bleasdale went on and on to an unimpressed Freeman about the need to put strict controls on hunting to conserve the game for the future. He quoted statistics of game animals taken a decade before, compared to those of the previous year. The numbers had fallen dramatically. Lions had been wiped out in many parts of the country, he said, and elephant and rhino were in great demand for their ivory and horn.

'Do you know, Freeman, that if we're not careful there'll be no elephants left in all of British East Africa?'

Bill tut-tutted. 'Really?' he said.

'It doesn't seem to matter how the government tries to dampen down the demand, hunters and their rich clientele are prepared to pay whatever is necessary to bag their trophies. And poachers,' he added, almost curling his lip in disgust. 'The worst of the worst. Up here in the Laikipia we throw the book at them.'

Freeman picked up his papers and bade him goodbye. When he and Dan were safely outside, he said, 'What an old fraud. No elephants left. Too much slaughter. Too much chance of finding yourself on the wrong end of a buffalo's horns is more like it for Harold Bleasdale.'

He described to Dan how Bleasdale had been one of the best in the business, but at one time got into a tight spot when hunting meat for the rail gangs.

'The railway was all but finished, and we only had a few months to go on our contracts. Out near Fort Ternan, Bleasdale was hunting meat and shot a big buffalo. They said he must have got it in a lung. Plenty of bright red blood around the shoot, but he didn't drop. Bleasdale tracked him for a couple of miles, and finally came to a big patch of scrub with a sightline of no more than a few yards. Now I have to admit, going into that country after a wounded buffalo is enough to make a man take a few deep breaths, but Bleasdale was very pukka in those days, and rushed in after it.

'So Dan, you've taken on a few buffalos since you've been with me ... What would you be doing in a situation like that?'

'I'd be careful of an ambush for a start.'

'Exactly. And that's what Bleasdale walked into. His buffalo doubled back, and as Harold came charging along on the blood spoor, he walked straight into it.

'The buffalo was on him, scything its horns as they do even though Bleasdale hit it from five yards. It caught Bleasdale on the thigh and flicked him fifteen yards into the bush, before it dropped dead.

'All of that was made pretty clear to us in talks with his bearer while Bleasdale was getting patched up in the infirmary, but the part of the story that came to light only a few months later, after Bleasdale had recovered and quit, was about the extent of his injuries.

'He had deep wounds to his thigh and we all assumed he'd had an artery nicked. It explained how he lost so much blood and was, by all accounts, a very lucky man to be alive. But one of the hunters got drunk with the railway doctor when the show closed down, and he told him Bleasdale's injuries were a lot worse than we all thought.

'The buffalo had caught him on the leg all right, but it also caught his scrotum on the way past.' Freeman shrugged. 'Poor old Harold lost the lot.'

They walked on in silence for several minutes before Freeman added, 'Probably explains why the bastard's so cranky.'

At the end of Max's science class, Liz waited as he dealt with one of her fellow student's questions. She watched him, admiring his commitment to his profession. He was a member of the university staff everyone seemed to admire and respect.

When the student left she approached his desk.

'Hello, Miss Freeman,' he said. 'Won't you please take a seat?'

It was not something they had discussed, but whenever they met on campus, they were careful to observe the usual student–tutor proprieties.

'Thank you, Mr Dinter,' she said, taking the chair across the desk from him.

'Is there something I can do for you?' he asked.

She paused for a moment. 'I'm not sure I'm enrolled in the correct course,' she said. 'I mean, I enrolled in science, which is what I wanted, but now I'm not sure it will give me what I need for what I want to do.'

'And what do you want to do?'

She started by saying that her science course had little in it that appeared to equip her for the kind of tasks she expected to deal with.

'I need to know about animals,' she said. 'All animals, but especially wild animals, that is, injured wild animals, and how to treat them. Oh, I expect that treatment of domestic animals will provide my livelihood, but it's wild animals that are my main interest.'

'We don't offer veterinary science,' he said. 'Few universities do, and none here in Australia, as far as I know.'

'That's what I was afraid of, and now I worry that I won't be able to do all I hope to in Africa.'

'In Africa? Well ... have you taken the animal physiology subjects?'

'I have, but they're quite general.'

'Yes, it's not intended to be an intensive course.'

He stroked the short hair of his beard for a moment. 'Why don't we go to the library and I'll help you find something that might be a little more targeted to your interests?'

She thanked him and they headed that way, chatting about her studies and campus activities.

As they approached the library, Max asked her if she'd considered his request to meet her family.

'Um ... yes, certainly I have,' she said. 'Grandmother is just so busy, it's hard to find a day when she's free.'

'I understand, perfectly,' he said. 'All in good time, I expect.'

They entered the stone library building and he led her down the main aisle, pausing at the row labelled *500 — Sciences*.

'Here we are,' he said, and ran his fingers along the rows searching for a title. '*Aha!* This is the one you need. An excellent reference.'

He handed it to her.

She read the title aloud: '*The Physiology of Exotic Animals*.'

'By Herman Gottlieb,' he added, smiling. 'Another German. We seem to be popular in many things these days.'

She returned his smile, but with difficulty. The irony was simply too much.

* * *

After delaying so long to raise the matter of inviting a special friend to tea, when the moment arrived and her grandmother blandly agreed, Liz was left feeling stunned and exhausted. It was as if the effort to release the tide of anxiety was greater than holding it back. But when the day of Max's visit arrived — it was for Sunday afternoon tea — Liz had still not told her grandmother about his German background and she was engaged in a mighty battle between her conscience and her heart regarding how much of his background she could reveal.

She had deliberately avoided mentioning his surname, referring to him only as *Max — my science tutor*. She knew that by inviting

Max to afternoon tea it signified there was more than a simple friendship existing between them. There were many questions, all of which Liz could answer without revealing details of his heredity. When her grandmother asked about Max's age, Liz expected she might comment on the disparity, but she accepted the situation with equanimity. All seemed to be going well, but she remained in turmoil.

The morning flew by, and when her grandmother announced lunch, the butterflies in Liz's stomach had taken the place of her appetite. She tried to keep to her usual Sunday routine of study and her laundry tasks, but she couldn't concentrate on her books, and in her nervousness dressed for Max's visit far too early and then didn't want to risk spoiling her dress with laundry work.

And then Max was there. On the doorstep. A bunch of daffodils in his hands.

She stared at him, her smile frozen on her face.

He was calm. He said something about being a little early and hoped it wasn't too inconvenient. 'You can never trust Adelaide buses on Sundays,' he said. 'So I made an allowance, and what do you know? I ended up catching the earlier one. Are you sure I'm not too early?'

'N-no,' she said with a swallow to clear the lump in her throat. 'Please, come in.'

She led him down the hall, stumbling through a response to his *Unusually pleasant June weather* comment, to the back veranda where her grandmother was attending to the potted shrubs.

Liz made the introductions, which she thought she managed quite nicely without mentioning Max's surname.

'Mrs Freeman,' Max said, giving her a polite little bow. 'Delighted to meet you at last.'

Liz's grandmother smiled, obviously pleased by his courtesy. 'Likewise, Mr ...?'

'Max!' Liz interjected. 'He likes to be called Max. Don't you Max?'

'I don't mind at all,' he said. 'People seem to be so much more informal these days, don't you agree?'

'I do,' her grandmother said.

'Elizabeth tells me you've been terribly busy recently.'

Her grandmother's brow creased in thought. 'Have I?' she asked, looking quizzically at Liz.

'To Grandmother I expect one busy day is much like the next. Just ... busy. Or not.' Liz smiled and subtly changed the topic to something less threatening. Max and her grandmother joined the conversation, and Liz was again able to relax.

The time passed pleasantly enough, but when her grandmother reminded her about the afternoon tea they had prepared, and inferred it was Liz who should serve it, she became panicked again.

In the kitchen, Liz put the kettle on the stove and hastily threw scones, cream and jam onto a tray, then had to wait for the kettle to boil. She fretted that Max and her grandmother were outside on the veranda, exploring all manner of topics, now quite beyond her control. She peeped through the kitchen window. They appeared to be in polite conversation but the minutes ticked by and the kettle took an age to boil. She was in quite a state when, ten minutes later, she emerged through the flyscreen door balancing everything on the tea tray while trying to appear unruffled.

'My, my, you were quick,' her grandmother said.

Liz smiled and nodded.

The next hour passed smoothly, and when the chill of the afternoon prompted her grandmother to comment about moving inside, Max took the hint and made his farewells.

'Thank you for a wonderful afternoon,' Max said, and her grandmother nodded and smiled, saying it was a pleasure.

At the front gate he turned to Liz.

'I'm glad we finally managed to arrange this afternoon,' he said, taking her hand in his.

'So am I. It was nice.'

'Mind you, every afternoon — or morning or evening, I expect — is wonderful when you're part of it, Elizabeth.'

Liz felt the blood rise to her cheeks. 'Thank you, Max. That's very sweet.'

'And that's the second time you've called me *sweet*. Do you know that?'

'Is it? Well, it must be true.'

'I'm glad you think so,' he said. 'And if I may say so, I hope those feelings you have continue to grow. Then you may understand what I feel for you.' He raised her hand to his lips and kissed it.

Liz's heart soared with delight.

* * *

The Sunday omnibus service from Gepps Cross always ran late as it reached the north of Adelaide, and, although the city's notorious winter winds swirled around the bus stop shelter, flapping Max's thin suit coat, he didn't care. He felt elated by Elizabeth's words, and the smile of appreciation on her sweet lips warmed his heart. Now he knew that she cared for him — at least as much as a fraction of the love that he felt for her.

He was immensely relieved that the afternoon had gone well despite his bumbling, hesitant, almost inarticulate, ramblings.

He climbed into the bus and handed his two coppers to the conductor. He tried to forget the shaky start to the afternoon because the remainder of it had gone surprisingly well. Although Elizabeth remained discombobulated throughout the afternoon, he reminded himself that the principal objective was to meet and, hopefully, favourably impress her grandmother. He felt pleased and somewhat relieved that after a faltering start, he seemed to have achieved just that.

It wasn't until Elizabeth retired to the kitchen that the conversation with Mrs Freeman flowed freely. He was pleased to observe she was genuinely interested in his work at the university. Pleased too that she had an interest in his family and their wine-making business. She told him that many years earlier she had also had a business, and had sold it to, coincidentally, a German man. He couldn't say that he knew the Hertzogs, but mentioned that since there were many families of German descent in South Australia, it wasn't surprising. She was also interested to hear his explanation of why there were so many Germans in that part of Australia. He started to tell her about George Fife Angas, an Englishman and director of the South Australian Company, who arranged the finance to pay the fares of German peasants to Australia, but was interrupted as Elizabeth returned with the afternoon tea.

Yes, he thought the afternoon had gone swimmingly well. He had met Elizabeth's grandmother, and felt he'd made a good impression.

As the bus swung into King William Road, he allowed himself a smile of self-satisfaction. He had found a glimmer of affection in Elizabeth's eyes and had charmed the old lady who, as her guardian, had the power to say whether he could continue to court his beloved Elizabeth.

* * *

After waving Max goodbye at the garden gate, Liz entered the house and closed the door behind her. She leaned against the heavy timber door and sighed with relief, and a certain degree of happiness. The afternoon had concluded without any ructions about Max's family background. Indeed the matter of his heritage had not arisen as a point of disapproval. Nor should it, among civilised adults. And she felt a warm glow of satisfaction following Max's expression of his feelings for her.

She almost skipped down the hall, through the kitchen to the veranda, where she would gather then wash the crockery. To her surprise, her grandmother was where she'd left her in spite of the chill in the afternoon air.

'Grandmother, aren't you cold?' she asked.

There was a silence, giving Liz cause to think her grandmother hadn't heard her, but she replied before Liz repeated herself.

'No. Not cold.'

There was something in her tone that sent a flutter of concern through Liz's chest. She glanced at her grandmother but she had a benign expression, perhaps even a small smile. Reassured, Liz gathered up the plates, cups and cutlery, and was about to take them inside when her grandmother said, 'He's an interesting character, your Mr Dinter.'

'Yes, I'm glad you —' Liz almost dropped the tea tray when she realised her grandmother knew Max's family name. She chose her next words very carefully. 'I suppose he told you about his family's vineyards in the Barossa Valley? And how they've been in Australia for years and years?'

'He did,' she said, her lips tightening in the expression that Liz had learned from her experience as a child that her grandmother wore when intensely irritated. She braced herself for a lecture and swore she'd be strong in her beliefs.

'He also told me how his father is a member of the German Club.'

'Oh, I didn't know that. I'm pleased that you had the time to have such a nice long —'

'So obviously the Fatherland is still very much a part of their lives. Just like all Germans. Stuck in their selfish ways. Ruling everyone around them. Running the show.'

Liz could think of nothing to say. It appeared her grandmother was about to launch into one of her tirades and Liz knew she would have to defend Max or else be unworthy of the affection he held for her. But her grandmother's next words stilled her voice before she could begin.

'You will not see that man again,' her grandmother said through tight lips. 'Not while you remain under my roof.'

CHAPTER 8

The fledgling British settlement in East Africa held many ties with the dominion in the far south of the continent. Early British East Africa administrators sent agents to South Africa to raise awareness of the opportunities available to white settlers prepared to take up land for farming purposes in the new settlement. Although the northern flow of immigrants was steady rather than torrential, there was a strong community of interest between the two British outposts. Events that were of interest to South Africa were of interest to BEA.

Dan had a newspaper open on the table he shared with Bill Freeman at Tommy Wood's hotel, which had become their preferred drinking place after Freeman determined the Norfolk was too *toffee-nosed* for his liking.

'It's full of British aristocrats these days,' he'd said by way of explanation. 'And when that Lord Delamere cove rode his horse through the dining room ... that was too much.'

'It was just for a lark,' Dan had said.

'I don't care. There's no need for that sort of behaviour where people are trying to have a quiet drink.'

The entitlement to a *quiet drink* was a principal part of Bill's personal concept of human rights.

Dan quite liked the more stylish surrounds of the Norfolk, but didn't care enough to protest. Wood's did have the advantage of being close to the station and therefore was first to get the latest delivery of newspapers from England.

'They're a fiery bunch over there in the Balkans,' Dan said, his head over the open page of *The Times*.

Freeman looked up from his copy of *The Field* magazine — in his view a far more thought-provoking publication than any of the newspapers. 'Another war, is it?'

'Yeah. This time between themselves. And it could get worse. They're saying here in *The Times* that it could spread.'

'So, who cares? It's too far away to worry about.'

'Some think it could involve Germany and England, and if it does it won't be far away any more. Don't forget that German East Africa is not far south of here.'

'German East! A bunch of drongos. There's no need to worry about that lot.'

'Germany and Britain aren't all that friendly these days. Don't forget what they did in the Boer War, arming the Boers and supporting their cause.'

'Don't be ridiculous. Any trouble over there in Europe won't worry us here,' Freeman said with a great deal of confidence.

'Why not?' Dan asked.

'Why? Because nobody cares about England or Germany out here.'

'There are some here who'd disagree with you on that. There's a lot of talk against the Germans. It's even in the local newspapers.'

'What nonsense.' Freeman said, returning to *The Field*.

'Maybe, but Hoschke was driven out of town.'

'Hoschke's Saddlery went out of business because Hoschke charged too much. It had nothing to do with him being German.'

Dan felt some degree of sympathy for Freeman's argument. It seemed preposterous that the shambolic town of Nairobi and its inhabitants could become sufficiently aroused to invade what was, from all accounts, the equally shambolic country to its south. But he'd seen the rise in nationalistic sentiment in outback Australia and had himself felt the rush of blood to defend mother England's interests in faraway Africa. The experience had greatly disillusioned him. He could never again be persuaded to fight a war declared in a distant country to fight for issues unconnected to his homeland.

Freeman had returned to reading *The Field* and Dan was about to resume his newspaper reading when he noticed a member of the constabulary talking to Tommy Wood, who nodded in the direction of their table.

From the corner of his eye he watched the officer pull the hem of his blue serge tunic down, stretch his neck to release the pressure of his collar and walk towards them.

'Mr Freeman?' he said, addressing Dan.

'I'm Freeman,' Bill said, looking up at the man standing beside the table. 'What is it?'

'I've been directed to ask you to accompany me to the district commissioner's office, sir.'

'Oh? Why so?'

'I'm not at liberty to say other than it's a matter to do with your hunting licence.'

Freeman shot a glance at Dan.

In the face of Freeman's stunned silence, the policeman asked them to accompany him.

Dan and Freeman remained silent as they followed the constable down Victoria Road to the DC's office.

When they were fifty yards from the office, Freeman spoke.

'What do you reckon?' he asked Dan in a low voice.

'Maybe our licence is overdue for renewal,' Dan said. 'Have you paid it this year?'

'Of course I have.'

'Are you sure?'

Silence, then, 'Well ... pretty sure.'

When he heard Freeman's equivocation, Dan felt reassured the matter was trivial. At worst, it would simply mean a small fine, but when they mounted the steps at the administration's offices, through the window they could see the DC had a visitor.

Freeman groaned. 'What the hell is Harold *bloody* Bleasdale doing here?'

* * *

Bleasdale appeared very indignant. Dan thought he looked like a man who had just found his wife in bed with his best friend. He sat tense and upright in the seat opposite the district commissioner, his thin lips pursed into two thin white lines.

After he invited Dan and Freeman to sit, the new DC, Frank Trail, spoke. 'Now, Mr Bleasdale, would you kindly recount the story you told me earlier this morning.'

'Certainly, Mr District Commissioner,' he said, noisily clearing his throat. 'On the morning of May fifth, I was on patrol of the northern section of Baringo, up near the old caravan road, that is, at the —'

'Can we just get to the important part, Harold?'

'Oh, yes, of course,' Bleasdale said, flustered. 'I came upon Mr Freeman here, and he asked me to weigh and tag his tusks. Which I did at Rumuruti. He claimed it was old ivory he found buried along the caravan road. Well, I had my suspicions, of course. I mean how lucky would you be to find buried ivory? I've heard of the Maasai finding some, but that was before they were all relocated to the southern reserve, and —'

'Harold ...'

'Sorry. As I was saying, I weighed the ivory, tagged it, and locked it in the cells until I got back from my patrol. It wasn't until George Gregory came back from leave that I was able to have the ivory brought back to headquarters, and although I wasn't obliged under standard procedures and —'

'You had it reweighed,' the DC interjected.

'Correct. I had it reweighed.'

'And what did you find?'

'I found that the ivory was five hundred and sixty-four pounds. That is, fourteen pounds lighter than it had been eight weeks previous. Only five hundred and sixty-four pounds. And I said to myself, well, well, well ...'

He paused to give Freeman a piercing glance.

'Go on,' the DC said, unsuccessfully trying to hide his irritation.

'Exactly fourteen pounds lighter. Now, Freeman said it was old ivory that he'd found buried. So the ivory should have been the same weight, but as I said at the start, I had my suspicions. And this proved it.'

'It proves nothing,' Freeman said, crossing his arms and glaring back at Bleasdale.

But Dan knew they were in trouble. They hadn't counted on the ivory being weighed twice.

'Green ivory always loses a few pounds as it dries. Old ivory doesn't.' He turned to Freeman with a triumphant expression. 'The ivory was poached, which ties in with the three dead bull elephants I found in the Kerio Valley forest. Three good-size bulls they were, easily able to give up that amount of ivory between them. And,' he said, drawing himself up to full height, 'I found casings that match Freeman's 450 and his mate's 500. I therefore recommend that William Freeman and his assistant be charged with hunting without an appropriate licence, concealing evidence and making a false declaration on the ivory certification.'

* * *

The Game Department charged Freeman, as the owner of the safari company, with ivory poaching. Dan was charged with being an accomplice.

The magistrate's hearing was not for another month, but it was a month within which Freeman could speak of nothing but Harold *bloody* Bleasdale.

'How could he know where to find those bulls?' he asked, not for the first time.

Dan had learned to treat such questions as rhetorical. There was no way of knowing.

'How could Harold *bloody* Bleasdale know we'd hoodwinked him?'

'He's an old hunter. Maybe he's wise to the tricks.'

'Nah! He was never that clever. Someone's snitched on us.'

'Who would do that?'

'Any one of those white hunters out there who are as desperate as us, and need clients.'

'Do you think John Hunter would do that? Or Bill Judd?'

'... No.'

'How about Alan Black?'

'Nah, 'course not.'

'Perhaps it was Flash Jack.'

'Orright, orright. Now you're being bloody ridiculous. But I want to know who done us in.'

'What do we do when we lose our licence, is more the question,' Dan said.

'I've given that some thought too,' Freeman said. 'I'll say you weren't with me. You stayed back in camp. It was just me and the tracker that went out after the ivory.'

Dan thought the chief game warder was unlikely to believe that Bill Freeman could bring down three bull elephants alone, but he didn't dare utter it.

'How will that help?'

'It should mean you'll keep your licence. At least the business won't fold.'

It didn't faze Dan to be the sole operator of the safari business. He'd been practically running it on his own for some time, and he suspected it would secretly be a relief for Bill to take a long rest from the game. But he worried that the penalty might involve gaol time, and he wasn't sure if the older man's health could endure it. He thought it better to also keep that concern to himself.

'Let's wait until the day comes and see what we can do,' he said.

* * *

If the chief game warder doubted that Bill Freeman brought down the three bull elephants alone, he didn't say so during the Game Management Tribunal, and Dan and his hunting licence were safe. But the head warder, though he spared him prison, stripped Bill of his licence.

Before Freeman had time to rise to protest his innocence, the tribunal went further. They declared that since Freeman Safaris' principal had lost his licence, the company must be wound up unless they could show good cause, within two weeks, why they should continue to operate. Bill was stunned.

'They can't do that,' he demanded of Dan after the hearing. 'Can they?'

'They can. They did.'

203

'Well,' Bill spluttered. 'They won't get away with it.' In the face of Dan's silence, he added, 'But why?'

Dan sighed. 'The Game Department have been looking at ways to control over-hunting. They think they can do that by removing the licences of small operators. Like us.'

'Well, they won't bloody-well close *me* down,' Bill ranted loudly. 'I'll appeal it in court.'

His intention sent alarm bells ringing in Dan's head. The appearance at the Game Management Tribunal was as close to the authorities that Dan was prepared to go. If, as was likely, he was called to give evidence in court, his real identity might come to light, and his crime of desertion exposed.

'Bill … Let's think about this.'

'What is there to think about? I've gotta fight it.'

'It'll cost us a lot. And we're broke.'

'We've got the Vandervold safari coming up.'

The Vandervold safari was a major contract, and promised a fee that would turn their fortunes around.

'You won't have a licence.'

'*Damn!*'

'What if I bought you out?'

'Bought Freeman Safaris?'

'Yes. For a year. Until you get your licence back.'

Bill thought for a moment. 'Yeah … You still have your licence.'

'It's worth a try.'

'It is … I'll do it.'

* * *

Although Dan had been the *de jure* owner of Freeman Safaris for only a short time, he'd been the *de facto* operator for a couple of years. He felt no qualms about leading the Vandervold expedition, though Bill Freeman still insisted upon being involved.

Dan didn't care if Freeman wanted to continue to be involved in the safari operation, but he was sixty-nine, and for the first time since he'd known him, Dan thought he looked his age.

'Bill, why don't you let me hire the *wapagazi* for the Vandervold safari?'

'Because with all the big safaris under way, our usual Kamba porters are booked up. And this Vandervold chap says he wants the best of everything. So you know what that means. A real tin bath, caviar, French wine. If I can't find some Nyamwezi in the next couple of days, we'll have to use Kikuyu. And I know the local chiefs better than you do.'

'Then let me do the provisioning.'

'We're going to the Mara River in Maasailand. We don't know enough about the country down there yet,' he insisted. 'Why don't you take the Pokot for a quick recce? We'll be in a better position to do the provisions when we know what to expect.'

'Why does Vandervold want to go to Maasailand? There's only a couple of hunters I know who've been out there. From what I've heard, it's pretty wild.'

'Maybe, but it's what Mr Vandervold wants, so ...'

'So, I'd better take Korok for a look-see.'

'Exactly. I'll go upcountry for the porters, but make sure you're back by the end of the month. We have a lot to do before we get started. And I don't need to tell you: this has got to be a success. We need that damn money.'

CHAPTER 9

It was a cold July afternoon. Liz wrapped her tartan scarf over her coat collar and rode the four blocks to the tea house on Pulteney Street where she leaned her bicycle against the veranda post outside the shop. As she entered, she spotted Max at their usual table. He smiled and gave the little wave he often did.

When she slid into the booth opposite him he reached across the table and pressed his hand on hers. 'It's wonderful to see you again,' he said.

She laughed. 'Wasn't it you I saw at the front of the lecture room this morning?'

'Ah, yes, but at that time we were surrounded by others. It's these times we share together that I need.' He squeezed her cold hand again, and it warmed her.

'How's your grandmother?' he asked.

The cheery atmosphere was abruptly sucked from the room, and Liz struggled to maintain her smile. She was still grappling with her grandmother's ultimatum, unable to obey her demand and afraid to reveal it to Max. 'She's quite well,' she said.

'I'm pleased to hear that,' he said. 'Earl Grey?'

'Um, yes, please.'

He went to the counter to place their order, giving Liz time to organise her thoughts. The dilemma posed by her grandmother's stern directive was a constant concern. She felt that Harriet's prejudice was no reason to end her relationship with Max. It was unreasonable, but so long as she lived under her roof she felt obliged to obey her edicts.

She liked Max and knew she should deal with the situation, but couldn't. It would raise the question of precisely how much did she love Max, and she wasn't sure if she was ready to directly address that matter.

The whole affair distressed her, as she felt she was now deceiving both of them.

It was too much for her to think about. Her examinations were coming up over the next few weeks, and she had too much work ahead of her to prepare for them. She decided to put the matter of her grandmother's ultimatum aside for another day and resolved to simply enjoy her time with Max.

He returned carrying two steaming cups. 'Your Earl Grey, my dear,' he said, placing the tray before her and taking his seat again. 'Yes, a remarkable woman, your grandmother,' he said, returning to his thoughts. 'I enjoyed our little chat.'

Liz's heart sank. 'Max ...'

'I especially appreciate her interest in your education. It's not common to find a person of her age with such progressive views. It's quite a revelation.'

'Yes ... she's ...'

He was lost in thought for a moment, not noticing her stumbling prevarication.

'A matter came up during our conversation that we didn't pursue, but I wish we had. I think it was after I mentioned our family's connection to the land, which seemed to spark an interest in our family background ...'

He paused, and tapped his finger on his lips in thought.

She held her breath, feeling certain he was about to reveal he had seen through her grandmother's polite deceit, which would expose Liz's complicity.

'I can't quite recall the point she made,' he continued, 'but it made me think about a matter that quite intrigues me. Do you know, Elizabeth, there's such a deal of anti-German sentiment here in South Australia that it worries me at times. Worries me and surprises me too. I consider myself an Australian, but at home we still hold to many of the old family traditions. That's not to say we're anything other than totally loyal to the British Empire.

'I have to admit that some of my uncles are more supportive of the Kaiser's activities in the Balkans than most of us, but if it came down to it, I'm sure they'd support Britain's side. Unfortunately, many people here and in the Barossa think we're all on the side of Germany. Some folk are actually quite abusive towards us. Perhaps you heard something of that at the football.'

He turned to her, and she made a non-committal shrug.

'Well, it was quite uncalled for. It makes me wonder what will happen if, as some people say, a war is coming.'

Liz had heard similar predictions and her grandmother, reading about the situation in the *Adelaide Advertiser*, would often make pronouncements like: 'I wish the British bulldog would show his teeth to the Kaiser's lot.'

'Oh, but listen to me,' he said, reaching a hand across the table to squeeze her fingers. 'Here am I, spoiling our short time together by talking politics. Come, would you like a scone with your tea?'

Liz looked at her cup. It was untouched and now probably quite cold. 'Thank you, Max, but no thanks. In fact, I'd better be getting back to the library. I have a big assignment to submit in a week or so.'

'Certainly,' he said, rising quickly to his feet as she grabbed her coat and scarf from the spare chair. 'When can we ...?'

But she was at the door and onto her bicycle to avoid his question.

* * *

Her time with Max had unsettled her and, instead of studying her anatomy references, she merely sat in the empty library staring at, but not seeing, the pages. She liked Max very much, and he'd made no secret of his feelings for her, so why was it so difficult to tell him of her grandmother's stipulation, and ask his help in resolving the problem?

Finally she admitted her study period had been a waste of time, and gathered up her notes and books.

As she hurried from the library building to her bicycle, the biting wind caught under her unfastened coat. It billowed around her body as she struggled to button it closed. The wind had gathered in strength since she'd left the tea house and now, as she swung into the seat of her bicycle, she realised it was already quite dark and she would be late home: much later than she'd planned.

The pathway through Wellington Square was dark and the chill wind caught her full in the face, biting at her cheeks and causing her eyes to water and her vision to become fuzzy. She could barely see her way, but it was a path she'd travelled so often she scarcely needed to look.

The branch on the pathway was under her front wheel before she realised it. The bump sent her bicycle into a leap and the handlebars skewed when her frozen fingers lost their grip. The wheel hit the pathway and turned at a sharp angle, sending Liz vaulting over the front. She came to a shuddering, scraping, sliding halt on the gravel pathway. Her coat took the brunt of the fall and she moaned, more for the damage done to her only winter coat than from any pain.

She'd barely regathered her senses after the shock of the fall, when she was again jolted. A dark figure stood over her, snarling and grabbing at her. She fought him off, but he was strong and he came at her with greater determination, pulling at her coat and throwing her around in his efforts to drag it from her.

She flung her arms about, sending punches into the darkness, not thinking to scream or even to cry for help, and then her coat was gone and she felt her tartan scarf burn her neck as it was drawn into a throttling tightness.

* * *

It had been more than a fortnight since their rendezvous at the tea house and Max had not seen Elizabeth anywhere on campus. All formal classes had concluded for the half-year break, so it wasn't difficult to imagine she'd simply decided to remain at home to study, but her hasty departure from their last meeting had left him vaguely disturbed.

There had been occasions in their times together when he felt his fondness for her had been reciprocated. But at other times she seemed withdrawn and reluctant to share her thoughts with him.

He wasn't entirely inexperienced with members of the opposite sex, but in his teenage years, most social occasions had been confined to family gatherings. It wasn't until his university days that he'd made a struggling entry into a mixed social life. Even then, his invitations to parties and outings were slow to emerge. It wasn't until his second year that he heard from a classmate, who had become a close friend, that many of his fellow students were a little intolerant of outsiders.

'You mean they don't like people from the country?' he'd asked, wondering how anyone could find the cheerful folk of the Barossa Valley in any way objectionable.

'That's not what I meant,' he'd said, appearing to regret raising the matter. 'It's because of, you know … you being a German.'

Max had been too stunned to respond. He was an Australian and had never considered himself to be an *outsider* by any measure.

After the mid-year break finished, classes resumed, and it was with some relief that he spotted Elizabeth in the hall on her way to her anatomy lecture. Adelaide had been reasonably mild for July, but Elizabeth appeared pale and wore a blue cotton scarf loosely thrown around her neck and shoulders. He caught her eye and smiled. She returned it, fleetingly, and waited for him to join her.

'Elizabeth,' he said, resisting the urge to place his hand on her arm. 'Welcome back to classes.'

'Hello, Mr Dinter,' she said.

'Ah, yes … Miss Freeman. Are you well rested after the half-year break?'

'I am, thank you.'

'Excellent. And rushing to a lecture right now, no doubt?'

'Yes,' she said, adjusting her scarf to sit higher on her neck.

'I wonder if you would pop into my room when you have a moment. A small issue with your, ah, last assignment.'

She said she would, and continued to her class.

Max watched her go, admiring the gentle sway of her hips, but again felt that there appeared to be a barrier between them.

He shrugged off his concern. Most likely it was simply the normal reserve they both adopted while under the scrutiny of staff and students.

It wasn't until days later that he discovered it was much more serious than that.

* * *

'I'm sorry it's taken me so long to come to see you,' Elizabeth said when he opened his office door to her. 'I've been so very busy with arrangements for the new semester.'

'Of course,' he said. 'I understand. Please, Elizabeth, come in and make yourself comfortable.'

He indicated his visitor's chair as he closed the door behind her.

Max took his seat behind his desk.

'How have you been?' he asked. 'I noticed you looked a little pale when last I saw you in the hall.'

'Yes … well, I had a small accident while riding my bicycle. A bit of a fall.'

'Oh, no! Were you hurt?'

This seemed to distress her, and she tugged her scarf higher on her shoulders.

'I'm sorry,' he added. 'I'm not very gallant, am I?'

Never comment unfavourably on a lady's appearance, he said to himself.

She gave him a small smile, but couldn't hold his gaze for long. 'I was unwell for a few days. But … you wanted to see me?'

'Um, yes.' He cleared his throat. He'd hoped for a warmer reunion. She'd been so much more relaxed in his presence before semester's end. Now she seemed to have withdrawn. 'I was hoping … that is, I was thinking, now that I've met your grandmother …'

No. This is nothing to do with Elizabeth's grandmother. The subject of the conversation is Elizabeth.

He cleared his throat again.

Must stop doing that.

'Now that we've become close and, um, I've met your grandmother, I was wondering if it's time to meet my parents.'

'Your … parents?'

'Yes. In Joseph's Creek. We could spend the weekend together — with your grandmother, of course.'

My God! I hope she doesn't think I have sleazy ideas!

'Naturally, we wouldn't go unchaperoned. In fact, I intend to discuss everything with your grandmother.'

'Max —'

'Wait. Please wait. What I'm saying is, I would like to ask your grandmother for permission to ...'

No, no, no. This isn't going at all like I planned it.

He came around from behind his desk and, dropping to one knee, he took her hand in his.

'Elizabeth ... My darling Elizabeth. I am very, very fond of you. And I hope that in some way you share similar feelings about me. And if so, I wonder if you would do me the great honour of being my wife.'

Her surprised expression grew as he made his stumbling proposal until, at the end of it, she simply stared at him. Her scarf fell from her shoulders, revealing a dull purple bruise on her smooth white skin.

'My dear, what happened to you?' he asked, raising his hand to tentatively touch her throat.

'It's nothing.'

'Is that from your fall?'

She covered her face with her hands and began to weep.

'Elizabeth ... Darling. What's happened?'

She took a deep breath, swallowed, and began to explain between her sobs. 'Going home.'

'Yes?'

'After our last meeting at the tea house.'

'Go on.'

'Just before semester's end.'

'Yes?'

'I was riding home in the dark, and I ... I was attacked in the park.'

It was inconceivable. His mind raced through all her possible meanings, but it led to only one conclusion. He was lost for words. He reached for her, but she was on her feet.

'I must go,' she said, trying unsuccessfully to hold back her tears.

He clumsily wrapped his arms around her, unable to speak.

She was sobbing, but accepted his comfort for a moment, then broke the embrace. 'I'm sorry,' she howled. 'I'm an absolute mess. I must go.'

'But …'

She fled from his office, leaving his door ajar.

* * *

Max sat in the confined space of his office until the winter sun fell through the bare branches of the oak tree outside his window and disappeared behind the library building. He couldn't expunge the unbearable thought of his sweet, innocent Elizabeth being ravaged by some brutish thug. Images of her body being invaded by another man drove him mad with disgust and rage.

He craved revenge. As a normally peaceful person, he was amazed at the level of physical violence he felt he could gladly inflict upon Elizabeth's attacker. He would beat him, pulverise him, strangle him. He would cut his body into strips and feed the pieces to the Adelaide Zoo's lion. There was no punishment so horrible, no act too cruel to inflict upon the man who had defiled his most precious.

By the end of the afternoon, he was exhausted by the emotional storm that had swept him from anger to frustration, sadness to compassion, but as he sat in the gathering gloom of the Adelaide winter he realised there was another, unexplored emotion that had lurked just beyond consciousness and that he had struggled to keep buried.

It was a hideous thought, one unworthy of an honourable man. He was ashamed of it and each time it reared its head he forced it back into the dark depths of his mind. It was base. It was barbaric. But it would not leave him and regardless of the utter shame he felt at its existence, he couldn't deny it.

He had placed Elizabeth on a pedestal: she was a shining beauty, a symbol of all that was pure and good. Now her image had changed. She was no longer that paragon of purity. She had been sullied by her attacker and, although he knew it had been no fault of hers, he now considered she was no longer the person he had previously adored. The term *damaged goods* refused to leave his head.

With such a fundamental change in her situation, was she still the same woman he'd fallen in love with? Could he ever look at her and feel the same tenderness that he'd felt before the brute had his evil way with her?

He brooded until the darkness reminded him he should go home. He stood, stiff from the tension in his back and shoulders, and packed his leather case in a streetlamp's light falling through the high casement. At the door he glanced back to where the papers due the next day lay unfinished on his desk. He sighed. Tomorrow would be difficult. His world had changed that afternoon and all his energy seemed to have been expended trying to resolve a new and difficult situation. He walked back to his desk and stared down at the students' assignments for a few moments, strongly tempted to simply ignore them, and go home to a cold dinner and a sleepless night. Then he angrily swept the papers into a pile and shoved them roughly into his case.

He felt wretched, but at least he'd made a decision about what must be done. He had proposed marriage to Elizabeth and he would not add *breach of promise* to his other failings. He would not desert her now. They would marry and there would be no discussion about her loss of innocence.

* * *

The invitation to attend a meeting with the dean of faculty came as a surprise to Max. He'd already completed his discussions about the curriculum for the coming year, and had received his endorsement to implement it. But the meeting was not only unexpected, the formality of the invitation was also a surprise. *Dean of Faculty, Prof Edward C White, would appreciate your attendance in his office at 4pm on 29th July 1914.*

'Bright Eyes' White was Max's head of faculty and his nominal boss although on a day-to-day basis he dealt more usually with the senior lecturer. Professor White and he seldom met formally and only on rare occasions crossed paths at staff meetings, but Max found him to be a reasonable man, and a fine academic.

Max knocked on the door, and entered after hearing the Dean's invitation.

Professor White peered up from the newspaper he had spread over his wide Huon pine desk.

'Ah,' he said, 'Mr Dinter. Come, come. Take a seat if you will.'

Max settled into the padded leather. 'You wanted to see me, Professor?'

'I did,' he said, pausing to glance once more at the open page of the newspaper before folding it. 'Dashed bad show. Another war over there, I suppose.'

'Professor?'

'Austria and Serbia.'

Max shrugged. 'I haven't read the papers today, but European politics are so convoluted. Ever since the Archduke … what's his name? … Franz Ferdinand?'

'Yes, that's him.'

'Ever since he was assassinated it's been brewing, hasn't it? Austria demands this, Serbia takes that. They sound like squabbling children. Where will it end?'

'In another Balkan war I suspect,' the professor said breezily. 'If it's anything like the last two, it'll all be over in about five minutes.'

Max smiled with him.

'Anyway … thank you for coming,' the professor said, frowning as he sat back in his chair, the famed blue eyes clouding in concentration. 'There's this matter of a girl, that is, a young lady … It seems that someone noticed her coming from your office in quite a state. Dammit, I don't know why these things can't be settled in the normal way. Well, that's beside the point, really. The thing is, there's been a report. And procedures, etcetera, etcetera, so I am required to raise the matter with you.'

'I understand, Professor. I don't mind.'

The report could only have been made by a staff member, and he wondered who would have felt obliged to raise it with the dean rather than discuss it directly with him.

'Yes, it's quite correct. I had a meeting in my office with one of my female students last Thursday.'

He thought carefully. He didn't want to lie to the dean, but he had no intention of revealing Elizabeth's identity nor her traumatic experience, to anyone. The poor girl was having enough trouble keeping her emotions under control following the rape without the whole campus knowing the sordid details.

'She came to see me on a routine matter, but she'd had an accident on her bicycle a few days beforehand, and she was still quite shaken by the fall. When I enquired about her well-being, she became quite overcome.'

'An accident, you say?'

'On her way home from the university.'

'But nothing too serious.'

'A heavy knock, a few scrapes, but I don't believe there's any persisting injury.'

The professor looked down to a page he had on his desk and took a moment to scan it, before he nodded. 'Hmmm, I don't see that we need to take this matter any further. I'll see to it. Thank you for coming, Mr Dinter.'

'Thank you, Professor.'

It was only when he left the office that Max started to feel uncomfortable with the whole affair. He had always thought he was on good terms with all his colleagues. He certainly didn't believe any would have thought him capable of taking liberties with a student.

It worried him that someone out there thought so badly of him that they would try to stain his reputation.

CHAPTER 10

After Dan returned from the reconnaissance trip to Lake Magadi, he found Bill recovering from an attack of malaria. His skin had a yellow tinge, and he appeared exhausted from the frenzied work provisioning for the safari while Dan was away.

'Absolute rubbish,' he said to Dan when he suggested he take a day to rest. 'It's not my first attack. Won't be my last. You should see the letters Vandervold's flunky has sent me. I've had five already.' He pulled a slip of notepaper from his shirt pocket. 'Here's one: Bone-handled meat knives — set of twelve, checkerboard and pieces, silver champagne bucket, ice-making machine. An ice-making machine! Where in blazes will I get an ice-making machine? And Vandervold arrives next week. I don't have a moment to scratch myself and you want me to rest.'

'At least sit while I tell you about the track to Lake Magadi.'

'What's to know? Outram and Cunningham've been there,' he said, citing two of the most famous white hunters in the land.

Dan resisted the urge to reply that Outram and Cunningham were young men, extremely experienced, and with a team of trek-hardened porters.

'It's lava country, Bill. The lake's salty, in fact, corrosive to the skin. It took the Pokot days to find a couple of waterholes and wheedle the whereabouts of another couple from the local Maasai. Even then, it's touch and go whether we can get beyond the lake to the better country. Why in blazes do you want to go in that direction? Why not go up through Kijabe like Judd does?'

Bill Judd was one of the few to lead safaris to the Mara region because of the concern about belligerent Maasai warriors.

'What are we? Railhead Johnnies? Freeman Safaris don't use railway lines. Let the cheap operators use the trains. We do it right. If you're not up to it, I'll lead the Vandervold safari myself.'

Freeman's vehemence caused Dan to realise he'd struck a nerve. He shrugged his agreement. Although he hadn't fully explained the dire conditions of the track to Magadi, he knew that when Freeman was in such a mood, if Dan persisted, he would merely become more stubborn. Better to leave the conversation for another time.

Two days later, Bill fainted while inspecting a load of dried goods.

Dan ordered him into the shade and poured him a mug of water. 'Bill, I'm putting my foot down. We either take another route to the Mara or you leave it to me. You're in no condition to take this safari. I've only seen the first part of it. Even the Pokot had trouble reading the land. The going is really rough.'

'And you think this old fool isn't up to it, don't you?'

'Not at all,' Dan lied. 'There's just no need for you to push yourself. Take some time to recover from the malaria. We've hired all the porters, and —'

'Including thirty Kikuyus. You don't know how to handle Kikuyus, and I do.'

'We have a good headman. He can —'

'I've been on all our big safaris, and I'm still fit and strong enough to go wherever you can, young fella. And don't forget it.'

But Dan remained concerned. That first part of the journey through a land of poisonous soda lakes and razor-sharp black lava fields would take a heavy toll on men and beast alike. Beyond that was a climb over the high Loita Hills before reaching the Mara River. It would test any man, but Dan knew that if Bill found he wasn't able to complete the safari, the injury to his self-respect would be far more severe than any physical pain he might endure. He decided to let the old man have his way.

* * *

Cornelius Vandervold arrived in Nairobi by train on a bright July day with a score of chop boxes and suitcases. He wore a black homburg and a cape thrown back over his shoulders, apparently to allow him to throw his arms about, which he did often while directing the small army of railway porters marshalling his luggage. He was a man of about sixty or so years, but there was no sign of age in his tall, straight stance, and his keen eyes missed nothing.

His great-great-great-grandfather, Bernhard Wiggerink, had been a Dutch farmer from the village of Vold, who arrived in the colony of Nieuw-Nederland in 1654. When the English seized New Amsterdam and renamed it New York, the family adopted the name Van der Vold and later, Vandervold.

By the middle of the eighteenth century, the colony had become a major port, and Vandervold family members worked in the ship-building industry as labourers and artisans. A generation later, Cornelius Vandervold began building vessels of his own.

The family rapidly accumulated wealth so that, years later, his son was well placed to enter the railway business. By the time he was born in 1850 — the only child of Cornelius Vandervold II — the young Cornelius was in line to inherit one of the country's largest fortunes, which he did upon the death of his father in 1890.

Cornelius Vandervold III had no inclination to run a railway, or to build ships, and was content for others to manage the business and his considerable investments. He wanted adventure, and he decided to seek it most recently in the newly opened land of British East Africa.

The porters loaded Vandervold's mountain of luggage on a wagon Dan hired from the assemblage outside the station and with Vandervold in one rickshaw and he and Freeman in another, they made their way down Government Road to the Norfolk.

After Dan and Freeman arrived at the hotel, the staff quickly whisked away Vandervold's luggage while the manager arranged for tea to be served at a table in a reception room off the main lobby. Vandervold made small talk for ten minutes before he got to the point.

'Mr Freeman, Mr Sutherland,' he said. 'I am prepared to pay you and pay you well for this expedition, but in return I want to see the best hunting this country has to offer.'

'I'm sure you won't be disappointed with what we've arranged for you, Mr Vandervold,' Freeman said, smiling confidently.

'Excellent. I don't wish to sound pretentious, Mr Freeman, but I am not a man accustomed to second-hand goods. I don't want to find myself walking in another man's shoe prints, if you know what I mean.'

'That's exactly why we've chosen the Mara River for you, Mr Vandervold. There's hardly been a white fella's boot touch the dirt up there. The game hasn't been made skittish by dozens of safaris and hundreds of porters. And we're taking a route that's never been used before, just because I knew you wanted to have a special experience.'

'As I said in my letter to you, it's the reason I chose your company over your competitors.'

This was a revelation to Dan. So much for his speech about *Railhead Johnnies*. Freeman had made a commitment before he knew the safari was feasible.

Freeman shot Dan a glance, but continued, unabashed. 'You'll see more of Africa than any white man ever has.'

'Very good. But tell me, why is it that no one's been on this unique route before?'

'Ah,' Freeman said. 'That's where my colleague, Mr Sutherland, comes in. He's reconnoitred the whole track for us.' At this point he turned to Dan and made an expression, unseen by Vandervold, that implied he must speak positively about the expedition.

'Yes ... I've only recently returned.'

'And ...? How did you find it?'

'It was ... very interesting.'

'Plenty of game?'

'Oh, yes.'

'And the going ... is it difficult?'

'Ah, yes. I must say that it is. But we've done all this before. There's no need to worry. Just leave all the arrangements to Freeman Safaris.'

Outside again, Dan turned on Freeman. 'What the hell have you been telling him?'

'A little self-promotion never does any harm.'

'But that track's a hellhole. Hard enough for me and the Pokot on a light safari. But this American bloke has a mountain of supplies, and wants the world.'

'We can handle him.'

'No, Bill. It was your big mouth that got us into this. I don't want anything to do with him. You handle Vandervold in camp, and I'll handle him when we're out hunting.'

* * *

The safari assembled outside the Norfolk Hotel and, in accordance with Cornelius Vandervold's request, departed at the gentlemanly hour of eleven with a great deal of pomp and bugle-blowing. It was not a big safari by East Africa standards, only one hundred and forty porters, but quite large considering there was only one client. Dan had kept an eye on Freeman in the days leading up to the journey and by the time the safari moved off he noted that, although his skin was still sallow, Freeman was able to keep pace without any visible sign of tiring. He was a little reassured — and given that the line of porters made only twelve or fifteen miles a day, his partner was not required to keep up a rigorous pace.

Bill marched beside Dan at the head of the column. The client, Vandervold, rode in a small trap pulled by an Abyssinian mule, with his entourage of personal servant, chef and secretary following.

'That won't last,' mumbled Freeman about the trap. 'It's either the potholes or the tsetse flies. One way or another, the horse will be dead or the trap busted, and he'll be walking by the time we reach Lake Magadi.'

They made good time out of Nairobi, pitching camp on the Mokoyeti River where Vandervold suggested a bottle of champagne be broken out in celebration.

In the morning, Dan found that twenty-five of the inexperienced Kikuyu *pagazi* had debunked during the night, taking their pay advance and new boots with them.

* * *

Korok stood on the highest of a jumble of gigantic grey cubes — granite monoliths originally thrust from the molten body of the earth, cleft by extremes of heat and cold, then tossed into untidy piles as if by a god annoyed at having his work undone.

He moved from one foot to the other, easing the discomfort of the hard hot surface against his bare soles, as he scanned the surrounding landscape. He could not only remember each landmark he'd noted when he and Dan searched for a suitable route to Lake Magadi, he connected them into a sequence as if they were a line of arrows drawn in the sand: the peculiar pointed hill; the chalky white patch on a rise in the south where last season's rains had cleaved a fresh face; the twisted limbs of a stunted tree at the base of a granite pyramid.

The more challenging task had been to find a course up the Rift Valley escarpment to the hills in the west accessible by the porters carrying heavy loads. There were only a few potential paths, and most contained at least one major obstacle. At the point of despair, they stumbled upon a gorge that wound its gentle way through sheer cliffs to the plains above the valley. It was a small opening among a score of almost identical openings in the face of the escarpment. Finding it again now would test his powers of observation to their limit.

The *most* critical task, however, was to locate water, and Korok spent the hours at dawn and dusk searching for the rock hollows, the depressions in the earth, the small caverns in stony crevices that caught the rain and held it for days, weeks or perhaps months until the next downpour replenished them. He read the geography as expertly as a mariner might read his charts of latitude and longitude, tides and currents after many years at sea. In Korok's case, it was the skill learned by a people who could see an antelope and by its condition know how long it had been since it last drank; who could study an elephant herd and know if it was headed towards or away from a waterhole. The Pokot were people who must read the signs, or die.

Korok used the skills his father had taught him, but most of what he'd discovered of this land he'd learned from observation of his cousins, the Maasai. He was unfamiliar with this part of the Great Rift Valley, but by watching these herders wander their territory in search of scant fodder for their precious cattle, he knew they would camp near water if it existed. From his observations, such places were few.

Soon after setting off for Nairobi after the recce with Dan, he had received clues from an unlikely source. They came upon a group of Kikuyu porters returning to their homeland in the forests beyond Nairobi. Dan didn't seem to understand how strange it was for these traditional enemies of the Maasai to be there, but Korok did. He watched and learned as the white man chatted to the leaders. The answer to why the Kikuyu risked the heat, the thirst and the Maasai was in the blocks of rock salt they had tucked into large woven baskets. It confirmed to him that the Kikuyu's journey was not a whim, but an annual event that had probably begun centuries before the British forced the Maasai to move from their fertile northern land to this desolate place. White farmers' cattle now grazed the grasses the Maasai herds had once enjoyed in the north. Korok didn't understand why the formidable Maasai hadn't fought for what was theirs. It merely confirmed the view that the British were now the most powerful tribe, able to do as they pleased.

He took note of the Kikuyu's route, knowing they must know where water could be found, otherwise the annual excursion would not have been possible.

He put all this information together, and still it was difficult to imagine a course across this barren rocky land, where the grass shrivelled into wispy tufts and drifted on the wind, that would provide enough water to survive it.

* * *

Bill and the replacement *wapagazi* caught up with Dan and the safari before they had travelled a further fifteen miles. He immediately demanded to know why they'd not made better progress. Dan bristled at the inference.

'It hasn't been easy, Bill,' he said through taut lips. 'With the extra loads from missing porters to carry, I had to split the safari into two teams. Twenty-five men had to carry a sixty-pound load twice the distance each day. After a couple of days, they refused to go on, and I can't say I blame them in this heat. And we've had a helluvu time finding water. It became a matter of waiting for you to arrive, or ditch some of the load.'

'You didn't ditch any of Vandervold's stuff, did you?'

Freeman's voice was cracked with stress. It was only then that Dan noticed how drawn and tired he appeared. The dash to recruit new porters had taken much of his remaining strength. Dan regretted his torrent of bad news. 'No, Bill. We've ditched nothing.'

The older man let his breath escape in a sigh. 'Thank God,' he said, removing his broad-brimmed hat and wiping his brow. When he replaced it, he squinted through the glare at the barren, ash-grey hills, tinder-dry and strewn with lava rubble and boulders. The long rains had ended a little more than a month earlier, but the land already appeared to have thrown off any memory of them. The landscape was completely desiccated. 'What's the country like up ahead?'

Dan studied him for a moment. Freeman was struggling to meet the challenges, and Dan wondered how much he should tell him. 'Korok's been out from dawn to dusk, trying to find water. Most of the rock pools have already disappeared. He found a shallow depression yesterday that we spotted on our recce a few weeks ago. It was so fouled by game we had to boil it and strain it through a sock.'

'I don't suppose it'll get any better for a while.'

'It's much the same for the next sixty miles.' He weighed what he was about to say carefully. Freeman was a proud man, and stubborn. Dan knew he could manage the safari quite adequately on his own. In fact it would be easier for him if he didn't have Freeman's failing health to consider. But convincing the older man of that fact required tact; perhaps more tact than Dan possessed. 'So far we've been lucky, but in another day or two we'll be at the point of no return. No water until we reach the Ewaso Ng'iro River. It's about sixty miles away.'

'Five days for a caravan of this size,' Freeman said.

'If we're lucky. This lava rubble is taking its toll. Vandervold's cart fell to pieces shortly after we passed Kiserian village. I'm glad we didn't decide to use wagons. Then in a few days we have the escarpment to climb somewhere down there to the south. I haven't seen a more difficult track for a safari.' He paused, causing Freeman to turn to him.

'And you think I won't be able to make it,' Freeman said, with a narrowing of his eyes.

'Bill, I know —'

'You don't know nothing. I was leading safaris through country worse than this when you were still in short pants.'

'For God's sake, Bill, you're sixty-nine. And quite honestly, I can't afford to keep an eye on you all day in case you get into trouble.'

'I don't need you keeping your bloody eye on me. So long as I'm able to shoulder a rifle, I'll run Freeman Safaris the way I bloodywell like.'

'Aren't you forgetting something? I'm the owner of Freeman Safaris and it's my responsibility to see that everyone on our safari is safe. And you're not. You're weak from a bout of malaria and you should be in bed instead of out here dying of dehydration.'

Dan's words clearly struck Bill like a fist. He went white with anger, then in a voice fissured by fury, he said, 'I told you, I can look after myself. And I certainly don't need a coward — a *deserter* — to tell me how to run *my* business.'

CHAPTER 11

The sun and the reflected heat from the lava scorched his skin, but Dan felt the icy air pass between him and Bill Freeman whenever their paths crossed as the safari made its painful progress towards the caustic water of Lake Magadi.

Each night they'd sit at the campfire — their usual place to plan the activities of the following day — and coldly carve out the arrangements for the following days. The tough going meant more than usual care was needed on the logistics of even simple operations like searching for water and carrying it to the camp, ferrying supplies between the camps, and which of the two leaders would manage each activity.

Cornelius Vandervold was unaware of the friction, and continued to inject his opinions on the running of the safari, increasing Dan's frustration as he struggled to find ways to overcome the water scarcity without compromising the schedule they'd promised Vandervold.

'Well,' Vandervold said, rising from his seat across the fire. 'I'm off to bed, but I have a request. We've been tramping across these damn rock flats for days now. And I'm getting mighty bored with it. Reckon it's about time we stopped for a spell of hunting.'

Dan met Freeman's eyes briefly, but the older hunter turned his attention to the fire and gave it a desultory poke.

When they had shared responsibilities, Dan had asked Freeman to manage the client. It was enough, he said, to take rich and spoiled men hunting without listening to their whining while in camp. Freeman reluctantly agreed and Dan now knew what he was doing: he was making Dan pay the price for taking over the running of the safari.

'I'm afraid that won't be possible, Mr Vandervold.'

'No? Why not? There must be a few antelope around here. Haven't bagged a gazelle yet. We can take a look-see tomorrow.'

'My tracker says the next waterhole is a ten-hour march away,' Dan said as patiently as he could. 'So there's no time for hunting.'

'Be damned there ain't. You do what you have to do, but I intend going shootin' — alone, if I have to.'

Dan again glanced at Bill, who simply sat with his arms folded, staring into the campfire.

'I'm afraid I can't let you do that, Mr Vandervold.'

Vandervold stiffened, but before he could reply, Freeman spoke. 'My partner is a little soft, Mr Vandervold,' he said. 'You came to Freeman Safaris to hunt, and hunting you will get. Tomorrow at dawn, if that's convenient.'

'Mighty fine, sir. I'll be ready and rarin' to go when you are.'

It took Dan all his self-control to remain silent until Vandervold had left the campfire.

'What the hell are you doing, Bill?' he hissed. 'You know we have to watch our schedule. We're real low on water. Now why'd you have to tell him we'd take him hunting? It's a stupid idea. And you know it.'

'You said I had to manage the client's complaining, and I have. If you don't take Vandervold hunting, I will.'

Dan made a decision. Bad enough they would lose time hunting in a place barely able to support a blade of grass, but it would be worse if Freeman tried to do so in his physical condition.

'If we're sticking to our agreement, as you insist, then it's my job to take Vandervold out,' he said through clenched teeth. 'We'll rest the men during the day and do a night march to make up the time.'

* * *

An hour after Dan had departed with Vandervold, Freeman became agitated. He'd wanted to take the client hunting, but his strategy had backfired. He paced the length of the porters' line of tents, finding trivial misdemeanours and barking orders for their rectification. The Swahili headman followed him, shaking his head at the breach of the traditional chain of command.

When he returned to the shade-awning stretched across the front of his tent he sat for a moment, but he was thirsty and still agitated. He decided to do something about the shortage of water.

Mumbling to himself about the incompetence of some people, he struck out across the shimmering lava-strewn landscape alone. He'd not travelled far, stumbling and cursing at the rough passage, when he sighted a lone figure following him at a distance. He wiped the sweat from his eyes and peered again. Nothing.

He was headed for a rocky hill about a half-mile from the camp where he thought he might find a spring, but after walking for what appeared to be more than enough time, he couldn't find it.

'Dammit,' he muttered and veered towards the sun. 'Must have missed it in the haze.'

He reached for his water bottle and realised he'd left it in his tent. Turning back in the direction he'd come, he could see nothing of the camp, but again he thought, or imagined, he'd seen someone watching him from a distance. He resumed his stumbling march.

Freeman's head spun with fatigue and thirst. He was becoming weaker by the step and decided to take a brief rest before returning to camp. Ahead, a stunted gnarled tree threw a patch of shade over a tumble of rocks. Freeman moved carefully towards it, fighting back a wave of nausea induced by the heavy toll the heat and the walk had imposed upon him.

A low ledge of rock offered a convenient seat under the tree. Freeman stepped from the blinding sunlight into the shade and saw the sleeping puff adder the instant before he planted his booted foot on its expertly camouflaged back.

The snake reared and struck at his leg with lightning speed. The adrenalin rush sent Freeman's mind into a slow spin wherein the events immediately following unfolded so slowly he was able to observe them in exquisite detail.

Enraged and unable to escape from under his boot, the puff adder opened its wide triangular jaws for a second strike, revealing the soft pale innards of its mouth and its pair of needle-like, inch-long scimitars. As it sunk its fangs through his trouser leg and deep into his calf muscle, he noted the little pointed nodules on its head and the black slitted pupils of its yellow eyes. The triangular head flattened, and he felt the poison flow deep and cool into his flesh a second time.

He jerked himself backwards, and the adder escaped.

Lying on his back and staring at the sun, he waited for the pain to come, knowing that it would not be pleasant. 'What a bugger,' he mumbled to himself. 'Been worried I'd cop it after missin' a cat or an ele. Or a buff. Now look at me, floored by a fucking snake!'

Freeman had seen a few die from a puff-adder bite. First came the excruciating pain then, like drowning men, they struggled to suck breath into their lungs. He'd seen the terror in men's eyes as they fought for breath and slowly asphyxiated. If they survived that, hours later the flesh surrounding the bite area turned green and blue, and days later it putrefied and fell off in great black chunks. Few survived that long after the bite of a puff adder. Bill was grateful death would spare him from those consequences.

The moments passed and he dared to hope that the puff adder had somehow missed its mark, but within another minute he felt a red-hot poker stab deep into his flesh.

* * *

When the Pokot spotted Freeman fall, then minutes later heard his scream of pain, he guessed he'd been bitten by a snake and hurried towards him.

He'd been watching Freeman for days, ever since he'd returned bringing the new porters. He'd seen men such as his boss suffering from the subtle effects of fever without knowing they were. It was only when they collapsed, as he'd seen Freeman do when out of sight of the others, that they became aware of the seriousness of their condition. But the white man had kept the extent of his illness to himself, and Korok wondered why.

In his years on the railway, he'd seldom seen his white hunter, Turk, become emotional. In many ways he was like the animals he hunted. Silent, detached, self-centred. Perhaps that was why he was so successful at the hunt. He could remain calm in a crisis and was seldom troubled by the actions of others until, under extreme provocation, he would lash out with passion and fury. He'd seen him kill more than one man who had pushed him beyond his bounds. It wasn't until much later that Korok realised that Turk was an extraordinary individual; a product of the life he led and almost a species unlike other whites.

In Freeman and Dan he learned that whites, in common with the Pokot and every other tribe he observed, had their moods. The two white men had been close friends for as long as he had worked with them. They were different from one another, but seemed to be drawn together by those differences. In recent days something had happened to shatter their friendship and it had affected them in different ways.

The younger man had withdrawn, now reluctant to assume the role of leader that he appeared to enjoy to that point. Freeman had become irrational and belligerent, finding fault in everything around him. He quarrelled with Dan and struck out at any porter, cook or gun-bearer who irritated him. How much of this behaviour was a symptom of his physical condition Korok couldn't tell, but he'd kept a watch on him in case the illness became dominant, as it now appeared it had. The old man had stormed off alone into the trackless wasteland. It was a dangerous act for anyone, and often fatal for someone in Freeman's dehydrated condition.

When he reached Freeman he was writhing in agony and clutching his lower leg.

Korok quickly scanned the area and found the straight, thick track of a puff adder in the soft sand. Freeman was pale and his eyes revealed he was aware he was a man facing imminent death.

The Pokot dropped to his side and, pulling out his knife, he slit the trouser leg open and made a two-inch slash across each pair of fang puncture wounds. He put his mouth over the first of the cuts and sucked blood and poison from it, spitting the bloody mess to one side. He repeated the procedure with the other.

Helped by the tracker, Freeman struggled to his feet, but he was suffering from the early effects of the poison and was unable to walk.

Korok dropped beneath Freeman and let his body fall across his shoulder. With a mighty effort he hoisted him upwards and, on legs tottering under the bigger man's weight, made his unsteady way back to camp.

* * *

It was mid-morning when Dan headed back from the hunt, fuming. The landscape was almost completely devoid of cover, and the game they had spotted took to its heels long before they were in range. Vandervold had tired of the exercise within a couple of hours, and Dan signalled the men to head back.

When they were within a mile of camp, he spotted a runner coming towards them. It had to be bad news. He went ahead, leaving the client with the porters.

Farouk, the headman, met him at the edge of the camp.

'Snake bite, *bwana*,' he said, then told him all he had been able to extract from the Pokot.

'What have you done for him?'

Farouk shrugged. 'What can be done?'

When Dan entered the tent he examined Freeman's leg, now blotchy purple and clotted with dried blood.

'Get the Condy's crystals,' he said to Farouk, suspecting it was a pointless exercise but, driven by his panic, needing to do something — anything.

He kneeled beside Freeman's stretcher, and put his hand on his shoulder.

'Bill ... Bill, can you hear me?'

Freeman slowly opened his eyes.

'How are you?' Dan asked.

Freeman tried to wet his lips and Dan lifted the water bottle to allow him to take a sip.

'Reckon I'm buggered.' His voice was hoarse, strained by the effort to speak.

'No you're not. We'll get you back to Nairobi.'

Freeman shook his head. 'Puff adder.'

Dan's heart sank. 'The Pokot drained you. You'll be good-oh in a day or two.'

Bill shook his head and closed his eyes.

'I'll rig up a lighter. We'll leave right away. With a few good *pagazi* we'll be in Nairobi in no time.'

'Dan,' he said, his eyes now wide and his grip on his wrist surprisingly strong. 'Save it. You were right about this safari. Too bloody hard. But forget that. I said some stuff I shouldn't have oughta.'

'Bill, don't worry about —'

'Listen. I knew you did a bunk from the army first time I set eyes on you. Written all over your face. There're blokes who can do that sort of thing and not give a damn. But you ... It ate you up. 'Specially in the early days.'

'It wasn't the fighting. It was all the other —'

'Shh, *yeah*, I know. Listen, I didn't say that to roast you. I just wanted you to know I knew, and it didn't matter a bugger.' He paused to take a gulp of air. 'You didn't have to help me out that night in Mombasa. Took guts. That's when I knew you weren't no coward.'

'Jeez, Bill ...'

Freeman laughed. It was more like a rattle in his chest. 'Looks like you'll have Vander-*bloody*-vold all to yourself after all.' He squeezed Dan's hand. 'Do it. We need ... the company needs the money.'

He struggled for breath and Dan caught a glint of panic in his eyes.

'Wait on,' Dan said. 'I've got some whisky in my kit.'

He dashed to his tent and fished a half-bottle from his pack before rushing back to Freeman. 'How about a nip of Bells?'

Freeman's cold dead eyes stared at the canvas above him.

CHAPTER 12

War had been brewing for a long time, and now Europe's sticky web of alliances, old and new, entangled one nation after another in quick succession. In late July, 1914, Austria declared war on Serbia in retaliation for the assassinations of their Archduke and his wife.

Harriet, ignorant of her granddaughter's desolate mood, couldn't keep her head out of the pages of the *Advertiser* and supplied Liz with running commentary on the escalating crisis.

Russia was allied to Serbia, but Germany didn't expect her to intervene, and made a promise to Austria to give military assistance if needed. Russia mobilised and so Germany declared war on Russia, who called upon France to honour their defence agreements. By early August, Russia, France, Austria, Germany and Serbia were at war. Harriet was apoplectic with indignation.

'Can you believe it?' she demanded of Liz. 'First it's Austria and Serbia, and now, exactly as I said they would, those rotten Germans have declared war on Russia. What a cheek! We won't stand for it.'

Liz had learned that when her grandmother said *we* under such circumstances, she generally meant the British, except when Australia was pitted against them, as in the cricket, in which case they were the *god-awful Poms*.

'If the Germans invade Belgium, that'll be the end of it,' she said. 'We'll be at war and it'll serve them damn-well right.'

The political situation in Europe had one redeeming advantage — it distracted her grandmother from her demand that Liz sever her friendship with Max. Liz always listened politely, but wasn't particularly interested in the affairs of countries on the other side of the world. She had more pressing concerns. She hadn't seen Max for days; not since the awful afternoon in his office. But his proposal was constantly on her mind.

The attack in the park had emphasised her vulnerability. She had no one to turn to in a crisis. It had made her feel lost and alone in a surprisingly hostile world. Max typified stability and security and she believed he cared for her very much. He was clever and handsome and safe. If she was with Max, she could escape her grandmother's overbearing temperament. Why not accept his proposal?

* * *

On a fine Tuesday morning in August, just as Liz was preparing to leave for the bus stop — she had abandoned using her bicycle — her grandmother came rushing in the front door, waving that morning's *Advertiser*.

'They've done it!' she cried. 'They've gone and done it.'

'Who?' Liz asked.

'They've invaded Belgium, and we're at war.'

Liz stared at her. Had she heard correctly? Did she say that Australia was at war with Germany?

'You mean England is at war.'

'I mean the British Empire is at war. Britain, Australia, Canada, New Zealand. As of yesterday, we're *all* at war with Germany.'

The distant conflict was distant no more, and Max's fears about anti-German sentiment in South Australia came ominously back to mind.

* * *

Max had not seen Elizabeth for weeks. He hadn't been avoiding her, but given her revelation at their meeting in his office, he needed time to come to grips with her changed situation. As the weekend drew nearer, he decided to go home to Joseph's Creek to spend time with his family. He was concerned about how the declaration of war would affect them.

'The Schmidts had their barn burned to the ground,' his father said at the dinner table on the night of his arrival. 'The Schmidts! They've been here almost as long as us.'

'And the Bernings had the window of their bakery smashed,' his mother added. 'Beatrice Berning is a good woman. She is always helping out at the school fairs, and her husband is in the volunteer fire brigade. It's a shame.'

'Ach!' his grand uncle said. 'The government is too lazy to chase these people. They should be grabbing them and throwing them in gaol, like when I was a kid in Germany.' Old Uncle Klaus, who was the family's patriarch after Max's grandfather died, still had a thick accent and pronounced *Germany* as *Chermany*. 'The Kaiser was strong and the people were always well behaved. We never had any trouble in *zose* days.'

The Saturday newspapers bristled with war news and strident jingoism. There was no sympathy expressed for Australians of German descent whose businesses had been destroyed by such incendiary propaganda.

Max walked down Murray Street in Tanunda, recognising many of the faces. Those from German families nodded as he passed and some stopped to chat, but their 'Anglo' neighbours stood together in small groups on the street corners, watching them — people they had lived beside for years — with suspicion.

In Tanunda there were three Lutheran churches within a mile of each other. He turned down Jane Place to St John's, built by the first German families to arrive in South Australia, including the Dinters. The solid timber door was shut and bolted. Painted across it in crude red brush strokes was *Huns Go Home*.

He moved to the adjacent Lutheran school, which was also locked. On the classroom door was an official notice declaring the school closed until further notice under the provisions of the *War Precautions Act of 1914*.

Max stepped back and ran his eyes around the collection of classrooms. There was more red paint and vicious graffiti splattered over the bluestone walls. The buildings looked much smaller than when he and his siblings had attended classes and at lunch run wild in St John's playground.

Although there had been rivalry in the community in those days, it was good-natured. It would have been ridiculous to say the Dinters were anything other than a part of the Tanunda community.

He stopped at a number of German family farmhouses on his way back to his parents' house. He was amazed to hear the stories of discrimination they told. Across the Barossa Valley, many people were being ostracised. In fact he spent the remainder of his time in Tanunda listening to panicked friends and reassuring them that the present uproar against them was a temporary thing.

It wouldn't be long before he discovered how wrong he could be.

* * *

The plane trees in Jeffcott Street had recently burst awake from their winter slumber and were now covered with new green buds. Liz walked beneath them in dappled sunlight, deep in thought. She had been on a shopping excursion to the city, but was returning home almost empty-handed. The city's pavements had been crammed with people. They waved Union Jacks and cheered as the Adelaide Civic Band marched down Hindley Street thumping out 'Rule Britannia'. Columns of young men followed, singing and waving to the cheering crowds. She watched in amazement. Something very strange was happening. The normally staid people of Adelaide had been transformed overnight. Faces glowed with patriotic fervour. They danced in the street.

She had assumed that the war would pass her by, but she now realised she had underestimated the depth of Australians' loyalty to Great Britain. What she had thought was a friendship of convenience was far stronger. It appeared that her countrymen and women considered themselves bound to Britain and the empire by a red ribbon of brotherhood. But more than that, to prove they were worthy members of that empire it seemed they needed to surpass all others in demonstrating that loyalty.

The government fanned the fervour and many interpreted this as an invitation to rail against detractors. Her grandmother, who seemed to be on the end of a pipeline carrying official announcements, told her that more than a hundred Germans had been arrested in South Australia.

Liz's heart lurched at the thought that Max, now out of touch for over two weeks, might be one of them. She told herself he was Australian-born, and tried to put her mind at rest, but her concern lingered. Even if he wasn't incarcerated as an enemy alien, she worried about the added pressure that the war would place on their budding relationship. It was not only her prejudiced grandmother she now had to assuage, but almost the entire British-Australian population.

As she rounded the corner into Childers Street, she noticed a couple of horses tethered to her grandmother's picket fence.

She had a premonition of bad things to come, which was confirmed when she reached the gate and found two policemen coming out her grandmother's front door.

* * *

Max faced the three men in the vice chancellor's office, trying hard to concentrate on their questions, but his mind was in a whirl, trying to trace the steps, the imperceptibly small steps that led him to this point where he was fighting to retain his reputation.

It started with a letter he received from the dean. It referred to the report of the female student leaving his room in tears and appeared to be purely a procedural response to their informal meeting in July, but it made no mention of the outcome, which was that the dean thought Max had no case to answer. In fact, it made no mention of the meeting at all.

He next received a memorandum from Riley from the legal department, informing him that he would represent the university at the hearing. What hearing? Max had no idea what the memo referred to, but now his concerns began to mount, and he asked for an appointment with the dean. He was told the dean was unavailable.

The final piece of the puzzle arrived a few days later by way of a formal request to attend a disclosure hearing in the vice chancellor's office.

A *disclosure hearing*. Again, Max was in the dark, but his disquiet grew. The matter of Elizabeth's attendance at his office and her hasty and teary retreat had not been shelved as he'd thought.

The men sitting opposite him were the vice chancellor, Dr Arthur Wilkinson; Riley, the man who wrote to him from the university's legal department; and someone named Bennison — a short man with thick, rimless glasses, who was from outside the university and whose role Max had missed during the introductions as he realised that Professor White, his head of faculty, would not be present.

The questions came in rapid succession and ranged from his qualifications to his class load to his sporting interests and pastimes.

'Dinter ...' Bennison said. 'That's a German surname, isn't it?'

It was the first time that Bennison had spoken, and his question was so wide of the discussion to that point that it took Max a moment to grasp it. 'Yes, it is.'

Bennison nodded, and made a note on the paper attached to his clipboard. 'And I understand your father's name is Rainer. Is that correct?'

'... Yes.'

Bennison nodded again, and made another note. 'Any other German Christian names in your family?'

Max found it difficult to remain calm. He glanced at the other members of the committee. They were stony-faced.

'I can't say I've given it much thought,' Max said stiffly. 'On my mother's side we have: James, Agnes and Henry. I suppose Uncle Klaus might sound German, but what about Uncle Fritz who prefers to be called Fred? And Aunt Hanna could be taken either way. As you may be aware, Mr Bennison, many English Christian names come from the days of William the Conqueror ... So would you mind telling me what this is about?'

'Mr Dinter,' the vice chancellor said, interrupting, 'we're here to investigate a serious charge of sexual harassment against a female student in your office on ...' he glanced at his notes '... on 23rd July.'

'I discussed that incident with Professor White. A young woman came to see me on a curriculum matter. She had some issues of a personal nature and she left my office in an emotional state. Professor White found no reason to take it any further. And by the way, why isn't my head of faculty at this hearing? He could clear this up.'

The legal man said, 'A private discussion with your colleague doesn't constitute a hearing. This meeting will make the appropriate determinations.'

'A determination about what, exactly?'

'How would you describe your relationship with your students?' the vice chancellor asked.

Max had been expecting this question, but he was now flustered, and had difficulty in framing a reply. How did he interact with his pupils? He hoped he was approachable and friendly, but also professional and objective.

'I believe I have a very good rapport with my students,' he said.

'A friendly rapport?'

'Friendly enough to encourage them to approach me for assistance when required.'

'I see.'

Bennison sat forwards in his chair.

'And Mr Dinter ... you're a young man, not very much older than your students. Do you find your female students are attracted to you?'

'I have no idea, Mr Bennison.'

'Then perhaps you can tell me if you find some of them to your liking.'

Max bristled. 'I'm sure that in that unlikely event, I would not let it prejudice my professional student–tutor relationship.'

'But you did, didn't you?' Bennison said. 'You lured a young woman into your office and made improper advances towards her and she fled for her own safety.'

Max's knuckles tightened on the arm of his chair. 'I did no such thing,' he said through gritted teeth.

'That is not what we've heard.'

'From whom did you hear such a scurrilous accusation? I deny it absolutely!'

'Mr Dinter, please,' Dr Wilkinson interceded. 'Let us not become emotional.' Turning to Bennison, he said. 'That allegation is not in my briefing notes, Mr Bennison.'

'I have made some investigations of my own prior to this hearing, Vice Chancellor.'

'Really?'

The vice chancellor appeared to have further to say on the matter, but instead said: 'Gentlemen, we are here to investigate an irregularity which, although it raises some matters of a personal nature, can be handled in an objective manner.'

Max glared at Bennison, but kept his lips tightly closed.

After a brief silence, the vice chancellor spoke again. 'Mr Dinter, perhaps if you could give us the young lady's name, we could interview her and if, as you say, there was nothing untoward that occurred, the whole affair can be closed.'

Max's thoughts went back to the last time he'd seen Elizabeth. She had been greatly distressed. He couldn't expose her to the harsh scrutiny of these insensitive bureaucrats; especially Bennison, who seemed to delight in muck-raking.

'I don't believe I can impose upon her. As I said, she's had a traumatic experience, and in her emotional state I don't believe it is reasonable to expect her to present herself.'

The vice chancellor remained grim-faced. 'So you won't give us her name?'

'I'm sorry. No.'

The legal man frowned.

Bennison, the outsider, smiled behind the façade of his glinting lenses.

CHAPTER 13

The message didn't make sense. The district commissioner, George Webster, scratched his head and looked again at the radio operator. Bert Morris was one of a handful of whites in Karonga, and quite typical. He'd been in the colonial service for years, too many years in Webster's opinion, because he'd settled into the languor that was characteristic of men who lingered too long in Africa. He was sitting in Webster's visitor's chair awaiting further instructions with a blank expression and not the slightest interest or surprise at the contents of the message.

As a young man commencing his career in the colonial service, Webster had no intention of falling into the complacency that tropical postings often engendered. He'd been warned by his father, a man of some experience in such matters, having served with distinction in India. 'Keep your distance from the old lags,' he'd told him. 'And never fraternise with the local women.'

Nyasaland was merely a stepping stone and he was determined to do well as the DC in Karonga before moving on. The post had nothing to distinguish itself other than as the site of the high-frequency radio station providing the link between the surrounding British outposts and the high power station in England.

He did, however, recognise that men such as the radio operator could be helpful in untangling the inexplicable ways of the dark continent.

He read the telegram again. *Tipsified Pumgirdles Germany Novel*, it said.

'Are you sure you took it down right, Bert?'

The radio operator shrugged. 'Exactly as they keyed it, sir.'

Webster strolled to his doorway and gazed over the nodding heads of hibiscus flowers peeping above the veranda rail to the lake and the violet-blue hills beyond. A cloud of lake flies wafted over the tranquil waters of Lake Malawi. As always, the view was idyllic. It's no wonder they become addled, he thought.

'Maybe it's code,' the radio operator offered, offhandedly.

Webster mentally admonished himself. Code! His brain was still foggy from yet another night of sleep deprivation — blasted heat and unbidden erotic thoughts. A despatch from headquarters about coded messages had arrived a few weeks ago.

He grunted without acknowleding his radio operator's contribution and moved casually to his locked filing cabinet. He was tempted to send old Bert back to his radio hut, but thought he might still be useful.

Webster sat at his desk and, with the code book open before him, flipped pages until the message was deciphered.

He raised his eyes to Bert, who was watching him with mild interest, and felt the blood drain from his face.

'Bloody hell,' he whispered.

* * *

The stars waned as the first faint blush of day appeared in the eastern sky. Dan stood alone in the open patch of lava rubble, his gaze on the horizon where a tinge of blue-green spread imperceptibly north and south to backlight the ink-black hills. Blues and greens melted into muted scarlet. Around him the rocky ground glowed as darkly red as it had in its prehistoric molten state. Slowly the sky lightened through red to orange to yellow and soon became too dazzling to follow its unfolding palette.

The morning retained the chill of the previous night and an involuntary shiver ran down Dan's back, but with rude impatience to start the day the equatorial sun burst above the horizon and within seconds its first rays fell on him, warming his skin.

Inside, however, he remained cold.

The night had been endless. Between his bouts of sleeplessness he dreamed strange dreams. He was in a field of head-high grass that swayed and shimmered as unseen creatures circled him, making strange calls and growls. Vandervold was with him, incessantly nagging. He was oblivious of the danger, urging him on until Dan lost his patience and grabbed him by the throat and squeezed until his face turned blue-black — the colour of Bill's leg when he died.

He awoke in a sweat.

He'd left the camp an hour before the dawn, unable to sleep and not wanting to delay what needed to be done that morning. He was worried about finding a suitable gravesite in that stony wasteland and now that the sun was up, it confirmed his fears. He would be unable to inter Bill beneath the ground anywhere within a day's march, and carrying the body through the cauldron of the Great Rift Valley would be a mistake.

He returned to camp and told the headman to order the porters to each collect two stones and follow him and Vandervold as they carried Bill's body, draped in a piece of plain mericani cloth, to the site he'd chosen for the burial.

As the whole company of men gathered around, they put Bill's body in a shallow depression on the stony earth. Each man came forwards to place his two rocks on the body so that, at the end of the process, the corpse was covered by a small mound of stones.

Dan stood at the head of the cairn with the eyes of over a hundred and fifty men on him, racking his brain for the words to suit the occasion. Although he'd been in attendance at many gravesides during the war against the Boers, it had always been someone else's duty to bury the dead and say the words. He felt sure that individuals chosen to speak at graves had an innate ability to do so. They could find, if not praise, then at least some redeeming traits the deceased possessed that could be mentioned to comfort the bereaved. His inability to recall anything from those occasions made him feel neglectful of his duty to prepare for days such as this.

He tried to recall something heroic to relate about Bill. Dan knew he'd faced off savage lions, charging rhinos, belligerent elephants and all manner of animals in numerous tight spots, but nothing that any other white hunter wouldn't do as part of a day's work.

Bill's account of his wild night in Kimberley town came to mind. It was the night before he'd set sail for Adelaide. According to Bill, he was shouting drinks for everyone in the bar in celebration of his great good luck on the gold fields. The men — tough, thick-necked types who would happily brain a man for the contents of his gold satchel — slapped his back and tried to get him drunk enough to drop his guard. But Bill, young as he'd been, was wise to them.

Bill said he was also wise to the attentions of the young ladies in the bar who draped themselves all over him. One in particular, Dulcie, was especially appealing. After a dozen or so drinks, he whisked her away from the bar and spent a night of passion with her before leaving her asleep and exhausted when he hurried away to catch his departing ship. A goddess, Bill had said, and after his gold like everyone else. Bill said he left Dulcie with nothing but a small nugget he put beside the bed to express his gratitude.

Even if it was an exaggeration, the story told much about Bill Freeman, a man who could make the best of any occasion, and if he didn't, his recollection of it would never acknowledge it.

Upon reflection, Dan assessed the Kimberley story as inappropriate for the occasion, and dropped the idea.

Now he wondered if he should have chosen to conduct the simple ceremony in private. What did these men know of his friend, William Freeman? To them he was the boss: a man who employed them for a short time, paid them a miserly amount for carrying sixty pounds for a good part of every day, and occasionally berated them for being lazy or clumsy. Looking around the faces from the many and varied cultures and tribes he expected to find indifference, but regardless of how the men viewed Bill, all of them showed respect for his passing. It somehow made Dan feel better about leaving him buried in such a desolate place.

Bill Freeman had been his friend, mentor and sometimes father figure. He had given him a chance and stood by him. He'd kept his secret safe.

Finally, he spoke.

'Here lies Bill Freeman.'

The heads that were bowed lifted to hear him speak.

'A white hunter.'

There was nothing more to say.

He stared at the men.

They stared back.

'May he rest in peace.'

* * *

It had been a month since Bill's death and three since the safari had snaked its way out of Nairobi. Following Bill's death, Vandervold had shown a surprising degree of empathy, and in deference to Dan's loss, was prepared to call off the safari. Dan thanked him but declined. Bill had wanted it that way, and he'd been right — the company needed the money.

Vandervold was ultimately completely satisfied with his safari. In the trans-Mara the savannah was blackened by an enormous number of wildebeest and other plains game, and the big cats and other predators followed them in numbers. The American had in the end a handsome set of trophies salted in readiness for the taxidermist. Lion, cheetah, kudu, buffalo, leopard and many more. He would have plenty to brag about back home in Manhattan.

When the Ngong Hills came into sight on the horizon, Dan allowed himself to begin thinking of the life he would resume in Nairobi. He blissfully contemplated returning to a soft bed, a hot bath and a cold beer at Wood's, though he was dreading dealing with Bill's paperwork and shambolic records. There were also Bill's personal effects to be sorted. It would be both an emotional and mental strain. He also needed to complete the letter he'd begun to Liz soon after Bill's death.

More than once during the safari his conscience nagged him about writing to Liz. He had no excuse for delaying it. He could have sent the letter back to Nairobi with a runner. But then he rationalised that he'd not written in over a year, and what difference would it make delaying the bad news for another month? He doubted she'd be returning to Africa to visit Bill's grave. Indeed, he didn't expect her to return to Africa at all, despite her ideas about being a veterinarian to lions and wildebeest.

They were within a day's march of Nairobi before Dan understood why the Maasai villages they had been passing along the foot of the Ngong Hills seemed so different from usual: there was no sign of the arrogant young warriors who would ordinarily stand by the track and watch the safari pass with aloof indifference. The usual clusters of giggling women, owl-eyed children and old people were present, but the young men were nowhere to be seen.

It wasn't until they reached Nairobi town that he learned the news that had already thrown the lives of every inhabitant of British East Africa into turmoil.

* * *

There was an inordinate display of flags in town. They fluttered from every building, tall or small. Outside the Theatre Royal, now draped in Union Jacks, was a long queue of young men. Dan interrupted a conversation between two upcountry types who stood with shouldered rifles and ammunition bandoliers watching the line edge forwards.

'It's war, matey,' came the incredulous reply. 'Where've you been?'

'What war?'

'Germany.'

His first thought was that a European war was many thousands of miles away, but then recalled that German East Africa was a mere seventy miles from Nairobi. At Lake Magadi his safari had almost been in German territory.

'And are you and all these men enlisting?'

'These are the Johnnie-come-latelies,' the man told him. 'You should have seen the crowds here earlier in the month. A line of men, hundreds long.'

In addition to fighting men, the empire also needed logistical support. Vehicles were scarce, but there were thousands of natives able to be press-ganged to act as porters, and Dan found hundreds of black Africans decked out in khaki. The mystery of the evacuated Maasai villages was solved: the Maasai warriors would not carry loads for the military operations, or for anyone else for that matter. *May you have a hand of leather* was a Maasai curse meaning may you be condemned to a life of manual labour — an intolerable situation. Carrying supplies was the work of women, and demeaning for warriors. Rather than be forced into such servile labours, the warriors had clearly quit their homes and marched into the bush.

There were many irregular outfits he could join, but Dan wasn't keen. He wanted nothing to do with war or its officialdom.

He busied himself demobbing his own army of porters.

* * *

Dan sighed as he screwed up another page and tossed it towards the wastebasket. It hit the overfull receptacle and bounced out to roll under the low table upon which was an empty flask of whisky and a shot glass.

Dan took another clean sheet from the top drawer and stared at it before noticing that Bill's old desk chair had started to wobble again. He reached down and slid the piece of linoleum under the leg with the missing rubber foot.

He pushed the clutter of unpaid bills and unopened envelopes to the farthest edges of the desktop hoping the extra space would help clear his mind.

My dear Lizzie, he began again.
No doubt you will be surprised to receive my letter after all this time.

He couldn't recall writing, and hoped he hadn't forgotten to reply to her last letter. He was not a good correspondent, struggling to remember aspects of his life that she might find interesting. His writing was either a string of hunting stories or a missive full of repetitions and platitudes. Liz's letters, on the other hand, came replete with news of her life in Adelaide, where there were picnics and interesting friends and stimulating subjects studied at university.

He tried to imagine her appearance these days. His memory was of an eleven-year-old with twigs and grass seeds in her long fair hair, looking almost boyish in her baggy shorts and floppy wide-brimmed hat.

> *I think it must be a year now since I last wrote, so please forgive me, but as you are surely aware, I am a poor correspondent, and a forgetful one at that. Even now it is difficult for me to write as I must inform you of some very bad news.*

This was roughly the point where all his previous attempts floundered. He simply couldn't find the words to tell her Bill was dead. If she was still eleven and on the Limuru farm, he would sit with her and explain, then hug her when she began to cry and tell her that time would soon mend her sorrow. Now her letters exuded such sophistication he realised he no longer knew Bill Freeman's granddaughter, and had no idea how to compassionately inform her of his death.

> *It is with great regret that I must inform you that your grandfather, William Freeman, has passed away.*

He was about to add, *after being bitten by a snake*, but thought better of it. How could a man who hunted dangerous game — lion, buffalo, elephant — die from the bite of a reptile not much more than a yard long? But she would surely have questions about the cause of death. He took up the pen again.

> *He died at camp after receiving the poisonous bite of the most dangerous snake in Africa while leading a big safari into untravelled country.*

That was better.

> *We buried him in the land he loved where he now lies in peace.*

He placed the pen on the desk's cracked leather inlay and went to the outer office where he fished another bottle from the otherwise empty filing cabinet drawer.

As he poured straight whisky into his shot glass, he thought again about Liz and how this news would intrude upon her idyllic life in faraway Australia.

CHAPTER 14

'There'll be no further discussion, Elizabeth,' Harriet Freeman said. 'There's a war on. And it's your patriotic duty.'

'But Grandmother,' she said, determined not to give in without a fight, 'I don't know anything about sewing.'

'Anyone can sew buttons on a uniform, my dear, which you will do while I carry on the dressmaking.'

'What about my course? How will I finish my degree if I'm sewing all day?'

'For goodness' sake. Everyone knows the war will be over by Christmas. You can resume your course after that.' She paused a moment before adding acerbically, 'Anyway, it'll get you away from the influence of that German teacher of yours.'

It was the first time her grandmother had mentioned Max since the afternoon tea when she warned Liz to stop seeing him.

'Oh, yes. You didn't think I knew about your continuing little trysts with Herr Dinter, did you?'

The conversation was quickly getting out of hand. It had started innocuously enough with her grandmother proudly announcing she had signed up with the Interior Ministry to assist the war effort. She explained that many patriotic individuals and businesses would be providing workers.

When Liz had asked how her grandmother, a dressmaker with a clientele of housewives, could afford to give up her time to assist in the war, she learned of Harriet's quite cunning strategy. While receiving full payment for her efforts, she also hoped her involvement via the war effort with the broader textile industry would assist to re-establish her profile. She could see it as a renaissance of her position as a trusted supplier for the fashion industry. And as Liz had only just learned, it would put a distance between Liz and Max, which she hoped would cause the budding relationship to wilt on the vine.

Liz felt powerless. As a guest in her grandmother's house, she could hardly dictate terms, but the war effort meant nothing to her. She had none of the patriotism that inspired her grandmother. Bad enough that she had to defer her course, but who could say how long the fighting would last? It might be years, not months. And what of Max? He had become very dear to her and the thought of losing contact with him was distressing.

Unable to mount any further argument she retired, defeated, to her bedroom, but not before her grandmother told her she should make her arrangements at the university so that she could commence her new role on the following Monday.

Liz closed her bedroom door and leaned her weight against it. On her bed was the unopened letter from Dan that she'd collected from the letterbox when she arrived home. The stamp and unmistakeable handwriting confirmed it. She needed something to lighten her mood and although Dan was not a scintillating correspondent, his letters brought Africa back to mind and invariably cheered her.

My dear Lizzie, he began.
No doubt you will be surprised to receive my letter after all this time ...

* * *

Max stubbed out his Capstan and, feeling the need for another, fidgeted with a pencil instead, rolling it across his desk and drumming it on the polished timber until it annoyed him. He had spent most of his free time since the disclosure hearing in his office hoping to hear from his superiors, and feeling like a condemned man awaiting his sentence. He didn't regret concealing Elizabeth's identity from them. It was the honourable thing to do, and he felt the members of the committee would ordinarily have respected his position, but these were not ordinary times.

The Adelaide newspapers' rhetoric became even more inflammatory as the country became consumed by patriotic fervour. Letters to the editor were strongly worded against people of German descent. Editorials raged against the insolent Germans greedily ravaging Europe. The community was baying for German blood. Even second-generation German blood would do.

German businesses were shunned and many closed. It appeared to Max there was an unofficial campaign to rid the business community of German surnames. Even long-standing members of the city council were forced from office. Claus Krichauff and Jorg Neumayer, men previously esteemed for their civic contributions, suddenly quit office.

Max wondered if such a purge could strike an academic community such as the university. He thought it quite unlikely for intellectuals to be swept up in the mindless xenophobia, but Bennison was not from the university and his questions had given Max cause for concern. He tried to discover more about Bennison but the dean's office would only say he was a government official. His role in the internal investigation was not defined, and when Max had refused to divulge Elizabeth's name, his eyes shone like a predator who had just sniffed blood.

On top of all the concerns about his position at the university, there was still the matter of Elizabeth, which continued to cause him to lose sleep. He hadn't seen her in more than a week, even in class, because his mood had made it difficult for him to concentrate and he had cancelled a number of his tutorial sessions.

He was now thoroughly sick of himself. He threw the pencil to his desk and stepped outside to stretch his legs. He had planned for a brisk walk around the university grounds, but upon arriving at an empty bench, flopped down on it and dropped his head in his hands.

His career, his reputation, were disintegrating around him, and the woman he had once cherished had been through a traumatic experience that had caused him to reassess his future and his feelings about her.

When he lifted his head again he saw Elizabeth some way off, walking towards a group of her friends. All the emotions of the previous weeks came sweeping over him, and in the knowledge he was presently invisible to her, he felt able to look inside his heart and reassess his feelings for her.

If he couldn't again feel the deep affection he once held for her, then it would mean she had become lost to him and he must give up all his wonderful plans for their future.

* * *

Liz had resigned herself to her fate and as soon as she joined her classmates in the university quadrangle before first class, she told them she had some bad news to convey.

'Today's my last day at school,' she announced.

'What?'

'My grandmother has volunteered us to help with the war effort. As of Monday, I'll be taking leave from my course to help her.'

'How wonderful,' one friend said. 'What a simply smashing idea!' said another.

As they excitedly chatted about what each of them could do to help the brave men who would defend Australia's shores, Liz realised how different they were from her. Did none of them see what was going on around them? Politicians and the press were feeding a frenzy of righteous rage at the threat that Germany and her allies posed to Australia. The mood of the public was getting quite out of hand, and from what she knew of Max's situation, the consequences were affecting innocent people's lives. Meanwhile hundreds of young men, boys really, came streaming into the city from their farms and homes to queue at recruitment booths, itching for a chance to join the *fun*. Country towns were being stripped of their young men. The streets of Adelaide were festooned with streamers, and had become a parade ground for the army. Military bands had replaced motor vehicles and buggies.

Her attention returned to the conversation when she heard someone mention that the authorities had interned another hundred German nationals. None of them seemed to have made a connection between this and their science tutor and his German surname. It gave her some comfort to know that none of her friends, nor any within the student body had considered Max to be anything but completely Australian.

As the chatter continued about the war, Liz put voice to her scepticism about the German threat to Australia.

'How could a country like Germany, so far away from Australia, mount an attack, let alone an invasion?' she asked.

'Haven't you heard?' one of the girls said. 'There's a German warship somewhere near India that's sinking everything.'

Liz hadn't heard, but India was still a long way off and, anyway, the issues that led to war had arisen from actions taken by the European powers and were surely none of Australia's business. Great Britain and the European powers should resolve them.

India. It was closer to British East Africa than to Australia and she felt quite sure that Africa would not be silly enough to get involved.

And nor should Australia.

* * *

Max hadn't been searching for Elizabeth, but when she suddenly appeared in his field of vision, it was as if he was seeing her for the first time.

She was wearing a deep olive-green woollen coat with a brown velvet collar. She'd told him she liked to wear clothes that were a little big for her, and therefore quite comfortable. Unlike many of the other females of her age, she didn't seem to care too much about fashion. The cold Adelaide morning had prompted her to don a brown velvet hat with a feather plume.

He studied her in earnest and familiar characteristics reappeared. He'd forgotten how she fetchingly inclined her head to one side while listening to another's point of view. He was very flattered when she paid him the compliment of such close attention, and he could see that he was not alone in that regard. Elizabeth had the ability to make others feel that everything they said was important. And now she was talking, gently lifting her hand, palm upwards, seeking agreement for some point she'd made and smiling that sweet engaging smile when her listener obliged. He loved her smile. It made his heart sing, and all the things he loved about her came rushing back to him.

He covered the distance between them without consciously planning to do so, and as he drew nearer he noted that her brown ankle-length woollen dress clung to her thighs, and her well-rounded breasts peeped between the open flaps of her coat. He couldn't remember seeing her more beautiful.

When she noticed his approach, her eyes widened in surprise and she sucked on her top lip, which she did when confused.

Max ignored the others in her group and went directly to her.

He could see that she held her breath.

'Elizabeth,' he said, and his voice came fractured by the tightness in his chest.

'Yes ... Max?'

'I ... I ...'

* * *

When she saw Max striding so purposefully towards her, Liz was surprised. He seldom approached her while she was with her friends.

She watched him come, wondering what lay behind his quite strange expression. He was unsmiling, even stern. He appeared to be on a mission, with something important to say, and prepared to have nothing and nobody stop him.

When he reached her, in fact was standing so close to her that she thought he was about to kiss her, her friends fell silent, and the silence emphasised the tension that hung in the air.

The frown he wore as he approached dissipated, and he looked deep into her eyes for a long moment.

'Elizabeth,' he said, taking her hand gently in his.

She stammered a reply of sorts.

'I ... I love you. Please marry me.'

* * *

Liz wrung her hands and paced within the small confines of her bedroom. After an hour, during which time she rehearsed a number of speeches, she straightened her shoulders, opened her bedroom door, and walked confidently down the hall. By the time she reached the kitchen where her grandmother, stern-faced as ever, was preparing to make a cup of tea, her resolve almost deserted her.

Taking a deep breath, she said, 'Grandmother.'

'Hmm? Yes, Elizabeth?'

'I have some exciting news.'

Harriet looked over the rims of her glasses, mildly curious.

'Max has asked me to marry him.'

Harriet returned her attention to the boiling kettle, which she took from the stove to the kitchen table. She stood beside her chair and poured the boiling water into the teapot.

Liz began to think she'd not heard her correctly.

'You mean that German has asked you to be his wife,' Harriet said.

'Yes ... I mean, no. Max is an Australian.'

Harriet still kept her eyes on her task. 'And you have accepted?'

'Yes.'

'Of course you have,' she said, now turning her gaze on her. 'But you will retract. I absolutely forbid it. No Freeman will ever consort with the enemy. Certainly not while you're living under this roof. Do you hear me, Elizabeth?'

Liz swallowed hard.

'I'm sorry, Grandmother, in that case I must leave.'

'Leave? That's quite impossible. You have nowhere to go.'

Liz folded her hands in front of her. 'Max's mother, Johanna, has kindly invited me to stay,' she said, softly. 'Until the wedding.'

Harriet stared for some moments at her steaming cup before lifting her eyes to Liz. Her granddaughter saw anger and frustration, then finally, defeat, as she sank slowly to her chair. Liz had never seen her grandmother appear so disconsolate, and was briefly tempted to withdraw her words, but a moment later Harriet's familiar spirit returned.

'Very well,' she sniffed, 'it appears you have made up your mind.'

Liz waited for more, but her grandmother lifted her cup and saucer. It rattled as she walked from the room with it.

Liz watched her go, then walked down the hall to her bedroom, where she pulled all her clothes and personal items out of cupboards and drawers and crammed them into two battered leather suitcases. It was too much for her to manage alone. She selected the most important items and put them into one suitcase, which she placed at the front door. The other would have to remain with her grandmother until she was able to collect it.

In the sitting room, Harriet was sitting on the sofa, her tea almost untouched.

'Grandmother ... I'm going now. I'll be back sometime to collect the rest of my things.'

Harriet sat stony-faced for a long moment before saying, 'I've made you welcome in my home as any grandparent should. I've offered you sustenance and moral support. I've stood by you in your travails, but when I ask for your assistance in a matter very important to me, and which I feel should be important to you, namely to support your country against a savage enemy, I have received nothing in return.'

'That's not it. Don't you understand? Max has proposed marriage. And I have accepted. We are engaged. I was hoping to receive your blessing.'

'Do you love him, Elizabeth?'

The question took Liz quite by surprise. It had never occurred to her that her grandmother had *love* in her vocabulary. But that was absurd. Harriet Freeman had been married. She and her grandfather had a child together — Liz's own father. For the first time she saw her grandmother as a woman, and she felt compelled to be as truthful to her as possible.

'I ... I'm not sure, but ... I think I do.'

Harriet appeared to release her hold on her emotions. Her shoulders slumped and she looked terribly sad, but the veil dropped over her eyes again and the flinty tone returned. 'He's German, Elizabeth. Don't you know anything about these people? Haven't you read the Bryce Report on German atrocities? They're not like us.'

Liz did not bother reiterating Max's nationality. 'All I know is that Max has asked me to be his wife and I've accepted.' Even she thought the response insipid, so she added: 'He is very fond of me. Very fond.'

'I've watched how hard you've worked for your qualifications. I haven't said much, but I've noticed. It's not been easy for you, I know. But now you are acting just like your mother. You're a silly, *stupid* girl.'

The words stung. Tears threatened to roll down Liz's cheeks, but she turned away before they could be seen. She was torn between her need to take control of her life and slighting the only family member she'd known for ten years. 'With respect, Grandmother, Max is not the person who instructed me to leave university within six months of the end of my degree.'

Harriet said nothing, but her already cold face turned to ice.

At the door Liz paused, one part of her fearing her grandmother would try to dissuade her, and another hoping she would. With a final glance down the hall to the kitchen, she picked up her suitcase, closing the front door quietly behind her.

Outside, Childers Street appeared very cold and unfriendly. At the gate, she looked back at the picket fence, the path through the tidy front garden, the tessellated-tile veranda. It had been home. Regardless of her prejudice and her overbearing manner, her grandmother was family.

She had Max, but she wasn't sure if that was enough.

* * *

Max arranged a room for Elizabeth at the Young Women's Christian Association boarding house in the centre of Adelaide. Male visitors were discouraged and Max was only allowed to visit her in the parlour. Even then they were under the almost constant scrutiny of one of the female staff, who popped into the parlour frequently during his time there.

He listened sympathetically as she told him of the altercation with her grandmother.

'Perhaps I should have got to know her better before we announced our engagement.'

The burden was too great to keep from him any longer. 'Max, I have to tell you that getting to know my grandmother better wouldn't make it any easier.'

She told him of her grandmother's obsessive dislike of Germans. She found herself trying to make excuses for her by describing the malicious trickery that led to the loss of her business. 'Of course it could have been anyone, but Grandmother seems to blame anyone of German heritage for what those two men did way back then.'

He nodded and said he understood.

'It's even worse now,' he said. 'My parents are really feeling the brunt of this anti-German sentiment. They're talking about moving away from Joseph's Creek. Can you believe it? It's their home and livelihood, but they've seen old friends turn against them — even those who know my father is Australian-born. Dad thinks that starting again somewhere else will put an end to it. But I know it won't.'

'I'm sorry for your parents and I'm ashamed of my grandmother,' Liz said.

He reminded her that his mother had said she would be most welcome to stay as a member of the family at the Tanunda farm until they were married.

'Are you sure they won't mind?'

'I'm sure they will love you as much as I do.'

She smiled and touched his arm, just as the maid re-entered the parlour. She gave them a stern look that made both of them smile.

'I'll rearrange my Friday classes and take you up to Tanunda on the train,' he said. 'We can see each other every weekend.'

'But won't I see you at classes?'

'Classes? But I thought you had quit your course.'

'Oh, I'm re-enrolling immediately. That was only meant to be temporary. While I worked with my grandmother on the army uniforms.'

'I see … Well, we haven't set a date for our wedding, but I was hoping we would only have a short engagement.'

'Yes, certainly, if that's what you want. But what has that to do with completing my degree?'

'Ah. Well, as I say, we haven't talked about such matters. You have a lot on your mind, poor thing. Let's just keep our plans focussed on the immediate future. There's a morning train to Tanunda on Friday. We can have the whole weekend together to see you settled in.'

He rose to go as the housekeeper made another sweep of the parlour. When she exited, Max bent down and quickly kissed her.

'There,' he said. 'That's one the maid didn't see.'

She smiled at him as he departed, but their conversation left her feeling a little uncomfortable.

* * *

Harriet climbed from the bus in King William Street and headed towards the building she was informed accommodated the people she needed to see.

Her decision hadn't been hasty. Long before she raised the matter of voluntarily working for the war effort, she had considered the problem of Elizabeth's infatuation with her much older German tutor. The age difference was a significant impediment, she believed, but even now, at the thought of her granddaughter fraternising with the enemy in such a shameless manner, she puffed her cheeks in indignation. It would never do.

She climbed the stone steps using the broad stone balustrade for support. At the second landing was a pair of heavy timber and glass doors with long brass handles that carried the tarnish of countless hands. On the glass panels, in gold lettering, was inscribed COMMONWEALTH OF AUSTRALIA.

Below them in a smaller font were the words *Interior Ministry*.

The entrance foyer was cavernous. Across a wide expanse of cold grey tiles was the receptionist who listened to the reasons for her visit before directing her down a corridor to a door marked *Special Investigations*.

The man sitting behind the desk continued to scribble on his writing pad until she became annoyed and politely coughed.

After another moment, he looked up at her as if she had committed a misdemeanour. She lifted her head and looked down her nose at him. She didn't care if she'd interrupted his concentration; she was there to exercise her patriotic duty.

Harriet prided herself on her ability to sum up a person's character after only a brief contact. Her first impressions were seldom far off the mark. She didn't like this man. And she particularly didn't like the thick, reflective spectacles that concealed his eyes from her and, in her firm opinion, also concealed his thoughts.

CHAPTER 15

Neither Governor Heinrich Schnee in German East Africa nor Governor Sir Henry Belfield in British East Africa were prepared for a war between their respective nations. Each had a mere two and a half thousand men in uniform, most of whom were *askaris* — Africans who had been enticed into service as guards and given limited training.

In Dar es Salaam, on the eve of war, Governor Schnee was making final preparations for the twenty-fifth anniversary of the *Schutztruppe* — the protective troops — and the official opening of the colony's Central Line Railway, which ran nearly eight hundred miles from the capital to Lake Tanganyika.

Schnee, a proud German patriot, received word from Germany's colonial office to say that the Imperial Navy did not intend to defend German East Africa and that the governor should offer no pretext to the Royal Navy to attack their undefended maritime installations. Schnee begrudgingly declared Dar es Salaam to be an *open port*, as defined under the terms of the 1907 Hague Convention.

But there was a German light cruiser, the *Königsberg*, in the Indian Ocean and the Royal Navy discovered that Schnee had allowed colliers to head to sea for a refuelling rendezvous. He also quietly ordered the mobilisation of the *Schutztruppe* and refused to disable the high-powered radio station that could be used to communicate with the *Königsberg*, incurring the ire of the British navy.

The military zeal displayed by Schnee and his *Schutztruppe* commander, Colonel Paul von Lettow-Vorbeck, were not initially matched in British East Africa, where Governor Belfield took a more lackadaisical attitude to the declaration of war.

When District Commissioner Webster's coded message was relayed from Nyasaland to British East Africa and trumpeted from the rooftops, it created a stampede of volunteers. Belfield was overwhelmed by the surge and responded slowly to the need to equip and accommodate them. He refused to allow government officials to enlist and for the first few months had not ordered the internment or deportation of German civilians. Nor did he encourage reconnaissance missions across the border — an oversight that would soon be found to be highly costly.

If Belfield had hoped to keep the lid on hostilities in the African protectorates, the British Navy had no such intentions. In retaliation to Schnee's blatant failure to conform to the terms of his own open-port policy, the HMS *Pegasus* and HMS *Astraea* bombarded the Dar es Salaam radio installation and the railway station early in August.

A month later, the *Königsberg* crept quietly into the Rufiji delta — a labyrinthine series of mud flats, islands, heavy jungle and blue-water havens. There it lay at anchor like a sleeping crocodile, resting before the hunt, while German settlers provisioned it with fresh fruit and vegetables and Governor Schnee smuggled coal to her in various small craft.

Refuelled and victualled, the *Königsberg* steamed to the British protectorate of Zanzibar, just off the German East Africa coast, where she exacted ultimate retribution on the HMS *Pegasus*, sinking her for her role in the bombardment of Dar es Salaam only a month earlier.

The *Schutztruppe* launched a number of raids into the coastal strip north of the border, including during October, an attempt on Mombasa itself. But the Royal Navy had been planning a major attack on German East African soil, which in November they launched at the port town of Tanga. However, by a brilliant piece of deduction, von Lettow-Vorbeck had anticipated the British and moved his forces from Dar es Salaam to fortify Tanga. There he would face formidable enemy forces in the form of the Royal Navy and troops of the protectorate and Indian Expeditionary Forces. What should have been a resounding and possibly decisive victory for the British degenerated into farce and in later years became a case study of a military disaster.

Dan had forgone his usual watering hole at Wood's hotel, instead choosing to return to the Norfolk, where most of the white hunters drank.

One of the regulars at the Norfolk's veranda bar was Harry Milstead, who had been among the first settlers to arrive in British East Africa, and who when his wheat crop failed for three consecutive years turned to leading hunting safaris. Harry was very well connected to senior people in the administration, and was a reliable source of information, especially since the declaration of war when the newspapers were placed under government censorship.

Dan joined Harry at his table and the older man pulled a crumpled packet of Woodbines from his coat pocket, offered one to Dan, then lit them with a Lucifer.

'They say the war'll be over by Christmas,' Harry said, squinting through the smoke as he puffed his cigarette alight. 'I've got my doubts.'

'Why's that?'

'If the rest of our military men are as dunderheaded as the lot that made the attack on Tanga, we're in trouble.' Harry went on to explain that the Royal Navy had had eight thousand troops, navy artillery and supply ships. The Germans were outnumbered ten to one, but mismanagement of the attack had turned it into a rout.

'Apparently, the war in this part of the world is directed not by the War Office, but by the Colonial Office and the India Office. A real shemozzle. I heard that it took our fellows three days to get organised. By then the Germans had dug themselves in and set up their defences. In the panic, we left behind weapons, ammunition, even uniforms.' He shook his head and took another long draw on his Woodbine. 'A bloody disaster.'

They sipped their beers in silence for a moment or two.

'We might have a bit of a fight on our hands,' Harry said, reflectively. 'I'd love to have a go at it, but they won't take me. Too old they say ... But what about you, young Dan?'

Harry wasn't the first to enquire about his intentions regarding active service.

'I don't know, Harry. I'll give it some thought.'

Harry nodded and screwed up his eyes as he took a heavy draw on his battered cigarette, now reduced almost to his nicotine-stained fingers. 'Yeah. Reckon it's about time you did,' he said.

* * *

As Governor Belfield dithered about his response to the war, a number of patriotic settlers took it upon themselves to organise a motley collection of irregular troops ready to defend the borders.

There were Arnoldi's Scouts, Wessel's Scouts, Ross's Scouts and the Plateau South Africans, which included many Boers who had fought the British just a dozen years earlier. Each had their own self-styled uniforms, some with feathers fluttering from slouch hats and others favouring the more practical double terais.

Russell Bowker, with his distinctive peaked cap formed from the face of a snarling leopard, formed Bowker's Horse, while Monica's Own, named in honour of the governor's youngest daughter, were the most stylishly regaled. The commander was an ex-Lancer and had his men fitted out with bamboo lances hurriedly crafted in the railway workshops. Red and white pennants fluttered jauntily from the heads, but they lasted no longer than the first parade — they startled the mules, causing a most inglorious stampede through the Government House gardens.

Men came from all walks of life and many nationalities. White hunters, poachers, train drivers, settlers, miners, butchers and bakers flocked into the Nairobi House recruitment office. Nationalities volunteering included Swiss, Australians, Americans, Indians, Swedes, Italians, and even a Turk, until it was discovered that Britain was at war with Turkey and the man was interned.

Perhaps the most extraordinary military unit in British history was the Legion of Frontiersmen or more formally, the 25th Battalion Royal Fusiliers. Among its members was the twenty-seven-stone American millionaire, Northrup McMillan, the sixty-three-year-old veteran hunter Frederick Courteney Selous, Texan cowboys, a number of circus performers including a clown, several former members of the French Foreign Legion, a Buckingham Palace footman, a retired Honduran army colonel, various Arctic seal poachers and a Scottish lighthouse keeper. They were to quickly gain a reputation for bravery and heavy drinking, leading some to rename them the Royal Boozaliers.

Colonial pride soared as the citizenry watched men in uniform parade along Nairobi's wide streets. News from abroad was scarce and, in the absence of bad news, confidence grew. The Germans would be sent packing in a matter of weeks. However, across the border, the Germans had other ideas.

Colonel Paul von Lettow-Vorbeck, the crafty head of the *Schutztruppe,* sent a party of reservists and *askaris* to capture the British East Africa border town of Taveta. The German colonel knew that the topography of the area, being between Mt Kilimanjaro and the Pare mountains, would be easy to defend with as few as a hundred men against a force many times larger.

In Taveta, the Germans were less than seventy miles from the Uganda railway — the lifeline of the protectorate — which they tried, but failed to blow up at the end of August. But the audacious attempt sent shock waves through the formerly sanguine British East African community.

Rumours, half-truths and exaggerations escalated overnight.

One report had it that the *Königsberg* had escaped the Rufiji delta and was en route to bomb Mombasa.

A patrol was hastily despatched to Kijabe on the Rift Valley escarpment to investigate a sighting of lights from enemy aeroplanes. It was found instead to be Venus, which was unusually bright at that time of year.

One enemy patrol *did* advance up the railway line towards Nairobi, but had used an inaccurate British map and had become lost in the waterless Taru Desert. They were captured, almost dead from dehydration, and brought to Nairobi to much relief and celebrations.

In the midst of the mad helter-skelter to enlist and find adventure in a war fought on the sweeping African savannah, Dan felt increasingly isolated.

He couldn't enlist because he might be discovered as a deserter from the Boer War, which would likely lead to a court martial and death sentence.

However, by resisting the rush to enlist he risked attracting the very attention he feared.

CHAPTER 16

It had been a perfect November day. Now the late afternoon sun tinted the vines pink, and the long shadow of the gum tree at the gatepost fell across the dirt track. It almost reached the big tent and canvas awnings that had been erected on the Dinters' front lawn for the engagement party. Inside, the tuba *oompah*ed. A washboard accompanied the timpani player and a piano accordion vied with a couple of fiddlers for lead. Max's father swung his wine glass in time, and his mother sang and clapped her hands in accompaniment.

Liz sat beside Max and was very happy, and also slightly drunk on her third glass of sparkling wine. She was pleased with the alterations she'd made to her pale blue lawn dress: she'd attached lace to the collar and cuffs and along the hem of the ankle-length skirt. Johanna had added the waxed orange blossoms from her own wedding dress, stitching one to her collar and another in place of a belt buckle. Her new straw hat, festooned with delicate cream flowers and pale blue ribbons, was Liz's only extravagance.

Around them Max's family and friends laughed and danced and, in ones and twos, came bleary-eyed to present their compliments at the main table. They wished them *Den Segen Gottes* and *Mögest du viele Kinder haben*. Max laughed and said such things must wait until they were married.

The Barossa Valley German community had banded together to erect the awnings and tent, and festooned the guy ropes and poles with red, white and blue bunting. Masses of flowers decorated the tables, and among the bouquets of spring flowers strewn along the long bridal table, where at each end stood an enormous flower vase, were several long-neck bottles of beer and a balthazar of sparkling wine. The trestle tables arranged in rows before them were littered with glasses, bottles and empty plates. The festivities to celebrate the engagement of one of the Barossa's finest sons to his beautiful fiancée were in full flight.

Elizabeth had approached her meeting with Max's parents in September with trepidation, but Rainer had given her a bear-hug and Johanna had cried and kissed her warmly. She took up residence in the guest bedroom of the sprawling Joseph's Creek farmhouse and soon felt comfortable alone with Rainer and Johanna while Max was at university.

During the few short weeks leading to the engagement party, as Liz and Johanna worked together, she felt a closer bond to her future mother-in-law than she ever had with her own mother. At last, she felt a part of a family, in fact part of a community, for the Dinters' extended family and friends were generous in their affection.

Although she still had plans to return to complete her studies in the new year, it depended upon Max, who told her there were some matters he must attend to at the university. He wouldn't tell her what, saying only that it was staff business and he didn't want her to get involved.

In all the confusion and excitement of planning for the party, her grandfather's death had quickly faded from memory. She had been saddened by his passing, but they had never been close; like her mother, Bill had only corresponded at Christmas. It was Dan who provided the real link to her earlier, vivid African life, and she realised perhaps it was the loss of one filament of her connection to the continent that she grieved, rather than the old man himself.

Elizabeth guessed that Freeman Safaris could be hers if she cared to claim it. But she thought it most unlikely her dream of returning to Africa to work with animals would be realised in the near future, if ever.

As the sun dipped to the horizon, Rainer rose unsteadily to his feet, calling to the bandmaster to rest his men. The drummer gave a drum roll, and ended it with a crash on his cymbal. The guests returned to their seats and Rainer quietened the last of the loud talkers with a good-natured bellow for silence. 'My friends,' he said. 'Thank you for coming to our little party.' He waited while the wry comments died. 'My firstborn has come home,' he announced to great applause. 'And brought with him the lovely Elizabeth to be his wife. Future wife. The Dinter family welcomes her. We *all* welcome her.'

Liz blushed at the loud applause and spontaneous toasts offered to her from around the tables.

'It hasn't been easy since I lost my son to the city,' Rainer continued. 'Now he's come home like the prodigal son. After all the love we gave him ...'

Liz caught the look Johanna gave her husband and he changed his course.

'Anyway, he's home again, and tonight we are celebrating a very happy event, which is —'

A shrill whistle interrupted Rainer's speech and the crowd turned as one to the entrance to the tent, where an army officer stood at the head of six soldiers.

Without a word he marched down the aisle between the rows of trestle tables. His men, with steel bayonets fixed to their shouldered rifles, moved to the perimeter of the tent. When the officer reached the main table he brusquely told Rainer to sit down so he could address the crowd.

Max pushed back his chair and went to stand with his father. 'What's this about?' he demanded.

'We are having a private function here,' his father added. 'You have no —'

The man shoved a paper into Max's hands. It had a coat of arms and official seals. He quickly scanned it. *Enemy aliens* and *detention* appeared in sub-headings.

'Now, if you don't mind,' the officer said, and walked to the front of the table. 'Ladies and gentlemen. Your attention please.'

Max returned to his seat and took Liz's hand in his.

'Max, what is it?' she asked.

His fingers closed tightly around hers, but he said nothing as the officer began to speak. 'I hereby advise that the following men will be detained under the provisions of the *War Precautions Act of 1914*. Such persons will immediately accompany my detachment to Keswick Barracks for assessment.'

There was general uproar as voices rose in anger.

The officer ignored them and commenced reciting a list of names.

'Gregor Hadtwalcher, Heinrich Kavel, Edmund Heindrich, Hans Dubotzki ...'

Liz held her breath and when it appeared that the army officer had completed his list, she breathed easily again.

But he continued.

'Fester Bauer, Peter Treue, Klaus Dinter, Rainer Dinter, Maximilian Dinter.'

Liz clung to Max's arm and held him tight.

'Elizabeth ... There's nothing to worry about.'

'What do you mean? How can they do this?'

'They can't. And they won't get away with it. We will just explain we are Australians. We have papers to show we were born here. Don't worry.'

'But this is impossible,' she said as tears clouded her eyes.

Max joined his father, Uncle Klaus and the others in the centre of the tent where minutes before there had been dancing.

The army man told them to form up, then led the nine men from the tent.

* * *

As darkness fell, Max climbed into a truck with *Finkelstein's Furniture* emblazoned along the sides. The army had obviously commandeered it and installed the long bench seats — two down each side and two more set back-to-back in the centre — that Finkelstein fitted when he hired it out as a picnic bus. Max and his father were last in but when the six soldiers took the seats at the back of the truck Rainer signalled to Max to move towards the front.

The soldiers relaxed and sat back with cigarettes and pipes, chatting and ignoring their charges, who sat in silence.

'Reckon we taught the Hun a lesson the other day,' one of the young soldiers said, to no one in particular.

'You mean the *Emden*?'

'Yeah.'

'What happened?' asked another.

'We sunk her. The *Sydney* did. Sunk her out near the Cocos Islands.'

'Where's that?'

'Dunno, but must be bloody close.'

'S'truth.'

'Yeah, this proves it. They're definitely heading for Australia.'

The story had been front page in the *Advertiser*. The *Emden*, a German light cruiser, had been prowling the Allied ports of the Indian Ocean. After a short battle at sea, the Australian navy's ship, *Sydney*, had sunk her.

'Maybe this sea battle so close is why we have been chosen,' Rainer said to his son.

Max shook his head. 'I doubt it.'

Rainer waited for his explanation, but when none was offered, he said to Max, '*Sprechen sie Deutsch?*'

'*Sie wissen, ich tue,*' Max replied.

Rainer shrugged, and continued in German. 'You've been away from home so long, I wasn't sure.'

Max ignored the gibe. His father seldom missed a chance to remind him of what he perceived to be Max's disloyalty when he left the farm to join the university staff years before. Even now, as they faced an uncertain period ahead, he stubbornly refused to understand his son's aspirations or at least to respect him for trying to achieve them.

'Under the circumstances, is it wise to be speaking German?' Max asked in a low voice.

'*Ja.* Because I have something to tell you and,' he nodded towards the soldiers, 'better to be sure.' He moved closer. 'I have a friend, a Dutchman. He captains a merchant ship. It is often in Port Adelaide. He can take us away.'

'To where?'

'To the Dutch East Indies. A neutral country.'

'And leave our home?'

There was a long pause.

'It is better than being thrown in prison.'

'You won't be thrown in prison. I know what this is about.'

'What is it?'

'Look at the others,' he said, indicating their fellow detainees. 'I'm pretty sure these men are all German-born.'

Rainer ran his eyes around the group. '*Ja*. Even Uncle Klaus.'

'Correct. And you and I were born here — an issue we can readily prove. So we have nothing to fear. They will keep us for a few days, then let us go.'

'What about Klaus? He is very German, and he's not well.'

Max looked at the frail old man. He suffered from diabetes and he could see his asthma was causing him to struggle for breath. 'I've heard men over seventy-five can be given some leniency. Maybe he'll get home detention.'

'Ah, but how can we arrange that?'

Max had a theory, but he wasn't prepared to expound it until he could test it. And he guessed the test would come soon enough.

CHAPTER 17

The Keswick Barracks sat behind a barbed-wire fence on the Glenelg road. When the Tanunda group arrived around midnight, it looked dark and foreboding as they were led to their dormitory. Now, in the bright morning sunshine, with the magpies warbling their morning songs, the mood in the barracks dormitory that accommodated them lifted. There was an air of unreality about it and some men even made jokes.

After a breakfast of bread and tea, delivered by a stony-faced kitchen orderly, a sergeant entered and explained they would be interviewed by an officer later in the day. Then he referred to a paper he took from his pocket.

'Maximilian Dinter?' he asked, running his eyes around the men.

'Yes?'

'You're to accompany me now.'

Max picked up his suit coat from his bunk and without a word, followed the soldier out into the grounds. They walked in silence to one of the offices in the administration block, where he was told to sit. The sergeant then left him there alone.

The sloping light of morning fell across the desk to the leather-covered chair. Along one wall was an empty bookcase. The straight-backed chair Max was using was the only other furniture item. Nothing hung on the walls and no personal items were anywhere on display. It was an office nobody used.

After he'd waited a quarter of an hour, the door opened behind him and Bennison from the university disclosure hearing came in, strolled around the desk and took his seat. He immediately began to polish the lenses of his glasses. An ID card hung from his lapel: *Interior Ministry. Special Investigations.*

When he was done with his specs, he rested his elbows on the desk and smiled the vaguely snide smile Max remembered from the hearing.

'I thought you might be behind this,' Max said.

'It's procedural.'

'Bullshit. I'm Australian-born. Even my father is Australian-born. You have no reason to detain us.'

Bennison smiled again and his eyes disappeared behind the reflected light of his spectacles.

'Perhaps, but the Act enables the government to detain people when a member of the public comes forwards with information about a person with a connection to the enemy.'

'That's rubbish. I have no connection with the enemy. Who's made those accusations?'

Bennison smiled, steepled his fingers and tapped them together. 'I'm afraid that's confidential.'

Max compressed his lips. It was an effort to control himself. He was playing games with him. Bennison knew he and his father were not foreign-born. It was a stunt designed to threaten him, in the same way that he'd concocted an allegation that there had been a sexual assault in his office. What Max didn't know, was *why*.

'Who are you?' he asked. 'Why were you at the hearing at the university and why are you hounding me now?'

'Don't flatter yourself. You're just one of many we are investigating.'

'*Special Investigations*,' Max said, referring to his pass. 'What does that mean?'

'It means I do what needs to be done. It means I make sure our war efforts at home are not compromised by the activities of unfriendly elements. In this case people like you and your lot, Mr Dinter.'

'My *lot*! I'm every bit as much an Australian as you.'

'I doubt that.' The smile returned. 'Let me get to the point,' he continued. 'It's really quite simple. We want your kind out of the public service and all government instrumentalities. The public are in a panic about an imminent invasion and they don't want any Schmidts or Schroeders in places of power. And they don't want any Dinters implanting foreign ideas in the minds of our best young people.'

'You're really stupid enough to believe that, aren't you?'

'Stupid am I? We'll see about that! Because I can tell you one thing, *Herr* Dinter: I'll get you thrown out of the university one way or another.'

It gave Max a moment of satisfaction to see that Bennison had finally lost his composure. 'If you think your enemy alien plan is going to get me to resign, you're more demented than I thought.'

Now back in control of his emotions, Bennison's maddening smile returned once again. 'It's served its purpose,' he said calmly. 'It has allowed us to have this little chat without the inconvenience of a witness or a record of our meeting.'

Max understood. There were probably no provisions for appeal or legal representation under the wartime Act. 'And what is it you feel such a burning desire to say? I've already told you I don't intend to quit the university because of your xenophobia.'

Bennison removed his glasses and paid great attention to them as he slowly cleaned them again. 'This little exercise is merely a preliminary. As you have guessed, I won't be able to hold you or your father for more than a few days. Maybe a fortnight. But I do want you to see our facility at Torrens Island, where your dear old Uncle Klaus will remain for the term of the war. I can assure you it has none of the comforts of Keswick. In winter the wind blows like the devil through the old quarantine station. In summer, it's an oven.'

Max remained silent.

Bennison sighed and sat back in his chair. 'Look here, Dinter, there's no need to make this harder than it need be. Sooner or later I'll get you thrown out of the university. You've already had one dubious situation involving a female student. We might unearth others. Understand? So face up to it. You have a lovely new fiancée. Why not resign and take the easy road?'

'What do you know about my fiancée?' Max snapped.

'Only that she's a very good-hearted girl. Didn't press charges against that poor wretch.'

'What are you talking about?'

'About the vagrant the police picked up at ...' Bennison paused and his irritating, self-satisfied smile spread. 'You don't know anything about the police involvement, do you?' He seemed genuinely surprised.

Max cursed himself for allowing Bennison into his mind but said nothing.

'It was the usual sweep through the parks for vagrants. They found a notebook in the coat pocket he wore and were able to trace her. But as I say, good-hearted. Even the Abo who stole her coat was impressed when she refused to press charges. She let the codger keep it. She said he probably needed it more than she did.' He shook his head in admiration. 'She said that if he'd asked, she would have let him have it. The only damage done was a chaffed neck where he dragged her scarf from her.'

Max couldn't contain himself. 'Are you saying there was no, no ... physical attack?'

'Of course it was physical,' Bennison said, then realised the implication behind the question. Again he smiled. 'You thought she was raped, didn't you?'

Max stared at him, trying to cover his discomfort.

'Well, now. Isn't that odd? Your fiancée has been keeping secrets from you.' Bennison tapped the desk with the end of his pencil. 'Why would she do that, do you suppose?'

Max reddened and felt like smashing his fist into Bennison's maddening smile.

'No doubt you're just dying to ask her that question, but it'll have to wait. First you go on a little holiday to Torrens Island.'

* * *

The old quarantine station on Torrens Island had served its purpose well. The bare concrete floors, stone walls and corrugated-iron roofs housed those afflicted by the occasional outbreak of typhoid, smallpox or measles during the previous century, but the station was completely inadequate as a concentration camp for hundreds of enemy aliens who were therefore accommodated in tents on the muddy banks of the Port River estuary.

A few days after the men from Tanunda arrived, the spring weather vanished and the notorious chilly southerlies blew through the canvas town, causing the internees to put on all their available clothes in an attempt to keep warm. When the wind dropped, the air off the mud flats was rank.

In Max's tent, which he shared with a dozen others, he and his father did their best to protect Uncle Klaus from the worst of the chill, but the old man's asthma worsened alarmingly. Each breath demanded a fearful struggle and his lips turned blue.

The family's efforts to have the two Australian-born Dinter men released proved fruitful at last, but Uncle Klaus's case for home detention was denied. The ministry refused to give a reason.

Max was in no doubt about the reason, and the day after his release he went to the Interior Ministry's offices in town.

His resignation letter to Adelaide University was awaiting his signature on Bennison's desk.

Two days later, Uncle Klaus came home.

* * *

It had been a very difficult time for Liz since Max, his father and uncle were taken into custody. She and the Dinter family were consumed by efforts to secure their release. Obtaining access to the appropriate government department seemed impossible. Nobody in authority would accept responsibility for investigating their case. When they finally found the right department, they were repeatedly sent away in search of more and more obscure paperwork to prove birth date, place of birth, marriage dates, proof of ownership of their property. Just as they were at their wits' end, the two men were released.

A few days after arriving back in Tanunda, Liz and Max took the train to Adelaide together. He said he had some business to conduct in town. At her suggestion, they went to the tea house that had been their favourite haunt when she was attending university classes. During this he announced he was quitting his position at the university.

His news stunned her. He had been quite passionate about his profession whenever they discussed his work. His decision to become an academic had incurred the wrath of his father, but he stood up to him to defend the life he'd chosen.

'But Max, this has been your life. Why do you want to quit?'

He paused for a long moment. He didn't meet her eyes. 'It's time to try something different.'

'I see ... Do you have something else in mind?'

'No. Not at the moment.'

She asked him if he wanted to rejoin the family business on the land as his father had always hoped. Max said he was still thinking about it.

Struggling to get an insight into this turn of events, Liz asked him if something had happened to make him reconsider his profession.

'I really don't want to talk about it,' he said. 'I've made up my mind.'

Liz was upset that he had chosen to exclude her from such a big decision — a decision that had implications for both their lives — but was obliged to respect his wish. It was obvious there was something preying on his mind, and she wondered if it had anything to do with his false imprisonment on Torrens Island.

He said he needed time to establish himself in a new job outside his career as an academic, and suggested they defer their marriage until he was back on his feet.

'Yes, Max. Of course. If that's what you think you need to do.'

'It's only for a short time.'

'How long do you think?'

He shrugged. 'I don't know. Maybe a couple of months. There are plenty of opportunities around.'

He thought it best he stay in Adelaide, so Liz went back to Joseph's Creek to stay with his parents, feeling confused and a little lost. She tried to understand, but realised she knew very little about this man or his personality and moods.

* * *

Liz remained unsettled over the schism between her and her grandmother. Harriet was family, and she had precious little of that remaining. She decided to make a final attempt to heal the wounds when she returned to collect the remainder of her belongings.

Max borrowed his cousin's car and drove Liz to Adelaide on an overcast Saturday morning. When he rounded the corner at Childers Street, Liz asked that he park at the end of the block.

'Are you ashamed of your fiancé?' he asked.

'Of course not, Max. But I've told you about Grandmother. If you come in, it will only make matters worse.'

Max remained silent and tight-lipped. Liz patted his hand and climbed out of the T-Model.

The street was very familiar, but now seemed so very different. She paused for a moment at the picket fence, before summoning her courage. She swung open the creaking gate and walked up the short path through the arum lilies to the veranda. Her heels clunked noisily on the tessellated tiles until, standing at the solid timber door, she lifted the heavy brass lion's-head knocker and knocked. The sound echoed inside the house.

She could hear her grandmother's familiar tread approaching. Liz quickly pressed the lace collar on her navy-and-white dress into place, rearranged her handbag on her arm, clasped her hands in front of her, and tried to calm herself.

The door opened a crack, then the gap widened, but Harriet's face was obscured behind the flyscreen door. The silence was more foreboding than anything her grandmother might have said. Eventually, Liz spoke.

'Hello, Grandmother.'

'Hello, Elizabeth.'

The face behind the screen door remained unreadable.

'I have come to collect the remainder of my things ... May I come in?'

The door opened and Liz followed her grandmother down the

hall to the sitting room. Once seated, she said, 'I'm sorry we have had a disagreement, Grandmother. I've come to say I'm sorry that things have turned out so badly, and I'd like to settle the differences between us.'

Harriet's lips were drawn tight. 'Settle the differences, you say. How can I forget what you've done?'

'But, what have I done, other than accept a man's proposal of marriage?'

'You know what I mean. But if you wish, I can remind you of the outrages being committed on innocents by Hun soldiers. I've read reports of mutilation and rape. One witness saw a mob of ill-bred German soldiers —'

'Grandmother, I don't think we need hear those stories again.'

'Of course not. You don't want to consider the truth, do you?'

Liz sighed. There was no point in attempting to find common ground. Her grandmother was too bitter. She stood and headed towards the hall and the suitcase in her bedroom.

'Elizabeth.'

Liz turned back to her grandmother.

'When you were leaving ... Something I said was ... I mean ... I shouldn't have said you're just like your mother. You're not. You're neither silly nor stupid. I withdraw that comment.'

Liz swallowed.

'And if you're as clever as I think you are, you'll see the folly of your plans and renege on your engagement.'

Liz turned to leave.

'Wait. If you do, I shall pay your ticket back to your mother. In Africa.'

Liz walked to her bedroom, took her suitcase to the door, then quietly closed it behind her.

* * *

Max sat in the T-Model with his head back and eyes closed. He could feel his temples throbbing. The smoke tendrils from his cigarette curled around him before drifting out into Childers Street while the bitter thoughts of the injustice of his detention stayed with him in the car.

Torrens Island concentration camp held over three hundred farmers, tradesmen, teachers, Lutheran pastors and other German and Austro-Hungarian men who had overnight become enemy aliens. Under the powers of the *War Precautions Act* the authorities could search homes, confiscate property, make arrests and hold people without trial. It also enabled the government to close Lutheran schools, churches and German-language newspapers, of which there were several to service the thirty-five thousand ethnic Germans in South Australia.

Max had spent only eight days behind the barbed-wire fences on the low-river mud flats, but it was cause enough for him to question his country's treatment of people outside Australia's British core. The Dinters had been accepted members of the community while things were going smoothly, but as soon as a threat arose, the herd began to distrust anyone who was not one of *them*. He and his family were suddenly pushed to the fringes of the society that had previously embraced them. They were considered security risks. They were increasingly harassed by nationalistic neighbours who had formerly been close friends. His parents were now talking about moving away from their life and livelihood. Although Bennison had a particular purpose in mind for persecuting Max and others like him, he was able to do so because the prevailing climate permitted it. His growing anger was made worse by the fact that he was powerless to strike out against it.

His detention also gave him time to think about the personal matters that had dominated his mind since learning the truth of Elizabeth's attack in the park. He repeatedly revisited the conversation they'd had in his office shortly after the event, trying to discover how he'd assumed she had been raped. He searched his memory for clues. He couldn't recall exactly what Elizabeth had said, but he clearly recalled she had implied she'd been sexually assaulted. Had she intended to mislead him and, if so, why? It was important to get some answers. Protecting her from a painful inquisition over her attack had led indirectly to his resignation from his university posting.

When he learned the truth from Bennison, Max had felt almost relieved. But when he thought about the following dramatic events that could have been avoided if he'd known the truth of the situation, he became angry. Now the outcome was irreversible: he'd resigned.

No matter how he tried, he couldn't put out of his mind the thought that Elizabeth was somehow responsible for what had happened. Had she been scheming to trick him into marrying her? Was it all a fabric of her imagination, or was her grandmother really prejudiced against people of German stock? The old lady had seemed friendly enough towards him. Maybe her grandmother wanted her out of her house for some other reason and Elizabeth latched onto him for security?

He shook the unworthy thoughts from his head. He was becoming unhinged with all the problems that were piling up against him.

The heat from the diminishing cigarette irritated his nostrils, and he carefully extracted the butt between thumb and forefinger and tossed it into the street.

Elizabeth was approaching down Childers Street, her big leather suitcase bumping her legs, making it awkward for her to walk. He swung out of the car and took the bag.

'How was it?' he asked, as he threw her bag into the tray back of the T-Model.

'Awful. Just awful,' she said.

Max leaned through the driver's side window and set the choke control. Then he went to the front of the car with the crank handle and gave it a brisk spin. The motor sputtered into life. Returning to the driver's seat, he adjusted the fuel mix and tossed the crank behind the seat.

'She can't accept the fact that we're to be married,' Elizabeth added.

'Hmmph.'

'She even tried to bribe me into accepting a ticket home to Africa if I called the wedding off.'

Max tightened the set of his jaw. His head pounded. He shot a glance over his shoulder and released the handbrake allowing the T-Model to shudder from the kerb.

'Do you want to go home to see your mother?'

'Mother and I are not as close as I'd like us to be. But yes, I would like to see her one day. Perhaps after we're married and I've completed my degree.'

Her degree was a matter that had been on his mind. Now that his connection with the university had been so callously and abruptly ended, he wanted her to have nothing more to do with the place. Regardless of that, he wasn't happy with the prospect of his young wife continuing to mingle with flighty young university students. She should be at his side, working to ensure their future.

'Why do you want to complete your degree? We'll be married soon. You won't have any need of a degree.'

Liz was silent.

Max turned to her to see if she'd heard him.

She was staring at him, open-mouthed.

'What?' he asked.

'Max, I'm stunned. You of all people. You know the value of an education. You know how important it is to me that I complete my studies. I've been working towards my qualifications for three years.'

'Qualifications! The only qualifications you'll need are in housekeeping and child-raising.'

CHAPTER 18

Max sat on the edge of the bed, staring at his fist pressed into the palm of his hand. His headache had not abated in days as he struggled with his feelings about Elizabeth.

He was also worried that his parents were still considering leaving their farm to find relief from the hostility within their community. The vineyard had been in their family for three generations and its success had been hard-won. Abandoning it because of prejudice was unthinkable.

He stood and lit another Capstan, which he hoped would relieve his headache. His whole body seemed to have become locked by the same frustration that had driven him to return to his small Adelaide flat rather than remain in Tanunda.

He'd told Elizabeth that he wanted to stay in Adelaide to search for a suitable position in the city. That was only part of the reason. He just couldn't deal with situations he could see no way of resolving.

He'd had no luck with the applications for jobs advertised in the situations vacant columns. His strong suspicion was that prospective employers avoided him because of his surname.

The walls of his flat became oppressively restrictive, so he stubbed out his cigarette and headed to the door.

The midday streets were busy with shoppers and office workers on their meal breaks. Max tried to find relief from his misery by gazing into shop windows, but everywhere were posters reminding the population of the wartime situation.

The most benign were those that targeted the older generation emphasising the need to contribute to the war effort: *The Road to Victory. War Loan Bonds — Buy Them Now!* Another depicted a small blonde girl clutching a war bond to her chest with the caption: *My Daddy bought me a WAR LOAN BOND, did yours?*

The posters that had always captured his eye, and that had the most compelling messages, were those directed at his generation. *Australia has promised Britain 50,000 more men. Will YOU help us keep that Promise?*

Other posters tried to stimulate enlistment by playing on people's fears of an imminent invasion by a savage and godless enemy. They were intended to stir emotions, and the one that showed a sub-human monster wearing a German helmet, reaching for a world spattered with blood, stirred Max's emotions to boiling. He blamed this form of propaganda for the emergence of the hatred that was now turning former friends against his parents and driving them from their home.

A new poster caught his eye. It was produced by the *Win the War League* and depicted two images of a young man. In the first, he was in uniform, proudly marching into battle. In the second, the same young man was shown sitting with a book. On the table beside him was a foaming glass of beer. A tennis racket rested against his chair. The caption read: *Which picture would Your father like to show his friends?*

It was crude but very clever, and it sparked an idea: what would happen if he attempted to sign up? When he was rejected because of his family's connection with the enemy, his parents could use the rejection papers to prove their son had at least made a noble attempt to fulfil his patriotic duty.

It just might cause a few of their neighbours to remember that the Dinters were loyal Australians trying to do the honourable thing.

* * *

A bleary-eyed sergeant opened the recruitment hall doors from within and seemed mildly surprised to find Max standing there. He looked him up and down without a word before turning on his heels to resume his routine.

When he came to his desk after raising the blinds, emptying the waste receptacle into a large black bin and opening a couple of windows, Max was sitting in the chair opposite him. The older man glanced at him again, this time with a slight frown, then pulled a sheaf of papers from a drawer and arranged all his pencils and pens before him.

He was a beefy man, too large for his uniform jacket. His reddish hair fitted his splotchy freckled skin. When it appeared he was about to speak, he stood and removed his khaki jacket, which he hung on a nail behind his desk.

'Now,' he said, deftly lifting up the slack of his sleeves. 'What do you want, young fella?'

'I'm here to sign up.'

'Well, bugger me!' he said with mock surprise. 'Anyone would think this was an army recruitment office.'

'I beg your pardon?'

'Infantry, mounted or artillery?' he asked impatiently.

'Um, I don't care. I mean, I thought you would decide.'

He thrust a hairy hand across the table, gesturing at Max's folder. 'Papers.'

Max rummaged in his folder, unwilling to risk asking what particular papers the sergeant wanted. He produced his birth certificate, driver's licence and degree.

The recruitment man shuffled through the papers.

'Dinter.'

Max stiffened, his prepared response on the tip of his tongue. When the sergeant remained silent, he said, 'I'm an Australian.'

The sergeant lifted an eyebrow at him. 'I don't care if you're a bloody Zulu. I'll sign anyone up.' He flicked to the next document.

Max felt cheated of his opportunity to vent. 'Even a German?' he asked antagonistically, now beyond caring whether he annoyed the army man. He was itching for a fight about principles.

'Even a German. So long as he's a resident of the country.'

With a shock, Max realised he was serious. He sat, stunned, as the sergeant completed his inspection of his papers.

'Can't help you, Dinter.'

Ah, here it comes, he thought. 'And why not?'

'A uni graduate. You smartarses have to go to HQ. Gotta see the captain.'

When Max remained seated, trying to understand, the recruitment officer went on, 'Officer material. Apparently.' His expression clearly indicated what he thought of the policy.

He slid the papers back to him.

Max slowly returned them to his folder as he collected his thoughts. This was an amazing turn of events. Unexpected, but very pleasing. He would not only be accepted into the army, he might even win a commission as an officer. It would make it doubly certain to stifle the anti-German sentiment directed at his family.

He rose, pushing his chair back with a creak on the polished floor.

Nodding to the sergeant, he walked towards the door.

'And Dinter ...'

He turned back to the sergeant.

'I'd think about using a different name if I was you.'

* * *

His letters always made her heart jump. Liz was never quite sure why. Perhaps it was the African postmark. It evoked memories of her time in the thickly wooded slopes outside Nairobi where the days burst into life a moment after the dawn, and the mornings grew hot and golden until by noon it was time to crawl into a shady place and read or sleep or just share your thoughts with whomever was near. Often it was Dan, who would plop himself down beside her and talk. She couldn't remember many of the conversations, but her favourites were about his adventures in the bush. Her only stipulation was that he mustn't include the parts where animals were hurt. It continued to distress her. So in Dan's stories the lions, cheetahs, rhinos and others always escaped to fight another day.

Or it might have been the way he addressed the envelope in his untidy scrawl — so emblematic of Dan himself — easy-going; unconcerned by convention; possibly even challenging it at times:

Miss Elizabeth Freeman,
Somewhere in the University of Adelaide.
South Australia.
Australia.

The letter had found its way to Joseph's Creek thanks to the diligence of the university's registrar.

She took it to the first gate and sat on the broad rough-sawn railing in the shade of the gum. On the reverse side, where the flap of the envelope sealed it closed, were the initials: *SWAK*. It always made her smile. She had learned the secret of the initials shortly after arriving at boarding school. One of the other twelve-year-olds — a girl who already had breasts — had a boyfriend who added the initials to his envelopes. Everyone thought it very daring, and Liz, not wanting to admit her special friend was more like a big brother, adopted the ritual. Dan had obligingly followed suit, and long after Liz had tired of the game, he had habitually continued to do so.

15th October 1914
 Dear Lizzie,
 I hope this finds you as the mail has been very tricky since the war began.
 Things around here are much the same although some parts of life have changed. Business is very slow. I closed the office to save money. I still have the postbox so you can still send letters there.
 We don't get the English newspapers until much later these days.
 The banks are even harder to deal with since the war in Europe started. But all this is business and I should not bother you with such matters.
 How are things over there in Australia? Is it still the same? The war is so far from where you are that I imagine people are not at all interested in the goings-on in the old country.

I saw your mother in Nairobi a few weeks ago. She was with her husband but I did not speak to her. They seemed to be in a hurry. She looks to be in good health. You never mention her. Does she write to you?

How is your grandmother doing? The winters must be cold in South Australia. Even the Darling Downs was cold in winter. Not like here except for July in the highlands. You probably remember it was a little bit cold in Limuru too.

Well, that is all for now. I will await your next letter and hope you are happy and well until then.

Your old friend

Dan

She slipped the letter back inside the envelope.

SWAK.

She missed his lazy smile and sympathetic ear, particularly at times like these, when her world was in turmoil and she felt she had no one to turn to.

Sealed With A Kiss.

She smiled.

* * *

Max read his commission statement again and smiled grimly. Having fortuitously discovered that he could enlist, he had embraced the idea enthusiastically. His only regret was that he hadn't known earlier that it was possible. It might have spared his parents from the ire of their neighbours. And he might even have preserved his position in the university until his demobilisation. Returned soldiers would surely be given first options on any jobs. Although that possibility remained a faint one, his position in the armed forces and his imminent departure for the Holy Land did solve another troubling concern.

He'd been unable to reconcile Elizabeth's behaviour in the affair of the supposed brutal attack with her behaviour since. Consequently he'd been having second thoughts about his hasty proposal of marriage.

Most people agreed peace would come quickly, but hopefully not before he was able to have a short stint overseas. It would give him time to reconsider his decision. If, in his mind, he was able to forgive her for her deception after that time, then they might be married as planned.

On the other hand, should he change his mind then surely a man returning from the trauma of war could be forgiven for having a change of heart.

* * *

Max arrived on the Friday morning train. Liz met him at the Tanunda station in the T-Model with his cousin. They always felt awkward showing affection when other family members were around, so Max refrained from embracing her. But on this occasion he remained more than usually quiet on the journey to Joseph's Creek.

Even after cousin Henk departed, Max took some time to return from his room, only emerging to be with her an hour before dinnertime.

It was Max's manner to slowly lead into serious matters, so as they strolled around the vineyards Liz waited patiently for him to raise whatever it was that he had on his mind. Eventually, while casually plucking unwanted suckers from the canes, he broached the topic that had been bothering him.

'Elizabeth ... I have something to tell you, but first, I have a question. The incident in the park, while on your way home from our meeting.'

'Yes?'

'I understand the police were involved.'

'Yes, they were.'

'I didn't know that.'

'No. Well, we've only really discussed it that once.' She looked at her boots in the dirt. 'I'm sorry. I haven't wanted to talk about it again. Even after the police came to me.'

'Perhaps. But it was fortunate that the incident wasn't a lot worse.'

'How can you say that? It was ghastly.'

'But not ghastly enough to take it to the police yourself in the first instance.'

'Max, what is this about? You're being callous and awful.'

'Why did you mislead me into believing the attack was something it wasn't?'

'I didn't mislead you. I don't know what —'

'If I had known it wasn't rape, I would have —'

'*Rape?* How did you ever come to that conclusion?'

'Well, I couldn't just ask you straight out. But if I'd known it was only an assault I would have made you go to the police.'

Liz bridled, her anger now flaring into life.

'*Only* an assault? May I remind you that it was I who was attacked? It was my decision to report it or not. You're not my father, Max, no matter how you appear to have assumed that position. You have no right to order me to do anything. And what do you mean *mislead you*? How dare you suggest I would? What must you *think* of me, to imagine I could tell such a lie? And what makes you think you can make choices about my life? Or prevent me from completing my degree for that matter.'

Max, white with rage, tightened his lips, then turned around and stormed towards the house.

* * *

A strained, brittle politeness existed between them through Saturday. They joined Rainer and Johanna tending the vines in the late afternoon. While the older Dinters were present they tried to act normally, but when they were alone, their conversations were brief and clipped.

On Sunday they went for a picnic on the river with family members and, after they joined the children in a boisterous football game, the tension between them eased.

Back at Joseph's Creek later in the afternoon, Max sat with Liz on the veranda.

'I need to tell you I'm going back to Adelaide tomorrow.'

The original plan had been for him to spend a few days at Joseph's Creek with her.

'I'm sorry for making a scene on Friday,' he added.

'I apologise for losing my temper.'

'I had intended to tell you something, but as it transpired, I didn't get to it. It's about our future. As you know, I've been looking for a suitable position, but with no luck. So I started thinking about a matter that has been on my mind for some time. I feel people are wondering why I'm not doing something about the war. And I think it would help my family if I could show I am. You know how badly they're taking the harassment from some of the Britishers around here. You may not know it, but we German-Australians can enlist.'

He glanced at her.

'Yes,' he continued. 'I was surprised too. I wish I'd known. It might have … Anyway, I'm sorry that I haven't consulted with you on this, but it was a conscience matter. I've signed up.'

It took a moment for the meaning to penetrate. She'd been too distracted by the odd feeling of remoteness that now existed between them. He was talking to her as if they were business partners.

'I will be joining my company in a few days. They've been training together for weeks. I expect we'll be embarking for the front fairly soon. Given this turn of events, I couldn't hold you to our engagement. After all, it's a war. Things happen. Naturally, I hope we can remain committed to one another, so that when I return, well … we can pick up where we left off.'

The remainder of his speech was lost in a host of thoughts. She thought she should have been distraught, but she wasn't. Deferring their engagement gave her a sense of relief, as if she had been granted additional time to complete a difficult exam paper.

'Of course, you can wait out my absence here.'

'Here? With your family?'

'My dear Elizabeth, but where else will you stay? Unless you want to return to your grandmother's house.'

The many repercussions of her choices now came flooding over her. She had no home. Returning to Childers Street was not an option. Anyway, she could imagine that Max would consider it the height of disloyalty if she did.

'No, Max, I won't be returning to my grandmother's house.'

But neither can I live here with your family, she thought. Oh, what am I to do?

* * *

Lieutenant Max Dinsdale stood at the rail of HMAT *Hymettus*, drew deeply on his cigarette, then flicked it deftly overboard. He watched the red tip fall through darkness and vanish in the troopship's swell as she surged through the blue-black waters of the Indian Ocean.

Max Dinsdale. It had been so easy to enlist under an assumed name; Max couldn't help but be amused by the pliability of the officers' recruitment process. He was Max Dinter of Joseph's Creek, Tanunda, but by some strange osmosis he was able to serve under the name of Dinsdale. It suited his purposes perfectly.

Now he was travelling with his new battalion to the Middle East to fight the enemy. They would join with the 9th, 11th and 12th battalions, to form the AIF's 3rd Brigade.

Max had started this escapade with what he now recognised as less than noble objectives, but was amazed at how good it felt to be accepted as a member of a team — the Fighting 10th — all proud South Australians. Even during the few weeks of training he'd found the camaraderie to be hugely uplifting. With his new identity he was soon able to forget his concerns about his German heritage.

Max Dinsdale had none of the anxieties of Max Dinter.

* * *

Liz stood at the stern of the SS *Oosterhout*, her silk shawl wrapped around her shoulders, watching the lights of Port Adelaide disappear behind her. Somewhere on the wharf, now lost in darkness, was her grandmother.

When Liz had made her decision to leave Australia, she went to Harriet with a proposition. Her grandmother remained civil but reserved while Liz explained that in return for a loan to buy a ticket to British East Africa, she would assist her on her war work for three months.

'A loan, you say,' Harriet said sceptically. 'If you and your fiancé want to run away to Africa, why doesn't he pay your fare?'

Liz hadn't wanted to reveal her changed circumstances, but she now had no choice. 'Max will not be travelling with me. Our engagement has been called off.'

Harriet's mood brightened. 'Oh! Well,' she said, folding her arms triumphantly, 'I must say, I'm pleased you've finally listened to some good advice.'

Liz resisted the urge to inform her grandmother that her advice had nothing to do with it.

'And there's no need for you to work for the loan. I don't think you should delay your departure a moment longer. This war may soon come sweeping down on us, and you'll miss your chance to get away.'

Liz thought it more likely that her grandmother was more focussed on consolidating the separation rather than worried about the enemy arriving on their doorstep overnight. 'Thank you, Grandmother. I may take a little time to repay the loan, but I will as soon as possible. Grandpa's safari company is still running.'

'I told you when Bill died, I have no interest in a safari company.'

'What I mean is, I should be able to get a good price for it and repay you.'

'As you wish. So far as I'm concerned, it's yours to do with as you please.'

Liz departed feeling relieved that there'd been a reconciliation of sorts, and even more relieved to be able to use some of her money for lodgings until she sailed. Regardless of how friendly Johanna and others were, continuing to live under the Dinters' roof had become very awkward for her.

The *Oosterhout*'s horn sounded a mournful farewell to the port. With its cargo of wheat and wool, she was bound for Batavia, where

Liz would then take a ship of the British India Steam Navigation Company to the port of Mombasa in East Africa.

It was a consolation that her grandmother had actually shed a tear as Liz boarded. She had been in Adelaide for ten years and it was the first sign that her grandmother actually cared about her. Liz had cried too.

Max had already sailed to the Middle East when a brief note arrived from him. It was friendly but formal. He wished her well in Africa.

When she spoke shortly afterwards with Johanna Dinter there was no mistaking the pride in her voice, though she was clearly anxious about her son too. The almost daily reports of young Australian men dying in faraway places with barely pronounceable names were distressing.

Liz worried too: Max had been dear to her and, despite his recent show of hostility, she hated to think of him wounded or worse. Until his troubles, his hurtful accusations and his insistence that she bow to his demands regarding her life, his obvious love and devotion had given her a great deal of happiness. Now she wasn't sure that feeling could ever be restored. The test would come at the end of the war. If Max wanted to renew their relationship, he knew where to find her. Until then, she would have to assume his decision to break off their engagement had more to do with his diminished feelings for her than with his enlistment. And to consider herself entirely free of obligation to him.

Now even the port's lights were gone and the inky waters reflecting the navigation lamps in the ship's wake drew her eye out to where the depressing black ocean met the equally solemn sky.

Liz felt as though she was the only person in the universe, and a shudder ran down her back. She had cast herself adrift with not so much as a thought of how she would cope in Africa. Somewhere she had a mother, remarried and now living in quite different circumstances. Would she be welcomed? Indeed, could she even find her?

At the back of her mind there was Dan. As always. He had been her most constant link with her life in Africa. But it had been so long since they'd seen each other: she wondered how he might react to her request for assistance should things not work out with her mother.

But it was too late to reconsider. Africa was now the only home she had.

PART 3
DAN

CHAPTER 1

1915

Dan was carried along by the crowd cramming into the Theatre Royal. Inside the great hall with its Grecian columns and ornate plaster of Paris ceilings, he was immediately confronted by the heat and odour of the crowd. Fifteen hundred excited people, their gabbling voices filling the auditorium, waited in high expectation for the night's event to commence.

The most important day in the history of the protectorate, had proclaimed the *East African* that morning. It wasn't the usual patriotic palaver that had drawn him to the building on Sixth Avenue, though, but concern that the matters to be addressed that evening would put further strains on the operation of his safari business.

The article in the *East African* hinted that the main speaker would address the need to take more drastic actions if Britain was to win the war. The number of clients coming from traditional sources — the titled and moneyed classes of Europe — had declined, either due to straitened circumstances or in deference to the war. Dan was concerned that the measures mooted in the newspaper might cause his remaining clientele — rich Americans, many of whom thought the war merely a European skirmish of little consequence to their lives — to abandon their passion for hunting in Africa.

The brass band that had mercifully paused as he entered the auditorium struck up a rousing rendition of 'Yankee Doodle' as the unmistakeable three hundred and seventy pounds of Northrup McMillan clambered laboriously up the steps and through the red, white and blue bunting that festooned the edge of the stage.

He dabbed a white cotton handkerchief to his sweating forehead, and raised his hands to quieten the cheering, whistling crowd.

He pulled a page of notes from his coat pocket.

'General Tighe and staff,' he bellowed in his slightly Yankee accent. 'Senior government administrators, Nairobi councillors, ladies and gentlemen. Tonight we are honoured to have a great local identity and member of our armed forces share with us his thoughts on the war and how it affects us all here in Nairobi and the protectorate at large.' His smile encompassed everyone in the theatre. 'You all know this gentleman very well, I'm sure. Down in Mombasa his port delivers goods that eventually arrive on your tables; he probably supplied the timber used to construct your house. Who knows? He might even *own* your bloody house!'

A howl of laughter filled the theatre.

'But that is not meant to make light of the reason we are meeting here tonight. Ladies and gentlemen, our special speaker is a man who, at the tender age of twenty-two, went off to fight the fierce Ndebele with Mr Cecil Rhodes. He acquitted himself admirably in that conflict, nearly giving his life for the cause. But a little later he came to our attention as Cape-to-Cairo Grogan — a man who braved countless miles of savage country for no other purpose than to serve his empire, his sovereign and his country. A man who at twenty-four years of age conquered the continent of Africa for these ideals; ideals that he still holds most dearly.' He paused to draw breath, and to let the suspense build, before flinging a hand towards the front row and crying, 'Please welcome Captain Ewart Scott Grogan!'

The band struck up a military march as Grogan, wearing his captain's uniform with its braids and decorations, made his way to the stage. The fire-proof curtain went up, revealing a huge Union Jack suspended high above his head.

Dan looked around the theatre. There was not a space remaining, and the doors had been closed to keep more punters outside and prevent a dangerous crush. Those who had been unable to enter clung to the frames of windows that had been opened to cool the air, trying to get a view of the proceedings.

Grogan was in no hurry to silence the crowd, who were on their feet, cheering and applauding. Dan had to admire his sense of timing. The speaker waited until the theatre fell into total silence and then allowed the tension to build even more before commencing.

'Ladies and gentlemen. Fellow countrymen. My friends. I am here today to speak of honour. And duty, and ... empire.

'First, let me tell you we are in a period of our history when the very fabric of our way of life teeters on a knife-edge. Across the border,' he gestured towards the south, 'no more than one hundred and fifty miles away, lies the enemy. He is powerful. He is cunning. He is hell-bent on destroying your life and mine. Why? Because he knows that if he can destroy the protectorate — one small element of this great empire of ours — it will send a tremor through His Majesty's entire realm. If one pole or beam of our mighty British Empire falls, it imperils the stability of the whole structure.

'I come here tonight to speak to you, my friends. I am talking to you, Mr Administrator, Mr Trader, and you, Mr Settler.'

He paused, his pointed finger sweeping the auditorium and his pale blue eyes glaring as if to capture each eye in turn. 'Many have done what is expected of them. In that I include our men in uniform, both black and white, who are prepared to make the ultimate sacrifice for the empire. But there are others who do not do enough. I go so far as to say that every man and woman in this protectorate of ours can do more.'

Again he paused, as if daring anyone to disagree. The silence was profound.

'We must put this country on a proper war footing. The measures we propose cannot deliver victory of their own accord. Nothing has been achieved in the long history of our empire without the sweat and muscle of people such as yourselves.' Again he swept his arm around the theatre. 'And again it is to you — the sturdy stock of the empire — to whom we must turn if we are to seize victory. We must mobilise every able-bodied man to the cause. We must liberate the power within our numbers. There can be no exceptions. Everyone has a part to play. The answer is universal conscription.'

The roar of general acclaim meant that conscription, which had been soundly condemned only months before, had become popular. It indicated to Dan that the country was now motivated by either fear or patriotic fervour to support it, and that his determination to avoid the conflict would now be particularly tested.

'I say we should all play our part in this war. By that I mean our full part. Any one of you can walk into a club or pub in this town, and I dare say in any other part of the protectorate, and see a half-dozen young blades sitting with a beer at their elbow and an illustrated newspaper in their lap.

'Or you can take a stroll up the hill,' he pointed in the direction of Nairobi Hill, where most of the grand houses looked down on the town, 'among the elite and well-to-do and find a host of pretty gardens and tennis courts. You will ask yourself, no doubt, what is all this nonsense about a war? For you will see no sign of it up there. Oh, no.

'Government offices are populated by men on fine salaries, but doing nothing to help the war effort. I feel, and I think you will agree, that this is no time for slacking, for penny-ha'penny bits of business and pottering about in gardens. This is no time for tea parties and silly games. *We are at war!*'

The crowd leaped from their seats, shouting, whistling and stamping their feet.

Grogan encouraged them as his eyes glistened in the stage lights. 'I met a young man on the street who said he had a farm to run. He said that it was the government's job to run the war. I told him his outlook was that of a rabbit. But not even a wild rabbit who takes its chances in the bush with the daily battle to survive, but a white rabbit who sits in its cage waiting for someone to bring it a lettuce.'

Dan imagined that Grogan appeared to stare directly at him.

'Many men do their best,' continued Grogan, 'but we must remember this is a war like no other. There is no warrior class. There is no settler's class. We are all British subjects. We stand or fall together.

'We will win this war by the efforts of all people in the protectorate. We cannot allow the situation to arise where one man stays home to make money, while the men at the front do battle for a shilling a day.

'The War Council will keep us to the task. Our first duty is to our self-respect. We are members of a proud fighting race — the British race. We will brook no interference in our way of life. We will cleanse this country of the invader.'

His last words were barely audible over the building applause. He pressed on.

'When it's time for history to make its decision ... When the gentle folk of this generation and the next ask for an account of our stewardship ... Or when you stand before your God long after the dust has settled on the battlefield ... And when your children ask, "Daddy, what did you do in the war?" Let no man dare answer in any other way than to say: "I fought for the British Empire. And we won!"'

Grogan took a swallow from his water glass before the crowd surged to the stage and carried him shoulder high around the theatre.

Dan knew his days of running Freeman Safaris were numbered. He would either have to sign up for service, or be conscripted. Exposure as a deserter from another, more distant conflict appeared inevitable.

* * *

Dan stood outside the recruitment hall looking at its walls plastered with posters of young men waving the Union Jack. His conscience troubled him. He was no longer a naive boy of sixteen, but under different circumstances he would feel stirred to defend his adopted country against invasion from German East Africa. However, there was the matter of his service record and he suspected the military had a long memory for deserters.

His choices were obvious, but would it be better to enlist or wait to be conscripted? He retired to Wood's to nurse a draught lager and consider his options.

He sipped his beer and watched a group of young men striding boldly towards the station. They wore the uniform of the East Africa Mounted Rifles, recently formed from a motley collection of volunteer groups consisting of clerks, storekeepers, prospectors, elephant poachers, train drivers and many more. Dan knew of at least one white hunter among their ranks and decided he would rather volunteer than be called up.

At thirty-one, and having spent more than a dozen years learning bush skills, he felt he had more to offer than mindlessly following orders that made no sense. He had the experience and expertise to make a real contribution, but knew that a foot soldier had little control over where and how he would serve.

In the heady early days of the war there had been a rush to enlist. Men left their farms, barely bothering to put their affairs in order, leaving their womenfolk to pick up the pieces — to organise labour, pay wages and make sense of the finances. Up in the wild reaches of the Uasin Gishu almost the entire membership of the male farming community embarked *en masse*, arriving at Nairobi station girded with bandoliers of ammunition and bearing rifles of several diverse and ancient varieties.

Dan took another sip of his beer. He knew what he must do, but his fear of exposure remained.

Before enlisting, he decided to make use of the single elephant licence he still held. On his last safari the weather had turned bad and it was impossible to track the herd through the mire. His client had returned home with little to show for his money. The tusks, should he be lucky enough to bag a pair, would help to settle the last of his outstanding accounts.

A few days later, Dan put together a small safari and headed northwest. Around noon the line of porters arrived at the edge of the escarpment, and Dan stood to one side as the headman led them on their snaking descent into the Great Rift Valley, two thousand feet below. Dan could never move beyond that point, where the great chasm first appeared through the low windswept scrub, without first pausing to acknowledge the majesty of the sight.

Seeing him pause, Korok stopped too, but Dan waved him on. Contemplating the vastness of the valley was something he preferred to do alone.

His eyes ran over the broad belly of the rift, stretching through a shimmer of heat for forty miles before the distant wall of the Mau arose, smudged with purple forest and topped with wispy clouds. The valley floor wore the silver-green hues of the *leleshwa*, a plant favoured by the Maasai for its softness on the skin and pleasant camphor scent. Here and there were the cadavers of ancient volcanoes whose slopes resembled the creases on an old man's weather-beaten neck. Between those peaks where, thousands of years before, rivers of molten lava flowed, were the olive-green pinpoints of umbrella acacia trees. A patchwork of dark shadows scurried across this pale canvas as fluffy clouds made haste towards the far horizon.

The porters were out of sight beyond the escarpment's abrupt edge, but their melodious, sometimes melancholy voices came drifting up on the thermal eddies, adding poignancy to the rugged beauty. Carried on their song was also the scent of dry grass, hot earth and the slightest hint of decaying vegetation.

Here was the Africa he'd grown to love: rugged, wide, unchanged for millennia and yet never the same. In many respects it reminded him of Australia's outback with its big sky, drawing the eye insistently towards an indistinct blue haze on the horizon. The Great Rift Valley moved him in ways he couldn't explain. The vision transported him back through time to the very gates of the Garden of Eden, to witness the unfolding of a great narrative. His heart lurched at the thought of what the machinery of war might inflict upon this magnificent panorama with its desecrating wheel marks of cannon, its barbed wire, its blood and its hellish noise.

He sighed and reluctantly resumed his march in pursuit of the safari. At the bottom of the escarpment he caught them on the flat ground before the Kedong River. A couple of pack donkeys were already there, drinking. They were attended by four Maasai *moran* and a man whose features were hidden by a huge, wide-brimmed hat. The hat and the accompanying Maasai indicated to Dan that it could only be Lord Delamere, a man who was close to the Maasai and could speak fluent *Maa*. He was also known by his almost pathological fear of what he called *the deleterious effects of the actinic rays of the sun*. His double terai was a hallmark. Delamere, or simply *D* to his friends, owned over a hundred thousand acres in the valley.

'D! Good to see you again.'

'Young Danny. How are you my boy? Where've you been? We haven't seen you up at Soysambu for ages.'

'Sorry, D, I've been busy.'

Dan had first met Delamere at the bar of the Norfolk where D, severely inebriated, had made a hundred-pound bet that he could ride down Government Road and shoot out all the newly installed electric streetlights before the clock struck midnight — fifteen minutes away.

In the flurry of betting that followed, Dan rashly placed a ten shilling side bet on the third Baron Delamere, then became concerned when D could barely find his saddle's stirrup. He helped him up and decided to ride with him as insurance on what he now realised had possibly been a rash wager.

Delamere set off with less than eight minutes remaining and was doing well until he fell off his horse.

Dan assisted him to remount, and did so twice more before galloping with D to the finish line — the Norfolk's veranda — just before the clock struck twelve.

D was declared the winner, but a dispute arose because of Dan's outside assistance. With no rules in place to settle the argument, a fight erupted between the two sides of the bet. Dan and Delamere fought back to back. The drunken lord, whose sobriety had barely improved, still managed to land quite a few telling blows. The bet and the fight were declared a draw when the constabulary arrived.

Their friendship progressed and Dan had been invited to D's Soysambu ranch near Lake Elmenteita whenever he was passing. He had done so on a number of occasions, particularly after Bill died and he needed advice on the sometimes curious manner of doing business in Africa.

They sat together in the shade of a tree and Dan's man poured tea. From the amount of gear on Delamere's pack animals it was obvious he was embarking on a long journey, but he wouldn't say where. Dan had heard rumours that Delamere was working for the military as a scout or in some form of covert role. It was obvious it didn't involve the usual military paraphernalia of uniforms and barracks accommodation and Dan wondered if D had found a way to serve without the need to join the regular army. As a scout, he too could meet his responsibility to assist in the war, but would be outside the formal establishment. It would enable him to use his skills and avoid the risk of revealing any incriminating personal details to the military.

He decided to try to pry the information from D and told him he had been thinking about joining the military, but was uncertain about the role he could play. 'I'd rather find something where I could use what I've learned in the bush,' he said. 'Maybe as a scout or a guide. Something like that.'

Delamere was non-committal, but Dan persevered, and the discussion continued until D mentioned that Dan might find it useful to talk to an officer by the name of Captain Durkheimer.

'Durkheimer? Isn't that a German name?' Dan asked.

'It is, but I wouldn't mention it if I was you.'

'Who is he?'

'Just a fellow I've met. He may be able to help.'

The name sounded familiar to Dan. It brought to mind a scandal — something that had occurred shortly after he arrived in British East Africa — but he couldn't recall the details.

CHAPTER 2

Liz couldn't recall Mombasa. She'd left the port ten years earlier when she was just eleven years old. She couldn't recall seeing anything like the fleet of bobbing dhows, lazy fishing boats and the many small craft ferrying stores and people between wharf and vessels as there were now. However, if the three drab warships, bristling with guns that now stood at anchor in the Kilindini harbour had been there in 1905, she would certainly have noticed.

She had been grief-stricken back then, and torn about leaving Africa and her animals, but had told herself Australia promised picnics in the bush, swimming in the sea, cold nights and warming fires. She didn't mind going to school — she loved boarding school books and imagined the real thing would be just the same — and certainly looked forward to making new friends her own age. And there was ice cream in Australia.

But by the time she settled in Adelaide, she knew Africa was the place for her. The little of the Australian bush she saw was boring in comparison with what she'd left behind. Animals, when they could be found at all, appeared only in early mornings or in the waning light of day. She missed her warthog, chameleon and newly acquired dik-dik and tree hyrax. Winters were freezing and Adelaide's blistering northerlies dried her skin before a sweat could bead on her forehead. And ice cream wasn't as delicious as an over-ripe mango full of sweet juice that ran down your chin quicker than you could slurp it into your mouth.

Looking from the railing of her ship, across the sparkling sapphire waters of Mombasa Harbour to the white stuccoed buildings lining the shore, she could already sense the bustle and vibrancy of the town. Exotic aromas came on the warm breeze and palm fronds nodded above the shopfronts.

When the ship nudged into the wharf, men in colourful *kikois* and dazzling white *dhotis* jostled one another. Indian ladies with silken saris draped over their plump brown bodies strolled regally among the shops. Golden chains glinted and dangling baubles flashed like rainbows in the tropical sun. Sweating black bodies carried bundles and crates into the gaping jaws of the godowns.

Liz felt a thrill of exhilaration. It might have been in anticipation of living the excitement of Africa again, or simply a fear of the unknown. Mombasa wasn't home, but its steamy strangeness had already reminded her of what she'd forsaken when her mother decided she should be given a proper education in Australia. Now she was returning, her mission only partly completed, and without any certainty that she would find either Dan or her mother.

Dan was likely to be on safari for weeks if not months on end, and her mother, an even worse correspondent, hadn't acknowledged Liz's letter announcing her return. To be fair, she may not have had time to respond before she left. Liz wasn't even sure she was still in Athi River — her last known address.

A porter offered to take Liz's suitcase ashore.

She followed him down the gangway, leaving behind her last secure lodging, unsure of finding the only two people she knew on the continent.

* * *

The train from Mombasa pulled into Athi River Station early on an overcast morning. When it pulled out a few minutes later, Liz was left standing, suitcase in hand, feeling terribly alone.

Scattered around the station were a dozen small *dukas*, but no sign of the storekeepers. Beyond them stood a few more substantial buildings through which ran a strip of gravel road that quickly disappeared in the grassy plain. The savannah rose imperceptibly until it merged into the undulating hills in the northeast. Beyond the town a line of dense foliage marked the passage of the river.

An Indian man with a greying beard and deep sunken eyes, and wearing thick-rimmed spectacles and a navy jacket with red piping, came hurrying up to her. Around his neck hung a brass whistle on a loop of grubby white cord. 'Oh, my goodness! I was not seeing you, madam. A thousand apologies. And here you are. You are wanting Mr Grassby's School for Girls, yes?'

'Um ... No.'

'Not for Mr Grassby's School? Then you are not Mrs Pendelbury from Bristol?'

'No. My name is ... I'm looking for the farm of Mr, I mean, Monsieur de Clemenceau.'

'De Clemenceau ... de Clemenceau. Oh, but his farm is quite far.' He looked down at her shoes, then to her suitcase. 'I am thinking you will need a wagon, isn't it?' His head wobbled on his scrawny neck.

'That would be very kind.'

'Sadly, there is no wagon in the town these days.' He did indeed appear sad. 'They are all helping bring in the crops.'

'I see ... Then, what can I do?'

'Please,' he said, taking her suitcase, 'be sitting in my office. I will find my brother-in-law. He has a very fine motor car.'

Liz sat in the relative comfort of the stationmaster's office — a small cluttered room behind the ticket-window grille — feeling reassured that her stepfather was at least known in the town.

Liz had never met de Clemenceau, and the title of stepfather sat rather incongruously in her mind. She had been close to her poor father, and hoped that her mother's second husband avoided any familial overtures. Liz didn't want anyone trying to take her father's place.

* * *

Liz held fast to her hat as Mr Patel's old De Dion spluttered and bucked down the dusty road where high fences enclosed flocks of ostriches. A few minutes later they clattered through the yard gate and drew up beside the house.

Her mother came out onto the veranda, shielding her eyes against the morning sun, as Liz handed Patel her two rupees.

Patel smiled, showing his mouthful of yellowing teeth, then

pulled his goggles down, released the brake, and swung the car into an arc. He was out the gate before Liz had lifted her suitcase.

Liz's first thoughts were that the lines that ran down her mother's angular face from her nose to her mouth had deepened. So too had those on her forehead, but it was the tired and defeated expression that shocked Liz. Vivian Freeman had always been a feisty woman. There was little of that person in evidence as she came down the steps towards her in a floral house dress and long-sleeved white cotton blouse.

Vivian broke into a surprised smile when she recognised her. 'Elizabeth! It's you!' She threw her arms around Liz and hugged her. 'I only got your letter the other day. I wasn't expecting you for weeks.'

Her mother's waist had thickened. As she stepped back to study her, she brushed a strand of wispy hair from her face and tucked it behind her ear. 'Oh, it's so good to see you. Really it is.'

Liz said she was happy to be there, then added, 'I wasn't even sure you would be here.'

'Of course I'd be here. Where else would I be? But you must be hot and thirsty: come inside.'

The house was large and the parlour, where Vivian now led her, was opulently furnished. Oil paintings decorated the walls, and a crystal decanter and glasses sat on an ornate oak sideboard. The large Oriental rug that covered the lacquered timber floor had lost its pile in some areas, and above the fireplace hung a buffalo head with an enormous spread of horns.

'I know,' Vivian said, rolling her eyes. 'It doesn't fit with the Louis XIV chairs, but Marcel is such a sportsman. He loves to display his trophies.'

She called her housemaid and ordered glasses of cold water. Then she invited her daughter to sit. They chatted for a while.

'I was surprised to hear that you called off your engagement,' Vivian said when the conversation lapsed.

Liz had been brief in her most recent letter.

'It's the war, of course. When Max enlisted, he didn't want to hold me to our arrangement. You never know what might happen in a war.'

'Indeed. Marcel tried to enlist, but the government said he was needed on the farm.'

'For the ostrich feathers?'

'Oh, no. The feather business has been in dire straits in recent years. We're slaughtering them for meat these days.'

Liz recalled her mother's bitter arguments when her father refused her wish to return to England and asked, as diplomatically as possible, why she remained in Africa now that the feather business had failed.

'Marcel kept stalling, hoping the demand would pick up, and then the war came. But I expect we'll be heading back home as soon as it's over.'

'What happened to the ostrich-feather business?'

'It just blew away with the breeze, I used to say. It was a joke because you see Marcel blames the new-fangled motor car. Like that one of Patel's. Ladies just can't wear feathered hats in them. They don't last a moment.' She clucked her tongue. 'You should hear Marcel go on about it.'

'And now you sell ostrich meat. But who would buy it?'

'The army. They can't get enough meat.'

'So they can it and send it to the troops in Europe?'

'No. They send it to the border with German East. We've ever so many men in uniform down there.'

'In German East Africa? There was a piece in the Mombasa newspaper, but it sounded like a handful of German farmers making a nuisance of themselves.'

'No, dear. The newspapers are saying very little, but everyone knows there's a full-blown war in progress down there, and people are worried we might soon be invaded.'

* * *

Marcel de Clemenceau strode into the parlour and raised his eyebrows when he found Liz sipping tea with his wife. He was a man in his mid-fifties, of middling height, an upright stance that tended to accentuate his paunch, and thinning grey hair combed straight back from his forehead. When introduced, he took Liz's hand and gallantly kissed it.

'Enchanted,' he said, holding her hand for an uncomfortably long time. 'Vivian has spoken much about you, but never has she mentioned how beautiful you are.' He pronounced *never* as if it was spelled *nevaaaah*.

'Elizabeth is staying with us until she finds a place in town,' Vivian said. 'I explained we aren't really able to accommodate long-term guests.'

'It shouldn't take long, Monsieur de Clemenceau,' Liz added.

'Nonsense,' said de Clemenceau. 'You will stay for as long as you wish, *chérie*. And you must call me Marcel.'

'But really,' Liz said. 'It shouldn't take long to find something in Nairobi and —'

'I will not hear of it.'

He smiled.

Liz felt awkward under his gaze.

Something about his manner disturbed her.

* * *

Liz was in her bedroom searching in her trunk for an item of clothing when she had the uncomfortable feeling that someone was watching her. She swung around to find Marcel de Clemenceau leaning against the doorjamb.

'Oh!' she said. 'Monsieur … I mean, Marcel. You startled me.'

'A thousand apologies, *chérie*, but I found your door ajar and I just wanted to ensure you were completely comfortable.'

'Thank you. I am. And please, call me Elizabeth.'

His eyes did not meet hers. They were on the crisp cotton nightdress that she had pulled from the trunk. She gathered it into a ball and thrust it out of sight behind her back, her cheeks blazing.

'Ah, you have such pretty things.' His smile became a leer and anger threatened to overcome her embarrassment.

'Is there anything else you would care to see in here?' she asked, not bothering to conceal her annoyance.

He was impervious to her mood, and retained his arrogant smile.

'Not for the moment, *chérie*. But I am certain there will be opportunities for us to get to know each other a little better over the coming days and weeks.'

He backed out the door and Liz closed it firmly behind him.

Wringing her hands, she went to sit on the edge of her bed.

How can things possibly get worse? she asked herself.

She had cut all ties with Australia, and apart from Dan, her mother was the only person she knew in Africa. And Vivian was married to a cad.

* * *

Liz felt that Nairobi had grown and changed, but it was still ugly. The Indian markets had been moved from the river to a street in the town specially named for them — Bazaar Street. There was a new Stanley Hotel in Hardinge Street after Mayence Bent's hotel business outgrew her old premises.

The Norfolk, which had opened the same year Mayence's first hotel burned to the ground in the Great Fire of Victoria Street, now had a double-storey wing and a new arched front entrance, where Liz's rickshaw now stopped.

She paid the rickshaw boy and climbed the four wide timber steps leading to the veranda — also new — and for a moment surveyed the bustle beneath her on Government Road.

A line of skin-covered Maasai women passed by, leaning against the weight of enormous firewood bundles supported by a head strap around each shaven pate. An English lady bobbed past in her stylish buggy, driven by a liveried black man who gave the chestnut mare a touch with his long whip. A row of naked black children stood at the fence, peering round-eyed at the veranda crowd until they were chased away by the doorman.

The Norfolk had transformed that end of the town, and itself had become a hub of commercial activity, where upcountry settlers met bankers, stock traders and land agents, and deals were discussed on the veranda over pink gins and completed over dinner in the dining room. The reality of the Norfolk's position within the protectorate was validated by the railway, which now allowed for an unofficial stop on Salisbury Road. Here passengers could clamber down to the tracks and make their way along Government Road to the Norfolk rather than take the longer route from the proper station.

Liz had thought she would be escaping the reminders of war, but British East Africa had obviously embraced it with as much passion as Australia had. There were the usual posters exhorting young men to enlist, and another that called for *women with suitable demeanour and attributes* to volunteer for nursing positions. The idea appealed to her, which came as a surprise. In Adelaide she had felt no threat to Australia and no sympathy for the cause. Perhaps the newspaper stories, the posters and Max's enlistment had all had an effect on her, or maybe it was her greater proximity to one of the theatres — whichever, it now seemed that she had a responsibility to do something in response.

Young men in uniform were everywhere, including in the Norfolk, which, according to the manager, had been virtually taken over by the military for officers' accommodation.

'But I've tried the New Stanley. They're full too.'

'I'm terribly sorry, madam, but there's nothing I can do.'

She turned away, almost colliding with a tall, broad-shouldered man in uniform who saluted and gave her a slight bow.

'Excuse me, miss. I happened to overhear your conversation with George just now. It appears the army has caused you a problem.'

His voice and English accent gave him the air of a gentleman.

'I ... well yes, it appears so.'

'I may be able to help. A number of our officers will vacate their rooms soon, but alas, not soon enough to immediately solve your problem. However, I have a suggestion.'

'Yes?'

'I would be happy to share a room with a fellow officer until our chaps clear off for the border, thereby freeing a room for your use.'

'That's very kind of you, but I wouldn't dream of inconveniencing you in such a —'

'It's the least I can do. After all, it's the military that has caused you the problem, and it's the military that must solve it.' Turning to the hotel manager, he said, 'George, the young lady may have my room, as soon as you can arrange to have my things moved in with Caruthers. Can you arrange that?'

'Certainly, Captain Durkheimer. At once.'

His smile was warm when he turned back to her.

'Thank you, Captain,' she said. 'I'm indebted.'

'Not at all. And it's Richard.' He extended his hand. 'At your service.'

She took it and she could feel her face flush under his close attention. 'Elizabeth Freeman.'

'Delighted to meet you, Miss Elizabeth Freeman. Perhaps we'll meet again soon. After all, we're now neighbours.'

He clicked his heels, saluted, and strode from the foyer.

CHAPTER 3

Captain Richard Durkheimer had long ago learned to ignore the upturned eyebrows of those who found this most English of English gentlemen bearing such a non-English surname. His disdain for such plebeian sentiment resided in the knowledge that his lineage was impeccable.

His maternal grandmother, Amelia Huth, was of the merchant-banking dynasty of Messrs Frederick Huth & Company, where his father, also called Richard Durkheimer, had been senior partner for many years. His maternal grandfather was of the Manchester Hattons — a pillar of the textile industry.

It was true that his paternal grandfather was born in Bremen before moving to England and his father's only other sibling, Aunt Beatrice, had married a German and returned to Germany. The two families maintained contact, his Aunt Beatrice even bringing her son, Karl, to London for a prolonged visit when Richard was a boy. Although much older than Richard, he and his cousin Karl became close friends. Years later, Karl returned to England and stayed with Richard or other members of his family until 1914, when he returned to Germany.

But Richard was a proper Englishman, and British from the topmost hair of his fair head to his size fourteen feet.

He'd attended Harrow School before joining his father in the bank, and immediately began to agitate to be allowed to attend military college. His father resisted at first, but having served in the Irish Constabulary as a young man, where, he proudly boasted, he cracked the thick skulls of recalcitrant Irish farmers, he was sympathetic to his son's military aspirations.

As anti-German sentiment grew towards the outbreak of war, the questioning looks became more belligerent, but Durkheimer treated them with contempt. Being a tall, well-built man, if his very English charm couldn't win respect, a withering look almost invariably did. When all else failed, and when provoked beyond endurance, his temper would flare and he would beat his tormentor senseless. His reputation as a cruel man, capable of inflicting unrelenting brutality upon those who displeased him, was legend within the military.

Durkheimer had always desired an appointment in Africa, having heard much of the place from his cousin Karl, and achieved that ambition in his posting to British East Africa in 1902. However, an incident while taking to the field against the belligerent Nandi resulted in him being sent home a year later to stew upon the injustice of it.

When he returned to BEA at the start of the war as head of the East African Intelligence Corps, he was determined to redress those misjudgements.

* * *

Liz returned to the Norfolk feeling hot and dejected. Her daily visit to the post office, which she'd been making for weeks now, hoping to find there a letter from her mother or even her grandmother, had again proved fruitless, and when she went to the army's administration offices to apply to serve as a nurse, she had been rejected. The uniformed man told her she must first be assessed by the chief surgeon at Nairobi hospital.

She decided to return to the hotel for lunch, but the Norfolk dining room had a queue waiting to be seated.

A uniformed officer, sitting alone at a table for two, arose and came towards her. His face was familiar and she searched her mind desperately for his name.

'Miss Freeman,' he said in a crisp British accent.

'Captain ...?'

'Durkheimer,' he prompted her, and smiled. 'Good afternoon.'

'Good afternoon to you.'

When they'd first met she hadn't noticed how tall he was. He cut quite a dashing figure in the khaki uniform and the red leather belts that crossed his broad chest. His hair was immaculately parted in the middle.

'We meet again, and again I am in the fortunate position of being able to offer my services.' He indicated his table. 'As you can see, I have just arrived, and am doomed to eat alone unless you take pity. Would you care to join me for lunch?'

He made her smile and she felt better about the morning's frustrations. 'Thank you. It would appear there's quite a wait for a table.'

'Wonderful,' he said, stepping back to allow her to go ahead.

During the meal their conversation was on the effects the war was having on life in Nairobi. The captain was of the opinion that, despite recent setbacks, the war in Africa would not last more than a year.

'Do you come from a military background, Captain Durkheimer?'

'Not at all. Bankers, in fact. Do you know of Frederick Huth & Company?'

She said she was unfamiliar with the financial industry.

'Huth is from Mama's side. My father was a senior partner, and I might have continued the family tradition had I not bullied him into letting me go to Aldershot.'

She didn't care to reveal any further ignorance and refrained from asking where or what was Aldershot.

'I won my commission there in '99.'

'I see.'

For the remainder of lunch he entertained her with stories of his exploits in India and his previous stint in East Africa.

When they parted, Durkheimer took her hand, kissed it, and said he hoped he would soon have the pleasure of her company once more.

The morning had begun badly with her futile hope to find a letter from either her mother or grandmother. She would go to the post office again tomorrow, but the physical distance from her remaining relatives seemed to be causing a growing emotional distance between them. At times she felt rather lost and alone. The only other person she knew in Africa was Dan, but she'd been trying for days to find him without success.

Her lunch with Captain Richard Durkheimer had elevated her spirits. Finding herself the object of a handsome gentleman's attention helped to dispel some of the anxiety she felt at being alone in Nairobi.

She walked towards her room thinking it curious that two handsome men, both of German origin, had found her attractive.

* * *

It was a long walk to the post office. The hot wind swept the dust from the baked earth and swirled along Victoria Street in clouds of suffocating air. She entered the building expecting to find relief, but it was hotter there than on Victoria Street. The walls seemed to close in around her as she made her way to the counter.

The postal clerk, a profuse perspirer, came to the desk, mopping his brow. He always appeared exhausted and, as usual, waited for her to speak.

'Anything for Elizabeth Freeman?'

He nodded, said, 'Hmm,' and turned back to the rack of pigeonholes, where addressees were arranged in alphabetical order.

Liz's heart leaped in expectation.

'Here we are,' he said, peering at the envelope. 'Hmm, that's an interesting stamp. Don't see many of those hereabouts.'

As he turned the envelope, examining both sides in exasperating detail, Liz felt inclined to reach over and pluck it from his hands.

'Egypt,' he said, handing it to her, almost reluctantly.

She turned from the desk, muttering, 'Thank you,' and quickly studied the handwritten address:

Miss Elizabeth Freeman
c/- Nairobi Post Office
British East Africa Colony

The handwriting was unfamiliar. The sender was a Lieutenant M Dinsdale.

She thought the postal clerk had made a mistake and checked her name on the front of the envelope again. She knew no one by the name of Lieutenant M Dinsdale.

At the side counter among the wetting sponges and blotting papers, she tore it open and unfolded the single small page.

My dear Elizabeth, it began.

She ran her eye down the page then turned it over. It was signed *With all my love, Max*.

She turned back to the beginning.

My dear Elizabeth,

We have a lull in proceedings here. I won't bother you with the details (they would be censored in any case). Enough to say that it offers us all a chance to write letters to loved ones, and in my case, to contemplate my actions leading up to my hurtful words and our even more painful separation.

My darling, I have been a fool. I think of the things I said in anger and feel sick to my stomach. How could I think such nonsense? How could I be so blind? All I can offer in my defence is that the war placed a heavy burden upon my whole family and it drove me slightly mad.

On days like this I have plenty of time to contemplate my loss and on many occasions have taken up the pen to write this letter before losing my courage. The next time I face the enemy and possibly my demise, I curse my cowardice and fear I might have missed my last opportunity to tell you I love you and want you back in my life.

There will be no heroics in this war for me. Bravery is for men who have nothing to lose. If there is some hope to once again win your heart, it will be my motivation to survive and to beg for one more chance to make you my wife.

With all my love,

Max

PS: I am so pleased I enlisted and was accepted. It is inspirational to serve with so many brave fellows, fighting for our country.

Liz released the breath she'd been holding as she read the letter. Max's words had flown across the oceans to reach her at exactly the right time. She had been feeling lost and alone. Now Max had declared he still wanted her in his life.

For all his faults, she believed he truly cared for her.

It gave her hope that she and Max could find happiness and a life together after all.

Tears of joy welled up in her eyes. And tears of relief too, because she had begun to despair of finding anywhere she could call home in Africa.

CHAPTER 4

Without D's detailed description of how to locate Durkheimer's office, Dan may never have found it. Even then, he blundered into the wrong place before finding the offices in an unnamed building behind Hardinge Street.

The attractive young lady at the reception desk appeared unmoved by Dan's request to see Captain Durkheimer, refusing to even acknowledge that he existed. After he mentioned Delamere's name, she told him to wait, and then disappeared down a linoleum-floored corridor. A moment later she returned and he followed her to a door marked *Capt. Richard Durkheimer — Intelligence Unit.*

Durkheimer was standing behind his desk and ignored Dan when he entered, concentrating instead on a map that covered almost his entire desk while he puffed on his pipe. It gave Dan a chance to study him. He was a man in his mid-thirties, tall, fair-haired and well built. While he was wondering what kind of boss he would be, he remembered why his name was familiar.

It was from Dan's early days in British East Africa, during the time when the protectorate was still having difficulties subduing a number of the tribes. Durkheimer assisted in one punitive expedition against the Kikuyu and their cousins, the Meru. Dan couldn't recall the reason for the punishment, but the Kings African Rifles, with whom Durkheimer was an officer, had discovered that arbitrary stock confiscation was a useful reprisal for any rebellious behaviour. On one expedition his unit confiscated eleven thousand cattle, which prompted furious retaliation from the owners, who had done nothing to deserve it. Durkheimer's men killed fifteen hundred warriors.

A couple of years later he had been engaged in a campaign against the Nandi who, ever since the railway line was constructed across their land in 1899, had objected to its imposition. They received no concessions from the administration and so had engaged in a number of battles, often successful, against quite well-equipped military expeditions. Their successes became a matter of increasing concern, and were damaging the administration's status.

Dan had heard that Durkheimer arranged a meeting under a flag of truce with the Nandi *Orkoiyot* and, while shaking hands with him, drew his revolver and shot him dead. Another two dozen Nandi were machine-gunned. The matter was covered up, but the details later emerged and it went to an official enquiry, where he received a reprimand and was sent home. After a third enquiry, he was cleared of any wrongdoing.

Like many, Dan had been shocked by the stories circulating about this man, and now wondered if he had made the right decision to work for him. He ran through his options. He knew he was putting himself under increasing scrutiny as people wondered why a man of his age, without the excuse of being involved in an essential service, continued to avoid military service. Yet by joining the forces he would almost certainly be discovered to be a deserter. A non-uniformed role was the only way he could serve without enlisting.

Durkheimer glanced up at that point and Dan met his ice-blue eyes.

'D tells me you know the territory out beyond Magadi,' Durkheimer said.

'He spoke to you?'

'You wouldn't have got in here otherwise.'

'Yes, I know the Magadi area.'

Durkheimer returned to the map. 'What do you know of this area here?'

He stabbed his finger at a point southwest of Nairobi.

'That's Lake Natron. A salt lake.'

'Tell me about it.'

'It's fed on the west by a small river — the southern Ewaso Ng'iro — and hot springs. Probably arising from the Ol Doinyo Lengai volcano. The lake can get hot in parts. And it's caustic.'

Led by Durkheimer's questions, Dan gave him a more detailed description of the lake and its surrounding environment. At the end of his fifteen-minute interrogation Durkheimer nodded and took his seat behind his desk. Dan remained standing.

'Daniel Sutherland ...'

His eyes seemed to bore into Dan who had the uncomfortable feeling that Durkheimer could read his innermost thoughts.

'Why haven't you enlisted as a volunteer?'

Dan breathed again. He was prepared for the question. 'I don't believe the army is the right place for me.'

'Why not?'

'I'm a hunter and a tracker, and I don't think I'm cut out to be a soldier.'

'Then I don't want you in my unit.'

Dan shrugged. 'Suit yourself.'

He turned to leave. Durkheimer called him back.

'Why did you come here today, Sutherland?'

'To offer to help. And I believe I can do more to help in your line of business than I can as a foot soldier.'

'And what's my line of business?'

'Spying.'

'We prefer *espionage*.' Durkheimer's smile was humourless. 'However, if you prefer to use the word spy, then you understand the risks. You know that if you join our unit you will be collecting information on the enemy while not in uniform, and if you are caught by the Germans, you will be shot. You know that, don't you?'

'Yes.'

'You own Freeman Safaris.'

Dan was surprised by his knowledge and was tempted to enquire how he knew about the company, but imagined D had given him background information.

'Are you able to supply everything you need for any reconnaissance mission I might send you on?'

'Yes.'

Durkheimer was silent for some time, resting his elbows on his desk and making a temple of his fingers, which he slowly tapped together. 'I want you to keep up your safari business. It'll be your cover. If possible, always take a client with you while you're out there. Go as often as you can to the area I have just indicated on the map and elsewhere along the German border. You will keep your eyes open. Make observations. Report on troop movements. Anything of interest. Is that clear?'

Dan nodded.

'Very well. My assistant will take you to meet Lieutenant Conroy. He'll brief you on our unit's *modus operandi*. At the conclusion of every mission you will report to me, and only to me. You will not tell anyone of your role in this unit.'

'I've heard there might be conscription. What if I'm called up?'

'You won't be. Those who need to know about your work with us will be informed.'

Dan nodded, and headed for the door.

'And Sutherland ...'

Dan turned back to him.

'If you're captured, the British government knows nothing of you.'

* * *

Conroy spent the remainder of the morning with Dan, detailing the finer points of the articles of war dealing with intelligence, espionage, sabotage and counterintelligence. He then loaded a gunny sack with a code book, maps and a set of instructions about protocol.

'Keep these safe at all times,' he warned as Dan prepared to leave.

Out again on Hardinge Street, Dan decided he needed a drink. Around the corner from Durkheimer's office was the New Stanley Hotel, which Dan had avoided during the fuss of its grand opening. He took a table facing the street. Since the Norfolk had added the veranda that opened to tree-lined Government Road, all the hotels were following the trend.

'You've been avoiding me,' Mayence Bent declared when her imposing figure swept up to his table.

'G'day, Mayence. Not avoiding you, simply waiting for the grand opening celebrations to end. I see you've planted a tree.'

Mayence had gone a step further than the Norfolk, planting a fever tree among the encircling tables.

'Yes. I reckon it's far better having a tree in your hotel than just looking at trees on the street. I suppose you're tired of the Norfolk with all those army types filling the place.'

'I am. And I've also missed your sweet smile.'

'Hmmph. I suppose you'll want a lager.'

'Please.'

Before he'd had a chance to open his newspaper, Mayence returned and planted Dan's lager on his table. In the same motion she swept up his coins.

'Thanks, Mayence.'

'Have you been away again on safari?'

'Um ... yes, I have.'

There was something in her tone that made him glance at her. Mayence knew everyone in town and there wasn't much that she didn't know about the goings-on in Nairobi.

Her husband, Charlie Bent, had arrived in Nairobi years before to build the railway depot buildings, railway station and staff quarters before Ronald Preston's platelayers began the incredibly difficult assent of the Kikuyu escarpment, and the even more improbable descent into the Great Rift Valley. It was 1899 and no one in authority had planned to make Nairobi more than a whistle-stop, but Mayence felt otherwise. The swampy flat land around the Nairobi River was the last staging post for the attack on the most challenging engineering feat of the age, and Mayence convinced her husband to quit constructing railway buildings and to erect a hotel. It was a masterful business decision, and the Stanley Hotel, and the New Stanley Hotel that followed it, became popular accommodation and meeting places.

'Thought you might be doing a job for Captain Durkheimer. You've just come from his office, haven't you?'

'Durkheimer. Who's he?' Dan asked, taking a sip of his lager.

Mayence simply smiled and moved off, collecting glasses as she ambled among the tables.

He turned to his newspaper. The front page was awash with details of the disastrous Allied amphibious attack on the Dardanelles and Gallipoli. There were calls for Winston Churchill, the First Lord of the Admiralty, to resign.

Dan finished his lager, and folded the newspaper, but he remained seated, watching the passing pedestrians and planning the days following, during which he would prepare for his next safari — his first opportunity to do surveillance for Durkheimer.

His client was a rich American, who Dan had briefly met when he arrived in Nairobi. He was quite verbose and opinionated. Dan wasn't relishing the four weeks on safari with the man, but it would be his first assignment in his new position, and the man was prepared to pay well, so he hoped to make good on both counts.

An attractive young woman came from Sixth Avenue, swinging her hips in a lazy relaxed rhythm, almost cat-like. It appeared as if the effect was quite unintentional, and it was spellbinding. He watched her approach the hotel with unconcealed interest. When she was about to pass his table she caught his eye and, after a moment's hesitation, smiled at him.

Having been caught gawking at her, he was completely flummoxed by her audacious grin. It was something quite beyond his experience and now he didn't know what to do next. His amazement was compounded when she walked to his table, and said, 'Dan! I've been looking for you everywhere. How wonderful to see you!'

* * *

Liz had tried Dan's last known address, but the proprietor of the guesthouse said he hadn't been living there for some months. Her only other option was to explore the town and if she couldn't find him, then she'd find someone who knew him.

When she saw him sitting at a table in the New Stanley, it took a moment to confirm it was him. His cheeks had lost their youthful roundness, but that gave his jaw a more determined set. His hair was shorter, but as he lounged in his chair, an arm dangling over the armrest as he sipped his beer, he had the same air of self-confidence he'd always had — though when she spoke to him, he almost choked on his drink.

'Oh ... um ... Hello,' he spluttered, as he lurched to his feet. 'Do I ...? Wait a minute ...' His familiar smile emerged from behind his confusion. 'Lizzie?'

She threw her arms around his neck.

He hesitated a moment before giving her a hug. It was a hug a man would give his elderly aunt.

'Couldn't you recognise me?'

'You've changed.'

'I hope so. It's been ten years.'

'Of course it has, but ... you've changed.'

'You already said that.'

'Sorry. It's just that I never thought you'd ... change so much.'

'Dan, I was a little girl when I left.'

This appeared to confuse him further because he simply stared at her.

She had hoped for something a little more demonstrative.

'When did you get here?' he asked. 'And *why* are you here?'

She shrugged. 'That's going to take a little while. Can we sit?'

'Yes, certainly. Sorry. Would you care for a drink?'

She accepted his offer and ordered tea.

As they sat together, Dan with another lager, she with her tea, she told him about the recent events that had changed her life. Dan hadn't received either of her latest letters, so he not only didn't know she was returning to Africa, he knew nothing of her engagement, let alone the end of it. He was surprised.

'But you were so young to be engaged.'

'I'm twenty-two.'

He paused a moment. 'So you are. Where is your fiancé?'

'*Ex*-fiancé. He's in the army. On his way to the Middle East.'

She briefly told him about Max and how they'd met.

'Thirty-three? He's even older than me!'

'It's not a matter of age. It's about how you feel about each other.'

'And how do you feel about him, Liz?'

When she was a girl and Dan was her mentor and friend, she wouldn't hesitate to discuss anything about her life with him. But now it was different. They were no longer as close. Time, and distance, had broken the old bond between them. But even so, she wasn't sure she knew the answer to the question.

'We've decided to postpone our engagement because of the war,' she said.

'The war has changed everything.'

'Are you in the forces?'

'Um ... no, I'm not. I'm still in the safari business. In fact, your grandfather's safari business.'

'Oh. And how is it going?'

'Up and down. As I said, the war's changed a lot of things. About my only clients these days are Americans. They've got the money and the war doesn't appear to have bothered them.'

'I thought it was you,' a man on the footpath said.

He was short, hook-nosed and slightly stooped. Straggly grey hair sprouted from under the brim of an enormous hat.

'G'day, D,' Dan said, and they shook hands enthusiastically.

Liz watched Dan as he engaged in a brief exchange. He still had the smile and boyish enthusiasm she had so admired as a young girl. He glanced back at her.

'Liz, forgive me. Let me introduce my friend. Lord Delamere, this is Miss Elizabeth Freeman.'

'Oh, for goodness' sakes, Dan,' he said coming to the table and taking her hand in his. 'Take no notice of all that *Lord* nonsense. Hugh Cholmondeley,' he said, giving her hand a shake. 'People call me D.'

'Pleased to meet you, D.'

'Freeman! So you and Dan are in business together?'

'Liz has only just returned from studying in Australia,' Dan said.

'Welcome home. Studying what, if I may ask?'

'I was taking science at Adelaide University. I intend to work in the veterinary field.'

'Excellent. We can use smart young people in Africa. And Dan, you must bring Liz to Soysambu. She might find my various merino crossbreeds of interest.'

'Thanks, D. I'll keep that in mind, but I'm off on safari next week.'

'Then you should take her with you. Let the young lady refresh her memory of this magnificent country of ours.'

They exchanged farewells and Dan came quickly back to his seat to place his hand over hers on the table. 'What do you think, Liz? Would you like to join the safari to see how the business is going?'

'Why, yes. I'd like that. But what about your client?'

'The American? I don't think he'll mind if a lovely young lady joins us.'

Liz took a sip of tea, concealing her smile behind her cup, and enjoying the feeling of his hand resting lightly on hers.

* * *

Captain Durkheimer had been heading to his office when he spotted Liz ahead of him in Hardinge Street. Even from behind she was unmistakeable. Her walk, the way she swung her hips, was quite distinctive. She crossed Sixth Avenue ahead of him and stopped outside the New Stanley Hotel.

He was about to increase his pace to overtake her when she approached a man sitting at one of the kerbside tables. He paused on the corner.

The two were obviously known to each other because a moment after she made contact with him, the man rose and they embraced. Then she sat at his table.

Durkheimer narrowed his eyes. He recognised the man as Dan Sutherland, his new recruit.

What place did such a callow bushie have in the life of Elizabeth Freeman? The connection between Elizabeth and the name of the safari company that Sutherland controlled leaped into his mind. How could he have missed it previously? Perhaps they had only a business association.

Lord Delamere joined them and the dynamics of the situation changed. After speaking with Delamere, Sutherland returned to his table and took Elizabeth's hand in his.

Durkheimer's jaw tightened.

They were more than mere business acquaintances.

CHAPTER 5

The stores; the ammunition; hay for the animals; the irritating whine of disgruntled porters moaning about their loads; the client's endless flow of trivial questions. Dan believed that any normal person would be driven to distraction by the many different, often conflicting, demands made before a safari could commence. But a white hunter thrived on them. Each was a precursor to the challenge and the excitement of the journey, which was not only a hunting expedition, but an operation involving scores — perhaps hundreds — of porters, animals, equipment, stores, food supplies, ammunition and trade goods. He knew that every detail must be checked and rechecked if the safari was to be a success. In the worst case, inadequate preparation or an incorrect decision could mean death or disaster.

Since arriving a virtual ignoramus many years before, Dan had learned the trade of big-game hunting from many sources.

From his tracker he'd learned about animal behaviour. It was Korok who taught him that a stalked lion always turned to look at a pursuing hunter before disappearing into deep cover. The habit gave the hunter the best, and possibly last, opportunity to shoot. And that an old bull elephant could double back on an unsuspecting hunter and wait motionless for him to pass nearby before bearing down on him with lethal and surprising swiftness.

Bill Freeman had taught him about firearms, cartridges and the best choice of both for every type of game. He'd also been a good judge of human nature and Dan had picked up many tricks in handling cantankerous or pushy clients.

Dan's first meeting with his latest client, the American businessman, Bailey Tuckmore, was at his hotel.

They sat for an hour on the veranda of the Norfolk reviewing what Tuckmore had indicated in his cables that he wanted to hunt.

This was an obvious prerequisite, but was also important when determining a host of consequential considerations such as their destination and the terrain they would encounter. This in turn governed what animals, if any, could be used since some areas were infested with tsetse fly, which were generally fatal to pack animals. If they could not be used, then a greater number of porters would be needed.

The destination and route would also affect decisions on supplies and trade goods as travel through areas where tribes were amenable to trade would mean they could obtain fresh food on the road.

Tuckmore wanted to bag big cats and large, dangerous game such as rhino, buffalo and elephant — all the usual trophy animals. Dan casually enquired about Tuckmore's firearms. It was usually a touchy subject as he'd found that most hunters had an emotional attachment to their guns. The American said he'd brought a few to Africa. He mentioned his Springfield 30-06 and 405 lever-action Winchester.

'They're both American firearms,' Dan said.

'Damn right. The best.'

By the tone of his reply and the set of his chin, Dan suspected Tuckmore was another fierce defender of his country's reputation in firearms. The British favoured British weapons such as Holland and Holland or Rigby or Westley Richards. The Germans trusted their Mauser or the Mannlicher-Schoenauer. The cross-Atlantic rivalry amused Dan and he was not about to get involved in it. But nor would he risk his reputation by taking a client into the field with inadequate firepower for his chosen quarry.

When white hunters sat around a fire at night, as they did whenever they met on safari, the conversation inevitably turned to hunting, hunters and their firearms. The kills, the near-misses, and the mistakes were discussed and dissected in acute detail.

Bill Freeman had taught him about penetration capabilities of soft-nosed compared with solid projectiles, and in which situation they should be used. Solid projectiles were recommended on tough-skinned game like rhinos and elephants, but the soft-nosed bullet struck the soft skin of an animal such as a leopard with devastating results. The projectile started expanding upon impact, leaving a massive exit wound, which usually killed the animal quickly.

He knew that an accurate brain shot with a solid bullet was lethal, but risky, because the brain's size and its position made for a difficult target, but that most head, neck or forward spine strikes were likely to immediately incapacitate the game.

The broken bones of a shoulder shot would disable almost anything, as would any spine hit, but these shots were seldom fatal, leaving an aggressive animal paralysed or partially so until the hunter despatched it with a close-range finishing shot. Even a heart, lung or liver hit often allowed the beast to cover considerable ground before collapsing. It might typically take twelve seconds to bleed out from such a wound, during which time it could drag itself in pursuit of the hunter. Many a hunter had been killed by an aggressive, dying beast driven by the mindless urge to exact deadly vengeance.

'I'm not concerned about your very fine Springfield 30-06,' he said. 'For plains animals it's perfect. But the 405 Winchester ... It's quite good for lion, but it's not enough for elephant. Even for buffalo you'd need a near-perfect brain shot.'

'You have no need to concern yourself about the accuracy of my eye, Mr Sutherland. I can handle myself as well as any man. Better than most, I reckon. Regimental champion back in '97.'

Dan chose his words carefully. 'I didn't mean to suggest you lacked ability, Mr Tuckmore. I like to be on the safe side when it comes to dangerous game. And your 405 doesn't have the stopping power of, say, the 450 Rigby Nitro Express.'

'The Nitro Express ...?'

'Yes. It's quite a good weapon. Not American, I'll grant you, but excellent for the big boys. I can't allow you to go after large dangerous game on one of my safaris with the inadequate weaponry you've mentioned.'

'Inadequate weaponry ...?' Tuckmore's tone was menacing.

Dan cursed himself for his choice of words. There were ways to handle a client's ego and he'd broken just about every rule. He was now forced to soberly consider the likelihood of losing his commission.

'I'm sorry, but that's my rule,' he added lamely.

Tuckmore retained Dan's eye.

'Hmm ...' he said, and slowly rose from the table. 'I did say I brought a few pieces with me. Wait here a moment,' he said, before disappearing into the hotel.

Dan felt like a recalcitrant schoolboy and sat impatiently awaiting Tuckmore's return. If he was going to be sacked, he'd rather he do it without all the drama. He needed the Tuckmore safari as a cover for his reconnaissance mission, but consoled himself knowing that Tuckmore was always going to be an annoying client. His constant bragging and his superior, know-it-all smile were intensely irritating. He decided he was now simply fed up, and determined to give his client an ultimatum when he returned. He would either do it Dan's way and follow orders, or there could be no safari.

Tuckmore reappeared carrying an immaculate rifle case in oak, with the initials H&H in gold inlay. It had shiny brass hinges, leather straps, brass buckles and leather corner pieces.

He laid it reverently on the table and lowered himself to his seat opposite Dan before placing his thumbs on the brass latches. 'You want an adequate weapon?' he said, then with two sharp clicks from the latches, he lifted the lid.

Lying on the bright blue lining was the most beautiful hunting piece Dan had ever seen.

Its double steel barrels shone with the lustrous depth of a mountain stream. The wooden stock glowed as if lit by some mysterious inner source, and the scrollwork around the trigger guard was magnificent, showing an elephant's head surrounded by intricately engraved patterns. As he studied it further, a herd of previously invisible zebras appeared from among the swirling engraved vortices.

'The bespoke Holland and Holland Royal Double Rifle,' Tuckmore said in the hushed tones of a devotee. 'Takes the 500/450 magnum flanged Nitro Express cartridge.'

It was the best available cordite ammunition. With the power of an express train, one bullet could drop anything in its tracks.

Tuckmore quickly and expertly assembled the gun, which

made the reassuring throaty *clacking* sounds that only a precisely manufactured mechanism could make.

'Twenty-six inch. With extractors, naturally. Fourteen and five-eighths length of pull. Two years in the making. Over a thousand hours of meticulous work by the best gunsmiths in the world.'

Tuckmore had it in his hands now, turning it for the benefit of Dan, who reached a tentative finger to the scrollwork on the equipment cover plate.

'My own design and personal engraver,' Tuckmore said. 'See the zebras in the background? And the rhino and buffalo on the top?'

Dan's hand moved to the stock.

'*Juglans regia*,' said Tuckmore. 'Thin-shelled English Walnut — the best, the only wood for a gun stock.'

It was truly a work of art as well as a firearm with the power to kill Africa's biggest and toughest game.

'I was personally fitted out at the shooting grounds in Wembley before embarking for Mombasa. Five thousand foot-pound of kinetic energy.'

Dan was nodding, but was consumed by the beauty of the piece, and barely listening.

'Seventy-five guineas,' Tuckmore added as a *coup de grace*.

Dan stared at him. Seventy-five guineas. Enough to buy the Ford truck fitted out for safari work that he'd been coveting in *The Field*.

Bailey Tuckmore was rich, conspicuously so. Dan could forgive him for that, but what rankled was his smugness. Dan felt envious and inadequate. He wanted to knock Bailey Tuckmore off his chair. Instead, he congratulated him on his choice of rifle. 'Holland and Holland,' Dan said, struggling to find a comment capable of bringing Tuckmore back to earth. 'It's British-made.'

'I grant you that, but it was good enough for Teddy Roosevelt back in '98. And it sure as hell is good enough for me.'

* * *

The night was mild and lit by countless stars. Bailey Tuckmore sat quietly staring into the fire. Dan sat opposite him, head back, enjoying the stars and the tangy taste of Africa's night air. Occasionally, the pungent odour of Tuckmore's handmade *Belicoso Fino* drifted on the shifting air towards him, but it was not enough to spoil the rare moment of peace.

Tuckmore was a boaster. When he wasn't advising Dan on the correct management of the camp, he was regaling him, and particularly Liz, with recollections of his exploits. Dan wondered how it was possible for a man of no more than fifty years to have packed so much into his life. However, for that moment at least, Dan was grateful for the serenity and the simple enjoyment of listening to the sounds of the night.

The mournful call of a spotted eagle owl drifted from the acacia at the edge of camp, and from the direction of the Taita Hills, came the throaty call of a lion.

They had been on safari for ten days and the evening sojourn with tea or coffee had become a routine.

Liz joined the men around the fire, which Dan had let burn down to a gentle red glow. She had changed into a fresh white blouse now turned to soft pink in the firelight, and her fair hair shone like polished amber when she tossed it from her face. As she took her seat on the opposite side of the fire, a shadow flittered soundlessly overhead.

'Oh, what was that?' she asked.

'Probably a fruit bat,' Dan said. 'Have you forgotten all you knew about the bush?'

'Maybe I have. It's been too long.'

Tuckmore removed his cigar from the corner of his mouth. 'How long have you been away in Australia?' he asked, before stuffing his *Belicoso Fino* back into his mouth.

'It's been a long time,' she answered. 'About ten years.'

'I was in Alaska about ten years ago,' he offered tentatively.

But Liz was lost in thought. She lifted her eyes to the sky. 'I've missed it.'

The lion's plaintive moans came again. *Oom, oom, oom.*

'That lion sounds real close, Dan. Maybe we can go out for him tomorrow,' Tuckmore said.

'What makes you so interested in shooting wild animals, Mr Tuckmore?' Liz asked.

'Why, I've always had an interest in hunting, Miss Freeman. Kodiak bears in Canada. Grey wolves and tiger on the Amur River. Moose in Scandinavia.'

'It must be very dangerous.'

'Aw, shucks, so long as I have a rifle in my hands, it's fine. The worst situation I was ever in was in Russia, when an itty bitty spider bit me. It was a karakurt — hurt like hell, beggin' your pardon. I had to burn the poison out of me. See?'

He rolled back his sleeve to show a patch of wrinkled, shiny scar tissue on his forearm.

'I had to hold a lighted match under there. The only way to deal with the critter's poison. But I hadn't thought about Africa until Teddy Roosevelt's safari in '09. It got me real interested. Now take Roosevelt, he's a man —'

'But what I mean is, what enjoyment do you take from killing these beautiful animals?'

It appeared Tuckmore had never before been asked the question. He appeared edgy about the direction the conversation was taking, and took a moment to consider.

'I guess it's the challenge of hunting dangerous game. Man against beast. The stalk. The strategy. The position for the kill. Ma'am, out there it's kill or be killed.'

'I see ... then why do you hunt antelope?'

'Antelope?'

'Yes, I noticed you had the boys skin a beautiful kudu for you the other day. Surely a kudu poses no threat of kill or be killed?'

'Now that's different. Those other critters, the antelope, the zebra and the like, shooting them is so as to, you know, capture their beauty.'

'Capture their beauty? How is that so?'

Dan was enjoying Tuckmore's discomfort.

'What else can you do? There's no way to keep it to yourself. I just feel that unless I can kill the deer or the bear or, in this case, the kudu, I can't control it. Until it's there, lying at my feet, it can disappear. It's almost as though it doesn't exist unless I shoot it.'

Dan had heard similar explanations from other hunters, but he could see that Liz was puzzled by the concept.

The lion's call came again, more distant now.

Apparently taking her silence as an endorsement of his logic, Tuckmore turned to Dan. 'That fella seems to be getting further away.'

Dan nodded. 'He is. Don't worry, there'll be others.'

'I'm tired of all these donkey-ears we've been shootin'.' It was Tuckmore's manner of describing antelope. 'I wanna chance to test my Winchester on one of those big cats.'

'I expect my tracker will be back by morning. He'll have found something for us.'

Dan had sent Korok out to search for game two days ago. He wondered why he hadn't returned, especially since lion were clearly in the area of their camp. Perhaps the little Pokot was monitoring the pride's movements. Dan hoped he would be back in the morning. He didn't think Tuckmore's patience would last much longer.

* * *

Korok had followed the lion spoor for miles before losing it in the rocky outcrops west of camp. When he spotted the circling vultures he headed towards them, hoping it was the pride's kill of the previous night. He examined the evidence surrounding the carcass and was quite surprised by what he was able to read in the sandy soil.

He was disappointed to find that it wasn't lion that had taken the wildebeest. A pack of hyena, he guessed about six adults and three juveniles, had taken it down and torn it apart in the early evening of the previous day. Hyena were quite effective hunters, particularly at night, when their lack of speed was not such an issue. What usually followed was that any lion in the vicinity would chase the hyena off their kill, devour it through the hours of darkness, and when sated leave the remains for the original owners. This gave the hyena its reputation as a cowardly scavenger, when in fact they were often the killers.

But no lion had been present at this kill, meaning there were none around. Korok was puzzled by the unusual distribution of animals of late, and could only explain it as being caused by the nearby fighting, including heavy artillery, in the Longido hills. He sighed: it meant more hours scouring the countryside for lion spoor.

Before leaving, he made a wider examination of the area around the carcass. It caused him to reconsider his earlier assumptions. What he had taken as a wildebeest was in fact a donkey, and it had not been killed by the hyenas at all, but had staggered for some distance before collapsing. It was dead before the predators arrived. More surprising was that there were strange tracks and human footprints all over the area beyond the carcass. He squatted on his heels, rested his chin on his forearm and let the spoor tell its story.

After a few minutes, a smile creased his furrowed face.

* * *

Dan left camp with Korok an hour before sunrise, having told Liz and Tuckmore the preceding night that he would be gone on a scouting mission looking for prospective game.

When they were a few miles from the camp, the sun began to lighten the sky behind them. Directly ahead loomed the darkened but unmistakeable monolith of Kilimanjaro, rising like a colossus from the surrounding plains.

Dan called a halt and handed Korok a piece of biltong. They squatted on their haunches and chewed in silence, sharing a water bottle between them.

Dan watched the line of sunlight creep down the shining glacier-draped mountainside into the darkness of the fringing forest, and again went over the details that Korok had given him the previous day. It was important to understand them fully.

'Tell me again about the *Gerimani* you saw.'

The little man halted his vigorous chewing and cocked his head to one side as was his habit when thinking. Although he could understand English reasonably well, he used a convoluted and tortuous patois of Swahili, Pokot and English to express himself. He reinforced this with animated hand gestures and facial expressions.

Dan followed it as best he could, and gleaned a few more facts that he had missed on the previous rendition.

While tracking a pride of lion two days earlier, Korok had come across what he thought were the remains of a wildebeest — their recent kill. In fact, it was the almost totally devoured carcass of a German pack donkey. All that remained of the equipment, and a distinguishing one at that, was a metal cross buckle from a harness that lay glistening in the sand. The hyenas had consumed everything, including all of the leather harness, leaving only the tooth-marked metal buckle with the letters *1/FK* stamped into it. Nearby, Korok found the tracks of several men and a wheeled vehicle drawn by two surviving donkeys, and followed them.

Dan could imagine Korok's shuffling gait and the tuft covering his buttocks bobbing as he jogged along in pursuit of the stumbling Germans. He would have overtaken them quite quickly and then watched from a distance to determine their direction before hurrying back to camp.

When he returned to camp and showed Dan the buckle, he took it to his tent to consult the documents and code book that Lieutenant Conroy had given him. The initials stood for *1st Feldkompanie* — the German infantry company stationed at Arusha, about fifty miles on the other side of the German East border. As near as he could estimate it from Korok's story, he'd found the piece of harness within British territory. But what interested Dan most was the Germans' position and apparent direction. It didn't make sense. Dan had decided he must see it for himself.

Having completed his story, Korok returned to chewing his biltong, which he did with complete absorption.

Dan wondered again at the Pokot's ability to so comprehensively turn his attention from one task to the next. It was as if there was an electric light switch in his brain, illuminating only the area needing his attention at that instant.

Like the Maasai, the Pokot were semi-nomadic pastoralists,

moving their cattle as the seasons and available grass demanded. Their traditional lands were in the dry country north of the Laikipia Plateau. Dan had never travelled that far north, although Bill Freeman had before Dan joined the company. Korok was the only Pokot Dan had ever seen, and he wondered if all his tribe had the same ability to concentrate on one matter to the exclusion of all others.

They finished their simple meal and Dan asked Korok to again indicate which direction he believed the German column was now likely to be. He again pointed to the south.

'Towards Lake Jipe?' Dan queried, still doubtful that he had understood Korok the first time.

Korok raised his eyebrows. It was the only indication he ever gave to suggest he found Dan's actions or questions peculiar. Then he gave his usual single, unambiguous nod of his head that implied that he would waste no more energy repeating trivialities.

They walked on in silence until their shadows had shrunken to small blots on the red soil. Above them the sun was a brilliant white beacon. Dan was about to abandon the search for signs of the Germans, when Korok pointed. It took Dan some time to find it in the heat haze, but ahead was a diffuse cloud of dust that rose languorously from the flat plain.

They altered their course to skirt the dust cloud and found a rocky *kopje* where they concealed themselves and waited. After about an hour, the German column passed below them. Dan used his field glasses to investigate, and found the donkey wagon loaded with water containers.

Dan knew that General Malleson was planning to mount a campaign to dislodge the Germans from their defensive position on Salaita Hill, which was inside British East Africa territory, but here, surely, was an alternative solution. The Salaita hills obviously had no natural water supply, or what existed had failed, so the Germans were secretly carrying in water by donkey carts. It didn't take too much imagination to see that if Malleson blockaded the supply route to Lake Jipe and Lake Chala, the enemy forces would be forced to capitulate.

He pulled a piece of paper from his pack and scribbled a note, which he gave to Korok to take to the army camp at Mbuyuni. The information would be conveyed by telegraph to Durkheimer and then to General Malleson. Dan wasn't a military strategist, but it appeared clear to him that the changed strategy would be a sensible alternative to a full frontal attack on the hill, which would likely result in many lost lives.

As Korok trotted off, Dan headed back to camp feeling pleased with himself. It was only a relatively small piece of military intelligence, but it would have major consequences.

Dan felt good. He'd at last become a part of the war effort.

CHAPTER 6

About eleven in the morning they came upon a small muddy stream west of Amboseli. It was early, but Dan decided to call a halt as the stream, muddy and barely moving though it was, was likely to be the best water they'd find for a few days.

After supervising the setting of the camp, Dan went looking for Liz. The headman told him that she had gone to the stream. Dan decided to join her.

He was pleased that Liz had settled into the life and pace of the safari quite well. She had relinquished her full skirts and prim shoes for more practical jodhpurs and boots. And although she never attended a hunt, she refrained from turning her nose up when he and the client returned with the day's trophies.

He found her at one of the pools washing items of clothing. Others were spread over the rocks to dry.

'Dan. It's you!' she said.

'I'm sorry. Am I in the way?'

'It's just that I'm washing some of my things.'

'Oh.'

His eyes went to the rock and Liz quickly gathered up her underwear. Dan was uncomfortably reminded of another woman by another riverbank and swallowed. 'Sorry ... I'll go back —'

'No, it's all right.'

There was a long moment of embarrassed silence.

'We haven't spoken for quite a while,' he said. 'I wanted to know if there was anything you needed.'

'Perhaps a washerwoman.'

'Then let me get one of the porters to —'

'You'll do nothing of the kind. I was joking.'

They smiled together and he sat on one of the rocks beside her.

'But you're right, we haven't talked much lately,' she said.

'I'm sorry. It's been a difficult safari. Tuckmore is a ... Well, he's different. And the game has been hard to find. I fancy the soldiers passing through this part of the country have shot up everything in sight, either for fun or for fresh meat: it doesn't matter. What game there is have taken to hiding in the bush. It's only when Tuckmore and I leave camp and go out with just the gun-bearers that we see anything at all. It must be boring for you. You should come with us next time.'

'When you're shooting? No thank you.'

'It's not so bad, really.'

'Mr Tuckmore hasn't convinced me.'

'Tuckmore only sees what's at the end of his gun sights. There's more to the bush than that. You of all people should know.'

'I do love the African bush.'

'I remember when you lived in the hills outside Nairobi — with all your pet animals. You were never at home. Always running off into the bush. Do you remember that?'

'I do. Now that I'm back among the memories. When I was in Adelaide it was hard to remember that lovely farm we had in Limuru. It felt like my early life was an invention of my imagination.'

'You were a wild one back then. Now look at you.'

She had a tentative smile on her lips as she asked, 'And what do you see now?'

'You're no longer the pig-tailed Lizzie I remember. That's for sure. Now I see a very attractive young woman.'

'Thank you,' she said, then began to draw circles in the sand with a stick.

'I wonder what happened to the farm after your mother sold it,' he said.

'Mother says it passed back to the Kikuyus.' She threw the stick into the water. 'I loved it up there in Limuru. I wish she had kept it.'

'After your father died, maybe she just had to walk away from it.'

'I should go back. Those beautiful hills, the bush, the animals. It was so delightful.'

'All the more reason to see what I see out there,' he said indicating the surrounding savannah. 'I'll grant you it's not the Limuru forest, but when I'm out there I feel — I don't know — I feel connected with everything around me. The sky, the bush, the wildlife. Every day, every hour, every minute of it makes me feel so alive.'

She stared at him for a moment. 'Why, that's beautiful, Dan. But, why spoil it? Why go hunting?'

'The hunt somehow brings everything together. It becomes more real. More … amazing. There's no trickery in it like you see in the picture theatres. Nothing but the raw life of Africa being exactly as it is. When I'm stalking game, there's nothing to distract me. I can hear the flies buzzing, the grunt of a warthog, the keening of a fish eagle. Sometimes I can even smell the animal. Hunting allows me to get into his head. To think like he does. And the bush, well, it's different too. Not like when you're trekking and the porters are wailing and the wagons creaking. It's quiet like a church. It's like I'm in the Garden of Eden and God is watching.'

She was silent, watching him quite intently as he spoke.

'I don't think I could stand to see an animal killed.'

'Then you don't need to. I'll leave you behind when we are closing in, but really, you'll never know more about an animal than you do when you're stalking him. If you're after lion, you have to think like a lion.'

'Think like a lion?'

'Yes. I know you've seen lion before, but when you're stalking him, he acts differently. You have to get into his brain.'

'I'm not sure about that.'

'Try it. I dare you.'

She looked at him and caught his smile.

He knew she could never resist a challenge from him.

* * *

Liz sat on the edge of her camp bed with a page of writing paper resting on a book on her knee. It would be a very difficult letter to write.

She had been postponing her reply to Max. So much had happened since he wrote — her changed circumstances made it difficult to untangle the many directions her life might now travel. But when she thought of his courageous decision to enlist, she felt it was her duty to respond as positively as she could. His patriotism was inspirational, and had stirred similar strong feelings in her — feelings that she'd not previously experienced.

In spite of his strange behaviour back in Adelaide, she was fond of him, and had great respect for him. She couldn't deny she'd been thrilled to receive his letter. It had come at a low ebb in her personal situation. She felt unable to live with her mother and new husband, and she had no one else. Then she found Dan and rekindled their friendship. She could rely upon him if in need of help. And the dashing Captain Durkheimer had shown interest in her too. More than interest, really — he seemed quite taken by her.

Max's letter had raised vital issues, such as what would be *their* future?

Once her personal circumstances had improved she was able to see the Africa she'd loved as a child. She didn't know if her incomplete qualifications would equip her for a veterinary position in British East Africa, but she knew she wanted to be there, whatever the circumstances.

Liz thought it unlikely that Max would happily leave his family and his chance at renewing his academic career for a new life in Africa. He'd never expressed an interest in such a move. Beyond a few perfunctory questions, he'd not asked about her life there at all. He had already indicated he expected Liz to follow his interests at the expense of her own. It appeared that she would have to make a choice between Max and Africa. And the pull of Africa was too strong.

She would be careful to explain her reasons for declining his proposal, but felt honour-bound to be truthful.

Dear Max, she wrote.

* * *

Dan could always feel the ripple of excitement before a hunt. The gun-bearers chattered too much, joking with the porters and each other. It was all bravado since every hunting safari carried the danger of injury or death, no matter the precautions and preparation. Even Korok, the inscrutable Pokot, was unusually pensive. Dan was himself not immune to it, the more so when, as now, there was mounting pressure to find the elusive game that had been promised to the client.

And then there was Liz, who had agreed to join them on the hunt.

He wondered if he'd made the right decision to invite her. At the time he thought she wouldn't be a problem, but they were going after elephant — a dangerous animal, and Tuckmore had not proven to be the marksman he'd claimed he was. He would need to be extra careful. When they were closing in on the target, he would leave Liz in a safe area with Korok until the contact was complete. The terrain was suitable as it offered good visibility to find the trophy, but enough tree cover for Liz to find a secure hiding place.

Over the last two weeks, the safari had crept its way further northwest, making camp at likely hunting spots before moving on. They were now camped near Lake Shompole — an oasis of fresh water between the alkaline lakes of Magadi and Natron. Dan had found the area during the Vandervold safari, when Bill Freeman had stepped on a puff adder and met his untimely end.

Over previous weeks they had found plenty of good plains animals and taken a few, including a magnificent kudu bull with a full two-and-a-half spiralling turns of its horns, tipped with ivory. Unfortunately, Tuckmore hadn't had much luck with the big game he'd set his heart on, bagging a good-size bull buffalo and a cow, a rhino and a leopard in the first three weeks, but no lion or elephant. They were now approaching the end of the safari and making a final sweep along the Great Rift Valley before turning north towards Nairobi. The Lake Shompole region had always been a reliable place for all kinds of game. Dan felt confident their luck would improve there. It was also an area that he knew interested Captain Durkheimer.

The Great Rift Valley ran through German East Africa across the border into British territory before passing just west of Nairobi. If the Germans were to advance on the town, it was one of the most likely approaches they'd take. He was told to keep watch for any signs of German reconnaissance missions.

Shortly after leaving camp, they began to see plenty of plains animals. There were herds of the long-necked gerenuk feeding on the low-hanging branches of the toothbrush trees. They thrived in the stony landscape, as did the striking long-horned beisa oryx. But it wasn't gerenuk or oryx that was needed that day — the client had already taken a few of each — but the elusive lion and elephant that remained on Tuckmore's list.

Shompole was in a rare period when the often fluky flow of the Ewaso Ng'iro — the *brown river* in Kiswahili — had been refreshed by a distant rainfall that sent a flush of cleansing water through Shompole on its way to Lake Natron. Dan was confident they would find elephant there — he could almost smell them — and the Pokot had confirmed it with spoor on the previous day. Now Dan was becoming tense because Korok had been unable to find fresh evidence that morning.

As they crossed the deep green foliage of a feeder stream, a large herd of giraffe set off in their slow, rocking-horse gallop. The bull's head was above the acacia trees and its back was as dark as tar. The herd consisted of about twelve adults and half a dozen calves ranging from six-foot-high babies on disproportionately long legs to gangling adolescents. They wore various liveries shading from fawn to mottled mid-brown.

A little further on, the giraffes had alerted a female white rhino to their approach and she was off before they could get in range, shepherding her calf with the occasional touch of her horn on its rump.

They pressed on in silence. Korok was twenty paces ahead of Dan, who could occasionally see his shaved head and plaited *siliot* appear above the tall grass. Dan carried his 404 Jeffery and his gun-bearer had the Westley Richards Nitro Express. Tuckmore was next in line, with his gun-bearer following. Liz took up the rear.

A thunder of hooves indicated a herd of zebras on the other side of the river had caught wind of them and fled.

And then there was nothing.

For another thirty minutes they walked on as if in a city park, with only an occasional bird and the swaying of the tall grass to animate the scene.

Dan called a halt and waited for Liz to join him and Tuckmore.

'I think our wind has given us away,' he said. 'I'll give it another ten minutes before I abandon this and take a turn on the opposite bank. Are you all right, Liz? Otherwise I can send you back with my bearer.'

Liz said she was enjoying the walk, and Dan sent Korok ahead.

After fifteen more minutes, he decided to change tactics. He signalled to Korok, but the little man ploughed onwards, head down, buttocks up, ignoring his hissed calls.

Dan caught up to the tracker as he hovered over a steaming pile of elephant dung. As he did so, Korok looked up and flashed a hand signal indicating the herd was fifteen minutes ahead.

Dan checked the wind. It was in their faces. He decided it was time to find a place to leave Liz while the hunting party went in for the kill. He exchanged his 404 for the Express and indicated to Korok that they head towards the dark green line of riverine foliage, which was some two hundred yards away.

They started across a barren patch where the grass cover was thin. Beyond that, a wall of high, dry, elephant grass made a barricade about fifty yards deep before the acacias rose in the background, marking the progress of the river.

The Pokot stopped, frozen in a semi-crouch.

Dan raised his hand, halting the others.

Tuckmore joined him at the front.

The hair on the back of Dan's neck tingled.

Without hearing a warning of any kind, a lioness sprang from the wall of yellow grass in full charge.

Dan had the heavy Nitro Express in his hands. As he lifted it to his shoulder, he heard the *ping* of Tuckmore's Springfield, and the thump of the bullet finding its mark.

The lioness barely faltered. Hit in the shoulder, her forward motion was deflected for only an instant. She came on strongly, snarling in fury. Dan squeezed off a shot from the Westley Richards.

The explosion reverberated across the savannah.

CHAPTER 7

Liz had bathed, washed and combed her hair. She'd donned a fresh long-sleeved blouse, khaki skirt and soft mosquito boots. But she couldn't bring herself to join the men for tea at the campfire. Instead, she remained in her tent, tormented by the images of earlier in the day.

When it happened, it happened so quickly she had been unable to comprehend it. She had no time to be afraid. Only now, in the sputtering lamplight of her tent, with the soft *hoo-hoot* of an owl marking the passage of evening into night, could she recall the events leading up to the terrible moment when the lioness fell, dead, not twenty paces from her.

Before the animal charged, Liz had been aware that the breeze had disappeared, leaving them sweating in humid, lifeless air. The muted rustling sound of brittle grass stalks had gone too. There was none of the chirruping, humming or singing of insects and the birds had lost their voices. She had the feeling that comes before a thunderstorm when the air is alive, and the skin of the forearm shies from the touch of even the softest silk.

In this eerie stillness they approached a tall stand of dry grass, gold as the sunrise, standing between them and the line of acacias that defined the course of the river. Dan and his Pokot tracker had exchanged glances. She could sense unspoken messages passing between them. They had noticed the electric atmosphere too.

Only now could she explain the startling phenomenon that occurred as they stood facing the wall of grass. It wasn't the wind, but at the time she thought it had inexplicably returned to strike the grass, parting it in one long gash that rushed towards them like a fissure prising open the earth. In the next instant the grass wall opened immediately before them, and the lioness burst through in all her magnificent hurtling fury.

There was the sharp report when Bailey Tuckmore fired, quickly followed by Dan's shot — an explosion that sent him a half-step backwards.

The snarling face of the lioness, terrible and beautiful a moment before, exploded too, leaving a mass of blood and shattered bone where it had been.

It had become the image that defined her day, and she was sick to her stomach.

She felt she was somehow a collaborator; an accomplice. Worse, the Freeman Safaris company was hers and as such she was at least partly responsible for the carnage.

She would wind it up rather than have her name appended to any further frightful butchery.

* * *

Bailey Tuckmore lifted Dan's tumbler from the edge of the fire and reverently filled it from the half-empty bottle. He held the glass up to the moonlight, squinting through the deep amber liquid.

'There,' he said, nodding in appreciation at what he saw. 'That's a bourbon for you.'

He handed it to Dan.

'No more for me. That stuff makes my head spin.'

'C'mon, be a man.'

Dan accepted it, but reluctantly. It was his fourth glass, and although he wasn't a whisky drinker — in fact had rarely tasted it before — the taste was growing on him.

'What's it called?'

'Ahh, I told you already. Old Forester's genuine bourbon whisky. See? There's the signature on the label.'

Dan took the bottle. 'It says *George Garvin Brown*.'

'Does it? Well, I'll be dammed. Must be the distiller. Or somebody. Anyway, what do you think of it now?'

'It's not bad. Quite good, in fact.'

He had mostly been a beer man, lager in particular. He'd been drinking it since he was a young man on the Darling Downs where

Castlemaine XXX Sparkling Ale was known by all to be the very best.

'So ...' Tuckmore said, swaying a little as he leaned towards Dan, his glass raised '... to our lioness.'

They clinked glasses.

Dan saluted and took a mouthful.

Liz came from the tents now hidden in darkness, and took a seat opposite Dan. She looked radiant in the firelight, although a little more subdued than usual. Now that he thought about it, she'd been quiet since returning from the morning's safari. Perhaps he'd made the wrong decision to invite her on the hunt. He knew how she felt about animals: he should have foreseen that despite his precautions there was a chance she would see one die.

'Miss Freeman,' Tuckmore said expansively. 'Good evening. I'm glad you could join our little celebration.'

'Celebration?'

'For our trophy. Our lioness.'

'Oh ...'

'I was about to tell our leader here, Mr Sutherland, that I thought his choice of firearm was excessive.'

'What do you mean by that?' Dan asked.

'Lion, my boy. You don't need a Nitro Express for lion.'

'We were after elephant.'

'And you totally ruined my trophy.'

'Your trophy! You might recall that you missed with your Springfield. Then she was on us before we could think.'

'You have to learn to be quick, young fella. A hunter needs to be quick in mind and body.'

'I've managed to survive so far. It's how I make my living.'

'Pah! I was charging up San Juan Hill in '98 while you were probably still in diapers.'

'In '98 I was fourteen, and working with real men on the Darling Downs.'

'Tending sheep, I suppose. On foot. What do you call it? Droving? I was with Teddy Roosevelt's Rough Riders.'

'Don't tell me about horse-riding. We lived on horseback in the outback. And I don't mind telling you, most of the drovers reckoned Danny Sullivan was the best horseman on the Darling Downs.'

'Who's Danny Sullivan?'

'Sutherland … I mean, Dan Sutherland.'

'Hah! That bourbon sure got to you tonight. Don't even remember your own name. Sure you don't want another?'

Dan caught Liz's curious expression, and decided he'd said enough that night. 'No more for me. Have to get up early tomorrow.' He stood unsteadily. 'G'night.'

* * *

Dan came from his tent into the light of dawn, his head aching, his eyes burning and with a feeling in his gut like fire.

Liz was already at the mess tent, looking her usual beautiful self. 'Good morning, Dan,' she said.

'Morning, Liz.'

'I'm glad you're here before Mr Tuckmore joins us; there's something I need to talk to you about.'

'Oh, yeah? What's that?'

'It's about yesterday.'

'Sorry. Do you mind? I really need a cup of tea. Could you hold on for just a mo while I get one?'

She said she could, and waited for him to pour a strong brew, which he brought back to the table. He took a tentative sip.

'Ahhh … that's better.'

'As I was saying, it's about yesterday. I was shocked, no … revolted by what I saw out there.'

'Yeah, I've been thinking about that. I shouldn't have asked you to come along. I know you — it was a stupid idea. I mean, if you were a hunter you'd understand. I know of a few women who really enjoy it, but others are —'

'So I've been thinking … I don't want anything more to do with it.'

Dan looked at her over his steaming cup. He could now see she was quite upset. She was composed but her lovely blue eyes were growing misty with the emotions she was trying to contain. She was just too young and sensitive for a hunt. Maybe in a few years …

'I want to go back to Nairobi.'

'Really?'

'Yes. Really.'

'But we'll be there in another few days.'

'Now.'

He sighed. 'Well, if you must. I suppose I can release Korok and a couple of porters to escort you back. You should be there in a day or two.'

'That will do quite nicely, thank you.'

'I'm sorry you haven't enjoyed it.'

'And I should tell you I intend to wind up the company.'

'What?'

'It won't be immediate, of course, so it will give you a few weeks to find something else.'

He stared at her, his head now pounding even more. He ran a hand across his forehead.

'Liz, you don't understand. You can't do that.'

'I know it must come as a shock, but I simply can't —'

'No, Liz, you can't do it. You don't own the company.'

She studied his expression, realising he was serious.

'What are you saying? Of course I own Freeman Safaris.'

'I bought it from your grandfather before he died.'

'That's impossible. It was his pride and joy. Why would he do such a thing?'

'It was … He had a good reason at the time.'

'I don't believe you.'

He sighed and massaged his throbbing temples. 'You can check the company records. It's all legal.'

She stood staring at him for several moments, the blood rising in her cheeks. Then she spun on her heels and headed back to her tent.

* * *

They continued to hunt the shores of Lake Shompole for elephant, but although Tuckmore bagged a number of good-size game, he had no success with his tusker. On the second night after they had shot the lioness and Liz had stormed off to Nairobi, he announced he had run out of time, and asked Dan to head for home.

In the morning the headman roared his orders, but the men needed little encouragement to strip the camp. They had been on safari for three months — three months away from wives, family, friends and the comforts of the village. Their voices lifted in exuberant song as they packed the camp in preparation for their departure, and their final payday.

The song grew as new verses were added. All were stories of unbounded heroism and amazing physical prowess. Dan knew enough Kiswahili to smile at the lyrics. One voice — that of a tenor — told of how, in the face of deadly danger, he had saved the life of the *mzungu bwana* when he had been attacked by a wild boar. Another sang of the client with the beautiful rifle and poor skills. The verses would multiply until they marched proudly into Nairobi.

They were on their way by mid-morning and shortly their path took them through the area where, a few days before, Dan had shot the lioness.

The incident had been on his mind ever since. There had been something odd about the lioness's behaviour that day.

It was not unusual to find a lone male lion, or a couple of brothers, that had been evicted from the pride by the dominant male. They wander the savannah in search of an ageing male no longer capable of defending his harem from younger interlopers. But it was unusual to find a lone adult lioness. Also, in his experience, a single lioness would not attack a hunting party unless she was cornered. This wasn't the case in the open grassland where they had come upon her. She could have taken advantage of the heavy cover to escape. Instead she made a frenzied charge at them. He decided to take the small detour to the site of the kill, and told his headman to carry on, and that he would catch up.

Alone in the bush, his thoughts turned to the other disturbing event that had occurred the morning after that day — his argument with Liz.

He had handled the matter badly from the outset. While Liz was far away in Australia he'd had no reason to tell her he'd bought the company. She would have asked why, and he didn't want to tell her it was because her grandfather had engaged in illegal hunting and was prosecuted and very nearly gaoled. He had always intended to sell the business back to Bill when possible, and upon his death it was proper that he offer to sell it to Liz. But now the safari business was the façade he needed to serve in the intelligence unit. He couldn't let her close the company down. Not yet.

His surroundings were becoming increasingly familiar now, and he brought his mind back to what was quite a hostile setting. The tall grass and flat terrain made it ideal for the surprise attack of a few days previously. He began to wonder at the wisdom of pursuing his curiosity. The lioness had probably been part of a pride that may still be in the vicinity. He had his 404 with him, but as had almost been proven, an attack at such close quarters could be fatal.

He soon found the circle of flattened grass where the lioness had fallen. Again, an eerie silence fell over the place except for the low buzz of the large flies that hovered over what remained of the carcass after the scavengers had been.

He found the lioness's trail of parted grass and pushed along it towards the river.

Now the silence deepened. After pacing carefully onwards for fifty yards, he heard the faint babble of the tumbling river. In a few moments he reached it and took a deep, relieved breath as the clean sweep of the river opened up the view along the bank. There was nothing out of the ordinary. The river was shallow and narrow and flowing slowly towards the lake. He wondered what he had hoped to discover and felt a little ridiculous for making the journey.

He was about to leave when he noticed signs of a struggle on the sandy bank, and blood stains — no more than a day old. A few steps further on, he came upon tufts of fur, and in another few paces found the remains of a lion cub, although there was precious little remaining to provide the clues.

Now he understood. The lioness had left the pride to give birth in safety. When the hunting party approached, she reacted to defend her cubs. With her death, and without her protection, the cubs were doomed to be easy pickings for almost any predator lucky enough to happen along when the cubs left their lair to find their mother and her milk.

The mystery solved, he began to retrace his steps towards the towering grass. Just as he was about to enter it, he heard a strange sound. He listened, but it had gone. A moment later it returned — a barely audible mewing.

At the edge of the grass, under a tangle of shrubbery, he found a lion cub. It lay like a ragdoll, motionless, but when he touched it, its tiny head came up. It hissed and spat, and its eyes glared defiantly in his direction, although how clearly it could see him with those smoky blue orbs was uncertain. The struggle to hold its head up was too much, and it sagged under the effort.

Dan scooped up the cub, but it struggled and hissed, then gave him a feeble but nevertheless painful bite with its needle-like teeth. Dan grabbed it by the scruff and, in the instinctive response of every cat, it curled up its legs and hung there, immobile.

'Now what am I going to do with you?' he asked the dangling bundle.

He checked for any signs of its siblings, but as he suspected, he found none. It was amazing that an orphaned cub could avoid detection by the many predators in the area. Its survival, even for a few days, was extraordinary.

He looked at the cub, hanging limply from his fist. It was a male. When he loosened his grip on him, he made a faint hiss. He was not only a fighter, he also had a very strong will to live. His path from the den to where Dan had found him was in the direction his mother had taken before she died at his hands.

The cub's fighting spirit impressed him, and for a moment he entertained the idea of trying to save this tiny ball of fury, but immediately rejected it. He had no time for such an indulgence. Anyway, it would probably die.

The humane action would be to end its starvation. He placed the cub on the ground and unshouldered his 404. The cub's head bobbed with the effort of lifting it, but it began to crawl towards the dense foliage from where he'd found it.

Liz had often said that the person who interfered with nature would one day be punished for their irresponsibility by suffering a burden of guilt and regret.

He shook his head to dispel the sentimental nonsense, and lifted the 404 again ... but the Jeffery was a massive overkill. He tucked it under his arm, lifted the squirming ball of fur and walked back to the river.

At the water's edge he prepared to toss the cub into the lazy brown waters. Ten yards away, on the far bank, he spotted a crocodile he'd not seen when he first arrived. It watched him with cold topaz eyes.

Dan hated crocodiles.

CHAPTER 8

Liz returned to Nairobi, fuming with anger and frustration at Dan's treachery. She had planned to set up a business with the money gained from selling Freeman Safaris. The type of business was as yet uncertain, but she had in mind something to do with animal care. Now she needed gainful employment, but her thoughts were of Dan, and her mind went into another round of, *If only I had said …*

She was in just such a reverie while walking down Sixth Avenue when she very nearly collided with Richard Durkheimer.

'Oh!' she said.

'I do beg your — Elizabeth!'

'Captain Durkheimer,' she said. 'It's my fault entirely. I should be looking where I'm going.'

'If you had, I might have missed that lovely smile of yours. So I am quite pleased to have bumped into you again. So to speak.'

She smiled.

'I was just now thinking of you,' he said.

'Oh?'

'Yes, indeed. I saw your name, Freeman, on a sign for one of those safari companies on Government Road. I was wondering if by chance Freeman Safaris belonged to one of your family members.'

'Ahem. As a matter of fact, it does. Or at least it did. My grandfather, William Freeman, started the company many years ago and owned it up until his death.'

'I'm sorry to hear of your loss. Is the company still in family hands?'

'No. Ownership passed to one of the employees.' She didn't want to involve the captain in her family squabbles. It would not be seemly, but the matter was still raw, and she couldn't resist adding, 'But the Lord alone knows why.'

'I see. Then you are not involved in the business at all?'

'No.'

'If I might be so forward as to observe — you seem annoyed about it.'

'It's something about which I intend to further enquire, but it's all too boring, and far too fine a day to worry about, don't you think?'

'It is a lovely day. Are you out for a walk?'

'I have some errands to attend to.' There was a brief silence and Liz said, 'Well ... I mustn't waste any more of your time. I'm sure you have matters of state to attend to.'

'Hardly,' he said, laughing.

His laughter brightened what was normally a quite severe countenance.

'It was a pleasure to see you again. Enjoy your day.'

She thanked him and wished him a good afternoon.

'Oh, Miss Freeman,' he said, bringing her to a halt. 'I wonder if I might be so bold as to ask if you would do me the great honour of accompanying me to our King's birthday celebrations on Saturday afternoon next.'

Her immediate inclination was to accept. A birthday celebration might be exactly what was needed to restore her good humour, yet she wasn't sure if she should. Regardless of his rank and standing, Richard Durkheimer was almost a stranger. But then, it was war time, and things were different.

Seeing her hesitation, he went on. 'It's a chaperoned affair. I mean, all the senior officers and their wives will be there. And the governor. But I would be ever so grateful if you would attend with me. You see, if you don't, I will be seated with the other bachelor officers and be forced to endure the same tedious conversations that I hear almost every other day in the officers' mess.'

'Oh, that would be just too painful for words,' she bantered.

'Exactly. It's high tea at the Norfolk dining room. I believe they put on an excellent spread. Cucumber sandwiches — not that I am all that fond of them. Give me roast beef and mustard any day. But also scones with jam and cream.'

'Cream? Are we not at war?'

He smiled with her. 'Our quartermaster is a magician.' He paused, letting his smile fade. 'Honestly, it would be wonderful if you could accept.'

'I do owe you a favour since you so gallantly arranged for my room at the Norfolk.'

'Then you'll come?'

'I shall be pleased to.'

'Until next Saturday, then. Two o'clock.'

'Saturday. Yes.'

She continued on her way, pleased she had accepted. *And a toss for convention*, she thought to herself. High tea with the dashing captain might be fun.

* * *

When Liz returned to her room from breakfast, she found a letter from Dan, hand-delivered, she later learned, by his little tracker, who had remained lurking among the gum trees on Government Road.

> *My dear Liz,*
>
> *I am sorry for not explaining the situation regarding ownership of Freeman Safaris when you first arrived. It might have avoided the disagreement we had, but I have my reasons.*
>
> *My purpose for writing is to ask your help. The lioness I shot had a litter of cubs, one of which I rescued from the bush (and certain death).*
>
> *I have persevered with various milk mixtures but after at first showing some improvement, the cub has now worsened.*
>
> *If you can spare some time, I'm sure your training could make a difference. The Pokot will show you to our camp. If you hire a buggy, we are only a half-day from Nairobi.*
>
> *Your friend*
> *Dan*

She re-read the letter. A lion cub ... Rescued by a man who thought nothing of shooting animals for pleasure. She tried to imagine Dan attempting to spoon-feed cow's milk to an orphaned baby lion. The little animal would have probably initially responded to the rehydration the milk provided, but she was aware that many animals were intolerant to the lactose in cow's milk.

Her initial resentment at the man's audacity to dare to ask for her help quickly faded as she imagined the little thing lying at death's door.

She threw a few items into a bag and went in search of the Pokot.

* * *

Following his usual custom, not a word of unnecessary conversation passed Korok's lips as he directed the cart driver to Dan's camp. It was a mile beyond what had become known as Ngong village, which was no more than a large circle of cow-dung huts behind a row of six small *dukas*. The Indians who operated the slab-sided stores dispensed small conveniences such as tinned meat and tobacco to the elders of the local Maasai clan.

It was late afternoon and the camp was empty and silent. There was no sign of Bailey Tuckmore, or the safari's large contingent of porters, cooks and gun-bearers, who Liz supposed had been dismissed when the client returned to Nairobi. Only a couple of men fussed around a small cooking fire in the middle of a circle of three small tents. Another two ambled in with firewood.

Korok spoke brusquely to them in Kiswahili, demanding they fetch the *bwana*. Before anyone could reply, Dan came from one of the tents and regarded her for a moment before speaking. 'I'm glad you could come.'

'I'm surprised you had the gall to ask.'

The line of his jaw tightened. 'It's not for me. You're the animal-lover, aren't you?'

'The lion cub ... Where is it?'

He nodded his head towards the tent from which he'd come.

She entered the tent behind him. It contained a stretcher bed, a chop box and two gun cases. In a corner was what appeared to be a bully-beef crate, open and empty. There was an odour in the tent like sour milk.

'Sorry about the stink,' he said.

Inside the crate was the small, motionless form of a lion cub.

Her heart sank. She was too late, but from the little creature's appearance, it was unlikely anyone could have saved it, separated as it was from its mother at such a young age.

She guessed the little cat was less than a month old and still carried the spotted coat that was its camouflage and protection from other predators. Its paws seemed several sizes too big for it, and it was thin, with hipbones protruding like pointy knobs under a fur coverlet.

She had seen many animals die in the university's medical laboratory, but this was not a white rat, bred to die in the interests of science. It was exotic and uniquely beautiful.

'When did it die?' she asked, dejected.

'It's not dead. Yet.'

She shot a glance at him and then reached into the box to feel warmth under the silky cover of fur. As she lifted and felt the cub's small swollen abdomen, peered into its eyes, and checked for pulse, she peppered him with questions.

'He's been going both ends since about the first day I fed him.'

'And he's badly dehydrated. We don't have much time.'

* * *

Dan sat in silence as Liz examined the cub, then watched her spend the next hour dripping sugar water, with infinite patience, into the cub's prised-open lips.

She was very businesslike and, just as he had hoped, had become so absorbed in her task that she appeared to have forgotten their quarrel.

Having lost his nerve to dispose of the cub at the river, Dan had warmed to its fighting spirit, and was determined to save its life.

But he had to admit he hoped his efforts to save the cub were also a way of restoring his friendship with Liz.

'That's all we can do for now,' she said, sitting back on her heels. 'He'll sleep, and in the meantime let's go to the *dukas* to see what they have that might be of use.'

At the trade store she rummaged through the various bottles and tins, reading the ingredients before selecting some and discarding others.

'I have enough milk for a few days,' he offered in a bid to be helpful.

'No. I think the cow's milk is the problem. That's why he's bloated and suffering diarrhoea. We need to try something else. I have some glucose here that will add sugar and there's cornflour for body.'

She reviewed her selections.

'These other ingredients might be useful too. Let's hope they help.'

Back at camp Liz set to work with resolve. His recollection of her as a child was of a capricious girl, one moment lost in the pages of a book and the next dashing wildly through the bush in search of animals and insects for her collection. The woman now fussing over warming bowls and food mixtures, with a tuft of her fair hair hanging over her brow, was purposeful and determined.

They fed the cub a serving of Liz's concoction before dinner, but it was difficult to get enough of the sticky liquid down his throat. Most of it ran down his chin and after trying for an hour his coat was matted with drying formula.

Liz gave him a warm-water sponge-bath and Dan used a piece of *mericani* cloth to dry him. The cub raised a muted string of protests and the exercise seemed to exhaust him: he promptly fell asleep.

'We should eat something too,' Dan said. 'Then I'll move my camp bed into the stores tent so you can be near the cub.'

'He'll need feeding every two or three hours,' Liz said. 'And I could use your help. You can see how he squirms. If you have another stretcher bed, we can both bunk in here.'

He agreed and gave orders to set up another bed in his tent.

The camp cook had been discharged, along with most of the other staff. The porter who had been co-opted into kitchen duties prepared a formless mass of beans and canned meat that Dan and Liz ate sitting on chop boxes at the campfire. The night was typical for that time of year — still and mild. He heard the distant whine of hyenas.

Dan tried a number of times to lighten her mood, but Liz remained withdrawn.

'You're worried,' he said at last.

'Yes,' she sighed. 'I have no idea what I'm doing. I don't know if the milk substitute is too strong or too weak. Maybe the cornflour is too starchy.' She looked at him with misting eyes. 'It's trial and error, and if I'm wrong, he dies.'

'You can only do your best. That's life in the African bush. He would have died anyway.'

Her eyes flared at that. 'His life wouldn't have been at risk if you hadn't shot his mother.'

Her stinging rebuke came like a crack of lightning in the still night.

'If I hadn't shot her, she would've killed us all,' he said, indignant by her evasion of the obvious facts.

'It's not right, what you do. African animals are not here merely for your clients' enjoyment. They have a right to life.'

Dan tried not to scoff. 'It's what men do. We hunt.'

'Yes, hunt for food if you must. But killing for sport is senseless, and it's … it's cruel.'

He could understand how she might see hunting as a cruel sport, but it wasn't. He was a responsible shooter, always taking care to ensure his clients used appropriate firearms so that the game was despatched quickly and, so far as it could be practically achieved, painlessly. And when a poor shot missed its mark, he never allowed a wounded animal to escape and die a slow and painful death in the bush. He would go after it regardless of the risk and put an end to its suffering. He didn't see any real distinction between game hunting and butchery. He was about to press his point, but Liz was becoming distressed.

'It's not always like that,' he said, mildly. 'Anyway, thank you for coming. I was worried I might not be able to save the little bloke.'

'Why are you?'

'Why am I what?'

'Trying to save him.'

He thought the answer self-evident, but given the heated exchange between them, perhaps not.

'I don't like to see animals suffer. Especially young-uns.'

'And yet you can shoot them. Curious.' Her anger vented, her tone had become dispassionate. Analytical.

'Actually, I love animals,' he said, and it brought back memories of Meg. 'I had a horse once, but ...'

It was a painful recollection. Watching his pretty bay mare slowly starve to death had been more than he could stand. He endured the sight of her suffering for days and weeks, hoping that decent fodder would soon arrive or the company would come upon some good grazing as they tramped across the veld. But they found none, and Dan hadn't the heart to shoot her, as he should have done, before she got so bad. Instead, he watched her die. Slowly.

'So, as I was saying,' he said, coughing to clear his voice. 'I appreciate you coming all the way out here to help.'

'I just hope we're successful.' Liz still wasn't herself. There was a cool formality in her voice.

'The other reason I wanted you to come was to explain about the company.'

'... Yes?'

'Old Bill ... that is, your grandfather ... he found himself in a spot of bother.'

'What kind of bother?'

He winced. 'I don't really want to go into —'

'What kind of bother?' she insisted.

He sighed. 'With the authorities. He — or maybe it was me too — got the bright idea to get some ivory so that —'

'You mean poaching.'

'Um, yes.'

'But why? Freeman Safaris takes paying clients on hunting trips. Although I don't approve, at least it's legal. So why was it necessary to break the law? Why poach?'

'Bill thought it would be a way to get some cash. Business had been quiet and the bills were coming in thick and fast. He thought he had a foolproof way of cashing in on some ivory.'

Thankfully, she didn't press him for the details of Bill's hare-brained plan to make new ivory into old.

'Well, it didn't work and they were going to force Bill to close the company, so he sold it to me — temporarily. The plan was that I would sell it back to him when the probationary period ended but —'

'Probationary period?'

'Look, it's complicated. Bill's licence was suspended for a time and I took it over until it all blew over.'

He could sense that this didn't explain why he didn't now offer the company to her, Bill's heir.

'I will be happy to sign the company over to you to do with it as you wish ... But I can't yet.'

She fixed him with her clear, grey-green eyes. 'Is it because you're using the company to avoid doing your duty in the war?' Her voice was cool, but there was no mistaking her disapproval.

For a moment he was tempted to reveal the real nature of his use of the company, but instead he said, 'I need to keep the company under my name for the duration of the war.'

She nodded, and the conversation faltered until a little later, Liz said goodnight and went to her camp bed.

Dan watched her go, then turned his attention to the fire, watching it slowly burn down to black coals.

* * *

Liz awoke to the sound of the cub's hungry mewing. Dan was already up, fumbling with the paraffin lamp. By its light she fed the cub although it again struggled against Dan's gentle restraint.

They engaged in desultory conversation as they cleaned and dried him. Nothing more was said about the awkward exchange at dinner.

Liz had always liked and admired Dan. He'd seemed so strong in the old days. Discovering he was a coward had shocked and disappointed her. She would have to reassess her opinion of him. It was hard to respect a man who dodged his responsibilities.

After the pre-dawn feed, Liz fell into a deep sleep. When she awoke, Dan was nowhere in sight. She peeped into the crate. The cub was still asleep, its thin rib cage rising as it took short, sharp gasps.

Rubbing her eyes, she poked her head out of the tent into the blinding light of morning to find Dan, a study in concentration, working on the top of one of the chop boxes.

'What are you making?' she asked.

'Oh, good morning. I'm making a feeder tube.'

He had a number of pieces of India rubber tubing of various lengths and diameters. They were fitted one into another to form a tube that started out at about an inch in diameter, reducing to less than a quarter of an inch over its short length.

'A feeder tube? What do you mean?'

He grinned. 'Come with me. Let's see if our little man is ready for breakfast.'

He wasn't, but Liz thought it was best to rouse him.

She watched as Dan pinched closed the narrow end of the tube and poured a little of the formula into the wider end.

The cub initially resisted Dan's rubber tube, but shortly after, responded by sucking on the end of the artificial teat.

'I was thinking about it all night. I could see the spoon we've been using wasn't right. We needed a teat of some sort.' He chuckled. 'The *dukawallah* wasn't too pleased to be woken so early. But look at this! He's taking the milk without most of it running down his chest.'

Liz was pleased for the cub and amused by Dan's boyish enthusiasm. They looked down on the cub like a pair of proud parents. It was the first time she'd felt happy since she arrived in Ngong.

Dan turned his head up to her, and smiled.

It was infectious. She laid her hand on his shoulder.

'Congratulations, papa,' she said.

He laughed.

If only he had done the honourable thing, and enlisted, she thought.

CHAPTER 9

During the following days Dan and Liz saw the cub gain in strength and vigour. The India-rubber feeder made it easier to administer the milk formula. It avoided the mess, and the cub seemed to be responding well.

'Look at him,' Dan said as he held the cub in the crook of his arm. 'He's after fresh meat ... Mine!'

The cub had captured his free hand between his paws and was contentedly gnawing on his thumb and at the same time emitting a soft growl.

'It's a healthy sign,' she said, laughing at Dan's pained expression.

'Ouch! Not so fierce!' he wailed. 'He's got teeth like needles.'

'Think of it as your contribution to the rehabilitation process.'

'Oh ... that's nice. Let's see how much dedication the doctor has when it's *her* turn to provide the teething bone.'

In between feeds they went for walks or sat in the long shadows of afternoon, talking about the different paths their lives had taken during the years they had been separated.

Liz explained the difficulty she'd had determining the course of her study. She had wanted to treat animals, but there was no veterinary course available in Adelaide University, so she took subjects in a science degree that she thought would be useful.

'It caused quite a few questions,' she said. 'There had been only a few women in the whole country who wanted to study science. Most people thought I was wasting my time. Others thought I should be taking arts. "It's more what young ladies do," they said.'

Dan listened to her with growing admiration. Her early years had been overshadowed by her parents' often venomous relationship. Losing her father, whom she relied upon to balance her mother's strident control, had been a terrible trauma. Then living with her grandmother, who by all accounts was no better than her mother, would have added to the load of study that her degree demanded over those years. She'd left Africa as a child and returned as an accomplished and confident young woman.

She talked too of Max and his family's involvement in the wine-making industry. Dan had the sense that she looked back on her time with her tutor-fiancé with such detachment that it appeared she now saw him as part of another person's life.

Dan had no such stories of accomplishment. To his ears, his hunting stories were repetitious; his accounts of the many different, often challenging, personality types among his clientele, trite. He did, however, discover his stories of her grandfather's antics kept her entertained and laughing.

'He could tell stories, all right,' he said. 'Nobody believed him, but he was never boring.'

On the sixth day, they were sufficiently confident about the cub's condition to leave him sleeping in the closed tent under the staff's care while they set out for the nearby Ngong Hills.

The morning was misty and Dan said he feared the visibility might disappoint them. But as they climbed, the wispy filaments of cloud floated away like gossamer veils on the warm air that rose from the grassland.

Climbing the topmost peak, they gazed out over the spectacular Great Rift Valley where ancient volcanoes defiantly held their gnarled heads high above the valley floor. To the north was the Aberdare Range, its blue-green swells rolling away like those of a deep and distant ocean. Slightly to the east of them were the swiftly rising foothills of snow-capped Mt Kenya.

'It's so ... lovely,' Liz said. 'No, that's not right. It's not enough. It's ... powerful. Like all creation's forces have been released in this one place, pushing and pulling the earth until these mountains and plains and everything came together in exactly the right places.'

She felt Dan take her hand and she turned to him.

'Look,' he said, pointing to the south.

Above the low mist that still obscured the savannah rose Mt Kilimanjaro, its glacier peak floating on the clouds: a glistening sentinel in the sun.

It took her breath away, and, she squeezed Dan's hand. 'This is the most beautiful place in the whole world,' she whispered.

The layer of mist eddied like an ocean around the mountain.

'But we've already been to the most beautiful place in the world.'

'... What do you mean?'

'Limuru ... Don't you remember?'

'Of course,' she said, delighted by the recollection. 'It was my first trip outside Nairobi.'

'You were a little girl.'

It pleased her to know they shared a memory. 'Ten,' she said.

'Little enough.'

'And you shared your blanket with me.'

'You were a strange one,' he said, chuckling. 'You said, "Do you think we'll ever see anything as lovely as this again, Dan?"'

His smile transported her back to the ridge at Limuru, high above the mist-filled valley.

Dan had been there through the best of times — sharing her joy overlooking the most beautiful place in the world. And the worst. When he stood beside her at her father's grave, he drew her to him to rest her head on his chest. He always found a way to lift her up when life turned harsh.

He thought she was a strange one. Perhaps she was, but when she left Africa, she had already been in love with him — in her eleven-year-old manner.

Now she yearned for the return of the simplicity that allowed love to flourish without complications.

'We should head back,' she said. 'We have a baby to care for.'

* * *

The lion cub had been lethargic and uninterested in his milk during the evening feeding. Liz reminded Dan that it wasn't unusual, and thought he was merely tired and, as had been the case on similar occasions, suggested that he would again be active and hungry for the night feeding.

He lit the paraffin lamp and they sat together until nine, chatting.

Occasionally one or other would glance into the crate and make reassuring but unconvincing remarks.

Later, when sleep claimed her just before midnight, he covered her with a light blanket, and in the throw of the sputtering lantern watched her gently breathing and thought back to the previous afternoon at the top of the Ngong Hills. She had never looked lovelier. Her face shone with the flush of the climb and when she loosened her hair and shook it free, the wind caught it and threw it around her like a golden mane.

In the preceding days, they had become close as they worked together to restore the little cub to good health. On Ngong he wished he could have told her of his intelligence work because he knew she thought he'd done nothing for the cause, and he could read the disappointment in her eyes.

Around three, when Dan checked on him, he found the cub hot. His little chest rose and fell in short, panting breaths. He thought about waking Liz, but there was no point. Together they could do no more than watch and hope.

He decided to let her sleep on.

* * *

The lion cub died before dawn.

Dan sat on the edge of his camp bed, elbows on his knees and his chin in the cups of his hands. Occasionally he lowered his forehead into them and massaged the creases on his brow, easing the dull pain that lay just behind his eyes. He ached all over, and with a conscious effort he released the tension in his shoulders, letting them drop.

Liz was on a canvas-backed chair, a crushed handkerchief in her hand, which she periodically raised to her nose.

When he went to rouse her to break the sad news, she came instantly awake, and by the look in her searching eyes, knew she already guessed what he was about to tell her.

He nodded to confirm her fears and her tears welled in her eyes before tumbling down her cheeks to her crumpled cotton shirt.

'I should have taken more care,' she said.

'We did all we could. He was a fighter … but just too young.' He tried to speak matter-of-factly, but his throat felt dry. He needed a drink.

'I was so sure we had the right formula for him. He was starting to pick up. He was doing so well.'

'I thought he would make it too,' Dan said. 'But that's life.'

He stood and took a step to Liz's side then placed his hand on her shoulder for a moment. She covered it with hers. Then he went to the back of the tent where the crate sat and stared down at the tiny unmoving figure.

A casual observer may not have noticed any difference between the animal sleeping yesterday on his *mericani* cloth bedding, and the same animal now equally motionless, but dead. It was strange, he thought, how attached he had become to the orphan, and he wondered how many more orphans he had created in his role of white hunter. He instantly put that from his mind.

'I'd better remove the … the cub. I'll get a couple of the boys.'

He turned to Liz and found her watching him. There was sadness in her eyes but also something else. It was as if she had been studying him, perhaps seeing him in a different way.

* * *

The man standing before her as the tent lightened imperceptibly in the first touch of dawn, bereft and grim-faced, was so different from the character she had thought him to be, it rendered Liz lost for words. She felt she should reach out to him, to say something comforting, but he was a white hunter. His emotions were surely different.

That's life.

Yet he'd been touched by the cub's death; he had tried so very hard to save its life. At times, from her darkened camp bed, she had watched him tending to the cub. She could sense his concern by the way he gently cradled the infant as it squirmed away from the feeder, and how he had patiently cleaned it after the feed so that the souring milk didn't stink and harden on its downy coat.

She simply stared at him in silence, wondering who he really was, this white hunter who could face a charging lion yet couldn't stand in uniform with his fellow-countrymen to defend the empire. 'I don't understand you,' she said at last. 'How can you be the hard-headed hunter at one moment, then be saddened at the results of your profession in the next?'

'Maybe I'm not as hard-headed as you think I am.'

'You were always going off shooting when I was a girl. You were *the great white hunter.* The consummate professional. Or so you would have had me believe.'

'And did you believe me?'

'No. I saw another side of you. Until now, I'd forgotten how kind you were to me. When I had no playmates you'd take me fishing. We'd sit and talk. You made me little toys from string and wire. You'd find me when my parents were having one of their big fights, and take me away until they shouted themselves to a standstill.'

He shifted his weight from one foot to the other.

'You were nice to me.'

'You were a little girl. How else would I behave towards you?'

'Well, I'm not a little girl any more.'

'Yes, well ... I'd better see to this matter.' He indicated the crate with an inclination of his head.

'Nothing more can be done now,' she said. 'It can wait.'

He shrugged, but took a step towards the front of the tent.

She stood and put her back to the tent flap, blocking his path. 'It's all right to be sad.'

'I know that.'

'Are you sad?'

'It happens.'

'You can't admit that this little lion cub's death has upset you, can you? It might cast doubt on your ability to hunt. You're afraid that it might reflect upon your manliness.'

'I'm not worried about that ...'

'Then you're worried that to express how you feel might make you too human.'

He hesitated. 'I'm not sad.'

'*Tell* me.'

'I feel ... just so bad. It makes me wonder if it would have been better that he'd died in the first days, before I got to like him. Then I wouldn't care so much.'

'There! You cared. Was that so hard?' she said, taunting him.

'Why are you doing this?'

'Because I'm trying to understand you. I used to know you, but now I'm not so sure. The Dan Sutherland I knew would have gone off to defend his country in a moment.'

'I ...'

She could feel his anger rising, but at last she was close to knowing what was in his mind.

He grabbed her and kissed her roughly on her mouth. He crushed her to him and, after a moment's resistance, she let herself fall into the shape of his body, which pressed so close to her that she could feel the tautness of his midriff and the strength of his arms encircling her.

He broke off and she gasped. Then she pulled his head down to her and kissed him, this time softly, though the heat of their embrace stirred her. They remained locked together. His hands explored her body and his kisses became more and more intense. She felt an urge to know him, to be part of his body.

He whispered, 'I want you.'

'Yes.'

He fumbled with the buttons on her cotton shirt and she pulled it over her head.

Now, with only the soft chemise covering her nakedness, she felt shocked at her boldness and paused.

Dan had torn off his own shirt and she was drawn to touch the firm brown flesh of his chest.

Her jodhpurs were a struggle. She fell backwards onto the camp bed and he ripped them over her bare feet.

He threw off his clothing and lowered himself into her arms.

* * *

They lay on the narrow camp bed in the heat of the tent, their bodies fused together by perspiration, neither prepared to break the spell that bound them.

Liz had been at first stunned by the pain of their union, then awed by the intensity of the emotion that followed. She wanted Dan. Had wanted him since she was a girl, not knowing what it meant.

But there was a flaw in the perfection of the moment. She didn't understand his answer to her enquiry as to the reason he held on to the safari company. His response appeared to be a denial of his duty.

She felt too inhibited to raise the question again. Perhaps an oblique approach would be better. 'I made some enquiries around the town to see what I can do for the war effort,' she said.

He was gently stroking her naked back with his fingertips, but paused for an instant when she made her statement.

'I see.'

His caresses resumed.

'I've put forward my application to join the nursing brigade. There are so many people out there doing the best they can to keep the Germans at bay. Volunteering for the nurses is the least I can do.'

She held her breath and waited, but he kept his silence.

CHAPTER 10

Liz mouldered in Nairobi for endless weeks as her medical unit's labyrinthine organisation prepared their move to the medical base on the Taveta track, which was set in a sheltered fold of land surrounded by dense bush. She had finally made it to the base about a month earlier and was still trying to understand the routine. She had been received on her arrival by Mary Carmichael, known to all as Sister Mary.

'The first thing you need to understand, love, is that there *is* no routine,' she said. 'Unless you can call late nights, early mornings and no time to call your own in between a routine.'

Mary had been a nurse with the Australian contingent during the Boer War, and had stayed on after she fell in love with a local. They were married in Durban and later lured to British East Africa by the offer of land for farming. After a decade struggling to coax a piece of barely arable land near Voi into a productive farm, she watched her husband die of hard work. She returned to nursing and was among the first into the field at the beginning of the East Africa campaign. By virtue of that experience, plus the fact that she was over forty and by far the oldest of the nursing staff, she had become the *de facto* coordinator and instructor for new nurses.

'I suppose I can understand that,' Liz replied. 'It's just … you know, it would have been nice if someone had showed me around and told me what I was meant to do when the casualties start arriving.'

Mary smiled. 'When it happens, and we haven't seen much of it yet, there's nothing that can prepare you for it. You just do what you can. You do what you must. What experience have you had, dear?'

'None, really. I was studying science at Adelaide University. Third year.'

'Near enough. Major McClimont wants me to train an understudy on anaesthetics. Do you know anything about chloroform?'

'No.'

'Ether?'

She shook her head.

'That's not a worry. We don't use ether. The Americans are keen on it. Reckon it's safer. Anyhow, let's concentrate on chloroform.'

She had handed Liz a textbook entitled *On Anaesthesia*. 'Have a go at that. If you have any questions, come and see me.'

* * *

The War Office wanted a speedy and successful conclusion to the East Africa campaign so that forces defending that far-flung corner of the empire could be redeployed to the European theatre. Early in 1916, they appointed a new supreme commander, General Jan Smuts, to achieve this objective in the most expeditious manner possible.

Brigadier-General Mickey Tighe wanted to make a good impression on Smuts before he arrived in the East African theatre of war in mid-February by expelling the Germans from their toe-hold in British territory. For good measure, he also intended to inflict a trouncing on Colonel von Lettow-Vorbeck for his impertinence. The Germans had shown far too much pluck for his liking. They needed to be taught a lesson.

Tighe assigned to the campaign General Wilfrid Malleson, who had under his command four thousand members of the South African Infantry Brigade, most of whom were yet to reach twenty years of age, and who had arrived in Mombasa in mid-January — just four weeks before the campaign commenced in earnest.

On 3 February, together with members of 2nd Loyal North Lancashires, 2nd Rhodesian Regiment and 130th Baluchis — six thousand men in all — the brigade marched to the base of Salaita Hill and demonstrated in force, but were unable to draw the Germans into an exchange. They then returned to their base at Mbuyuni, where they engaged in a week of manoeuvres — the extent of the brigade's field training.

Based upon ground and air intelligence sources, General Malleson estimated the Germans' strength at three hundred men, with no artillery and only two machine guns. Both he and General Tighe believed the correct strategy was to make a frontal attack on Salaita from the north, and sweep the Germans off the hill.

The officers ordered the men to tie grass to their helmets, prompting a great deal of hilarity as the South African and British troops marched out of Mbuyuni with eighteen artillery pieces, forty-one machine guns and two armoured cars, dubbed *kifaru* — rhinos — by the *askaris*. Morale was high, as could be expected in company with such a powerful force of men and equipment.

They camped the night of 11 February 1916, in the refreshingly cool air within sight of Lake Jipe, the Pare mountains and the snows of Kilimanjaro. Ahead lay the dense Taveta forest, but the terrain between the forest and the British lines was like open parkland.

Malleson had only one small irritant — Brigadier-General Percival Beves — the commanding officer of the South African Brigade.

'Wilfrid,' he said. 'I'm worried.'

Malleson sighed. 'What is it, Percy?'

He knew Beves was a favourite among the troops for the very reason he was a nuisance to him: he was overly cautious when deploying his men.

'We've marched our men from Observation Hill to Salaita and back again. And we've had aircraft swooping all over the place for weeks. Lettow-Vorbeck can have no doubt about our intentions. We've lost the element of surprise.'

'Have you forgotten we have six thousand troops at our disposal to Lettow-Vorbeck's three hundred or so?'

'We don't know how many he might have in reserve in Taveta or Moshi or wherever else. Lettow-Vorbeck's no fool.'

Malleson, who had been a career staff officer before being sent to East Africa, dismissed the South African's concern, saying that with their overwhelmingly superior numbers, the assault would be over before Lettow-Vorbeck could respond. Malleson kept his personal opinion to himself, but was of the opinion that the Boer's indirect method of attack by rapid flanking manoeuvres was a vulgar form of war, unsuited to English officers and gentlemen. He also dismissed Durkheimer's suggestion that the Germans could be driven from Salaita by blockading their water carriers. General Tighe wanted a frontal assault, and a frontal assault it would be.

* * *

Shortly after dawn on 12 February, the assault of Salaita Hill began. The 7th South African Battalion, composed almost entirely of Australians and New Zealanders recruited in South Africa, charged towards the northern face through dense forest. They reached a half-mile clearing before the base of the hill, exhausted and dehydrated, and were forced to await the water carriers, who had been unable to keep up.

Other brigades assembled on the 7th's left and right flanks. All was in readiness for a frontal assault on the north side.

Two four-inch guns salvaged from HMS *Pegasus* opened fire on the fort and the surrounding heights of the hill. It was the signal for the howitzers and sundry other batteries to launch their bombardment.

The 'Fighting Seventh' advanced to within three hundred yards of the base of the hill, but things were not going as expected.

From the level of fire and the thunder of artillery, it was obvious that the Germans were better armed than Malleson's intelligence suggested. In fact, Colonel von Lettow-Vorbeck had at his disposal thirteen hundred men, twelve machine guns, a seven-pounder field gun and two light pom-poms. He was also better informed than the Allies thanks to his chief scout — a German East Africa farmer.

The commander of the 7th and his fellow officers on his flanks realised that the Germans were entrenched at the base of the hill rather than at its heights and therefore little troubled by the Allies' bombardments. They sent word to the gunners, but they were afraid to lower their sights because their troops were now too close to the enemy position.

Just as he had done at Tanga fifteen months previously, Colonel von Lettow-Vorbeck observed an opportunity and grasped it with breathtaking military skill. His reserves entered the fray.

Belfield's Scouts — sixty volunteers raised within British East Africa itself, who were charged with reporting upon any German reinforcements — were unable to get the information of the advancing German troops to the Allies engaged at the bottom of the hill, and Lettow-Vorbeck's surprise counterattack swept forwards.

A shambolic Allied retreat ensued. As the men fell back, enemy snipers, who had remained hidden as the Allies advanced, now opened fire on them, killing many. Others fell into deep pits that the Germans had dug as part of their defensive preparations. The holes were concealed with thin sticks and grass, and the retreating troops who fell into them were impaled or disembowelled on sharpened stakes wrapped in barbed wire.

What was planned as an easy victory for the British side had turned into a rout.

With only one stretcher per company, many of the wounded lay for hours awaiting medical evacuation to the field hospital.

* * *

Liz was in the mess tent when the first of the wounded began to arrive around mid-afternoon. At first it was a trickle of cases, and the nurses were called into theatre in an orderly manner. Then later in the day, the flow of ambulances, mule-drawn carts and any other conveyance that could be pressed into service began arriving in numbers.

Sister Mary came dashing into the mess tent. 'Nurse Freeman. With me, please.'

Liz hurried after her. Triage medics hovered over a dozen stretchers under an awning adjacent to one of the large surgery tents. A line of stretchers queued beyond the shaded awning into the late afternoon sun. Sister Mary paused to consult the nurse in charge.

The first man in the line was reclining with his arm thrown up behind his head to form a pillow. He had a bloodied bandage on his forehead and a cigarette hung from the corner of his mouth. He winked at Liz as she ran her eyes over the men in line. It was such a brazen act in the presence of such misery that she had to suppress her smile.

Another ambulance pulled in and from it came a most awful high-pitched howl. Orderlies rushed to the back of the vehicle and removed a man with a mass of bloodied bandages wrapped around his midriff. He was screaming. It was a sound Liz thought no human being could make. Two orderlies rushed to him to hold him down as another stabbed a hypodermic needle into his arm.

Liz watched in open-mouthed amazement until the morphine had temporarily, if not completely, reduced his pain. Mary's insistent hiss brought her back to her duty, and she hurried into the hospital tent after her, leaving the sounds of sobbing and moaning behind.

Inside the surgery tent, it was very hot, and the sweet odour of chloroform was almost overpowering. Boiling water bubbled in trays on three Primus stoves. Doctors hunched over their patients, attended by several medical support staff.

The bloodied sheet on an operating table was swept away and a clean one flung over it in replacement. Liz helped Mary spread it as the patient was carried in — a boy of maybe nineteen, his leg heavily swathed in bandages.

A nurse poured peroxide onto the bandage, which frothed vigorously. The boy-soldier flinched as the surgeon carefully unravelled the filthy material and the nurse poured more of the antiseptic onto the wound. When the knee area was exposed, Liz could see that the patella had been smashed to a pulp. She'd been warned of the effects of soft-nosed bullets.

The young man moaned, turning his head from side to side as if trying to shake the pain from him.

An orderly began to cut away the soldier's tattered uniform, revealing the pale skin, reddish pubic hair, gangly arms and protruding ribs of an adolescent. His good left leg and knee carried the scars of a boisterous boyhood. The other knee, and the leg below it, looked more like something found on the floor of an abattoir. It was obvious even to Liz — the least experienced member of the attending medical staff — that there was little chance that the leg could be saved.

The attendants strapped him onto the table and, when he was secured, quickly disappeared to attend to the next case.

Liz felt tears well in her eyes: neither the drug nor the veil of pain that clouded the young man's eyes could hide his terror.

When she took up her place with Mary behind the patient's head, she bent over the boy soldier to offer him some encouragement. 'You'll be all right,' she whispered, knowing she might well be lying.

She poured the chloroform onto a gauze pad held in what Liz recognised from her *On Anaesthesia* text as a schimmelbusch mask. Mary asked the young man to count to ten. He moaned, but commenced as instructed.

'Your mask,' Sister Mary whispered. 'Pull it down.'

Liz quickly pulled down and adjusted her own face-mask.

At the count of five, the patient faltered, made a sound like a small creature whimpering, and was still.

'Pupils,' Mary said.

Liz prised open an eyelid and found the pupil suitably dilated.

She watched as Mary checked the colour of the boy's fingernails. *On Anaesthesia* warned the anaesthetist to take care to avoid the many possible hazards of chloroform. It was thought to be less dangerous than ether, but the by-products of its use, namely phosgene and chlorine, could be fatal. Then there were its effects on blood pressure and heart rate. She wound the cuff of the sphygmometer around his bicep and took his blood pressure readings. His breath was scratchy and irregular, but Mary nodded that all was as expected.

The surgeon had left the table, but now reappeared, scalpel in hand. His assistant joined him, and both men examined the ruined leg in silence.

Someone came in and strung pressure lamps above the surgeon's head. In the strong light, the doctor's eyes appeared to retreat into the dark caves above his mask. 'About here?' he asked his associate, indicating a line across the leg.

The second doctor nodded.

The surgeon paused a moment and sighed, before slicing into the good flesh about two inches below the strong tourniquet wound around the thigh. Blood oozed from the thin red line like a spreading tide.

As he neatly cut through the hamstrings, quadriceps and other tendons, his assistant dexterously clamped off arteries and veins before the surgeon returned to suture and knot them.

Liz tried to avoid watching the macabre butchery, but the wonderful artistry of the veins, muscles and arteries of the man's limb held her in morbid enthralment. The operation was brutal but infinitely fascinating.

The chloroform odour wafted around Liz, but it wasn't necessarily the vapour that was causing her light-headedness. At university she had participated in the dissection of a cadaver, but lying on this table was a living human, a young man whose life lay in the hands of these unexceptional men now wielding instruments that would either kill or cure him. She was also acutely aware that she was not merely a bystander, but an actor in this game of life and death. She and Mary were administering the drug that kept the soldier unconscious of the pain but short of the downward spiral that might pull him beyond the point of no return.

The surgeon produced what Liz could only describe as a carpenter's tool, and began to saw through the bone. The sound was similar to one made by a workman toiling with wood. He worked quickly and expertly, and soon the leg was no longer a part of the body. It might have been an unnecessary appurtenance, which the doctor dropped into a waste bin as if it was an off-cut of a length of four-by-two.

The skilled lancet work had left a good-sized flap of skin to draw over the stump. The doctor inserted a rubber drain hose to irrigate the wound and the suturing was quickly completed.

Before she could quite regather her composure, the surgeons had moved on to the next operating table, where another of the wounded lay. The soldier was moved onto a gurney and the blood-spattered surgical sheet was whisked away. Suddenly Liz was alone at the table.

She tore the mask from her face and dashed from the tent, disgorging the contents of her stomach into the bushes.

She wiped a handkerchief across her mouth and sucked in large gulps of the cool moist air of evening.

A pack of hyenas whooped and yelped not far beyond the throw of lantern light. Even Liz could smell the bittersweet fragrance of fresh blood.

* * *

Liz had never in her life received a telegram. From all accounts, they seldom brought good news. The messenger from field signals must have had similar experiences. He disappeared as soon as he'd handed it to her.

She took it to her tent, and tore it open.

There was a sender's address that made no sense, then a string of cryptic words.

... regret to advise ...

... while storming an enemy stronghold ...

... mentioned in despatches ...

The words blurred one into another making little sense other than to say that Lieutenant Max Dinsdale had died in action.

She staggered to her camp bed, holding the stabbing pain she felt in the pit of her stomach.

It took time for the full import to strike home. When it did, she could scarcely breathe.

Max.

His last contact was his letter stating he loved her and hoped she would agree to marry him.

There will be no heroics in this war for me. Bravery is for men who have nothing to lose.

Her heart pounded.

She looked down at the telegram again.

Lieutenant Maximilian Dinsdale died while storming an enemy stronghold.

These were not the actions of a man determined to avoid heroics.

Her last contact had been the letter kindly but firmly declining his offer.

She felt sick.

Could her refusal, so thoughtless and ill-timed, have been the reason for his impetuous dash into enemy lines?

She dropped her face into her hands and wept.

She would never know.

CHAPTER 11

Liz cared for the men she treated for various combat injuries, and grieved deeply for those who died, but essentially they were strangers. Occasionally one soldier's demise would particularly affect her and she would shed tears, but it was left to others, far away, to carry the heaviest burden of their loss. She only realised the extent of that burden when she received the news of Max's death. It had shocked and stunned her. He had been a fundamental part of her life, and now he was gone. Forever. Knowing there were thousands — hundreds of thousands — of mothers, fathers, brothers, sisters and loved ones feeling far worse even than she did was almost overwhelming. She couldn't continue to carry the mounting emotional load, and made an effort to toughen up.

Although Sister Mary said there was none, Liz found it essential to establish a routine to manage the time between the drama of triage, the trauma of the theatre and the essential escape she needed from all of it.

There were certain parts of the field hospital that affected her more than others. The dreaded Admissions tent was where men arrived straight from the front, many of them suffering horrific wounds. There were others — men who had died on the stretcher before reaching her — that made her feel even worse. They were the young men who'd died alone without even the solace of a smile or someone to hold their hand before they passed.

In Resuscitation she would deal with the consequences of those injuries; the post-operative shock as men who had entered the war able-bodied and fit discovered they would now face a quite different life. What saddened Liz was that most men cared not about their reduced prospects of finding employment or living a life without pain. They had other, more personal fears.

'What chance does a bloke like me have?' one asked Liz as she chatted to him on her rounds. 'Look at me. No right arm. What woman would bother with the likes of me?'

Many smiled bravely or in embarrassment for burdening a stranger with such personal matters. Others had lost the ability to smile, like those shuddering as they came in with the walking wounded, so damaged in spirit by the trauma of battle that she thought happiness would forever be beyond them. And there was the young man who had his ear and lower jaw removed by shrapnel and who would quite literally never smile again.

Time was the only asset she had to heal her battered spirit, and it became an essential part of Liz's escape from blood, pain, cannulas, saline solutions, bedpans and bedding soiled by men lost in an ocean of pain, to go beyond the sentry line into the line of bush that concealed the tent hospital from view. It was peaceful, reminding her of Limuru and a time when the African bush was — if not quite a place of happiness — a refuge from her cares.

Before the telegram arrived, she would use her bush escape to revive her memories of Dan and their one night together. She would recall the look in his eyes when he took her in his arms, relive the firm and insistent press of his body on hers, feel his hot breath on her breast and the softness of his kisses as they later lay entwined on the small camp bed together.

Following the news of Max's death, the sacrifice he'd made for his country loomed in stark contrast to Dan's reluctance to serve. Max had given his life for his country — a country that had rejected him and his family; a country so ungrateful of his offer to fight for it that he'd felt obliged to change his name before making it.

Meanwhile Dan had given nothing.

After returning to Africa and finding Dan — her childhood hero — she realised she had never loved Max. But Dan was no longer her hero.

She could never love a man who relied on others to fight his fights.

* * *

Durkheimer had not heard from Delamere for several weeks and sent Dan to search for him along the border to the north of Mt Kilimanjaro. When he found him, he was to obtain what information he had on the German troop movements and bring it to the captain at the Mbuyuni army camp.

Dan took the Pokot and five days' rations on the train to Emali, where they were met by an army driver and his black African assistant in a tiny T-Model Ford. The car had been commandeered from a farmer at the start of the war, at which time it was already in a parlous state of repair. The pneumatic tyres had been replaced with solid rubber ones to overcome the constant problem of punctures caused by the flinty and thorny countryside.

They bumped and bounced over the dusty terrain until they reached the saltpans of Amboseli, where the Ford became bogged in the powder-dry pumice dust. They manhandled the little car out of several such bogs before giving up on motorised transport. They were by then no more than twenty-five or thirty miles short of the border with German East Africa, and Kilimanjaro was already massively in view. The driver and his assistant turned back and Dan and the Pokot continued on foot.

The snow-capped mountain hovered in the distance for the whole day of travelling, and when he and Korok camped that night beside a pair of umbrella acacias, the mountain's glaciers shimmered like an ocean clipper's sails, creamy-white under the full moon. The next morning they found the entire mountain had been swallowed by a mist. The two headed south until, around midday, they reached the foothills, where they swung east as instructed by Durkheimer.

Soon after, the sun returned in earnest and Dan decided they should rest in a *kopje* of rocks until late afternoon.

The Pokot found a shady perch above while Dan made himself comfortable under an overhanging rock. He let his mind wander to thoughts of Liz. He knew she was now stationed at the Mbuyuni Field Hospital and he was impatient to complete his assignment and join her there. She had been constantly in his mind over the months since the night they'd made love in his tent at Ngong Hills. It was a moment that had transported him from enchantment to love. He could barely wait to see her again, perhaps this time with the privacy and opportunity to hold one another once again.

Korok awoke him from his daydream with a finger over his pursed lips. He led Dan to the rock that formed a natural wall around their resting place and pointed into the hazy distance. A thin column of dust rose above a short line of men and pack animals. They were headed southwest towards Arusha in the German territory and would pass below them in the next few minutes. Dan nodded and indicated they would stay put until they passed.

But the column didn't pass. They drew up to the small waterhole that Dan and the Pokot had used a little more than an hour before, and it was obvious they intended to camp there for the night.

Shortly before dusk, Dan decided to take a closer look, and made it clear to the Pokot that he stay in their hideaway. He didn't need the tracker's skills, and stalking the enemy's camp alone would reduce the likelihood of being discovered.

Dan had about an hour's daylight as he made his way down among the rocks until he was close enough to observe the Germans' activities.

Dan had counted six men when in the hideout higher up among the rocks. Now he could see only five. At first he thought they had set a sentry and cursed himself for his carelessness. Then he spotted the missing man. He was wearing the unmistakeable double terai of the Right Honourable Hugh Cholmondeley, 3rd Baron Delamere.

* * *

Captain Richard Durkheimer sat alone at his table overlooking Government Road. The Norfolk's resident military contingent had gradually thinned as Colonel von Lettow-Vorbeck and his motley collection of black *askaris*, farmers and relatively small contingent of German soldiers and officers continued to outsmart and occasionally out-fight the Allies along the length of the border.

Durkheimer was enjoying a brief respite at the Norfolk before heading upcountry to tour his far-flung intelligence operatives in the field.

'Howdy,' the man said as he came abreast of his table.

'Afternoon.'

'It's mighty quiet around here. Mind if I join you?'

Durkheimer glanced at him. By his accent he was an American, made more obvious by his plaid jacket and striped trousers. He had a cigar in his hand that had a pungent but not unpleasant odour. He shrugged and extended his hand to indicate the chair opposite.

'Mighty friendly of you.'

'Not at all.'

The waiter arrived and he ordered a brandy on ice. Durkheimer waved away his offer and took a sip of his ale.

'It's what I've liked most about being in this beautiful country of yours.'

Durkheimer raised an eyebrow.

'The friendliness and all.'

'I see. You're a visitor then?'

'Last six months or so. Leaving tomorrow. I'm Tuckmore, by the way. Bailey Tuckmore.'

He stuck his cigar in his mouth and offered his hand.

Durkheimer took it.

'Durkheimer. Captain Richard Durkheimer.'

'Yessir, a mighty nice place. Done a bit of huntin'. Been all over the place. Exceptin' for the south of course. Don't wanna run into any squareheads down there.' He paused, raising an eyebrow. 'Durkheimer ... Ain't that, you know, a German name?'

Durkheimer fixed him with a flint-hard stare. 'I'm British,' he said.

The American chuckled. 'Course you are. Otherwise you'd be down there with old von Lettow what's-his-name.'

Reassured, he took a sip of his brandy. 'Got me a beautiful set of kudu horns, and a fine rhino horn. The young fella taking me out was a bit of an amateur at the game. I can tell you, I've done some huntin' in the US. Bear, moose, cougar. You name it.' He guffawed. 'He took me out after elephant and we bagged a lioness. As I say, not very professional.'

Durkheimer was beginning to wish he hadn't invited the American to his table, but felt obliged to feign interest. 'Oh, really? What was the company called?'

'Freeman Safaris,' Tuckmore said, then leaned back in his chair and took a puff on his cigar.

'Did you say Freeman Safaris?'

'Yessir. A young fella by the name of Dan Sutherland.'

Durkheimer was now mildly interested, particularly if Tuckmore had unflattering remarks to make about Sutherland.

'Danny Sutherland or Danny Sullivan. The guy didn't seem to know who he was after a couple of glasses of my Old Forester's.'

Durkheimer sipped his ale, ruminating on Tuckmore's comments. Here was an able-bodied young man, who may have changed his name and was reluctant to join the regulars, but prepared to work in or near enemy territory in the far more dangerous role of spy.

Curious.

He would make some enquiries.

* * *

Night was approaching fast. Dan watched as the soldiers went about pitching their tents and preparing their cooking fire. Delamere sat on a rock with his hands tied behind him.

Now Dan wished he'd brought his rifle along. And the Pokot. He had five Germans to contend with, and only a few hours of darkness in which to extract D from among them.

The men fanned out in opposite directions in search of fuel. The remaining man, the apparent leader, took Delamere to a large candelabra cactus tree and tied him to it. A spikey limb broke off in the process, and Dan watched as the soldier — a sergeant — tried to wipe the milky latex from his hands.

They cooked their meals in the brief twilight and the sergeant set a sentry. Dan kept his eye on this man as he strolled the outskirts of the camp before finding a comfortable rock to sit on, his rifle resting across his knees.

The men settled down to sporadic conversation. The moon rose an hour after sunset, giving light to the savannah. Dan could clearly see the sergeant studying his palm and rubbing it against the coarse material of his trousers. It was as Dan had hoped. The sap of the candelabra had toxic qualities — a few tribes used it as a poison on their arrows — and the man had smeared enough of it on his skin to be affected.

As the irritation became more intense, the sergeant's voice rose with what appeared to be German obscenities. The others in the camp at first found the sergeant's discomfort amusing, then one by one went to see for themselves what was causing the pain. Satisfied it was not fatal, they sauntered back to their places around the fire, but Dan had used the distraction to creep down the hill, moving from boulder to bush until he was only a short distance from Delamere.

The sentry passed close by him, pausing to relieve himself into a bush. He loudly farted, then moved on.

Dan slipped his knife out of its sheath and, in a crouch, crept quickly to Delamere's side.

'Shh,' he whispered as his blade sliced through the rope.

From the direction of the fire, the Germans' voices rose in heated discussion.

D struggled stiffly to his feet then followed Dan back up the slope.

Before they'd gone twenty paces, the sentry appeared in front of them. He'd not seen them until the last moment and his surprise was written all over his face as he opened his mouth to shout an alarm.

Dan lunged at him, and the soldier grunted before Dan was able to throw an arm around his throat. They both fell to the ground, the German's rifle clattering on the hardened earth. Dan had his arm around his adversary's mouth, gripping with all his strength, but although muffled, he thought the man's muffled voice could probably be heard at the campfire.

One of the Germans at the campfire shushed his comrades and called into the night, which had suddenly become very still.

'My knife,' he hissed to Delamere.

Delamere scrambled on hands and knees in the darkness, looking for the knife that had been knocked free in the skirmish.

Dan grabbed the knife from Delamere and in a single motion slashed the German's throat.

He gave out a strangled cry and fell away from Dan's grasp, clutching at his throat and making dreadful gurgling sounds as his blood gushed through his fingers. He kicked and jerked in a series of muscle spasms before he lay still.

A shout of alarm came from the campfire and the Germans began rushing up the hill. Dan and Delamere scrambled up the rocky hillside with the soldiers close behind.

A rifle shot from above sent the Germans diving for cover.

The Pokot, holding Dan's 404, was silhouetted against the sky. He let fly another volley. Like the first, it was well wide of the mark, but it gave Dan and Delamere time to escape.

Back in the safety of their hideaway, Dan slumped to the ground, Delamere, his breath coming in loud rasping gasps, dropped beside him.

The Pokot looked down at them. His small sharpened teeth appeared as he grinned.

Dan nodded his gratitude, but he felt sick.

He'd shot at the enemy in the Boer War — he may have even killed one — but a rifle is an impersonal weapon. It kills at a distance.

Dan had killed the German with a knife in his hand. It was as personal as it could be, and he knew he would always be able to recall the horror in the German sentry's eyes when his blade cut the carotid artery and the man knew with terrible certainty that he was going to die.

CHAPTER 12

Captain Durkheimer was peeved. When he arrived at Mbuyuni, he had sent word to the field hospital that he would like to see Elizabeth as soon as she was available. He'd heard nothing in response. His second note received a reply that suggested she would try — *try* — to meet him at three that afternoon. It was now four and she had still not arrived at the canteen tent as arranged.

He was peeved and disappointed. Between this and her failure to accompany him to the King's birthday event, Elizabeth had not lived up to his expectations. Indeed, she appeared to be quite unreliable and fickle.

He was about to submit to his impatience and abandon his wait when he saw her walking towards him. 'Ah, Elizabeth,' he said, smiling as warmly as he could under the circumstances. 'It's so good to see you.'

'Hello, Richard. I'm sorry I'm late. One of our nurses was sick and I —'

'Not at all. Not at all. I understand completely.'

An awkward silence developed. It appeared that Elizabeth wasn't in a talkative mood.

'It's been so long since I've seen you,' he said.

'Yes, it has.'

He waited again, but she made no mention of their arrangement to meet at the Norfolk.

'Would you care for a cup of tea?' he asked.

'That would be lovely. Thank you. But would you mind if we take it out here? I think I could use some fresh air.'

'Certainly. I'll be right back.'

The African kitchen aide handed him the cups, but Durkheimer insisted on a tea tray. The tea and tray arrived and he aligned the spoons so they were parallel to each other on the saucers and to the edge of the tray.

Not a word, he thought as he placed the sugar bowl precisely midway between the cups. Not a word mentioned about our appointment at the governor's high tea. Durkheimer knew why she had not attended as promised. Elizabeth had informed the hotel manager, who had informed him, that she would take a short safari to visit a friend in need. It could only have been Sutherland.

Having made much of his announcement to his fellow officers that he would be accompanied to the governor's party by a beautiful young lady, he had been forced to suffer their jibes and insults all that day and several following. He felt righteous indignation, especially since she showed no sign of remorse. In fact, had said not a word about it.

He smiled as he presented the tea tray.

She took a cup and thanked him.

'It was a pity about the King's birthday celebrations,' he said as pleasantly as he could.

Elizabeth, who had her cup to her lips, paused.

'Oh, Richard. I'm so terribly sorry. I forgot all about it. Can you ever forgive me?'

He beamed at her. 'For you, dear lady, anything.' Durkheimer didn't care for female capriciousness, and was not accustomed to being headed by the likes of Sutherland — a bumpkin. He had no doubt he would win Elizabeth Freeman, and when that was accomplished he would persuade her to become more steadfast and systematic.

As for Sutherland, he would find other ways to bring him to heel.

* * *

His orders were to immediately report to Durkheimer, but when Dan arrived at the Mbuyuni camp, he went instead in search of Liz at the field hospital. He needed to see her, to be with her. Her presence would take his thoughts away from the German soldier's death.

A nurse told him she was on stand-down for a few hours, and he returned to the camp to find her. When he did, she was with

Durkheimer outside the canteen tent. They appeared to be in a friendly conversation. He walked directly to Liz.

'Dan!' she said, but she made no move towards him.

Her subdued reaction took him by surprise, but he thought it was Durkheimer's presence. He took his lead from her.

'Hello, Liz,' he said.

In accordance with Durkheimer's orders, he gave no indication he knew his commanding officer. He nodded to him. 'Dan Sutherland.'

'Captain Durkheimer,' he replied.

Neither made a move to shake hands.

'And may I ask, why are you here?'

'I run a safari company in Nairobi.'

'This is a military installation, Mr Sutherland. You can't just pitch your tent anywhere around here.'

'I'm aware of that, Captain. My camp is down on the lake.'

'Then I suggest you remove yourself there.'

His tone was a little more severe than the pretence required. Durkheimer's vexed expression indicated to Dan that he had annoyed his commanding officer by interrupting his conversation with Liz. Dan, in turn, was annoyed by Durkheimer's apparent interest in Liz, and was not prepared to take a backward step.

'I will when I'm ready,' he shot back.

Liz intervened. 'Mr Sutherland is a friend of mine,' she said. 'I'm sure he only needs a moment.'

Durkheimer glared at Dan, but nodded to Liz. 'Of course. Perhaps we can continue this conversation a little later.'

He took her empty teacup and they watched him leave.

Dan moved towards her, but she remained distant, holding her hands folded across her pale grey-and-white nurse's uniform.

'Liz, darling. How are you?'

'I didn't know you were coming. Do you have a client?'

'Um ... no. I have a new client coming in a month or so, but ... Is there anything wrong?'

'Nothing. I'm just ... surprised to see you. And I'm a little tired.'

'I understand. Maybe tomorrow then?'

'Maybe.'

She couldn't meet his gaze.

'There *is* something wrong, isn't there?'

She looked down at her hands. 'I think I ... we ... acted a little hastily.'

He couldn't believe what she was saying. Had she not felt what he'd felt in those few hours they'd been together? Surely he hadn't imagined their intimacy? He tried to find words to express his dismay, but failed.

Realising she was about to flee, he spoke. 'Liz ... I love you.'

She looked at him now, tears in her eyes.

'Oh, no,' she said. 'I can't.'

She turned and ran towards the hospital.

* * *

Dan poured the canned meat into the pot and added the tin of mixed vegetables. He sat the pot on the fire, and when he remembered it, gave the bubbling mix a stir, but his mind was still with Liz. He was numbed by the shock of losing her at the very moment he realised he loved her.

When they made love he knew it was right. For years they'd had a special bond and now it had changed, intensified, but it wasn't until he sensed she was about to reject him that he realised just how deep his feelings for her were. He had to tell her he loved her before she made her decision to end it. He wanted her more than anything he had ever wanted in life.

When she said *No*, he wanted to stop the world from spinning. He wanted to freeze time to prevent her from saying, *I can't love you*, because he knew that if he had time, he could explain that what she thought of him was an illusion. He wasn't a coward.

But was that true? Hadn't Daniel Sullivan deserted his comrades in the face of the enemy, and for a trifling excuse? What was the life of a horse compared to his duty to stand with his fellow soldiers and fight for the empire? Would she understand that he had been too young to go to war? Would it make any difference?

The food sticking to the bottom of the pan began to burn, wafting pungent smoke into the sweet scent of cedar burning in the cooking fire.

He slopped the food into two dishes, handing one to the Pokot, and taking his to a convenient rock embedded in the dried mud of the lake.

The waters had receded beyond sight. A wide salty crust sat on the baked slime of the sweeping shoreline. In the moonlight it looked like a frosted cake decoration.

He poured himself tea.

One of the many disadvantages of being an undercover operator was that he couldn't join his comrades in the army camp. Instead, he must pitch his tent on its periphery like a leper, and spend his nights in silent contemplation. It made it even more difficult at moments like this.

Korok, never a conversationalist, sat on his haunches in the shadowy space between the throw of the firelight and the night beyond. In such a pose he could rest for hours with his chin on thin arms he folded across his knees. There had been times when Dan almost stumbled upon the motionless Pokot as he made his rounds of the camp before retiring.

The little tracker disdained canvas, preferring to find a shelter on the outskirts of the camp. A fold in the rock face, a tree trunk hollowed out with age, or a cover of banana leaves on a cleared space on the dirt appeared to be his preference.

He wondered what motivated the Pokot to stay with him, and he'd never asked. He presumed he belonged to a tribe somewhere up north. When old Bill was around, Dan could imagine the history they shared was a form of connection between them. Although the Pokot didn't appear to be the sentimental type, years on the railway, hunting with Bill and Turk to provide meat for hundreds of labourers, probably meant that some form of companionship, if not friendship, had developed between them. But why he remained with Dan was an even greater mystery.

Durkheimer came into camp as Dan was lighting a cigarette.

'I thought this'd be your camp site,' he said.

Dan offered the pack of Player's Navy Cut to him.

'No thanks. I have my pipe,' he said, and lit it on the burning end of a twig.

Dan wasn't inclined to make conversation and waited for Durkheimer to settle himself on a fallen acacia limb across the fire from him. Dan then debriefed him on his observations of troop activities in the border area following Malleson's failed campaign. He also told him about Delamere's capture and release.

Durkheimer sat puffing his pipe, occasionally clarifying a detail. At the end of it, he nodded, and said: 'Hmm.'

Dan knew it was the only recognition he would get for his work and wondered how long Durkheimer would hang around. He didn't like him. He was cruel and a snob. But what rankled most now was that Durkheimer appeared to have replaced him in Liz's heart. He knew it would be difficult to remain civil.

'You appear to enjoy this work,' Durkheimer said after a prolonged silence. 'Most men would rather work in a team. At your age, you could be a leader. What are you, thirty? Thirty-five?'

'I'm thirty-two.'

'How did you learn your bush skills?' Durkheimer asked.

'I don't know … Probably when I was a young bloke.'

'You'd been brought up on the land?'

'Yeah.'

'Was your father a farmer?'

Dan had never been one to easily share personal information, but was feeling particularly uncomfortable sharing it with an officer of the British army. He decided to change the subject.

'My dad was a drover. Like me. And what about yourself, Captain? What brought you to take up with the army here in Africa?'

It worked. Durkheimer had a fondness for talking about himself. Once started, he became easily immersed in the minutiae of his family history. He began with his mother's side, which was resplendent with titles and wealth, and then began again with his father, Richard Durkheimer II — a notable banker — and his German-born grandfather.

'Grandfather had only two children, my father and my Aunt Beatrice. And I'm an only son. So I'm the last of the Durkheimers — a fact of which Papa never fails to remind me.'

He rambled on about the German side of his family, blithely disregarding the irony of his military position.

It was obvious he had been close to his aunt and her son, Karl, who had spent many years living with them before returning to Berlin. He spoke fondly of his cousin, saying he had been his mentor throughout his career.

'Cousin Karl was more like a brother to me. A very close brother,' Durkheimer said. 'I'm not sure if you are aware of African history, Sutherland, but Karl Peters was a famous explorer in his day. Have you heard the name?'

'The name?'

'Yes ... Karl Peters. My cousin.'

Dan shook his head, bored beyond weariness by Durkheimer's palaver. 'Can't say I have.'

'Hmmph,' Durkheimer snorted in disgust.

From behind him, Dan heard a rustle in the brittle grass. He turned, but beyond the throw of light from the campfire he could see nothing but darkness. He did, however, notice that the Pokot had disappeared.

* * *

Korok stood invisible in the darkness. Only the firelight that might catch the flame of hatred in his eyes could reveal his presence.

The army officer Durkheimer had brought a reviled name to mind — Karl Peters — the man who had murdered his beloved cousin and age-mate, Tobeya.

Karl Peters — who had slaughtered his family, his clan and his tribe.

It was Karl Peters who had consigned Korok to live in an alien world until he had honoured the oath he'd taken to avenge his cousin's death. It was his deeds that had prevented him from returning to his pastoral life on his ancestral lands. Karl Peters had escaped punishment for all this. It was unjust.

Now here was Durkheimer, who had revealed he was Karl Peters's cousin. It was ordained by Asis that he be sent here so that Korok could repay the debt he owed his cousin by taking sweet vengeance.

A cousin's life had been lost. Another cousin must die too.

As much as he could understand it, Durkheimer said he was the last of his family. Just as Karl Peters had ended Korok's clan, then he, Korok, would end Durkheimer's clan.

The symmetry of the plan appealed to Korok's poetic nature. His lip plug moved on his humourless smile.

* * *

Liz was passing the New Stanley on her way to the post office when she heard her name called.

'Miss Freeman!' It was Lord Delamere, sitting with the proprietor, Mayence Bent.

'Elizabeth! Won't you join us?'

She liked D. He was a peer of the realm but not at all pretentious. In fact, from some of the accounts she'd heard, some of his antics were positively outrageous. 'Lord Delamere,' she said. 'Good afternoon.'

'Now, now, my dear. It's Hugh or D. Take your pick. Now, sit and have a drink with us. You know Mayence?'

'I do.'

Mayence offered her a drink. 'We're having champagne. Would you care for a glass?'

'Mayence! What a silly question,' Delamere said, with a slight slur. 'Of course she will. We're celebrating.'

'Celebrating what, exactly?' Liz asked.

'Ah, life, my dear. We're celebrating life.'

'It's the only answer I've been able to get from him all afternoon,' Mayence said as she poured the champagne for her.

They clinked glasses.

'What are you doing in town?' D asked. 'Last I heard, you were at Mbuyuni.'

'I'm on a seven-day leave pass. How did you know I was at Mbuyuni?'

He smiled and put a finger across his lips. 'Ah, I'm afraid I can't reveal my sources,' he said, lifting his champagne glass.

'Hah!' Mayence said. 'Take no notice of him. His Lordship just loves playing the spy. Him and Captain Durkheimer.'

Delamere drained his glass. 'Mayence, my dear! Another of the Moët if you would be so kind.'

'I'm not sure I have another. You may have drunk them all,' she said, and left them as she disappeared through the door to the kitchen.

'What did she mean about being a spy?' Liz asked.

'Ah, that's just Mayence. She believes everything she hears. Mind you,' he said with a smile, 'I may have been in my cups one night and spoken out of turn. However, the lovely lady is something of a gossip, and while she's gone, I just wanted to ask how you got on with young Dan in Mbuyuni.'

'Dan? How …? Um … what do you mean?'

'Just asking. I could tell by just looking at the pair of you when we met at this very table that he was smitten. You too, if I'm any judge.'

Liz flushed. 'It's … Well, it's not like you think. We're … just friends.'

'Hmm, that's curious.'

'What do you mean?'

'Well, I shouldn't say too much, but I camped a night with him before we parted ways. Let's just say that you, and your safety at Mbuyuni, were on his mind.'

Rather than pleasing her, thoughts of Dan made her heart sink.

In light of her silence, Delamere continued. 'It appeared to me that he thinks of you as more than just a friend.'

Liz studied him. Delamere was trying to tell her something she didn't want to hear. The whole weight of her problem of dealing with Dan and her conflicted feelings about him bore down on her. She released the deep breath she'd been holding.

'It can't be otherwise. We're … so different. I believe we should be doing all we can for the war. Even you — people say you're working with Captain Durkheimer. And at your age. No disrespect. Why can't Dan do his share?'

Delamere shrugged. 'Maybe you don't understand.'

'There's nothing to understand. He's more interested in running his safari business than doing anything worthwhile.'

Mayence returned.

'Just as I thought. You and your friends drank all but two of the Moët last time you were here.' She held out a bottle for Delamere to see.

'Piper-Heidsieck,' he said, reading the label and wrinkling his nose. 'Isn't he some kind of German?'

Mayence shrugged.

'Well that simply won't do. Don't you have something more ... French?'

'I'll check,' she said tartly, and stormed off.

Turning back to Liz, he said. 'Elizabeth. I'm aware I've had a glass or two of bubbly ... but I must tell you a man doesn't have to wear a uniform to do his duty. There's more than one way to serve your country.'

'I'm sure there is, D, but surely running a safari company isn't one of them.'

'My dear, I run a farm. And thanks to my big mouth and Mayence's ability to spread the gossip, most people also know I serve with Durkheimer's East African Intelligence Corps from time to time.'

Liz tried to read his eyes. 'Are you saying that Dan is using the company to do what you do?'

Delamere shrugged. 'All I can say is that if it wasn't for Dan Sutherland, I would most likely be in a Dar es Salaam prisoner-of-war camp today. If not dead.'

Liz nodded slowly. Her thoughts were rushing in several different directions, but one was paramount. 'D, I have a favour to ask of you.'

'Certainly, my dear.'

'Do you know where Dan is?'

'I ... might. Why do you ask?'

'I need to see him. Urgently. Will you take me to him?'

CHAPTER 13

When Captain Richard Durkheimer returned to Nairobi he found a telegram on his desk. The sealed envelope was marked *Secret*.

Drawing out his chair, he sat and took the envelope into his hands. He believed he knew what it contained, but resisted his urge to open it for a further several minutes until his anticipation had built to an almost unbearable state.

Even then he moved slowly, sliding open the top drawer of his desk, taking the sterling silver letter opener from it, and admiring the Durkheimer family crest emblazoned on the pommel.

He ran the point under the flap and enjoyed the crisp slicing sound as it cleaved the paper apart.

It was from army headquarters in Bombay. His smile grew as he read the contents.

For Attn Capt R Durkheimer.
  Confirming one volunteer by name Daniel Sullivan.
  Born Toowoomba Australia. 1st May 1884.
  22 June 1900 enlisted Queensland Imperial Bushmen
  (4th Contingent).
  Missing from active service Dullstroom Feb 1902.
  Believed desertion in face of enemy.

He slowly folded the report and slid it into his jacket chest pocket. Now he needed to plan his next actions. He had a number of options, but would take his time to evaluate them in his usual meticulous manner.

His easiest course would be to send out a contingent of military police to arrest the man. He immediately rejected it. Too crass. Bringing a criminal to justice whom he had personally investigated required a more individual touch. Durkheimer wanted to confront Sullivan with his crimes and to personally apprehend him.

An alternative was to inform Major General Britts of his intention to find and arrest the deserter. But by involving the line of command he might lose control of the whole process. His commanding officer might insist he take support personnel, or even veto his involvement. No, that was too risky.

Durkheimer needed no assistance with a colonial hick such as Sullivan. He knew roughly where he would be, having told him while they were in Mbuyuni to return to Emali and await further orders. He would have the element of surprise and therefore have the great satisfaction of bringing the felon to justice, single-handed.

He checked his gold fob watch. The supply train would be returning empty to the coast via Emali in less than an hour. He could board it unnoticed, avoiding any involvement by the military hierarchy.

He slipped his hand weapon from its pouch and unclipped the ammunition magazine. All was in perfect readiness.

Durkheimer placed his red-banded officer's cap squarely on his head, straightened his jacket, and strode to the door.

* * *

Dan returned to camp with the sun's rays burning into his sweat-soaked shirt and immediately sensed something, or someone, had been there while he and Korok were hunting. He had dismissed all his porters before heading to Emali, so it had to have been an interloper.

He looked at Korok, but the Pokot had set to work immediately on the gazelle carcass. When dried, it would keep them in meat for weeks.

He could find nothing out of place, but he had a strong feeling that the camp had been disturbed.

Dan ran his eye over the ground searching for spoor that might identify the intruder. His tent flap was untied and a water bottle that hung from the tent pole had been moved. He found boot prints around the tent that were not his. Large boot prints.

The visitor was human, and had been poking around his camp. *Why?*

He followed the boot prints to a stand of acacias and, sitting beneath them, his cap pulled over his eyes, was Durkheimer.

* * *

Dan couldn't find the Pokot. Korok occasionally disappeared for hours, sometimes days, when there was little to do, then reappeared without comment or explanation. Dan abandoned his search for him and gathered the firewood himself to roast a haunch of the gazelle.

Durkheimer was obviously in no hurry to reveal Dan's new orders and spent the afternoon sitting in the shade smoking his pipe. With dismay Dan realised he would be stuck with him overnight.

As the afternoon light faded, and the aroma of roasting venison mixed with the damp nutty air wafting in from the Emali wetland, Durkheimer joined Dan at the fire.

'You're too predictable,' Durkheimer said to Dan.

'Am I?'

'For a man who prides himself on his bushcraft, you were too easy to locate. It only took me a couple of hours to find you.'

'Water, shade, fuel. Where else would I camp? Anyway, I wasn't trying to hide.'

'Predictable. Like the rest of your kind.'

Dan peered up at him. 'What do you mean by that?'

'Typical white hunter. You don't think; you just react. Hotheads to a man. I've heard most of you Australians are like that. Ill-disciplined.'

Dan tightened his jaw and concentrated on turning the haunch.

'Comes from your bog-Irish heritage.'

A warning trigger sounded in Dan's head. He tried to ignore Durkheimer, who was being more than usually objectionable, but it wasn't easy.

'What are you talking about?'

'Bog-Irish and undisciplined. I don't suppose the military men sent to Australia can be blamed. I should think that dealing with convicts every day, most of them from Irish stock, could be quite disheartening.'

Dan stood and made a show of stretching his back. He decided to step away from Durkheimer and the vaguely disturbing direction the conversation was taking. He took a few paces towards his tent.

'Sullivan,' Durkheimer said from behind him. 'That's an Irish surname, isn't it?'

Dan halted. When he turned again he had set a blank expression on his face, but Durkheimer's vitriolic smile confirmed his concerns.

'Undisciplined. Cowardly. That's you, Daniel Sullivan, masquerading as Sutherland. A deserter — cowardly and dishonourable. Running from his comrades in the face of the enemy.'

'I didn't run from the enemy. And if you want to talk about being dishonourable, how would you describe someone who shot a man under a flag of truce?'

'What are you —?'

'The Nandi chief in '03. You were desperate to win a battle but the Nandi had you beat. You called the chief to parley. You shot him dead in cold blood, you *bastard*.'

Durkheimer pulled his pistol from its holder and aimed it at Dan's head, his hand shaking with rage. He cocked the mechanism and stepped closer to him. Dan stared down the barrel, but after an agonising pause, Durkheimer swung the handgun hard at Dan, catching him flush on the ear.

Dan fell beside the fire.

He seemed to be lying in the dust and ashes for hours, struggling to regain his senses. His vision ebbed and flowed. Each time his consciousness returned he briefly glimpsed scenes from a startling montage.

From the darkness a figure flew at Durkheimer, who responded by firing off a shot. The explosion resonated in Dan's aching head, and he squeezed his eyes shut against the pain.

An indeterminate period later, he saw the flailing *siliot* and flashing skinny buttocks of the Pokot, who was swarming all over Durkheimer, a giant in comparison. The military man had lost his pistol but was swinging haymakers at the little Pokot, missing wildly, until Dan heard the sickening crunch of one huge fist meeting Korok's finely chiselled jaw.

Dan fought the encroaching darkness, rising and falling like a dhow riding the storm swell on the Indian Ocean. He surrendered and fell into semi-consciousness, where he dreamed of Durkheimer, a blur in the moonlight, screaming like a banshee.

* * *

When Dan awoke the moon was up and the camp deathly quiet.

His head pounded and there was dirt and ash caked to the side of his face and when he brushed at it he found a crusted patch of blood on his temple that was painful to touch.

He dragged himself to his feet.

There was no sign of Durkheimer.

He called for the Pokot, who he imagined was in a fearful state following the blow the big man landed on him. There was no response.

He walked unsteadily around the camp until he came upon somebody lying in the darkness. It was Durkheimer. Dan felt for a pulse on his neck. It was cool to his touch. There was no heartbeat.

He went to his tent, lit the paraffin lamp, and returned to where Durkheimer lay.

The light fell on the body, and Dan recoiled in horror.

Durkheimer's face was black, as black as coal, except for eyes that were white and caught in the strictures of agony. They stared, frozen, into the purple night.

Korok was nowhere to be found.

* * *

Liz dropped to the tracks after Delamere, stumbling for a moment before regaining her footing in the loose ballast.

The train rolled on, revealing the Emali station bathed in the mid-morning sun. It was deserted, as had been the case for most of the stations they had passed that morning. The army supply train slowed while passing through, but rarely stopped.

They retrieved their haversacks from where they'd thrown them clear of the train.

'Down that way,' Delamere said, pointing south. 'That's where I camped years ago.'

She followed his arm. There was nothing about the country to distinguish it from what they'd travelled through for the last four hours. The Kapiti Plains, and the Athi Plains before them, were dotted with spindly scrub, the kind that seemed able to survive flood or fire. It mottled the blood-red earth with insipid green stains. In the distance, through the heat haze, was a grey-blue smudge of hills.

'Towards those hills,' he said, 'there's a fair bit of water. From memory it's an hour or two away.'

Now that she'd learned the truth from Delamere, Liz was anxious to find Dan and ask his forgiveness for thinking so badly of him. She couldn't endure the thought that he was out in the bush believing she didn't love him.

Delamere checked his rifle's magazine.

'Are you expecting trouble?' she asked.

'Not really, although the last time I was here there was plenty of game. A couple of the biggest lions ever taken in East Africa were shot just down the line at Tsavo.'

Liz took her eyes from Delamere's rifle and peered out into the shimmering savannah.

'We'd better get moving,' she said, leaving Delamere flat-footed on the railway line.

* * *

Throughout the night, Dan struggled to find a solution to his plight. An important officer of the military establishment had died under bizarre circumstances. And Dan was a witness.

He briefly considered returning to Nairobi to report the incident, but immediately rejected it. All his efforts to avoid scrutiny would be demolished. The death of an army captain under suspicious circumstances would prompt an intensive investigation, and Dan would certainly be considered a suspect.

It was obvious to Dan that Durkheimer had come to his camp not to give him a new assignment, but to arrest him. Dan imagined such a personal vigilante action was most irregular. Surely procedures demanded the military police be involved, but knowing Durkheimer's personality, Dan could understand why his commanding officer might choose to ignore such procedures when it suited his vanity.

It was therefore likely that Durkheimer had acted alone and in secret. Dan had no choice but to assume so, as it was the only explanation that allowed him to construct a plan to conceal his involvement.

By morning he was prepared. He would leave the body where it lay. If it was found, Dan must ensure there was nothing at the camp that could place him at the scene of the crime. If the body was not found, then it was unlikely that anyone could connect Dan with his disappearance. Durkheimer had many enemies.

The irony that his commanding officer might be suspected of desertion was fleetingly amusing, but realistically, unlikely.

Dan went around the camp to ensure he was leaving nothing behind that might implicate him. He'd decided to abandon the cooking pots and heavy gear, and dropped the fly poles and guys leaving the tent flat. Then he crammed all personal items into his pack and threw it onto his shoulder. Before leaving, he ran his eyes once more around the camp and its vicinities. His gaze went to where Durkheimer's body lay, uncovered.

'*Shit!*' he said, and dropped his pack. After a further moment's reflection, he went searching for something he could use to dig a grave.

He'd not touched Durkheimer's body after he'd found it during the night. In daylight it appeared much worse than it had in darkness. The skin was blue-black and already assuming the sheen caused by the distension of the putrefying flesh. Large fat blowflies crowded around the small patch of dried blood on the chest. Others were crawling into the orifices. The eyes, nose and mouth were a swarming mass. Dan felt the bile rise in his throat and fought it back.

With his head pounding and sweat dripping from his brow, he scraped out a shallow depression in the rock-hard dirt, then dragged Durkheimer's body into it. As he did, the dead man's jacket fell open, and a folded sheet of paper could be seen protruding from an inside pocket.

Dan thought for a moment, then slid the paper out and opened it. And there were the condemning words:

Believed desertion in face of enemy.

He crumpled the paper with more force than was necessary and lit it with a Lucifer from his own pocket. The ashes dropped onto Durkheimer's chest.

After an hour, he had covered the body with enough rocks to deter the hyenas, and stood looking down at it wondering what had transpired in Durkheimer's last minutes alive. The skin discolouration was extraordinary, and a memory of Korok's demonstration of the strength of his hunting poison came surging back to mind. Thinking of how such a powerful toxin could affect living tissue made him shudder.

He gathered up his pack and, slinging his rifle over his other shoulder, turned his back on the grave and his abandoned gear.

He and Korok had arrived unseen in Emali and his plan was to avoid returning to Nairobi via that same route, thereby avoiding any connection with the camp. Instead, he would board a train at night where it slowed to climb one of the rises further west.

He kept clear of the tall grass running along the edge of the soak. He and the Pokot had spotted a herd of buffalo in the shallows the day before.

A couple of miles from camp he heard the lion. A male was making its territorial moan: *Oom, oom, oom.* The terrain was slowly rising along skirting hills covered by a thin belt of thorn bush. Higher up the cover became thick with yellow fever trees and palms. It was ideal cover for predators. He gave it a wide berth.

Sometime later the lion calls fell away to the rear and he relaxed his vigil, concentrating instead on finding his bearings so as to join the railway at the desired point. He unwittingly wandered from the open grassy savannah, and by the time he realised it, the grassland was far off to his right and he was now well within the scrub.

A roar filled the space around him until nothing existed outside its reach. It snapped his attention back to his immediate surroundings. The lion was close; somewhere in the bush, and no more than a hundred yards from him. He unshouldered his Westley Richards, and although he knew the cartridges were correctly in place, he checked the barrels.

There was a deal of movement in the grass and woody scrub. Dan levelled his rifle towards it and slowly backed away.

The lioness came unhurried from cover, slashing her tail and pressing her ears flat on her head. It was a dangerous sign. Dan had the animal in his sights and was slowly bringing his finger to the trigger when two lion cubs came tumbling out of the bush. One made a playful lunge at its mother's tail while the other trotted to her and rolled beneath her, pawing at her legs.

But the lioness was staring at Dan with deadly intent. She lowered herself into a crouch and flattened her tail.

Dan fixed her in the Westley Richards's sights and held his breath.

* * *

After about an hour, Liz and Delamere reached the swamp.

'He could be camped anywhere along here,' D said. 'Let's go towards the higher ground. If he's not there, we'll cut back the other way.'

'Why don't we split up?' Liz asked. 'You go that way, I'll go this way.'

At that moment came the call of a lion.

'I think not,' D said. He patted his haversack. 'But we've got water and food enough for a couple of days.'

Liz turned to him with a worried look.

'Don't worry. I expect we'll find him well before then.'

They marched to where the swamp petered out and the terrain slowly rose towards distant trees.

'I'm sorry, Elizabeth, it looks as though I've picked the wrong direction. We'll have to double back.'

'Wait,' she said. 'Look. Is that someone following the line of trees?'

Delamere squinted in the direction she pointed.

'I can't see anything,' he said.

'Neither can I now, but let's go a little further, just in case.'

They hurried on, skirting the heavier cover.

Liz's heart was racing. Ever since she discovered the truth about Dan and the dangerous role he played in the war, she was desperate to find him and make amends. She had judged him most unfairly. If she had trusted her heart, she would have trusted him, but there had been so much turmoil she had let her cold head rule her. Sometimes she worried that Vivian and Harriet had succeeded in recreating themselves in her: that she was as unable as they to freely, bravely love another person.

She had a frightening notion that something terrible would happen to Dan unless she could find him and tell him she had been wrong and that she loved him. That she always had.

'There he is,' whispered D, pointing ahead. 'He looks to have a bead on something.'

Liz spotted Dan about a hundred yards away. She could see his raised rifle and followed its line into the bush. After a moment, she caught sight of a slight movement.

'A lioness,' she gasped. 'With cubs!'

Even she could see it was in an aggressive mood.

'*Shoot*,' she whispered. 'Why doesn't he shoot?'

They stood in silence, waiting for the explosive sound of the 500NE.

But he didn't fire. Instead he moved away. Step by slow step he backed away from the crouching lioness towards where Liz and Delamere stood, afraid that any movement would trigger the charge.

When Dan had crept backwards so he was almost to them, the lioness licked its jaws and disappeared into the tall grass with a flick of its tail.

Liz could see his shoulders relax.

After a final check in the direction of the lioness, Dan lowered his rifle and turned.

His eyes met hers.

Liz ran to him and he swept her into his arms and they kissed, long and hard, heedless of D's presence.

Then Dan stepped back and grinned at her, tears of joy glistening in his eyes. 'Darling,' he said. 'What are you doing here?'

'I've come to make sure you don't do anything stupid.'

They laughed together and embraced again.

AFTERWORD

THE GREAT WAR IN EAST AFRICA

By the end of the nineteenth century, European nations had invaded, occupied, colonised and annexed an African expanse twice the size of their home continent. At times the nations competing for territory almost came to blows, so the German Chancellor, Otto von Bismarck, convened a meeting of imperial powers to reduce the risk of war on the African continent. The Berlin Conference of 1884–85 signed the Congo Act, which codified agreements to manage the scramble for Africa.

Before 1914, the colonial governors of German East Africa and British East Africa regularly met to discuss matters of mutual interest. Both agreed the Congo Act of 1885 required them to remain neutral in the event of a European war. This suited governors Schnee and Belfield quite nicely since neither had military resources of any note and both were busy developing their respective jurisdictions.

The British military command, who were concerned that the German ports and radio stations in their African colonies could threaten commercial shipping, were the first to break the terms of the Congo Act. They attacked German outposts at Lake Victoria and on the Indian Ocean coast at Tanga and Dar es Salaam.

The East Africa campaign of World War I, deemed a *sideshow* by some, would in any other context have been considered a significant war. The Allies had one hundred and fifty thousand troops, support and ancillary personnel in the field. These were supported by a million African carriers who had been coerced to serve. In the Teita district, three-quarters of the able-bodied men served, reducing the area to destitution. The British Commonwealth forces lost over ten thousand men, but ninety-five thousand carriers died supporting their colonial masters.

The Germans had about fifteen thousand belligerents, incurring military losses of about two thousand. No accurate records were kept on the number of native carriers used by GEA. One estimate placed the number at three hundred and fifty thousand. If their losses were of a proportionate size to those of BEA, at least thirty thousand died serving German interests.

The biggest killer was Africa itself. For every man killed in action, thirty died of or were incapacitated by malaria, dysentery, pneumonia and other disease.

The financial cost for the British side was immense (£2.8 billion in today's terms) and the more than one hundred thousand lives lost on the Allies' side were equal to the USA's total World War I human losses or twice those of Australia or Canada or India.*

From 1904 to 1907 Colonel Paul von Lettow-Vorbeck served with the German imperial troops in their South-West African colony (now Namibia) before taking command of the German East African *schutztruppe*.

The Germans had studied the tactics used more than a decade before in the Boer War and ensured the commanders and NCOs of the *schutztruppe* learned the bush skills and ways to fight a mobile war as used by the Boer commandos.

Conversely, the British General Staff had not taken heed of the lessons despite their salutary and first-hand experience in South Africa. In Africa they fought a conventional campaign to secure towns, railways, strategic outposts and the like.

In contrast to this static war, von Lettow-Vorbeck hit and ran, engaging the enemy when terms were favourable, and retreating when they were not. He was considered by many to be one of the greatest guerrilla fighters in history. He led the Allies a merry chase from modern-day Tanzania, through Mozambique, Malawi and Zambia, engaging British forces and those of several of her territories in Africa as well as those of Portugal, Belgium, India and South Africa.

---

* Edward Paice, *Tip and Run: The Untold Tragedy of the Great War in Africa*, Weidenfeld & Nicolson, 2007.

At the height of the campaign Colonel von Lettow-Vorbeck was outnumbered ten to one, yet he held out until 23 November 1918 — two weeks after the end of the war — continuing to drain the Allied resources of troops, ships and material needed at the 'main show' on the European front.

Ultimately, it wasn't a defeat that ended his fight-and-flight campaign, but an agreement to cease hostilities signed by the powers in faraway Europe.

* * *

Although *Whisper at Dawn* is not intended to be an historical record of the incidents surrounding World War I, every attempt has been made to use correct dates and places for the historical characters and events. The known exceptions for this are the timing of Cecil Rhodes's control of South Africa's diamond industry, the date of the release of the Bryce Report and the opening of the Norfolk Hotel, which have been slightly altered to facilitate the narrative.

ACKNOWLEDGEMENTS

Once again I must thank my partner, Ms Wendy Fairweather, for her contribution in developing the outline for *Whisper at Dawn*, and her understanding when my characters chose to stray from their intended paths in the narrative.

Thanks to Ms Margaret Hosking of the Adelaide University library for the information she supplied on the history of Adelaide University.

I would also like to acknowledge and thank the following selfless friends and helpers who have continued to support me in my writing:

Ms Charlotte Smith, author and curator of the Darnell Collection (www.darnellcollection.com), for her expert advice on female attire in the early twentieth century.

My agent, Selwa Anthony, my editor Kate O'Donnell, my publisher Anna Valdinger and others at HarperCollins.

Many thanks go to my good friend James Hudson, whose enthusiasm, feedback and support in the early drafts were, as usual, extremely helpful.

I knew that tackling a story of the great white hunters of Africa would challenge my paltry knowledge of hunting and the killing capabilities of firearms and their ammunition, so it was with great relief that I could call on a real expert in that field. Thank you, Garry Keown, for again coming to my assistance. However, I must add that Garry is not responsible for the embellishments that were intentionally added for dramatic effect, or any errors that were not.